A Charleston Yankee

Michael D Mercurio

ISBN: 1500934860
ISBN 13: 9781500934866
Library of Congress Control Number: 2014915835
CreateSpace Independent Publishing Platform
North Charleston, South Carolina

Dedication

To my wife, Gillian, without whose love and encouragement this novel never would have seen the light of day.

ACKNOWLEDGMENTS AND AUTHOR'S NOTE

This work of fiction is set against a background of certain historic events that took place in Charleston, South Carolina, and around the nation. Other than the well-known political figures and others who shaped our country's future during that time, all characters are the sole products of my imagination. Their possible resemblances to any real people, living or dead, are purely coincidental. Any factual errors that may exist are mine alone.

Heartfelt thanks to my sister-in-law, Anne Lowenberg, who helped set me on the right course in the early stages of writing this book, and my good friend Lyndon Abbott, who read the story chapter by chapter as it unraveled and made invaluable suggestions.

Finally, I want to acknowledge the CreateSpace editorial team for their excellent recommendations and professionalism.

One

Summer, 1964

Reveille sounded at 0600 at the Charleston Naval Base marine barracks. The day was already on its way to becoming hot and humid as a resolute wind blew down the Cooper River, sending warm tidal waters lapping against muddy banks and carrying the scents of the Carolina Lowcountry marshes throughout the maritime facility. In the distance the rumble of incoming naval traffic merged with the sounds of the shipyard coming alive, disturbing the peace of the primeval river. The US Navy never slept, building and repairing its arsenal of ships to make ready for the day when the Cold War might turn hot.

After sleeping in beyond the bugler's call, I ambled over to the Spartan mess, located in a three-story redbrick building that also housed most of the marine guard. The majority of the enlisted men had eaten breakfast much earlier and had gone off to their various assigned tasks of providing security to the naval base. Only a few NCOs remained, shooting the breeze over their cups of joe. They glanced over at me and said nothing, but then why should they? I had as much utility to them now, being a civilian, as a rusty rifle without a firing pin. Ignoring them, I scoped out the chow line with its great selection—everything from cereal to bacon and eggs to French toast. I was hungover from partying the night before and not particularly hungry, so I helped myself to a small portion of scrambled eggs and a mug of coffee.

As I carefully sipped the strong brew and contemplated the long drive ahead of me, the door to the galley thudded open. Out came Staff Sergeant Lopez, all five foot four of him, wearing a gold cross entangled in his dog tags outside his skivvy shirt and an apron around his middle.

He came straight over and sat across the table. Before I could wish him a good morning, he said, eyeing the meager pickings on my tray, "Romano, you're eating like a bird. That's not enough to keep you going on the road today. How about me rustling up a farewell T-bone to go with those eggs? And maybe some home fries?"

Caught flatfooted by his generous offer and not wanting to seem ungrateful, I chose my words carefully. "Thanks, Lopez. You know I love your grub; everyone does. Just look at all the out-of-shape, lard-ass porkers we have walking around in the guard thanks to you!"

Choking back a laugh, he snorted.

"So I hope you'll understand that if the head honcho in the sky sent his personal chef down here to cook me a breakfast this morning, I would have to tell him, 'No, thanks, pal. I'm a bit screwed up from hitting the sauce too hard last night and don't have much of an appetite.'"

He chuckled. "Sure I do." His smile faded. "Romano, I'm glad I caught you before you left. There's something I've been meaning to say to you."

He paused for a second while his dark eyes darted anxiously around the mess. What the devil was up?

He stretched his small torso across the Formica table and said quietly, "It's good you've gotten out. You got fucked over in this command, and I know you'll do better on the outside."

Now I understood his furtive behavior: he was worried that dead commandants overhearing his blasphemous words might rain napalm down upon him. I appreciated his sincerity and felt vindicated that my transgressions against the corps—or at least some of its NCOs—were warranted. I thanked him and said, "But you know what really bugs me? They had the nerve to try to get me to re-up after all that happened. Can you believe that shit?"

"Sure! To them you were nothing more than a cog in a killing machine. They would have saved the government a buck or two by keeping you in and not having to train another guy to replace you."

"Christ, I never heard it put so coldly."

He shrugged, looking at me as though I were a naïve child. "It's nothing more than that."

"So what keeps you in to put up with all the crap?"

"Romano, you gotta understand that life here in the United States is more difficult for a Mexican American, but at least it's better for my family, even at the price of risking my neck if there's another war. My kids get to go to a decent school, and they don't have to face as much shit as I did. But don't think that when reenlistment came up, I didn't consider other possibilities. Anyway, that's water under the bridge. In a few years, I'll be retiring, and my boys will be able to take care of themselves. And it looks like my oldest will be going to college!"

"So then whaddya gonna do?"

His face lit up like a Christmas tree. "Open a restaurant in El Paso with my lovely wife, Consuela."

The sun rose higher, lightening the shadows in the mess. Lopez checked his watch, rapped the table smartly with his knuckles, and stood up. "Look, I gotta get back to work. It's lasagna night—your favorite. Would you like for me to reserve you a private table? With candles maybe?"

"Hey, I'm tempted, but I got a woman in New York who's been waiting almost five months now."

"Mmm." He nodded, smiling broadly. "A woman should never be kept waiting or denied. It's a mortal sin!" He winked. "*Vaya con Dios.*" He walked away, disappearing into the galley and out of my life.

I toyed with the food on my tray and felt conflicted. My self-imposed incarceration in the corps had come to an end, but what would the predatory world outside have in store for me?

After finishing my coffee, I double-staired up to the third-story barracks. In the room—large and lackluster, with fluorescent lights and gray Kentile floors—some of the 0400 to 0800 guard were squaring away their gear. Others were making up their racks, and a few were grab-assing, the fourth-most-popular form of entertainment after masturbation, booze, and women.

PFC Arnaud, a Canuck from Quebec, better known as Kong, was leaning against the bulkhead, staring into space with an unlit cigarette dangling from his lips. The door to his olive-drab locker hung open. Inside was a picture of a sexy pinup and a calendar marking off the days to his discharge. He stood slightly over me at six feet tall. He had a low, protuberant brow and knuckle-walking hands twice the size of those of most men. He was an OK guy, but when his demons took hold of him, we had to look out.

"Hey, Kong!" I called out to get his attention. "I wanted to say good-bye, and I'm looking for Pug."

"He's in the laundry room, doing his unmentionables."

"Ha! Very funny."

He grunted. "There's nothing funny about this bullshit outfit!"

"What's got a hair up your ass this morning?"

"Where the hell've you been, Romano? Haven't you heard what happened to Funk?"

"I was gone most of the day, getting my wheels ready for the trip up north."

"Sergeant Rutledge, that ass kisser, was returning to base yesterday afternoon and spotted Funk drinking on guard duty."

"Rutledge wasn't on duty?"

"Heck no! He was out joyriding with some WAVE bimbo he's been banging."

"So what happened?"

"He reported him to the sergeant of the guard just when Funk and his section of the guard were being relieved of their post, probably hoping to score some brownie points with those higher up in the command who hate Funk."

"Did the sergeant check it out or what?"

"No, he just wrote up the incident as described by Rutledge in the log. Anyhow, an hour or so later, Funk was slapped with a court-martial and marched off to the brig for safekeeping pending trial."

"Damn! That'll probably buy him some serious bad time and a general discharge to boot. He's been burned before."

"Exactly. And that bastard Rutledge knew it. My God, half of us are alkies, especially the lifers. He could've looked the other way. To mess up a guy like that when he had only four or five months to go to get out with lily-white paper is pure mean and ugly." He slammed his locker door shut, catching the attention of those nearby. They quickly turned away, seemingly not wanting to risk making eye contact with him.

Glowering at me, he continued, "And here I am, a Canadian putting it on the line for the good ol' United States, and I get busted down from lance corporal because I told Sergeant Kruger, that Kraut son of a bitch, to go fuck himself when he was riding my ass for no good reason other than to get his rocks off. You bust a man for that? Shit! It burns me that I didn't bash his head in."

"Easy, man. Easy!" I raised my hands, trying to put the brakes on his rant. "Men like Rutledge and Kruger wouldn't amount to much in civilian life, so they stay in for the benefits and especially the power and identity that rank gives them. They can't stand individuality; it threatens what they're all about."

"Hell, Romano, you should know that better than anyone. You tried to protect your guys against abuse by that maggot, Pratt, and got court-martialed because you challenged that yellow dog to drop his stripes and settle things out behind the barracks."

"That was my foul-up, thinking Pratt was a marine."

"Marine, my butt," he scoffed. "They all hide behind rank."

"Yeah, you're probably right. But as far as Pratt's concerned, fuck that Georgia cracker and the whole inbred state he came from. I beat the rap. I didn't lose my stripes this time around. And a guy in admin told me Pratt's cojones were on fire because I got off so light."

"Now there's a thought."

"What?"

"Setting him on fire!"

I laughed, but he just looked away and grimaced.

"Kong, you're a short-timer."

"Not short enough, man."

I gripped his shoulder and shook him hard. "Stay close to Gunny Starr. He ran interference between me and Pratt and some others. He's good people. He cares about the men."

Arnaud didn't seem to be listening really, only hearing the echoes of my voice. Then he shot his hand out, taking me by surprise. We shook, and he said, "Play it cool, Romano. Don't take any prisoners."

I left him still brooding. He probably never even knew my first name. I certainly didn't know his. It made it easier when you lost a man or men in combat, especially when you gave the order that got them killed. What a hell of a way to make a living—or do a dying.

Now behind schedule, I picked up the pace to the laundry room, where Pug Calder was bopping and shaking his skinny rump to the beat of "Short Shorts" on his transistor radio. We had buddied up while serving in the same company back in Lejeune. He was a little guy with a cutting wit, who played a mean sax and raced dirt bikes. What he lacked in size, he made up for with heart and determination.

I walked up behind him, and he cracked, "So how does it feel to be a civilian again?"

"I don't know. It's been so long, I don't think I'll ever be able to kick the marine habit completely."

"You'd better! Civilians won't appreciate our delicate way of expressing ourselves."

"Hey, shitbird, what the fuck are you talking about?" I said. We both laughed.

He threw his skivvies into the machine and turned on the wash cycle. He said soberly, "Romano, I'm gonna miss having you around."

His unusual display of emotion surprised me. I could only think to say, "Do us both a favor and knock off the hearts and flowers shit, OK? Look, I'll call when I get back to Charleston, after I finish my training in the insurance business."

He made a face. "You, a casket pusher? I still can't believe it."

"Come on, Pug, gimme a break, huh? I can't sing or dance. I've got to make a living somehow. The only job possibilities I had up north was being a blue-collar worker. I hate the thought of that. This job gives me an opportunity to wear a suit, keep my nails clean, and make some big bucks. And big bucks are what I'm out for. I'll be damned if I'm going to live my life on the edge of society, picking crumbs off the floor!"

"So what about the Mob?"

"Dammit! I told you months back I turned those goombahs down. No way in hell will I subject Julie to a life like that."

"Easy, man! Don't bite my head off. I was only asking to see if you were having second thoughts, in case you don't make it in the insurance biz."

"Well, I'm not. No matter what. Don't ask me again, you got it?"

"Yeah, I got it."

He shrugged, took out a cigarette, and offered me one. I waved him off. He lit up, took a quick couple of puffs, held the smoke a second or two, and then exhaled a steady stream through his nose.

"Romano, you've changed a lot since you started reading those deep-shit philosophy books. I hardly know your ass anymore."

"What ass?" I snapped. "All you ever wanted in me was some fast-fisted guy to raise hell with. Look, pal, we've had a lot of good times—drinking, chasing broads, and breaking heads together—but those days are over with."

Lost for words, he ground out his smoke in a tin coffee can, turned, and looked at me blankly.

"Seriously, Pug, maybe *you* should start thinking now about getting a real job when you get out. You have to prepare yourself for something other than playing sax in some honky-tonk."

"Hey, bub, don't knock the brass. It keeps me cool and flying under the radar—unlike you, the Italian tank, crashing through walls, wreaking mayhem."

"There you go again—always with the mouth."

"So what?" he said.

"I'll tell you what. You're married to a great girl. If I weren't married to Julie, I'd make a move on Maggie in a minute."

"You tellin' me you're hot for my old lady?"

"Jesus Christ, you're a royal pain in the ass! If I were hot for Maggie, she'd volunteer to be my concubine and never have second thoughts about you, friend."

He laughed. He had to know he was getting my goat.

"If you don't settle down and find a real job, numbskull, you could lose her."

Pissed, I turned and headed out. He yelled over the racket of the washer, "Hey, Mike, good luck, buddy!" When I looked back, he had the biggest shit-eating grin on his face.

I shook my head and smiled back. "The same to you, Bernard."

Next I hustled over to the admin building, hoping to find Gunny Starr. The first person I saw was Pratt, talking to the office pinkie who had prepared the papers for my court-martial several months back. Our eyes met for a second. He looked away, broke off his conversation, and hurried past me out of the building. The smell of his nervous sweat lingered in his wake. I was now a private citizen: no oath or contract existed any longer that shackled me and protected him.

A corporal was mindlessly filing papers, and I asked him if he had seen the gunny. "He's in the captain's office, having a powwow."

"Do you know how long he'll be in there?"

"Hey, man. Do I look like his secretary or something?"

I looked him up and down. "I don't know, man. Are you wearing silk panties and a garter belt under that uniform?"

He chuckled, and as he did, Gunny Starr came barreling out of the office. When he saw me he slammed on the brakes. "Romano! Why the hell are you still hanging around? Have you changed your mind and decided to re-up?"

"No way. I'd rather eat the peanuts out of an elephant's shit than do that."

Towering over me with his six-foot-three boxer's physique, he laughed. "So what are you doing here, busting my balls?"

I looked into the deep-set gray eyes that had seen the obscenities of war and then at the Silver Star and Purple Heart he wore. "Gunny, I've come to say good-bye and thanks for keeping me out of harm's way. If it hadn't been for you, they would have buried me six feet under with a stake through my heart and a dishonorable."

He rubbed his jaw hard. "I'm proud to have served with you, Romano. Never lose your fighting spirit." He leaned into me with his hands on his hips and growled, "Now get your civvy wop butt outta here!"

Sprinting behind the admin building to my hot '61 Ford Fairlane, I was euphoric. This was the moment I had dreamed about for four long years. I was free—truly free! I fired up the big 390 engine, shifted into first gear, and rolled out of the parking lot toward the main gate. Up ahead the American and admiral's flags stirred in the languid breeze in a grass-encircled island midway between the entrance and exit lanes. Lance Corporals Pulaski and Bell, two of the men from my time as corporal of the guard, were busy directing traffic. With no cars in front of me, I stomped on the gas. The Ford sprang forward like a tiger, wheels screaming and rubber burning. As I ran the gate, I gave them a one-fingered salute. I watched them in the rearview mirror laughing and waving. They were good men.

Two

I slowed my speed as I drove down the notorious Reynolds Avenue strip. Starting conveniently just outside the base, with its one- and two-story brick and stucco buildings, it was known for its many gyp joints, greasy spoons, pawn shops, finance companies, uniform shops, and ladies of the night—some professional, others not. Some navy wives, being lonely, sought male companionship and quick rolls in the hay. Others needed extra cash and offered their favors for a price. We hated main-gate guard duty on Friday and Saturday nights. Some wiseass, drunk swabbies would always feel the need to challenge our post, and an inevitable fight would follow. When trouble broke out on the strip, the navy shore patrol or the county bulls took care of it. They were indeed bulls; not one I saw was fewer than 250 pounds. Dressed in khaki uniforms, weighed down by heavy holster belts, they would post themselves beside their souped-up squad cars, close to where most of the action was likely to take place. They did an excellent job of otherwise ignoring the obvious vice that was going on.

As the five blocks of the strip faded from view, I made a right turn onto Highway 52, to start the first leg of my journey back to the Big Apple. The trip usually took between twelve and fourteen hours depending on the traffic, especially going through DC.

Up ahead was my favorite place in all of Charleston: the Port City Drive-in. I thought about Julie, with her luxuriant, chestnut hair and blue eyes, and the happy evenings we had spent there, enjoying the cheeseburgers and thick, addictive chocolate malts. But more than the food, it was the music, cars, and people that made the place cool, especially on Saturday nights during the summer, when flocks of southern belles wearing their most enticing outfits would preen and flaunt while perched on the fenders of hot Fords, Plymouths, and Chevys to the delight of their male audience.

Leaving behind the coastal lands and the ghostly gray shacks that dotted the roadside, I found myself hours later at the Rocky Mountain exit, where a black marine was thumbing a ride. I pulled over onto the soft shoulder, kicking stones and pebbles to the underside of the Ford and making a racket. "Where're you headed, private?"

"South Philly, sir," he replied.

"Get in. I can drop you off outside Philly—I'm going to New York."

"Thanks." He slid into the seat with an easy smile. He had a tall, wiry build, a light complexion, and facial features that spoke of a strong dose of white heritage.

I asked, "How long've you been in the corps?"

"A little over four months. This is my first leave, sir." He looked straight ahead, as if he were centered in the hatch of a drill instructor's office, ready for a dressing down.

"You must have just finished advanced infantry training at Geiger."

"Yes, sir."

"Hey, pal, knock off the 'sir' shit—I'm out of the corps. And you don't have to 'sir' any enlisted man."

"I know, but it's a hard habit to break after yes-sir-ing all the corporals and sergeants in boot camp."

"I had the same problem. My name is Mike Romano. What's yours?"

"McDaniel P. Simmons the third."

Laughing, I said, "It sounds like royalty to me."

"Yeah, my royal family goes all the way back to Africa."

I chuckled. *He's a bright bulb.* "I've been to Africa, and I never ran into any kings or queens."

"No kidding! You've been to Africa? Whereabouts?"

"From Simonstown around the Cape of Good Hope to Cape Town and all the way up the west coast, to Sierra Leone and Guinea, back in '61."

"Sierra Leone's where my royal family got on the boat, with lousy accommodations by all accounts, 'cept they didn't get off at Ellis Island but Charleston, South Carolina."

"I know all about Charleston—I was stationed there for a year and a half and left it just a few hours back."

"What were you doing there?" he asked.

"Marine guard at the naval base."

"Hell, I thought you came from Lejeune!"

"No, but I was with the Pogey Ropers at LeJeune for over two years."

"What're the Pogey Ropers?" he asked.

"That's the Sixth Marines! The pogey rope, or the fourragère, was a decoration given by the French to the Fifth and Sixth Marines for bravery in fighting and defeating the Germans during World War I in the Battle of Belleau Wood."

His face lit up. "That's where we got the name Devil Dogs, isn't it?"

"You got it. And the rope we wear on the left shoulder—it's a green-and-red braid with a spike on the end. The spike symbolizes the silencing of the guns. It was driven into a cannon muzzle, making it useless."

"So tell me more about Africa," he said, settling into his seat.

"Our mission supposedly was to present the American way of life to other nations and create goodwill. We gave out medical supplies, books, and food, and we competed in athletic contests with local teams in basketball, volleyball, shooting, judo—that sort of stuff. I was a member of the judo team and fought as a light heavyweight in smokers against the navy. Anyway, we held open ship in some of the ports, put on concerts, and did some parading around."

"Which places did you get to visit?"

"Let's see...Port Elizabeth, Simonstown, and Cape Town in South Africa and up to Freetown in Sierra Leone, Monrovia in Liberia, and then Conakry, the capital of Guinea."

"Sounds like one hell of a great trip," the kid said, wide eyed.

"Yes and no."

He looked puzzled.

"Port Elizabeth and Cape Town were great. The people greeted us with open arms. I married a local British girl there within a week from when we first met."

"Wow! you work fast, man."

"I guess I do. But when you find something you really want, something you need, you grab for it. Anyway, that's a story in itself. Back to South Africa. The place had drawbacks. Before we got there, we were told the colored marines and sailors would have special colored escorts to show them around, but they couldn't go on liberty with white marines and sailors."

"No shit!" he muttered. "Sounds worse than here."

"Yeah; and we white boys were told in no uncertain terms not to talk to colored girls for any reason, including asking for directions, because we could be arrested for solicitation."

"Damn, the government there must be run by a bunch of Nazis," he said uneasily.

"Except they call them Afrikaners. However, there was a lot more to the mission than met the eye. On our way up the coast, we'd stop on some beach, and then, while we were playing football and drinking beer, an underwater demolition team of three guys would go over the side for a little swim. The scuttlebutt was that they were studying tides and mapping out future beach landings. I never knew for sure. I hung out with those guys on the ship, but they didn't let on.

"When we entered the port of Conakry, I saw two Russian freighters, with the hammer and sickle painted in red on their smokestacks, unloading tractors. It raised the hair on the back of my neck being up close to the enemy.

"Around ten hundred hours, it was announced over the PA system that we could go on liberty, but then it was canceled because Communist sympathizers were throwing rocks at the sailors and marines who were trying to leave the port."

"What the fuck was going on?"

"A few hours later," I continued, "we were told we could go on liberty, but only in groups of five or more. We got a sheet of paper with French written on it—it explained who we were—that we could give to the local authorities if we got into trouble. My squad and I went on liberty about an hour later. As we left the port area, we came upon this wide dirt road."

I could see and feel it as I spoke: the kaleidoscope of greens that engulfed us, the smell of the jungle and the sea, and the heat and humidity that made our starched khakis cling to our bodies and dulled the leather of our shoes and the visors on our caps.

"Less than a half mile down the road, we came to a landscaped clearing that had a beautiful, two-story, white-plastered colonial building on it. We decided to stop and hopefully get a drink. It seemed to be some kind of country club catering to the local upper crust. Negroes dressed in white jackets were serving at the bar and in the restaurant. We bellied up to the bar. A dazzling woman with short-cropped hair and large, gold earrings was talking to a fat, sweaty white guy who kept mopping his neck with a handkerchief. Everyone kept admiring her gorgeous figure and shapely ebony legs." Now I really had the kid's attention. I couldn't resist. "Her hands fluttered as she spoke in French, and her taut breasts strained against the material of her white dress."

"Oh man, stop it! I ain't had a woman in half a year, and I've got a major hard-on. She couldn't have been that fine."

I laughed. "I made that part up just to get a rise outta you."

"Rise, hell!" He jabbed me in the arm, nearly knocking me through the door.

"Whoa, man. That hurt." *I would hate to get on the wrong side of this guy. He's powerful.*

"Sorry, sir." He looked as though he'd committed a crime. He was back in his boot camp frame of mind, probably thinking I would order him to drop and do a thousand push-ups.

"I had it coming, pal." I rubbed my paralyzed arm.

I looked at him sideways and continued my story. "After a couple of rounds, we decided we wanted to eat and were seated at a large, rectangular table. No sooner than we got our menus, the shore patrol entered with whistles blowing and yelling loudly that all liberty was canceled. We were ordered to return to ship immediately. On our way back, we found ourselves flanked by two pygmy-sized Guinean soldiers in tan shorts and long socks, pointing burp guns at us. They were gesturing with their weapons to keep us moving toward the ship."

"Damn. You guys musta been shittin'."

"You bet your ass we were. We had a hotheaded Mick called McGee who was eying the soldiers and cursing them loudly. Thank God they didn't understand English. Two of our guys grabbed him by the arms and told him to shut his trap, or he was going to get us all killed. We got back to the ship and asked guys what the hell was going on. No one knew anything. The next morning, around zero eight hundred, we heard the rapid clanging of a bell, and the announcement, 'General quarters, general quarters; all men to battle stations. This is not a drill. Repeat, this is not a drill.' I grabbed my M1 and rocketed up two steel ladderways. I almost lost my flip-flops on my way to the main deck, and I was flapping around in my undershorts. As I came through the hatch, one of the officers handed me two bandoliers of ammo. The lieutenants and sergeants posted men from stem to stern at port arms, overlooking the dock below, where three platoons of Guinean troops were lined up like tin soldiers with their rifles slung. *My God,* I thought, *are we going to war*? I wondered what it would be like to have to kill someone, but then I realized that my pecker was partly hanging out of my shorts. I was worried more about that than anything else, and I tucked it back in."

McDaniel roared with laughter. "Here lies Corporal Romano, winner of the Congressional Medal of Honor, who died in his skivvies with his pecker hanging out!"

I laughed. "It's peculiar how you get when you're in danger like that. Then minutes later, five people, two of them women wearing wide-brimmed sun hats, walked onto the dock and up to the arguing officers, theirs and ours. We learned later that they were from the French embassy. After a while, the Guinean troops did an about-face, and we were ordered to stand down. The word was the Guinea government claimed that one of our sailors had knifed one of the local Commies in an argument. The sailor said it was self-defense and that the other guy attacked first—I guess we'll never know the truth. But they came to the dock that morning to arrest him, and we weren't about to give him up. Those Frenchies intervening saved the day. We were glad to be the hell outta there after that."

"Man, that's some crazy shit. I can't believe that it all really happened."

"Well, it did. Look, I know it sounds exciting, but you gotta watch out for yourself in those foreign ports. We lost a guy. He was hammered to death in a bar fight by a native who crushed his skull with a ball peen hammer. Another fella was thrown through a skylight—crippled him for life. No one ever seemed to know who did it. Then you have the two-dollar hookers and their pimps trying to roll you while you're too screwed up to walk."

"I'm wised up to all that crap. I grew up in South Philly."

Nodding, I pulled out my pack of cigarettes and offered him one.

"No, thanks," he said. "I've got to keep my wind up and stay in shape."

I turned on the radio so we could both relax and not feel the strain of having to make further conversation. Staring down the road, I worried about the future of McDaniel and all the guys serving in the armed forces. A year back an old buddy from the Sixth, Spike, had come to visit me on his way to Atlanta. He'd asked if I was going to reenlist, and I'd told him no.

"Good," he'd said. "We're fixing to get into a big fight in Vietnam."

"Where in the hell is that?"

"French Indochina," he'd replied.

I had a general idea where that was. The Frogs had gotten badly whipped in some major battle against the Commies there and had pulled out of the country.

"So what's up, Spike?"

"After I left the Second Division, I was sent to Vietnam as an advisor to the South Vietnamese army, which isn't worth a damn. Every time they ran across the enemy, they wanted to bug out. One day a marine captain pulled out his forty-five and rammed it to the head of a Vietnamese lieutenant, yelling, 'If you don't stand and fight, I'll blow your fucking brains out!'"

"What the hell?" I said.

"It's worse than that, Mike. The government in Saigon is nothing but a bunch of damn hoods making money off of every conceivable vice, including drugs."

"Why are we supporting them?"

"They are the lesser of the two evils, and the government is worried about the spread of Communism. But here's what really gets to me: when they liberate a village from the North, they rape and pillage—a bad habit they picked up from the French. So how in the name of God do they expect us to win, with shit like that going on? Mike, that country ain't worth spit for us poor boys to bleed and die over."

I thought about telling McDaniel this story, but it wouldn't do anything except worry him. He had four more years to go, and I hoped he would be lucky. Anyway, he was fast asleep.

About ten miles short of the Virginia line, we came upon a whitewashed, wooden building with a sign advertising Jeb's BBQ within. I shook McDaniel awake.

"What's happening? Where are we?" he said, stretching his neck.

"Nearly in Virginia, and I'm hungry for some pulled pork and fries."

"Sounds like down-home cooking."

When we entered the restaurant, Hank Williams's "Cold, Cold Heart" was playing on the jukebox. The place was half filled with what looked like mostly locals and maybe a few tourists. We parked our butts at the counter and picked up the menus, and a hush descended over the place. In a flash, a perky young waitress, hair pulled back in a ponytail and wearing too much red lipstick, shot over to us and said flatly, "We don't serve no coloreds here."

"Whaddya mean? This is a marine serving his country."

"Don't mean a thing around here—we got rules."

McDaniel eyed me and mumbled, "Let's go."

I ignored him. "I want to see the owner."

"He's in the kitchen, cookin'." She smirked.

I said, "Well, go get him."

About a minute later, a stocky man in a dirty apron, with a salt-and-pepper crew cut and forearms the size of hams, came around the counter. "Didn't Lucy tell ya? We don't serve coloreds."

"Yeah, and I wanna know why."

"Hell," he sneered, "this is my place, and I says who eats and who don't. I was in the marines from '44 to '48, and I got out because that nigger-lovin', Jew-lovin' Truman forced integration of our armed forces. I'm proud to say the corps fought harder than all the other services not to do it. I don't like niggers. They're stupid, lazy, and untrustworthy, and I weren't gonna eat nor sleep with 'em or put my ass on a commode a nigger done sat on. And no way in hell was I about to take orders from any of 'em!"

Enthusiastic nods bobbed throughout the eatery. McDaniel grimaced, looked down at the counter, clenched his fists, and swallowed hard. I was dumbstruck.

"So you get your Yankee ass outta my place, or I'll have the both of ya arrested for disturbing the peace." He spat on the dirty floor, narrowly missing my shoe.

The crowd was now getting raucous in support. "You tell 'em, Jeb," came from a group of bully boys, one already on his feet. McDaniel grabbed me, yanked me out of my seat, and dragged me out to the car like a rowdy schoolboy. Just as we were pulling out of the parking lot, those wild-eyed yokels burst through the door, throwing beer cans and pop bottles, and one fired a pistol in our direction as we took off down the highway at full speed.

"Jeez, Mike! I appreciate you standing up for me, but that was fucking stupid, arguing with that Reb. This is the South, for God's sake. Major Klan country. We could've gotten killed back there. Haven't you learned anything about the South yet?"

"I guess not, McDaniel. I thought we were OK with us both being in uniform."

"Maybe it slowed them down some—gave us time to get outta there."

I hit the steering wheel hard with my fist and checked the rear-view mirror. Today had been a frightening revelation for me. The blatant bigotry and hatred of those people would be forever burned in my mind.

"McDaniel, how the hell do you people put up with it?"

"Habit, fear...but that's changing fast," he said with grim determination.

Hours later, with the sun almost down, I dropped the kid off in front of his blighted apartment building in Philly instead of just outside the city, as I had planned. It was the least I could do after what I had put him through.

I was on the Jersey turnpike doing eighty miles an hour to try to make up for lost time after dropping off McDaniel. The noxious fumes of the refineries greeted me. I revved up to a hundred to escape the stench and the yellow haze lingering over the highway. I was risking a big ticket, but what the hell—the speed was both exhilarating and empowering and helped ease the feelings of anger and helplessness brought on by the incident with Jeb. I was getting closer to home and Julie.

A flock of billboards advertised shows like *Hello Dolly, Funny Girl, Fiddler on the Roof,* and many more. I had never seen a Broadway musical or play or visited the Empire State Building. Neither had my family. We lived in the capital city of the world, yet we participated very little in what it had to offer. Could it be a class thing, or were we just oblivious to what was around us?

I entered Manhattan and found my way to Eighty-Fifth Street on the East Side, where Julie was waiting. My heart beat hard with excitement; five months was too long to be separated. The many phone calls and the letters Julie had written had done little to ease our longing and hunger for each other. I spent a day's pay to leave the car several blocks away in a parking garage. At the entrance of her apartment building, a pudgy, elderly doorman dressed in a worn brown uniform greeted me. He smiled when I told him who I was.

"Mrs. Romano told us you were coming. I'll call her up."

"Please don't do that. I want to surprise her."

"I understand perfectly, sir." He grinned and then opened the door as if I were Rockefeller.

Pulse racing and mouth dry, I stepped into the antique elevator that creaked up to the eighth floor. The door opened, and I quick timed it to apartment 807. I took a deep breath and rang the doorbell.

Three

She stood in the open doorway, softly backlit by the flickering candle glow. In a single moment, she pressed herself tightly against me and hid her face against my neck. I put my arms around her and felt her trembling beneath the silky black robe I had given her for her last birthday.

"Honey, what's wrong?" I asked.

Her voice catching, she breathed, "Oh, Michael, I've missed you so much."

I tipped her head back and saw the tears. "I'm here now." I kissed her hard and long. My voice was hoarse as I said, "So, Mrs. Romano, are you going to let me in?"

This time when she looked at me, a decided gleam appeared in her eyes. "Oh, *yes*," she murmured, walking me into the room.

I dropped my sea bag and took in the sight of her as the robe puddled around her ankles, leaving her in nothing but a wispy pair of black panties. I was exhausted and half starved, but hell, I was twenty-four and hadn't seen my wife for five months. I slid my hands down over her small breasts and settled them into the tender curve of her hips.

"I'm filthy," I managed to utter.

"So what?" she replied breathlessly.

Soon the khakis joined the silk on the carpet, and I backed her against the sofa bed. We stumbled as I misjudged the height of the low mattress, and we fell on it, locked together. We were almost frantic as we joined, touching, tasting, moving fast, and crying out as we found release from the long months of loneliness. I rolled us over onto our sides to take my weight off her and then instantly fell asleep.

Minutes or hours later, I awoke as Julie wriggled against me. The candles had all gone out.

"Oof," she said, "my leg's gone to sleep."

Adjusting our position stirred my passion awake again, and I began to react accordingly.

"Mmm," she moaned sleepily. Then she stiffened, her eyes opening wide. "Uh-oh. How could we have forgotten? Didn't you bring any rubbers with you?"

"No." Throwing caution to the wind, I began to stroke her hungrily.

She moved her hips against me and whispered, "It's really nice this way, isn't it?" That did it. This time we made love slowly, reveling in the sensation and ending breathless and sated.

Once my mind began to function again, it informed me that I had better eat, or I would probably die. Julie, lying naked and hair tousled, purred in a horrible French accent, "Would monsieur care to dine? We have all of 'is favoreeete dishes...jellied eels, ze pickled pig's feet, kidney pie..."

As she rolled off the bed, I swiped at her pretty butt, and she bounced across the room to a small alcove half hidden by a bead curtain. She started pulling cardboard containers out of the tiny icebox, setting them on the café table. As she moved about purposefully, I took my first real look at the apartment. It was essentially one small room, with the sofa bed, table, two wooden chairs, and not much else. A door led to what I assumed was a bathroom, which was confirmed when I went to check it out. Another door opened to a miniscule closet. She had fashioned a bookcase from a couple of boards, empty now of the books and photographs filling the packing box beside it. Her two battered suitcases stood next to the door.

I had lived in worse accommodations, but I was sorry Julie had to be in this dismal place.

"Baby, why didn't you tell me it was this bad?"

"I didn't want to worry you," she replied cheerfully, "and I knew it would be better with you here. Anyway, we'll be out of here tomorrow. Go shower off, and then we'll eat."

At least the water was hot, even if the pressure proved to be subpar. When I came out, dressed in a T-shirt and shorts, the table was set, new candles were lit, and a jelly jar of daisies was wedged between the dishes.

"I'm just crisping up some bread and reheating the lasagna," she announced. "Sit!"

"Can I do anything?" I reached for an olive.

"Absolutely not! Actually, yes—could you open that bottle of champagne?"

Champagne! This had the makings of a feast. "So," I said as casually as I could around a hunk of cheese, "you're really OK with going back to South Carolina?"

Julie turned and looked at me seriously. "It's not just OK—it's wonderful. I hate New York. I hate being dirty just from walking down the street. I miss our friends in Charleston. I even miss the food—well, the shrimp and grits anyway. I'm tired of people pushing and shoving and shouting. And this job has not been at all what I expected." She turned and pulled the bread from the oven. I sat there wondering what to say.

"I'm sorry, Michael. I didn't want to bitch. It just came out of me. It doesn't matter now. We're together. You have what sounds like an interesting job to look forward to, and I have that new position lined up at the Medical College."

"I'm sorry it's been that bad for you. If I had known I would be working in Charleston, none of this would have been necessary. But what happened with the job at the Flowers Hospital? The docs seemed like reasonable guys to me."

She sighed. "They are, I suppose, but setting up a new lab meant just that. I spent weeks unpacking huge crates of glassware and stuff, then washing it all, then autoclaving it, and so on. Then more endless weeks of making buffers and nutrient broth. I don't want to bore you. It bored me doing it, and it bores me talking about it. I don't want to be a lab tech for the rest of my life. I need to get my master's degree so I can do something worthwhile. But time enough for that. Let's eat!"

The next morning, happy but bleary-eyed following a night with little sleep, we had the apartment inspected by the real estate company that had leased it to us.

Our bags packed, we stuffed the sheets and still-damp towels into my sea bag; hauled out the cardboard boxes stuffed with my precious, leather-bound Harvard Classics; emptied the fridge into a paper sack; and headed for my grandmother's old house, where Gilda, my mother, and my stepfather, Arturo, still lived along with two of my uncles and their families, trapped in a commune of necessity since the Great Depression. Saying our good-byes was going to be hard. I loved them, and they had counted on my return. However, they had reluctantly accepted our reasons for moving to Charleston—notably jobs for both of us and a much lower cost of living. Other factors had affected my decision. As the time grew closer for me to return to New York, bad memories came back to haunt me. Most of all I worried that the inevitable demands my family would put on me would stifle my growth and jeopardize my relationship with Julie.

I once read that people moved on not because they knew what they wanted but rather they knew what they *didn't* want.

Relieved that my filial duties had been fulfilled, I accelerated rapidly from the toll booth onto the Jersey pike.

Julie enthused, "My God, this car is fast, and it rides so comfortably. And this black-and-white interior is beautiful."

"And we came out OK on the deal, considering the transmission was slipping on the old Hornet. Just think: if I hadn't gone down to

Morrison Drive to trade it in, we wouldn't be looking at a future in Charleston."

Julie paused for a beat. "So tell me about Mr. Dawson, the man who got you the job with the insurance company. I know he overheard you bargaining for the car and said you would make an excellent insurance agent, but that's all you told me."

"That's about it."

"No, I mean, what kind of a man is Mr. Dawson?"

"He's in his late fifties or early sixties, soft spoken, well dressed—a gentleman. He used to be a high school teacher in Alabama."

"Is he married?"

"No. After I interviewed for the job, he invited me to his house. He lives with a much younger guy who's a hairdresser, and a bunch of poodles. Oh, I forgot—he says he wants to meet you and treat us to a dinner some night."

"Sounds like fun!" Julie responded with a grin.

"You'll like him. He's a real charmer."

The heavens suddenly opened and let loose sheets of deafening rain. Slowing down, I turned on the wipers. Semis up front were splashing water onto the windshield, making it difficult to see through the liquid prism. I offered Julie a cigarette.

"No, thanks," she said. "I'm going to quit."

"Why now?" I asked.

"I don't like the smell of smoke in my hair and clothes, and it's better for one's health, especially if one is pregnant."

"Good God," I said faintly.

"We'll know in a few weeks," she chirped airily.

On that note, I fired up a weed and took a much-needed, long drag, inhaling so deeply I thought the smoke would blow out of my ass. London fog filled the cabin. Julie started fanning furiously at the smoke, opening the wing window and getting her clothes wet with rain. "Blimey, Michael, I never thought it possible that one drag could consume a whole fag."

I smiled evilly. "It takes a real man to do that."

"Well, real man, I have other criteria, and you do pass satisfactorily in most areas."

"Whaddya mean, most? I excel across the board."

"There's always room for improvement, my lad."

We chuckled and then pecked each other on the lips like two guppies. Julie sighed and lit up a cigarette. "The hell with it. I'll stop when we get to Charleston."

FOUR

Since we had a little time on our hands, I decided to take the scenic route along the coast back to Charleston. Julie had never traveled that way before, and I knew she would enjoy visiting some of the seaside resorts, especially Virginia Beach, where we walked the boardwalk, bought a few postcards to send to Julie's parents, and sunned for a while on the beach. Arriving at Morehead City, North Carolina, several hours later, I remembered my many deployments from there to Cuba, the Dominican Republic, the Mediterranean, and Africa. With great fanfare I announced, "This is where I shipped out to come find you, sweetheart."

"That's nice, honey," she said without inflection.

That's nice? That's all I get?

"Michael, it's after nine o'clock; we have to eat. It's a long ride to Charleston. And I need to go to the loo."

Ah, now I understood. It was nature howling, "Relieve me. Feed me." I was feeling a bit light-headed myself.

Up ahead on the dark beach road, we saw a restaurant—the Fisherman's Net. It looked like a place in which Long John Silver and his crew would be chowing down. Julie urged me to splurge a bit and celebrate my being a civilian and our new lives in Charleston.

"OK, but the place looks about two hundred years old. I hope it doesn't cost too much."

"Stop being such a worrywart, and live it up a little," she teased.

We climbed the weather-beaten stairs and opened the porthole door to the almost empty restaurant, dimly lit by old ship's lanterns on battered wooden tables. On the walls hung rusty anchors, moth-eaten fishnets, life preservers with ships' names, and dusty plastic fish.

"I just love this place. It's romantic and mysterious—something from out of the past," Julie said.

"Yeah, you might be right. I think we've entered the twilight zone. I hope the kitchen's clean," I grumbled.

She laughed. "It certainly beats another Howard Johnson's and you ordering two dogs with ketchup, mustard, and all your etceteras!"

"OK, OK. Let's put the feedbag on and party."

An old, skinny dude with a penciled-in mustache seated us and gave us menus. "Julie, I can hardly read this. It's so damn dark in here."

"Hush, you're too loud! For heaven's sake, I'll read it to you. Salads, clam chowder, fish stew."

"Yuck! Fish stew—makes me want to throw up."

"Me too." She wrinkled her nose. "Grouper, shrimp, flounder, chicken, and steak."

"I feel like a steak. How much is it?"

"Four ninety-five."

"Are they crazy? That's exorbitant! How much for the flounder?"

"One ninety-five."

"It certainly would've been cheaper at HoJo's, and I could have had my choice of thirty-two flavors of ice cream."

She gave me an exhausted look. "Listen closely, *my dear.* We can get a surf and turf and split it for five ninety-five."

"I bet the portions are small."

"Good! I couldn't help but notice those extra pounds you've put on."

"Hey, that's not fair. You're hitting below the belt now."

"You mean below the flab?" Julie tried to keep a straight face but cracked a grin. Then she snorted and began to chuckle. My spirits lifted, and I laughed too.

The steak and flounder proved to be delicious. We topped it off with coffee and three big scoops of chocolate, strawberry, and vanilla ice cream. Suddenly I felt a bare foot moving up and down my calf. Well, two could play at that game. I kicked off my loafer. We moved our chairs closer and began necking. The few late-night guests took no notice. We were really getting hot when the waiter startled us by presenting the check, an amused look on his face.

We paid up and were hurrying across the lot to the Fairlane with the obvious in mind when I veered away.

Julie said, "What's wrong?"

"Let's go to the beach and find a patch of soft sand between the dunes."

"OK," she replied breathlessly.

Kneeling on the sand, loosening each other's garments but not removing them, we pressed urgently against each other. The sound of the surf crashed against the shore, and a warm, salty breeze washed over our bodies. Caught up in the throes of passion, I screamed, "Jesus Christ!" I had been struck in the ass by a flaming arrow. Again it happened. I jumped up like a jack-in-the-box and almost tumbled, with my pants caught around my knees.

"What happened?" Julie cried. Then she shrieked, "Bloody hell!" and leaped up. We were under attack by a squadron of dive-bombing, bloodsucking, fucking mosquitos. Grabbing hands, we beat a hasty retreat back to the Ford, scratching crazily, all lust evaporated.

Julie said, "We're nuts! Look on the bright side: we had no protection, remember?"

I thought maybe I should cross myself like my Aunt Rosa and thank all the saints. "Maybe God ordered up those devils to attack us."

"Unlikely," she responded wryly. With that we cranked up the car and headed for Charleston, a good six hours away.

We drove through the night on Highway 17 and finally reached the stretch of road that cut through the densely wooded area of Mount

Pleasant, with its ubiquitous pines, palmettos, and live oaks. On the left, a new development was being built called Cooper Estates, which butted up against Shem Creek, with its small flotilla of shrimp boats. It would be an ideal place to live if you had the money. It was close to the Old City and the beautiful beaches of Sullivan's Island and Isle of Palms. On the right was Hobcaw, with the prestigious Hobcaw Yacht Club nestled among the moss-covered oaks where the Cooper and Wando Rivers merged. Looming up ahead in the early dawn light was the treacherous Grace Memorial Bridge, which spanned the Cooper River for well over two miles, its two narrow lanes divided by a double yellow line. Many Charlestonians went out of their way to avoid this dangerous bridge. I had often thought, passing over it, that it had been engineered with population reduction in mind.

Julie tensed and clenched her fists. "Here we go again, over this damn stupid bridge."

"Just keep your eyes closed, honey. It'll be over soon."

"What do you mean, over? As in dead?"

"No way I'm going to allow that to happen. We got a lot of living to do yet." All the while I was saying a few Our Fathers in my head. I was the least devout nonpracticing Catholic on the planet, but when you needed a god, you needed a god. I was glad the sun was coming up, and we wouldn't be confronted with glaring headlights from approaching vehicles. Another blessing was that we didn't have to navigate the roller-coaster bridge through dense fog, when a car traveling in the opposite direction would suddenly burst through the thick gray curtain like a demon, scaring the bejesus out of you.

Finally we were over the kamikaze bridge. We needed a couple of stiff drinks, but that was impossible given the hour.

"Michael, let's go to a motel. I'm exhausted. I need to sleep."

"Don't you want to see the apartment first?" I asked.

"No. It's too early, and we'll disturb the other residents. I need some rest. I can't think clearly."

I was a little crestfallen—I wanted her to see how great our new place was compared to anything we'd had in the past. But she was right. I was wiped too, and we would have a big day ahead of us, shopping for furniture and other essentials. "Where do you wanna go, baby?"

"Anyplace that's close. I don't want to roam all over the city with you looking for a deal."

"How about the St. John Hotel? It's a few blocks away, on the corner of Meeting and Queen."

The tired, old hotel still maintained some of its regal charm from an era that predated the Civil War. Julie looked the place over.

"Are you OK with this, baby?" I asked.

"As long as it has a bed with clean sheets and a decent loo, I don't care."

Despite the noisy window air conditioner and mattress springs that moaned like a dying harpsichord when we sat, the sheets were indeed clean, and the bathroom was good enough. However, it probably had not been updated since 1902, when President Teddy Roosevelt bedded down at the old place.

We slept like the dead for eight hours straight. I awoke with a start and shook Julie. "Let's get moving. It's two in the afternoon."

"Oh my God. I can't believe we slept that long." She stumbled out of bed, yawning and mumbling to herself.

"Let's hope it's not too late for us to buy some furniture and get it delivered today, or we'll be spending another night here," I said. As we left, Julie looked back wistfully at the bed.

Fewer than thirty minutes later, unbathed and somewhat unkempt, we entered Goodman and Sons' furniture store on King Street. Pug's wife, Maggie, had recommended it highly, telling us it had the best prices and selection in town. As we paused, trying to get our bearings, a well-dressed, courteous assistant in his fifties greeted us. We asked him where we would find Mediterranean-style furniture.

We picked out a bed, a chest of drawers, a night table, a couch, and a small dining room set with six chairs. We found our salesman, and I handed him a list of all the items we had selected. At that point, Julie asked for directions to the ladies' room. She was getting out of Dodge: it always made her nervous when I started bargaining.

I learned early in life from my Neapolitan grandmother, Maria, who used to take me shopping in Little Italy on the lower east side of Manhattan, that only a fool would pay the asking price for anything. After haggling for a few minutes, we reached a tentative agreement on the total price. Just as the salesman left to see if he could get it approved by some unseen person in the back office, Julie returned.

"Is it over yet?"

"Not until some higher-up gives the OK."

"Crikey, Michael, this is so stressful. I wish you didn't always have to do this."

"Hey, relax. I'm trying to save us some bucks."

"I know." She sighed and reached into her purse for a cigarette. Then she changed her mind, put the pack of cigarettes back, and pulled out a pack of gum.

After a few more tense minutes, the salesman returned, smiling. He clapped his hands. "We have a deal."

"Cool!" I responded.

"What about delivery?" asked Julie.

"Don't worry, ma'am. The store is more than happy to oblige you due to your circumstances. We'll make a special delivery this evening."

We thanked him, paid in cash with part of the money we'd saved and gotten from our families as wedding gifts, and rocketed out of the store.

Keeping up the hectic pace, we found ourselves in Woolworth's on King Street, with a crowd of shoppers wandering up and down the fluorescent-lit aisles between rows of inexpensive merchandise.

"Michael, I'm really going off. I feel faint."

"What's wrong, baby?"

"I'm hypoglycemic. I need to eat something."

"What the heck is that? Is it serious?"

"No, it's just my blood sugar is low. We haven't eaten since Moorhead City."

"I could go for a bite too, and I have a headache coming on," I said. "Do you have any aspirin?"

She rummaged through her bottomless purse, retrieved a small tin, and handed me two small pills.

"Give me another one. This is going to be a doozy."

She answered sharply, "You'll upset your stomach."

"It's my stomach. Let me be the judge."

"Have it your way, he-man." The stress was getting to us.

Only a few people were at the lunch counter, drinking sweet teas and colas and eating ice cream. As we were scanning the menu, we caught the eye of a bespectacled colored waitress in a white uniform who was talking to another customer at the far end of the long counter. She came over to us, took a pencil out of her pomaded hair, and asked if we were ready to order.

Julie replied, "I would like a grilled cheese sandwich with fries and a cup of coffee, please." She looked at me. "I'm just going to the loo to freshen up. I'll be back in a sec."

"Hey, d'ya need me to come along?"

She cocked her head and enquired sweetly, "So what are you going to do in the ladies' room?"

The waitress brought her hand to her mouth to keep from laughing as Julie walked away, and then she asked what I would like to have.

"Give me a burger with the works, a bag of chips, and a bottle of bourbon."

She chuckled. "Seriously, sir, what do you want to drink?"

"A beer would be fine, thanks."

Sighing mightily, she said, "Gimme a break."

"OK, I'll have a root beer with three cherries in it."

"Well, I *surely* do thank you." She walked away, shaking her head.

Left alone, I swiveled on my stool while drumming out a beat on the counter. I was antsy to get going. Finally we were served our meal, and we finished it quickly. I dropped a buck fifty on the counter and swigged down my drink. Then we roamed the store, picking up pots and pans and cleaning supplies.

At the checkout, Julie handed the cashier a twenty, and I asked her how she was feeling.

"Fine," she responded. "The carbohydrates did the trick. What about you, Michael? You still look peaky."

"About the same," I said, trying to ignore the escalating pain behind my eyes.

"Let's just make a short stop at the grocery store. It's been a hectic three days. You should rest."

She got no argument from me. I was feeling extremely ill.

Ten minutes later we pulled up at a small supermarket on the corner of Smith and Vanderhorst, in a predominantly colored neighborhood only two blocks away from our new apartment in Radcliffeborough. It was the only viable location for us since we couldn't afford two cars. Julie would have a short walk to the Medical College, and I would be working in the city of Charleston.

While we were checking out of the store, Mr. Davies, the owner, greeted us, and he introduced us to his son, Tom, and daughter-in-law, Karen, who worked with him. They were gentle people with warm, caring demeanors.

Julie remarked as we left, "You know, those people reminded me a lot of Mr. and Mrs. Herrick. They lived in the village of Shadywell in England, where I lived as a kid before we moved to South Africa. They ran the only grocery and post office in the area. They helped so many families get through hard times by letting them buy food on credit. They delivered supplies and mail to the old and sick and looked in on them regularly. One day the village was hit by a terrible storm. There was lanky, old John Herrick in his wellies, directing traffic and carrying kids across the flooded streets for their mothers. They even delivered candles to the old folks when the electricity went off."

"Sure doesn't sound like any store owners back in New York. If you didn't pay up, they probably would've had your fingers broken."

Reaching our destination, we climbed the metal stairway to our new apartment, which overlooked Rutledge Avenue. Juggling shopping bags, I opened the door. Julie walked in, set the groceries down, and then walked around the apartment with an eagle eye, with me following her closely.

Turning, she smiled at me. "This place is great. You did a jolly good job. It's modern, roomy, bright—and we finally have a real kitchen we can work in together. I love these light oak floors. And being on the top floor will be a lot quieter." She paused to catch her breath. "Our new furniture will fit perfectly. And when we can buy drapes and a few rugs, it'll be very stylish." I was so relieved my girl was happy.

Suddenly she quieted and stared at me. "Michael, are you OK? Is your headache getting worse? You look positively gray."

"I feel like my head's going to explode. The aspirin didn't work. I guess it's the stress." A wave of nausea suddenly hit me, and I ran for the bathroom, half blinded by the pain. I heaved my guts up with seemingly no end until, finally exhausted, I removed my head from the commode. I splashed cold water on my face and returned to Julie in the empty bedroom.

"Are you feeling better, honey?'

"A little, now that I've thrown up."

"Is something else upsetting you?"

"It's silly, but I'm worried to death about starting insurance school on Monday."

"Why?"

"I'm afraid I might fail, and then what will we do?"

"Oh, Michael, don't fret so much." She placed her hands against the sides of my face and brought my aching head to rest against hers. She said lovingly, "I think I know you better. You will *not* fail. If anything, you'll excel. Don't doubt yourself. Trust me." She wrapped her arms around my waist and rocked me gently. I felt the headache subsiding. She was magic.

And then, thank God, the furniture arrived.

FIVE

Sunday afternoon found me at the Wade Hampton Hotel in Columbia, South Carolina, where I was to take the insurance course. Julie had been as sorry to see me go as I had been to leave, but she was full of plans for the coming week. Most important, we were having a phone installed at the apartment. Julie would call me with the number. I had kissed her before leaving and said suggestively, "Maybe I could stay a little while longer?"

"Uh-*uh*. You need to get cracking. Anyway, you do know that too much sex is bad for you, don't you?"

"Oh yeah?"

"Yeah. We don't want it to fall off." She'd giggled wickedly. What a send-off! As I'd driven away, I'd carried the image of Julie waving good-bye, her hair curling wildly in the humidity.

At the hotel, the assistant manager, who had the bearing of an English valet in service to some rich nobleman, welcomed me warmly. How long had he practiced his act in front of a mirror to perfect it?

"Mr. Romano, I'm to give you this envelope, which has a set of instructions from your company, and to inform you that you will be sharing room five zero four with a Mr. Lowery, who has already checked in."

"Thanks, pal," I replied. He looked slightly affronted. *What's wrong with "Thanks, pal"?*

He reached across the counter and handed me the keys, saying with a slight bow, "I do hope you and Mr. Lowery will have a comfortable stay with us."

Comfortable for me would have been having my own room—at least then I could scratch my balls in private. But then again this arrangement beat trying to get some sack time while listening to a concerto of seventy marines snoring, belching, and farting and having to share a john with twelve crappers in a row with no doors or even partitions.

A few minutes later, I was inserting the key into the lock of room 504. I belatedly wondered if I should have knocked. Well, it was too late for that. I pushed open the door with luggage in hand.

Lowery was stretched out on his bed, watching a small black-and-white TV. When he saw me, he reared up and walked over in his stocking feet to introduce himself. "Hi, I'm Owen Lowery from Greenville." He held out his hand.

"Mike Romano from Charleston." We shook. We were about the same age. He had a boyish face and an easygoing manner. I liked him right away. He told me that he had recently gotten out of the air force.

"Why?" I asked.

"I missed my family, my friends, and my high school sweetheart—she's now my fiancée—back in Greenville, where I grew up."

Boy, are we at opposite poles in life experience.

"So what about you, Mike?" he asked.

"I got out of the marine corps about a week ago. I'm a New Yorker."

"I guessed that, with that Yankee accent."

We both laughed.

"But unlike you, I dislike my hometown. Also, I had a love-hate relationship with the corps, and the hate won out."

"Gee, I'm sorry to hear that."

"That's life," I replied. "But I got married to a great girl while I was in the service. That made up for everything. We decided to settle in Charleston, my last duty station."

The more we talked, the more I relaxed, allowing my true nature to emerge, which was unusual for me with strangers.

We decided to have dinner together and turn in early after watching his favorite TV show (and mine)—*Ed Sullivan*—so we would be bright eyed and bushy tailed for our eight o'clock class the next morning in one of the hotel conference rooms.

We rose early after a good night's rest and were standing outside the classroom in a crowded hallway with about forty other guys wearing name tags, smoking furiously, and talking loudly. The tension level was high. I was surprised to see Sal Fanelli, a slim, balding, fifty-something staff manager, standing in the crowd. I walked over to him and reminded him of our brief meeting a couple of months back, when I'd been interviewed for my job.

"Oh, yes," he said, staring at me in recognition. "You're Dawson's new protégé. How's it feel to be out of the marines?"

"Great, sir."

"I felt the same way when they discharged me from the army back in '45."

"Sir, are you going to be one of our instructors today?" I asked.

"Oh, no. This training is now mandatory for new agents and staff managers. It's been a long time since I've been in a classroom." He sounded disgruntled and seemed somewhat nervous. Knowing that he and probably others were as worried as I was made me feel better.

When the course director appeared, the men snuffed out their cigarettes, and the mood became subdued as we all followed him into the classroom and took seats at folding tables. After the last man pulled his chair noisily into place, a silence fell. At the front, the instructor was writing on a moveable blackboard. When he finished he turned sideways to examine us with a piercing look, tapping the board with his chalk.

"I'm Mr. Tylke, your course director." He repeated his name with more emphasis. I detected a warning not to forget it or make fun of it.

The grade-school clown in me emerged. *Ah, Mr. Tickles, pleased to meet you. I can't tell you how tickled I am to be taking your course.*

Then: *Stop that shit, Romano. One minute you're a nervous wreck, the next minute you're a comedian?*

Mr. Tickles—no, Tylke—looked down at the floor, fingers pressed together while he collected his thoughts, like a Baptist minister ready to launch into his sermon. "Does anyone know when insurance was first invented?"

Everyone looked blank. I don't think any of us had any idea.

"Take a guess, gentlemen."

A couple of hands shot up, mine not included. "Yes, Mr. Richards." He nodded toward a short fellow in the front row.

"Two hundred years ago, at the time of the Industrial Revolution?"

"Good try, Mr. Richards, but incorrect."

Next he pointed to a big guy sitting in the back row who looked like a Clemson fullback. "I'll guess five hundred years ago, sir."

"Why do you say that, Mr. Bundy?"

"Well, it sounds like a good, round number to me." We all laughed, including the instructor.

Hey, he's not such a bad sort.

Then a twig of a guy wearing a pink bow tie and a mischievous look blurted, "I know, sir. Back in biblical times, when Noah was selling travel insurance to folks booking passage on his ark!"

Mr. Tickles smiled pensively as the class once again erupted in laughter. When quiet fell, he said, "Mr. Rooney is closer than he knows. The earliest record we have of the concept of insurance goes back five thousand years, to the ancient Chinese."

We all glanced at one another, looking flabbergasted.

"To protect against total loss of cargo being shipped on dangerous rivers, they divided the goods between many vessels so that if a ship were lost, the owners would not suffer a total loss. This is called spreading the risk and is the basis of all insurance companies today. Next we have the Greeks and Romans, who, in about six hundred BC, developed the first form of life and health insurance. They set up benevolent societies, or guilds, that cared for the families of sick or deceased members and paid funeral expenses."

He went on for a good while, giving more examples of types of insurance throughout history. The first fire insurance had been instituted in Charleston, back in colonial times. Given its history of destruction by fire and being the instigator of the Civil War, that was probably a good thing. Finally he began the history of the Cardinal State Insurance Company, of which I was now, hopefully, an employee.

"The Cardinal State Insurance Company was established in 1920, and our main office is located in North Carolina. We cover eleven southern states, and up until recently we were a weekly premium insurance company, selling what is known in the business as industrial insurance. Most of our customers still come from the lower classes. However, beginning today, all new agents and staff managers will be required to take this course to become more proficient in insurance overall and to learn about our new line, which will target the upper classes and be sold on a monthly basis. We will compete with much larger companies, expand our present markets, and open new ones. What this will mean to you is opportunities to bring home bigger paychecks and chances for rapid promotion."

I was elated by what he said. Lowery and I looked at each other and nodded.

Tickles continued, "Study hard, gentlemen. Get to know your product well. And by the way, a grade of seventy is required to pass this course."

Then he passed out thick study booklets covering the four days of course work, which included insurance vocabulary, types of insurance, calculation of premiums, state law, ethics, and a canned insurance presentation we would have to memorize and recite in class. Everyone seemed to dread the last part the most. Somewhere in there we stopped for a quick lunch break. Finally, at four thirty, class ended. After working through a blizzard of terminology and definitions, we were in desperate need of drinks and smokes.

Owen and I headed out of the hotel in search of a liquor store to buy a bottle of whiskey before it closed at sundown. On the way, I noticed a Confederate battle flag flying atop the state capitol. Hadn't anyone told them the Civil War was over, and they had gotten their butts kicked?

After finding a red dot store, we bought our booze with the agreement that we would use it for medicinal purposes only. The prescription called for one shot before dinner and two before going to bed. When we got back to the hotel about ten minutes later, I got a message slip with Julie's name and a phone number. I ran up to the room. Owen had already poured two hefty belts of the sour mash. He politely took his outside while I called Julie.

She'd been busy. She had already called my mother and checked in at the Medical College to complete her paperwork for the job. While there she'd dropped in on Rina Avery at the lab to say hello and to thank her for helping her find her new position. Tom and Rina had invited us to dinner on Saturday at the Sailfish Restaurant, a marvelous seafood place on Folly Road. Julie had also met some of our new neighbors, including a nurse next door who worked at the Medical College Hospital.

"But enough about me. How's the course so far?" she asked. She chuckled when I told her about Tickles and then warned, "Just be careful you don't slip up and call him that to his face. You do want to pass this thing."

We wrapped it up with "I love yous" and promises to speak the next day. I was hungry as a bear and went to find Owen.

We decided to eat in-house, to save more time for studying. After hamburgers and fries, we returned to the room and began studying in earnest.

I was sitting on the edge of the bed in my shorts, perusing the study material. Owen said, "Why don't we study together and quiz each other, to make sure we have all the bases covered?"

"Sounds good to me, Owen."

We finished our labors at around eleven thirty. Owen felt we had everything down pat. I wanted to put in another forty-five minutes of review, and I retreated to the bathroom, pillow in hand, where I wouldn't disturb Owen. He was already sound asleep and snoring loudly.

Somewhere in the distance was a faint lateral glow of light followed by a menacing rumble. A storm was approaching. The glow became brighter and the rumble louder. I had to get up and find shelter. But my legs wouldn't move. I tried to lift myself on my arms, but they were too feeble. Suddenly the storm rolled over and around me, and I smelled black powder. The earth was shaking and breaking, as if hell were trying to release its demons. Gray, red, and blue shapes were whirling around me, screaming. My heart raced as I lay there paralyzed. A gray form loomed over me with brutish, hate-filled eyes, a bayonet poised at my throat. The fiend grinned as he thrust his spear forward. I raised my hands helplessly, yelling, "No, no, no..."

"Mike, wake up! You're having one hell of a dream." Lowery shook me awake. I heaved myself out of the tub, stiff as a board.

The next three days passed in a blur. Owen and I scored aces in class quizzes and participation, and I delivered the canned talk with Shakespearian flair. At nine o'clock sharp on Friday morning, Tickles handed out exam papers. We had two hours to answer one hundred questions. The class was silent except for the occasional nervous cough and the whisper of turning pages.

About midway through, Mr. Fanelli tapped my shoulder. I turned to see what he wanted, and he gestured for me to show my answer sheet. I looked to the front of the room. Mr. Tylke was halfway out the door, speaking to an assistant. He had his back turned to us. Surreptitiously I positioned my paper for him to copy and fervently hoped no one would catch on. I continued the exam. The answers came to me like pennies falling into a slot. Owen and I finished with thirty minutes to spare. We turned in our test papers, shook hands with Tickles, hurried to our room, grabbed our luggage, and quit the hotel. We said our farewells as we headed for the parking lot, stripping off our jackets and ties.

Six

When the alarm went off at seven o'clock, Julie and I hit the floor running. After quick showers, coffee, and cornflakes, we were out the door to begin the first day on our respective jobs. A few minutes later, I was on the Ashley River Bridge, looking down at some lucky boaters on the sun-speckled river as they left the marina. I envied their freedom and the serenity and excitement the waters would provide.

Taking the left fork off the bridge, I cruised down Savannah Highway to the pseudocolonial office building graced by two stunted columns at the front entrance. Here was the Cardinal State Insurance Company. I pulled into the parking lot, killed the engine, took a deep breath, and strode purposefully inside. Room 103 was at the end of an unadorned hallway with gray carpeting. I paused to compose myself and then walked down the corridor, tightening my grip on my brand-new attaché case, and crossed the threshold. Two secretaries I had met earlier were hard at work.

"Good morning, Mr. Romano," said Ida. She was a good-natured, motherly woman who wore too many rings on her plump fingers, which had typed up my employment contract at light speed.

"The top o' the morning to you, Ida and Ellen," I said cheerfully, trying to imitate Barry Fitzgerald, the Irish actor. They smiled graciously.

"May I get you a cup of coffee?" asked Ellen, a dark haired girl of about twenty. She had a figure reminiscent of Popeye's girlfriend, Olive Oyl.

"Yes, please," I said. I wanted to continue the congenial mood.

Coffee in hand, I sat in the waiting area, watching flocks of agents coming in and lining up like two-dollar bettors at a racetrack in front of the reception counter, greeting the secretaries, making various requests of them, and getting messages and mail.

Mr. Dawson entered, and I shot out of my chair.

"Good morning, Mike," he said cordially as we shook hands. "Nice suit."

"Thank you, sir. I bought it at Perlitz's men's store."

"Great place to shop for apparel—I go there often."

"I agree, sir, but it's expensive."

"It's well worth the money. It will pay off handsomely when doing business." He checked his watch. "My goodness. It's almost eight. I need to get you seated before the morning meeting begins."

Most of the twenty-some agents were already in their chairs. I ended up in the front row under Dawson's eagle eye. Mr. Dawson would oversee my training over the next four weeks. I would work with him day and night, learning the business and preparing to take the state licensing exam. Mr. Randall, the general manager, began the meeting with a loud and enthusiastic, "Good morning." He looked over at me. "I want us all to welcome Mike Romano, our new agent, recently out of the marines. Please rise, Mike." God, I felt embarrassed as I stood and they politely applauded.

"We all know that the marines are hard chargers." He had that right. "I'm expecting he will give you leading agents some real competition. Especially you, Miss Kitty Kelley," he said, pointing to a woman seated across the room from me. I turned and saw this older gal in her midfifties, with a face that had seen too much sun. At one time, she must have been a real knockout.

She laughed, looking directly at me. "If he ever beats me out for leading agent, I'll treat him to a catfish dinner and a bottle of bourbon on Wadmalaw Island—and give him a night he'll never forget!" The office rang with wild laughter and catcalls.

I responded, "Miss Kelley, I may be inexperienced, but when I'm challenged I give it my all. If by any chance I might win, could we change the entrée to a steak and make that two bottles? I'm a drinking man, honey!" Mr. Dawson was struggling to control his gentlemanly demeanor. Kitty was laughing the hardest, and she threw me a big kiss, which I happily received.

Finally everyone calmed down, and Mr. Randall began a pretty boring meeting, telling us that we were behind on our production goals and needed to pick up the pace. In addition, the home office would be visiting us within a few weeks.

When the meeting ended, some of the agents came over to introduce themselves. Many were not well dressed. Their trousers needed pressing, and their shoes were scuffed. They wore frayed short-sleeved shirts and cheap ties.

After the introductions, Mr. Dawson and I, along with a half dozen other agents, crossed Savannah Highway to a place called Bilbro's Diner. Even though I'd had breakfast earlier, my mouth watered as I listened to the others order eggs and sausage and home fries. I decided on the shrimp and grits—Julie's favorite. As we were chowing down and talking, I found myself enjoying the camaraderie of my fellow agents. They heckled each other mercilessly and told off-color country jokes that cracked me up. Listening to their southern accents, I was taken back to Jeb's BBQ and wondered if any of them were like those good ol' boys. I dismissed the thought immediately; I liked these guys a lot.

At around nine thirty, Mr. Dawson and I headed downtown in his light-blue Cadillac Eldorado convertible. I felt like a big shot as we cruised into the old city with my arm slung over the back of the white bucket seat. It was so comfortable, I could have gone on riding all day.

Driving down Rutledge Avenue, passing by Hampton Park, Mr. Dawson cleared his throat and glanced over at me. "The area you'll be working in is predominantly colored. Most of the people are poor and have little or no education. What you'll mostly be selling is burial insurance. Most of them want fancy funerals—what they call big send-offs. They have so little in life, but the one way they get something special is by dying. If you make it a point to treat them with respect and sell them only what they need and can afford, you should be successful. Unfortunately many agents are prejudiced, which the Negroes are quick to pick up on. Couple that with a lukewarm work ethic, and they sell very little insurance. Simply put, what this means to you is that your competition is weak."

I guess I won't be selling any monthly $5,000-plus policies out here, much less doing any estate planning.

"Mr. Dawson, I really appreciate your advice. Anyone doing business with me will be treated with respect and fairness. Also, where the coloreds are concerned, I have the utmost sympathy for them."

"I'm glad you feel that way. Unfortunately this land is the embodiment of many of the ills throughout America. But changes are afoot that may set things right."

"I hope you're right, sir, but it's been an uphill struggle."

"Listen, Mike, I want you to relax and not be so formal with me. The name's Jim."

"Thanks, Jim," I said, feeling that I might have found a new friend.

When we arrived downtown, Jim parked the Caddy in a downtrodden area. We collected weekly premiums and canvassed for new business when time allowed. It was hard, hot, sweaty work that required a lot of walking and climbing stairs. The nonstop pace, interrupted only by a quick lunch break at a small eatery on Calhoun, went on for more than eight hours.

We had made our last call around seven. Jim said, "That's it. Let's head back to the office so you can pick up your car."

Back in the vacant parking lot, Jim said, “Rest up tonight. Tomorrow will be tougher.”

Fifteen minutes later, with those words not yet faded from my memory, I came through the door shouting, “Hey, babe, I’m home. Let’s party!”

Julie appeared from the kitchen wearing a white T-shirt and light-blue short shorts. She looked yummy.

“Come over here and give your lover man a big hug.”

“No,” she said, fending me off. “I’ll give you a kiss, but keep your hands to yourself. I’m not about to go rolling around with you on the floor while dinner’s cooking. Anyway, it’s too hot for hanky-panky.”

I dutifully obeyed, hands clasped behind my back. She put her hands on my shoulders and on tiptoes gave me a sedate kiss.

“If we’re not going to fool around, let’s eat,” I said. “I’m so hungry I could eat a whole hog off the spit.”

She gave me a curious look. “Do I detect a southern accent?”

“If you do, it’s a southern New York one.”

“You sound like one of the Rebs out of *Gone with the Wind*.”

“Could be. I spent an hour with a bunch of southern boys, eating breakfast. It was a lot of fun. And you can’t be with Jim for several hours and not have that old Alabama accent rub off on you a bit.”

A buzzer went off in the kitchen. “Michael, open a bottle of wine while I drain the pasta.”

“OK, babe,” I answered. After uncorking a bottle of Chianti, I stripped down to my undershirt and adjusted the rotating fan to blow tepid air toward the dining table.

Minutes later she reappeared.

“Looks great, Julie,” I said, admiring the large bowl of spaghetti and meatballs.

As I lost myself in the food and the wine, Julie said, “So what’s with this Jim thing? Up until now, it’s been Mr. Dawson with a capital D.”

“We got to know each other today.” I gave her a rundown of our early morning conversation while riding to the debit.

“What the heck is a debit?”

"It's just a geographic area designated by the company in which an agent collects and sells insurance. In my case, it covers a good part of the west side of the city."

"Blimey, that's a lot of territory to cover in a week."

"I don't have a week to cover it. By no later than five on Thursday afternoon, I have to be back in the office to reconcile my book. And that can take many hours. It'll be easier if I just get a bite to eat after we're done at the office, so don't worry about dinner. And there'll be nights when I'll be working late, depending on what hour I can meet with clients to sell them policies. I'll be able to give you a heads up on that."

Julie sighed. "I guess that's the price we'll have to pay to get ahead."

"Anyway, today we worked in our own backyard, right here in Radcliffeborough. Jim gave me some historical background that's really interesting. You know how we think of South of Broad as being the smartest area to live in? Well, only a few of the original Charleston families still live there today. Apparently a couple of hundred years back, the wealthy planters were making their move from South of Broad to Radcliffeborough."

"Ah, that explains those once beautiful plantation houses we've seen around here that've been chopped up into diddy apartments. So who took over South of Broad?"

"The merchant class, who the planters looked down on."

"Sounds like the landed gentry in England. They thought work was beneath them, and a day's activity should consist of drinking, chasing a fox, gambling, and ordering a young maid to bed for a little debauchery."

"The southern boys had one up on their European cousins: their own harems of brown sugar that were getting lighter with each generation. That was certainly evident today, judging by the many mulattos I saw." I paused. "You know, Julie, I identified somewhat with the people and the families I saw today."

"How so?"

"Many of them have absentee fathers, and the mothers and grandmothers seem to be the only security for the children. According to Jim most of the mothers have to work or abandon their kids altogether, leaving it all up to the grandmothers or the streets. If it hadn't been for *my* grandmother watching over me while my mother worked at the chewing gum factory, I would have been at a total loss. Also these kids are growing up with the added problem of racial discrimination." Pausing to refill our wineglasses, I said, "Enough of that. Overall it's been a good day. Jim sold a couple of policies that will help increase my paycheck, and I enjoyed hanging out with him. How did it go with you today?"

Her cheeks pinked up, and I realized she had been dying to tell me about it. "I think this is going to be a really interesting job. I met Dr. Herschaft for the first time today. He hadn't been there when I'd left. He's an infectious diseases doc, but he also has some great research studies going. He has a big lab on the second floor of the research building and two other techs who do the routine stuff. He gave me a bunch of papers to read. I'll be doing the actual experiments. I also told him I'm interested in going for my master's degree in microbiology, and he seemed very supportive. I also met a really famous surgeon who is a burn specialist who's coming here next year. One of the projects will be on infections in burn patients. And I'm going to be involved in running the micro labs for the medical students. Me, teaching! It's amazing—I came back at just the right time." She finally stopped to catch her breath. I raised my glass to her, and we toasted each other in mutual delight.

Seven

After four days on the debit, in ninety-degree weather and suffocating humidity, I was alive and well on Friday morning, albeit a few pounds lighter. The office buzzed with loud chatter and laughter. Mr. Randall walked into the room and nodded to Mr. Fanelli, who was standing in front of a fifteen-foot blackboard that listed all the agents' names and the three categories of insurance we sold. Everyone quieted down.

Mr. Randall said, "I know y'all are tired. It's been one helluver hot week. Let's get down to business quickly, so we can all leave early." He looked at the first name on the board. "Mr. Mitchell, please report."

"Life weekly; two dollars, fifty cents; no health; no monthly."

Mr. Fanelli chalked in the results. "Mr. Sharpen."

"Life weekly; three dollars, twenty-five cents; no health; no monthly."

"Mr. Ogden."

"Sorry, nothing to report."

Fanelli posted three large zeros. Everyone shifted in their seats, looking embarrassed for Ogden. I silently vowed that would never happen to me, even if I had to buy the insurance myself.

"Miss Kitty?"

"Life weekly; seven dollars, thirty-five cents; no health; fifteen dollars monthly for five thousand coverage."

The group applauded. Kitty, all aglow, took a bow as if she had won an Academy Award. She looked my way and winked. I gave her a thumbs-up.

After a dozen or more reports, Fanelli called on Jim and me.

"Life weekly; four dollars, fifty cents; one health; no monthly," Jim intoned. We received polite applause.

When the reports were completed, Mr. Randall smoothed out his mustache and loosened the bottom button of his jacket. He announced that some small changes were being made in office procedure, and we would receive a memo about them early the next week. He repeated what he had said on Monday about needing to pick up production and that the big boys from the home office would be descending on us soon. I sensed that the sword of Damocles might be hanging over his head.

Next he wished us a good weekend. "Come back Monday with a fire in your belly and ready to sell."

As I was closing my attaché case, Jim and Mr. Randall walked over to me, looking deeply concerned.

"Mike," Mr. Randall said mournfully, "yesterday I received your test results from Columbia."

Nervous sweat popped on my brow.

He placed his hand on my shoulder like a priest preparing a man for the gallows. "You scored one of the highest grades in the class. Ninety-two."

He and Jim fell about laughing, but not me. Blood pressure dropping round my knees, I blurted, "You had me shittin' bricks!"

Jim said, "Mike, we were just having fun. Honestly, we're proud of you, and we think you'll be very successful."

Randall pulled out his wallet and presented me with a twenty-dollar bill. "Take your wife out and have a good time on Jim and me."

I thanked them and shook their hands. Then I excused myself, saying, "I have to go buy an air conditioner. Julie and I are sweltering in our apartment and haven't managed a good night's sleep since we moved in."

I headed out of the door like quicksilver.

After buying an air conditioner, I drove home and lugged it up the steps to our apartment. Out of breath, I set it down in front of the window and rested awhile. When I opened the box, I discovered I needed a screwdriver to install it. No way in hell was I going back out into the heat. A kitchen knife would do the job just fine. Having successfully installed the brackets with only a couple of knife wounds to my hand, I slipped the air conditioner into place. I was very pleased with myself. Then, when I tried to plug it in, I discovered that the cord was three inches short of the outlet. A cannonade of vulgarities flew from my mouth.

Calming down a few minutes later, I once again braved the tropics to seek out the much-needed extension cord. When I returned I plugged it in to the unit, stripped completely down, threw my sodden clothes in every direction, grabbed a beer from the fridge, collapsed on the couch, and fell asleep.

As the day wore on, I heard the front door latch click. Still half asleep, I looked over at Julie, who was standing there with her mouth hanging open.

"What the hell are you doing lying naked on the couch?" Then she eyed the room. "My God, this place looks like a Chinese laundry gone amok." Still standing at the wide-open door, she was unaware of the blissful coolness of the room. I silently pointed to the heavenly box. She closed the door, walked over to the air conditioner, and briefly admired it. Then she quickly undressed and bounded over to the couch, where we both fell asleep.

An hour later, locked in a frigid embrace and trembling, we awoke, got up, turned off the air conditioner, and took a hot shower together.

At eight the Port City Drive-in downtown was hopping. We ordered our usual favorites and discussed the day's events.

"I got my test results back from Columbia." I paused for a second.

"Well, are you going to keep me in suspense?"

“I got a ninety-two!”

Sighing, she shook her head. “That’s fantastic. I told you that you would do well. You had no need to worry.” She paused for a beat. “You know, we’ve been married for two years, and some things about you I still don’t get.”

“What are you driving at?”

“I’ve lived through you being court-martialed, thrown in the brig, and fighting guys twice your size, and you never wavered. Why did you get so bloody unnerved about having to pass an insurance exam?”

“I told you that night when I got sick: we had a lot riding on my passing. That’s different than fighting some gorilla or telling some NCO to go fuck himself.”

“I don’t buy that. There’s something more.”

“I was just stressed out by the trip, the test, and a run-in I had with a few hicks in North Carolina.”

“What happened?”

I told her as she nervously fiddled with her wedding band.

When I had finished, she said, “I’m proud of your stand at that redneck place even though it frightens me to death thinking what could have happened. It reminds me of something I once read: all that is required for evil to prevail is for good men to do nothing.”

She asked me for a smoke. I sensed she was tense: I certainly was. I pulled out a pack and lit one for her.

After a beat, she said, “ Michael, you know I love you, but I don’t think those were the only reasons for your having to pass that test.”

“Jesus, Julie, let it go. So what if I’m not some tower of strength? Isn’t it enough that I love you and have the responsibility of building a good life for us?”

“Michael, we’re a team, and I participate in this building of a good life. You knew when you married me that I’m not a woman who wants to stay home all day, wheel a pram around, bake cakes, play bridge, and have tea parties.”

“Yeah, yeah, OK. I know all that, but I feel I have the major responsibility for supporting us.”

"Well, get over it. There may come a time again when I make more money than you. Didn't I earn more than you when you were a lance corporal? Did you feel diminished in any way then?"

"No, but I was stuck at that miserable pay grade and couldn't do anything to change it. Now I'm earning a helluver lot more and have the chance to make some serious money down the road."

"So am I to feel like less of a person because you earn more than I do now? Well, I don't. It would be stupid if I did, and you should feel the same way. And what did that crack about being a tower of strength mean?" She glared at me. "I told you how much I love you. All I'm trying to do is understand you better and help you in any way possible." Then, to my horror, she began to cry, the tears streaking down her cheeks, onto her blouse. She angrily brushed the salty flood away with her fist. "I was worried to death how ill you became that night, that's all."

God, I felt terrible. I took her hand. "I love you, babe, and would be lost without you."

She smiled weakly. "You know, you can be a real twit sometimes."

Chuckling, I said, "I know. And maybe you are right about my reaction to the damn test. The earliest recollection I have of something like it was when my mother left me on the very first day of school. I threw up on and off for a few weeks. Then when that ended, I started getting these killer headaches."

"Oh, you poor thing! What d'ya think was the cause?"

"You know about my drunken father. He put a knife to my throat when I was four and threatened to kill me. He beat my mother and me regularly until she left him when I was five."

"Yes, that was bloody awful." She grimaced.

Just talking about it stirred up the deep feelings of insecurity and vulnerability I'd been fighting since that time.

"I was in constant fear that he would come back and get me somehow. And with me being the youngest and smallest in my class, I was easy prey for the bullies, which just made it worse. By junior high I'd had enough of being beaten up and scared. I rebelled and started lifting weights, wrestling, and boxing. Around then the headaches stopped. At sixteen, weighing about a hundred sixty pounds and standing five foot ten, I knew I could take care of myself. I gained a reputation as a badass. No one wanted to screw with me. However, I was cutting classes and got thrown out of school that year.

"Honey, let's face it: I didn't have the best education. I only got a GED while I was in the corps. If it weren't for the reading I do, I'd be stone-dog ignorant. I felt insecure taking that insurance course and exam. The fear of failing and losing your respect and the difficulty it would have caused us economically may have resurrected those old demons."

"Oh, Michael, how could you possibly think that? You really believe that my love for you is so shallow?"

"I'm sorry. I felt I have to be the main provider. I would have walked away from myself if I had failed."

My throat tightened as I looked away from her. "I guess we're all damaged children living out our lives on a stage that terrifies us."

EIGHT

Julie was quiet as we ate breakfast the next morning. I reckoned she was still upset about the argument we'd had the night before. I was also out of sorts. I couldn't reconcile what Julie had said about our relationship. I still believed I had to be the main provider and direct our lives into the future. Anything less was unacceptable to me. Also, whether Julie realized it or not, a woman needed a man to be that way—and I wasn't thinking about keeping the *little wife* imprisoned in the home, barefoot and pregnant. We couldn't get around basic instincts. No matter how much cultures changed, they were built into our genes.

When the phone rang, I hustled over to the kitchen, expecting my mother to be on the line, laying a guilt trip on me for forgetting to call her the previous week. She needed me to tell her that I loved her more than life itself and that my bowels were functioning. However, it was Tom Avery, and he sounded distraught.

"Mike, we'll have to cancel our dinner arrangements. Rina and I are catching the noon flight to Boston. My dad had a heart attack yesterday in his courtroom while he was hearing a case."

"Damn! How is he?"

"We don't know anything for sure yet. My mother was barely coherent last night when she called. But he's conscious and on oxygen.

I'm sorry we won't be able to take you out as planned. When we get back, we'll make it up to you."

"That should be the least of your worries. You don't owe us anything."

"You and Julie are good friends, and Rina and I think the world of you."

What he said touched me deeply. Never could I have imagined just a few years back that I would have a friend who had grown up in Boston high society and who was a history professor. The divide between us was enormous, but for some reason we clicked. It had been a fortuitous day, more than two years ago, when Rina, Tom's Burmese wife, and Julie had been teamed up in the same lab.

"Tom, I hope your dad recovers quickly. Julie and I will keep him in our prayers."

"Thanks. I'll give you a call when I know what's going on. Give our love to Julie."

Hanging up, I felt like a damn phony. I would hope, and Julie might pray, for his father's recovery. For me praying would be like knocking on the door to a house knowing no one was home. The words had just popped out of my mouth—social conditioning at its finest.

"What's going on?" Julie asked as I sat down and looked at my cold pancakes. I took a sip of tepid coffee and told her.

"That's so sad. Oh dear, poor Rina!"

"Why poor Rina?" I asked.

"You know what Tom's family thinks of her."

"No, I don't. What are you talking about?"

Julie hesitated. "I thought Tom would have told you."

"For God's sake, I have no idea. Spit it out."

She fidgeted with her fork. "Please promise not to pass this on to anyone. I don't know if Rina meant for me to tell you. Tom's parents were so upset when he announced that he and Rina were going to be married, they threatened to disown him."

I was stunned. I knew nothing of this. "Why on Earth?"

"Because she's Burmese. I guess she's a little too dark skinned for their taste, even though she comes from a very old and respected family in Burma. That's why Tom left Harvard and took the position down here. They were married in Charleston. When they do visit his parents, the mother treats her like the hired help."

"Good Lord, I can't believe this. Rina's such a lovely woman. Has she had any problems with the folks down here?"

"Sometimes in stores, but it's mostly been OK. They've made good friends here, especially at the college, and everything's been fine with them. And of course with us. Anyway, Michael, I guess that changes our plans for this evening. I was really looking forward to seeing them."

"I know. So was I. We haven't all been together since you left." I thought for a moment. "Hey! I know what we can do. Let's eat early, go to the movies, and pig out on popcorn and candy. We could see that new James Bond flick, *Goldfinger*. The guys in the office have been raving about it. One of the stars is a hot-looking chick called Pussy Galore who flies an airplane."

"That's so *rude*!" Then Julie said with a sly smile, "But I just love Sean Connery."

We stood at the back of a very long line in front of the movie theater, inching our way toward the ticket booth. Julie looked at me and said, "Hey, you're a million miles away."

After taking a final drag on my smoke, I flipped it into the street and watched the embers flicker as they hit the asphalt. "Do you remember a year back, when there was that big demonstration along King Street?"

"The one where the coloreds were demanding integration of businesses and fair hiring practices."

"At the time it happened, there was scuttlebutt in the guard that we might be called out to help maintain order."

"You never told me that."

"It was only a rumor. I didn't want to worry you. But I was really disturbed by the thought that I might have to patrol the streets of an American city with a weapon in my hand and perhaps use it against citizens of this country. Some yahoos in the guard were actually looking forward to doing battle."

Julie squeezed my hand. "Thank God it didn't happen."

I reached into my pocket, pulled out a stick of spearmint gum, and folded it into my mouth. It seemed I always had to keep something going there: cigarettes, gum, my fingers, whatever.

"Yeah, but it sure frightened the hell out of the Charlestonians, and I don't think they've gotten over it yet, worrying that something else might be coming."

"Justifiably so. What do they expect?"

"You know, Julie, it wasn't up until that time that I started to realize how bad the coloreds have it. Do you remember that blacklist the demonstrators published? The one with the names of the local businesses that discriminated against them?"

"Yes, I do."

"Well, we're standing in front of one of them right now, waiting to buy our tickets."

"Julie, Julie!" a voice called from behind us as we filed out of the theater. Turning, we saw our neighbor, Melanie Warren, standing on tiptoes and waving above the crowd. She was a wide-eyed, fair-skinned nurse with butterscotch hair whom Julie had befriended after we'd moved into our apartment. I hardly knew her other than having exchanged a few polite greetings.

Coming up to us, she bubbled, "Wasn't that a great movie? And that Sean Connery is so cool!"

"He certainly is." Julie replied.

I did a mental head shake. If I were Julie, I would have rolled my eyes. However, the word *cool* sounded so hot coming from Melanie's

Lowcountry lips. A guy standing by her side, looking ignored, was suddenly taken by surprise when she latched on to his arm and jerked him toward her like a hooked grouper.

"I want you to meet my beau, Eric Mattson."

Beau? Good grief!

"He's a lieutenant in the coast guard."

Well, whoop-de-do. With a moniker like that and his Scandinavian looks and reddish hair, he should have been in the Viking navy, marauding the coast of England, not protecting ours.

With introductions completed and synthetic smiles exchanged, Melanie enthusiastically urged us to join them for a show at 300 King Street. Julie and I looked at each other. Being new to the downtown area, we knew very little about its venues of entertainment. Awkward in my ignorance of the place, I said, "What's going on there tonight?"

Both of them looked surprised. Eric responded, "Haven't you guys been there?"

Obviously not, knucklehead!

"It's a club owned by the Wayfarers. They're performing there tonight."

"Hey, I heard about them," I said. "It's some folk group that's supposed to be very good."

"They're better than good," Melanie said excitedly. "They're excellent."

"What do you say, Julie?"

"Well, I don't know. It's getting late, and it's been a rough week."

"Aw, come on, honey, it's not even nine o'clock."

Melanie wheedled, "You'll love the music, Julie, and the songs. I promise you, they're super."

"What time do they start, then?"

Eric checked his watch. "In about fifteen minutes. And the show lasts around an hour."

"Well, OK, let's go," said Julie.

"Atta girl, baby!" I said. "I know we're going to have fun."

She smiled at me reluctantly.

As we turned away from the theater, I noticed a group of coloreds exiting on the tail end of the crowd. They had confined themselves to the balcony. I wondered why, given the new law. Were they fearful to sit somewhere else? Was the old law still being enforced? Were they ignorant of the changes? Or were they just comfortable being among themselves? From what I could see, nothing had changed.

After we found a table at the club and ordered drinks, the girls excused themselves to make a pilgrimage to the ladies' room. To get a conversation going, I asked Eric how long he had been in the coast guard.

"Two years," he responded.

"Do you like it?"

"It's OK."

"Are you going to stay in?"

"No."

"What're you going to do when you get out?"

"Don't know."

Boy, talking to this guy was like pulling teeth. I tried a new tack.

"What's your favorite baseball team?"

"Don't have one."

Mamma mia, what will it take to get this guy to open up short of putting a firecracker up his ass? I took a long, fortifying drink of soda. "So, what do you do for relaxation?"

He brightened with unabashed enthusiasm, telling me he had recently bought a twelve-string Martin guitar.

I sighed with relief. "What's the difference between a twelve-string and a regular guitar?" *If he says six strings, I will kill him.*

Then he launched into a definitive treatise about the attributes and advantages of both, which had my head spinning. The return of the girls and the start of the show rescued me.

The four Wayfarers, dressed in black suits with white shirts and thin black ties, hit the small stage with energy, strumming their instruments and kidding around. Then they announced a new album they had made live at the World's Fair. Julie and I looked at each other; I was impressed.

Their performance left no room for a lull in the collective high spirits, especially when they sang a humorous song about an ill-fated romance between Sally the crab and Herman the lobster: "Crabs walk sideways, and lobsters walk straight, and you can't take a crab for your mate." I promised myself I would see the act again. Given Julie's cheery mood, she must have felt the same. As we departed, we thanked Melanie and Eric for a great evening, and we agreed to get together again soon.

Nine

Back on the debit, collecting and selling along St. Philip Street, Jim suddenly staggered behind me as we descended the exterior stairway of a two-story, sun-bleached tenement. He grabbed hold of the railing to steady himself and then sat heavily on the steps.

"I can't take this heat any longer. I feel really nauseated," he said weakly. I had seen these signs before, in the corps. Pallor, nausea, and excessive sweating: it was heat exhaustion. I knew I had to get him cooled down and hydrated quickly.

"Jim, give me the keys to the car." Fumbling in his pants pocket, he came up with them. Then, dazed, he rested his elbows on his knees and cupped his face in his hands.

"Don't worry, I'll be back in a jiffy. You'll be OK."

He didn't answer.

Pounding my way over the ancient slate sidewalks, I saw hardly a person, cat, or dog on the streets. A few minutes later, I returned in the car with the air conditioning going full blast. I assisted Jim inside. He rested his head listlessly against the side window and closed his eyes. I made a hard U-turn on a one-way street to save time. Running lights and stop signs when I could, I raced through the neighborhoods of Charleston toward his home. I turned off East Bay onto Mariner's Lane and came to a screeching stop in front of a small, white, clapboard townhouse. I walked Jim slowly to the glossy, Charleston-green door and into the house. His live-in, Lloyd, was in the front room, dusting, with three black poodles lounging about.

He became extremely upset when he saw us in the doorway. “Oh my God, Jim! Is it your heart?”

Heart? Had I made a mistake? Should I have rushed him to the hospital?

“Please calm yourself, Lloyd. I’ll be OK,” Jim said. “I’ve just taken a bit too much sun, that’s all.”

As I steadied him, he lowered himself carefully onto the brown leather couch. The dogs bounded over to him and licked his hands and face anxiously.

I turned to Lloyd, who was standing frozen and horrified, his deep-blue eyes fixed on Jim. “Lloyd, please get some water and ice. We need to get him drinking and cooled down.” Luckily the air conditioner was doing its job, but we needed more than that.

When Lloyd returned, Jim grabbed the water glass and started drinking greedily. He looked surprised when I pulled it away from him. “Jim, you must sip slowly, or you’ll throw up.”

He nodded.

With the help of a somewhat calmer Lloyd, I stripped Jim down to his shorts and patted him down with ice cubes wrapped in a kitchen towel. After a while he said, “Get me a blanket, Lloyd. I’m freezing.”

“No,” I said, “at least not for another few minutes.”

He flashed me an angry look, but it was gone in a second when he must have realized what I was doing. The minutes passed slowly. Jim hunched over on the couch and tried to wrap himself in his own body to get warm.

“Any nausea, Jim?” I asked.

“No. I’m sure I’m OK.”

“Can I get the blanket now?” asked Lloyd.

“Yes,” I replied.

I felt confident that the crisis had passed. “Jim, you need to rest up for a couple of days to make sure you’re fully recovered. I’ll have no trouble handling the debit on my own.”

"I know—you're catching on quickly." He pulled the coverlet tight around his shoulders. "Lloyd, I want you to drive Mike back to the office."

"That's OK. I'll grab a cab," I said. "You need Lloyd to watch you for a while, and I really think you should go see your doctor."

"Mike's right!" said Lloyd firmly. "I'm cancelling all my appointments at the beauty parlor this afternoon, and I'm taking you to the doctor."

"Lloyd, I'm a grown man. Don't baby me."

"You're an *old* man, and you need to be checked out. I won't have it any other way."

Jim slumped his shoulders in resignation. "I guess I won't have any peace until you get your way." They looked caught up in the stress of the moment and seemed to forget I was there.

A couple of hours later, I was back on the debit, trying to collect from Mrs. Scruggs, who ran a small hair-dressing business out of her house.

"Mrs. Scruggs, this is the second time today I've come back to collect your insurance!"

"I'm working here—cain't you see that, white boy?"

"Yes, ma'am," I said politely, trying to conceal my irritation. I planted myself firmly in front of her. The place smelled of sweet shampoo, iron-straightened hair, and collards. "But you have only one customer, and she's sitting under a hair dryer. It will take only a second for me to mark your book."

One hand on her bony hip, she angrily opened a cigar box, pulled out a few notes, slammed the box shut, and flung the crumpled money onto the kitchen counter. I shoved it in my pocket, initialed her book, thanked her, and left.

Livid as all hell, I was reminded of having locked horns with colored marines. A misunderstood word or look was all it took to get a fight or argument going. Colored on colored or white on white and the look and the words would have gone unnoticed. *Jesus,* I thought, *how the hell are we ever going to get around that?*

A couple of days later, I walked into the office and saw Jim hard at work, balancing Big Burl Woodrow's book. On the two brief occasions I had met Burl, he had been dressed in khaki pants; brown, scuffed boots; and a short-sleeved shirt. He had a red bull neck, weighed at least three hundred pounds, and stood around six feet. He was a true son of the Confederacy. Sal Fanelli had told me at one of the morning breakfasts that Burl dressed that way because he collected his debit along the primitive dirt roads of Wadmalaw Island, in a beat-up World War II jeep. It was dirty work collecting that debit; the locals didn't give a damn how you dressed. On the few occasions he had gone out with Burl, he couldn't understand a word the islanders were saying.

When I asked why, Sal responded, "They speak Gullah."

"What's that?"

"Some peculiar African-English dialect, I think. I don't really know. But Burl understands them. He's invaluable to us out there. He's been doing it for almost twenty years. He's an avid boater and fisherman who holds court most nights at the Adams Creek Marina on the inland waterway. They call him the night mayor."

Jim waved me over as Burl got up from the desk. Greeting me, Burl said in his gruff voice, "How'd it go for you this week, marine?"

"Fine, Burl. I think I did OK."

"Good. But don't let those niggers ever get the upper hand."

"Yeah, OK." I turned to Jim. "Welcome back to the world of the living, Jim. How do you feel?"

"Great, Mike. The three days' rest did the job. Lloyd sends his regards."

"Tell him thanks," I said.

"I will. How did things pan out the rest of the week?"

"Not too bad. I had a few rough patches, but they were nothing I couldn't handle."

"Like what?" He looked concerned.

"I had a face-off with a woman who runs a hair place on Quince Lane."

"Mrs. Scruggs?"

"Yeah."

"Let me guess. She made you come back a couple of times to collect."

"You got it, Jim."

"She's done that to every agent and manager who ever tried to collect from her. Don't take it personally."

"OK, but she's a real pain in the ass."

"Anything else?"

"Yeah. I ran across this badass in Jacob's Row when I went to collect from Catherine Dupree."

I told Jim how she had been all busted up—black eye, cut lip. When I'd asked her what had happened, she'd lowered her head and said nothing. Mr. Bad had picked up a revolver from the nightstand and told me it was none of my damn business. Then Catherine handed me her receipt book with a warning glance. I recorded the payment while the guy fondled his Colt .45, glaring at me. As I was about to leave, he asked me where I was from. I told him. Then he said I'd better watch out for my white ass out there, especially at night.

"What did you say?"

"Nothing. I was stupefied. But the threat was very clear."

"I would stay away from him if I were you. He sounds like a psychopath. Try collecting on another day or at another hour, when he might not be around."

"I'll figure something out. Everything else went pretty well for the week. Most of the people were pleasant or indifferent." Then I opened my attaché case and produced seven contracts.

Jim pushed his chair away from his desk and stared at me, aghast. "My God, what have you done, Mike? You're not licensed yet to write up contracts."

"Yeah, I know. But I left the witness line for you to sign. You'll recognize the names. Some of them we spoke to about additional insurance last week."

"What about receipts?"

"No one asked me. And if they had, I would have told them the truth—that I didn't have any on me." I grinned innocently. "Look, nobody's been hurt, and everyone's been well served. I just didn't want to lose the opportunity to make a sale or two."

"All right, all right." He raised his hands, "Let's just keep this between you and me." He scrutinized the contracts and signed them. I knew I was dismissed.

TEN

Menotti's Italian restaurant was buzzing on Friday night. Pug's wife, Maggie, a Charleston girl with a pre-Raphaelite face and trim figure, had called Julie. She was excited that we were back in town to stay and suggested we get together at seven for dinner. We accepted without hesitation—or at least Julie did. I had my doubts about the Italian offerings; I would have preferred to take my chances with Caruso's Pizzeria, which Sal Fanelli had recommended. He swore on the head of his dead mother that the pizza and lasagna were as good as anything up north. However, custom prevailed, and the ladies made the choice.

We stood behind a large group of people in the foyer. An old lady posted at the dais was greeting guests. She reminded me of my grandmother: salt-and-pepper hair pulled back tight into a bun, no makeup, five feet tall, and wearing a black dress so typical of Italian women from the old country. Shuffling behind the crowd ahead of us, we finally stood in front of the elderly matron.

"Buona sera, signora," I said.

She looked at me blankly. Julie interjected quickly, "We have a reservation in the name of Maggie Calder."

The old gal nodded, looked at her book, and ran her finger down the page. "Yes," she said with a half smile, "please wait. I'll have you shown to your table."

How could she not have understood me? But then I remembered a time in Brooklyn when I was twelve. Uncle Enrico's mother had invited us to Sunday dinner with her family. The meal consisted of many courses that took hours to consume. Toward the end of the feast, while they were eating chestnuts and drinking wine together, my grandmother from Naples got into a fiery argument with Enrico's mother, who was from Palermo, over the correct pronunciation of the word for *umbrella* in Italian. Soon random insults began to fly back and forth.

"Maria," Isabella said, "you been in America for fifty years, and you hardly speak a word of English."

"Why should I?" my grandmother responded in her mother tongue. "Italian is a far more beautiful language." Then she added, "My husband, Alberto, is retired. Your Giuseppe is still laying bricks!"

Isabella was indignant. "Well, we have a new car. Yours is a jalopy!"

Enraged, Maria lunged for the heart. "Our house is paid for in full, so don't you fucking tell me I don't know how to speak Italian correctly!" With that she waved to us all to get up and leave. We dutifully obeyed. George Bernard Shaw said that Americans and Brits are divided by a common language; but they have nothing on the Italians.

I was chuckling to myself at the memory when a hostess appeared and ushered us to our table.

"Hey, Pug, Maggie. How're you guys doing?" I said as they rose from their seats. We embraced and shook hands, delighted to see each other again.

"Julie," Maggie sang out, "I can't tell you how much we missed y'all!"

"I missed you too," Julie said happily.

Clutching his chest and faking tears, Pug turned to me. "Oh, I would have died if you hadn't returned. I would've been at a complete loss without you."

"Knock it off, babe," said Maggie. "Be serious."

"OK, pumpkin." Then in a terrible English accent he said, "I'm so elated that you have returned to dear old Charles Towne. Our lives have been an utter bore without you."

Laughing, I grabbed him and planted a big kiss on his cheek. He responded in kind, to the surprise of Julie, Maggie, and the curious diners around us.

"Leave those two clowns to themselves," Julie said. She and Maggie pulled their chairs closer to each other, faces only a foot apart, and talked quietly.

"OK, Pug, bring me up to date on what's going on at the base."

"A lot of crap you're not going to believe, Mike."

"Try me."

"Funk beat the court-martial for drinking on post!"

"No shit," I blurted. Julie gave me a reproving look. "Sorry," I said, looking her way. "How did that happen?"

"Funk called his buddy, Kong, from the brig and asked him to call some lieutenant commander's wife he was shagging."

I laughed. "That sounds like Funk."

"Yeah—and a couple other guys we know. Anyway, he told Kong to ask her for two hundred bucks to get him some war-wounded attorney who wears an eye patch."

"I know that lawyer. I met him once or twice when I was a brig guard. He's good."

Pug nodded. "The day of the court-martial, Funk marched into court with his attorney, looking like a man destined for the firing squad. Less than ten minutes later, he walked out, laughing and shaking the attorney's hand."

"So what the hell happened?"

"The attorney asked Sergeant Rutledge if he could have been mistaken about seeing Funk drinking on post. Could it not have been possible that what he took for a mini bottle of liquor was actually a bottle of cough medicine? Rutledge, the idiot, said he didn't think so, but it *was* possible. So the attorney asked the captain to drop the charges on the basis of reasonable doubt."

"Wow, what a story! I can't believe it was that easy."

"There's more, Mike. Funk hit a home run, and for whatever reason got an early release."

"What incredible luck that guy has."

"Yes and no. On the day of his release, Funk, being Funk, managed to get himself arrested in Georgia for busting up a roadside bar and assaulting the owner, who he claimed cheated him out of all of his dough in a crooked poker game."

"Moron! He should have known better than to gamble with locals he doesn't know."

"Yeah, but let me finish. Since he had no money and no family to help him out, the court appointed him a public defender, who stuck him with a six-month sentence in some Macon jail."

"Jesus," I said, "it's weird how life can turn on a dime."

A waitress came to take our orders. I ordered spaghetti and meatballs with a house salad. Julie, perhaps sensing that my mood had changed, looked at me questioningly. I raised my hand slightly and mouthed, "I'll tell you later."

Maggie asked, "What's going on, Pug?"

"I'm just bringing Mike up to date on the news from the base."

"Oh." She sighed, shaking her head.

Julie said, "Will somebody please tell me? I can't stand the suspense."

"I promise I'll tell you everything later tonight, but Pug and I haven't finished."

Pug interjected, "There's a lot more I want to let Mike in on."

Julie shrugged and went back to speaking with Maggie.

"What d'ya mean, there's a lot more?" I asked.

"Sergeant Kruger is in the hospital with a severe concussion and a face that barely looks human."

"What happened? Did he get hit by a truck?"

"He wishes! Someone waylaid him when he left the NCOs' club four sheets to the wind."

"Couldn't happen to a nicer guy," I said without the slightest concern.

"He was clubbed from behind, and whoever it was did a Mexican hat dance on his face." The image made us chuckle.

"Any suspects?"

"Yeah, about a quarter of the guard." We laughed again. "They've got the Office of Naval Intelligence investigating, but I doubt they'll nail anyone."

My mind flashed back to Kong saying it was eating him up that he couldn't bash that Kraut's head in. I felt in my bones that he had done it.

"Mike, what are you thinking?"

"Nothing."

He looked at me suspiciously, which unnerved me.

"What goes around comes around," I said. "I've got no sympathy for that son of a bitch. I hope this will make for a major disposition change."

"If it doesn't, it might where Rutledge is concerned. The rumor mill has it that he's jumping at his own shadow, driving everyone crazy in admin, and bugging the hell out of the ONI investigators every day for information."

Not surprising, I thought. *While Kong is still around, there is one more head to bash.*

Our conversation had left me a bit uneasy. But dinner arrived, and I was starving. Tasting the sauce, I almost spat it out. It had an odd, mushy texture and was extremely sweet. Julie noticed my reaction, but I didn't complain, not wanting to offend Maggie.

Julie asked Pug what he intended to do after discharge. Before he could answer, an ebullient Maggie piped up, announcing with great pride that he was going to Palmer College, to get an associate's degree in business and become a certified public accountant specializing in taxes.

I almost snorted soda through my nose—to the dismay of Julie and Maggie. Head down, Pug continued eating as if none of us were present.

"How 'bout that, old buddy? Me a casket pusher and you a high-priced bookkeeper. Who woulda thunk it?"

Looking up, he said, "Don't rub it in, Mike."

"Well, you certainly did with me, pal."

The women looked confused but held their tongues.

"Yeah, I know. But I took to heart what you said about responsibility the day you left. I've got to make a living somehow. I'm good with numbers. It runs in the family. My father's a county treasurer in Delaware, and my mom teaches high school math."

I always had Pug pegged as a blue-collar kid like me and most of the guys in the corps. "Did you sell your horn?"

"Hell no. I'll never give that up. Besides, I'll need it to pick up a few extra bucks on the weekends, doing gigs."

Following up, I asked, "Will the veterans' benefits cover the tuition?"

"Yeah, with a little left over. My parents volunteered to kick in with any extra we might need. My mother was ecstatic when I told her I was giving up dirt track racing. She said it was good to see I finally had both feet planted on the ground."

We all chuckled at that.

"No happier than I am, Bernard!" said Maggie.

Julie nodded in agreement, but I knew how much racing had meant to him and what a sacrifice it was.

He said, "I guess we all have to grow up sometime."

I felt sorry for my friend as he uttered those words with stoic resignation. I hoped the quick wit, dash, and flash that had drawn me to him would not be dimmed. As long as he was blowing that sax, he would be OK.

After finishing our dinner with coffee and dessert, I bid Old Lady Menotti *buona notte*. She looked at me stone faced. Then I said, "Good night, *signora*."

She responded, "Good night, sir."

As we left, Maggie asked, "What did you say to her?"

"I said good night."

"No, I mean before that."

"I said good night in Italian."

Both Pug and Maggie laughed. Maggie said, "Mrs. Menotti is Greek, although her husband's Italian. She comes from Schenectady, New York."

"Dammit." I laughed. "I knew she spoke a different dialect."

Now Pug and Maggie looked confused. Julie crossed her eyes and shook her head.

On the way home, I began to tell Julie about my conversation with Pug, but she interrupted me. "Maggie told me about all the goings on in that nightmarish guard. God, I'm glad you're out. Maggie's on pins and needles, worrying that something will happen to him."

"Pug gets along with everyone. Next time you see her, tell her not to worry." After a pause, I said, "You know, I think I've got that weird sauce figured out."

"It wasn't all that bad. Just a little too sweet."

"Well, not to my taste buds. You could have poured it over vanilla ice cream."

"So what do you think was in it?"

"Applesauce."

"How do you know that?"

"Sergeant Lopez and I were talking one day about various kinds of pasta sauces, and he told me that the Greeks put applesauce in their ragù to sweeten it."

ELEVEN

A few days after hooking up with Pug, I was sitting on the granite steps of the downtown federal courthouse building. The flower ladies were busily setting up their colorful displays along Broad and Meeting Streets. I would be taking my State licensing insurance exam, which would be much harder than the original test for employment with the company.

From my roost, I could see the county office building, city hall, and St. Michael's Episcopal Church. The natives called this city crossroads the Four Corners of Law. Feeling somewhat apprehensive, I lit up a cigarette and perused the insurance licensing book for one last time, though I was cocksure I knew the material well and would pass the exam. Traffic along Broad began to pick up, and more people entered and exited the courthouse, which also served as a post office. I put my book away and checked the clock on the steeple of St. Michael's: it read eight forty-five. Soon the banks, insurance companies, and real estate offices would be open for business along with government buildings and many law offices.

The temperature was rising, and the suffocating humidity would not give up its tenacious grip on the Holy City. I loosened my tie and unbuttoned my collar. Mornings like this reminded me of the Land of the Lotus Eaters. But instead of a narcotic fruit causing the general state of lethargy, it was the mind-numbing weather. I was convinced that the slow southern tongue was a manifestation of the clime. Jim once told me that if you ever needed to see a lawyer in Charleston during the dog days of summer, make sure you got to the office before two in the afternoon. If you didn't he'd be gone for the day, seeking strong, ice-cooled refreshments in the company of his brethren. However, the practice traditionally extended into the winter months.

When the bells of St. Michael's chimed nine, I was being handed my exam paper. Sometime after ten I completed the test, feeling good. Leaving the building posthaste, I rounded the corner onto Meeting Street, passing by the church's ancient cemetery, to get my car. Had any of its inhabitants been sent to the gallows by the Brits on the very site of the beautiful building I had just left? I thought if anyplace in Charleston was worthy of a haunting, it should certainly be the courthouse—but so far no one had reported sightings.

I peeled the Ford away from the curb and headed for the office. Man, was I feeling cool as I hit Lockwood Drive doing better than sixty and listening to a rock station. Fifteen minutes later, back at work with no traffic citations, I saw Sal, who was filling in as my trainer while Jim was on vacation.

"How did you do?" he asked.

"Great! I know I passed."

"Good. Let's get something to eat. I'm starving. Then we'll hit the debit hard and do some serious selling."

After dodging traffic on Savannah Highway, we slid into one of the red vinyl booths at Bilbro's. As we looked over the menu, a cute waitress with big, hazel eyes came over to us. "What y'all like to have, gennelmen?"

Sal checked her out from head to toe. "What I would like to have, darlin', isn't on the menu."

I suppressed a laugh. She looked blankly at Sal.

"Only kidding," he said with a wolfish grin.

"Uh-huh."

"Give me a burger, honey, with fries and an iced tea."

Turning to me, she smiled. "And you, sir?"

"I'll have the same, thanks."

She reached across me, exposing her well-defined cleavage in her tight, peach-colored uniform. She brushed my hand slightly while picking up the menus. She smiled again. Then she turned and walked away, her cute little tush dancing rhythmically into the kitchen.

"Hey, Sal. Don't you think she just might be jailbait?"

He laughed. "Mike, if I had a half hour with that sweet thing, I would be willing to do life in prison!"

I shook my head. He had the libido of a sixteen-year-old.

My bladder was screaming. "Excuse me, Sal. I gotta make a head call."

"OK. But remember, if you shake it more than twice, you're playing with it."

Cigarette butts and chewing gum were afloat in a sea of yellow waste in the urinal. I flushed, unzipped, and started to pee. On the wall were three condom machines offering all kinds of colors, textures, and lubricants, all guaranteeing maximum pleasure and having her ask for more. I thought it a miracle of science that one size fit all. Blissfully relieved and washing up, I read the graffiti carved, inked, and penciled on the beige wall.

"If you want a great blow job, call Bruce." *No, thanks!*

"Tina and Louise are looking to make it a threesome." *Hey!*

"Impeach Earl Warren!" *What the fuck?*

Coming out of the john, I stopped to drop a few coins into the juke. The Wurlitzer kicked in and played the classic "Blue Suede Shoes."

"Mike, you like that rock and roll stuff?"

"Yeah, I dig it Sal."

"I don't much care for it, but the wife loves the music. She's always shimmying around the house listening to it while she cleans and dusts. Drives me crazy."

I laughed, "I thought you guys were from the big band era."

"We are. But try telling her that."

"How did the two of you get hooked up?"

"We met at a USO dance when I was in the army."

"Did you see any action?"

"Mind your own damn business."

"I meant during the war."

"No. I was lucky. I served as an interpreter in a POW camp for Italians in California. Had a great time, and lived like a king. The Italians did all the cooking, cleaning and laundry, and even pressed our uniforms. They were really happy to be out of the fighting. Nice guys," he reminisced. "Security was so slack that toward the end of the war, they were given weekend passes to the town near the camp. Women loved 'em and the men hated 'em."

"Why?"

"I guess it was because they were pussy-eaters. The local boys weren't into that."

I about choked on my coffee as Sal chuckled at my reaction. Then I asked him if anyone had heard from Jim.

"No, but I know he's enjoying his vacation in Florida. He goes every year to Coco Beach. I think he has family and friends down there. He wouldn't have gone if he didn't feel you were ready to take over the debit. He told me he has the utmost confidence in you. After seeing you in action, I have to agree. You pick things up quickly."

"Thanks, Sal. Without sounding like a mutual admiration society, I think you're a great salesman. You have people eating out of your hand, the way you joke and make them laugh—that's a real gift. It's hard for them to say no to you."

"Yeah, maybe I missed my calling. I should've gone into vaudeville."

When Sweet Thing returned with our grub, she looked at me mischievously. "Sir, is there anything else you might need?"

"No, I'm fine, thanks."

She cocked her head at Sal and said with a come-hither look, "How 'bout you, big boy?"

I cracked up, and Sal turned the color of the booth, vanquished. She turned on her heel with infinite grace and a big grin and walked her great walk back to the front of the restaurant.

"Sal, she really nailed you. I thought you were going to stroke out."

"I almost did. She's one hot tamale."

Midway through eating, Sal paused, looking down at his plate as if in a trance. I pretended not to notice. After a few seconds, he looked at me somberly. "Mike, there's something I need to get off my chest."

I tensed, wondering what had changed his mood so dramatically. "OK, Sal. Spill it."

"I'm embarrassed I copied off your exam. I panicked when I got to those questions about estate planning and annuities. That's all new stuff for me."

"That's all right. I didn't mind." I was lying. "I probably would've done the same, given your position. I'm glad I did OK and didn't fuck you up."

"You did better than OK. Dawson told me your grade. A green agent scored so high and me so low. That's humiliating."

Nuts! I hoped my good deed wasn't going to boomerang on me.

"I barely passed with a seventy-four." Damn, that was low. "If I'd failed, I could've been demoted or worse. I'm still worried about the low score. Mike, I gotta ask you: did you tell anyone?"

"Not a single soul. I never gave it a second thought."

He still looked doubtful, turning his head away from me and sighing.

"Look," I went on, "I like you a helluver lot, and I want to be your friend. Besides, we paisans have got to look out for each other. If we don't, the fuckin' Irish will be pissing all over us again. So don't worry, OK?"

He laughed as if he were trying to punch a hole through a cement wall. But I felt that those words had struck home, reminding him of our common blood. "You're all right, Michele."

Returning with Sal to the debit in his '88 Olds, I tried to avoid the stares of the plastic Jesus, Virgin Mary, and Saint Anthony affixed to the top of the dashboard. I wondered if I should drop a quarter in the ashtray, light up a match, and say a prayer.

"Hey, Sal," I said, pointing to the altar, "does it work?"

"Well, the wife seems to think so." He laughed. "She hasn't had an accident in more than three months, since she first stuck them up there."

We arrived at our destination with no dents or scratches—only running one red light—and I knocked on the door of Mary Middleton's home on Coming Street.

An ancient, mahogany-skinned woman answered. We stepped back, hit by the overpowering smell of mothballs and kerosene inside her tiny, one-room apartment.

"Cardinal State Insurance Company," I announced.

"Oh, are you the gennelman who collected from me last month?"

"No, ma'am, I'm new. I'm Mike Romano, and this is Mr. Fanelli. He's training me."

"My goodness," she said, "they come and go so often, I cain't hardly keep track."

Sal interrupted, "Well, we found you a good one this time, and I'm sure he'll be staying."

"I surely hope so," she said in a tired voice. She turned and tottered painfully over to a beautiful chestnut hutch that held at least a half dozen photographs of white children ranked across a shelf. She barely had enough room to squeeze between the hutch and an expensive-looking rice bed to open the top drawer and get out her receipt book. As she handed it to me, I asked who the children were in the pictures.

"Oh," she replied with pride and affection, "those chillun I raised over the last fifty years. That one on the right is my baby boy, Tad. I raised him from when he was no bigger than a pea in a pod. He now have three grown chillun of his own and is the president of a big bank. The one next to him is my darlin' little Miss Penny. She a grown woman now, with two sweet little girls. She a lady of high society—live in a big house on LeGare. She still come see me sometime."

She went on to give bits and pieces of the life stories of the other children, all beautifully dressed, smiling out from the past in their silver frames. I was struck that all of those children had grown up to take on positions of power and money. I wondered about their last names, so I asked her. She rattled them off; many of those names could be found on street signs and statues in Charleston and in history books. Clearly they and their parents were all offspring of former slave owners, and the children Mary had loved had evidently done nothing meaningful as adults to end the discriminating practices against her and all Negroes in Charleston and South Carolina. If anything they had helped to maintain them.

On the bedside table was a lone photograph of a colored child. I pointed to it and asked who it was. Her withered old shoulders slumped, and she became teary eyed. "That's my Gerard."

"What is he doing now?" I asked.

"Ah, me," she said, sighing. "He was killed some forty years back by the po-lice for what they called *resisting arrest*. They never really tol' me what he done wrong."

"That's terrible," I said. "I'm so sorry, Mrs. Middleton."

"Don't matter much now, 'cause I be in heaven soon with my baby." She paused. "The Lord sets all things right in the end."

Why the hell isn't He doing anything now?

I marked her book. "I'll take good care of your insurance, ma'am." I shook her cold, bony hand gently.

She looked at both of us and smiled. "Y'all fine gennelmen. I hope the Lord see fit that we meet each other again soon."

We walked away in silence.

TWELVE

Finishing the hot and emotional week with Sal, I was ready for a lot of cold beer, partying, and loving. I opened the refrigerator and grabbed a brew, and then I heard the staccato clanging of footsteps on the rear metal stairs to the kitchen. I opened the door and was surprised to see Julie, out of breath and red faced, with two large shopping bags in her arms.

"What're you doing home so early?" I asked.

"We finished our experiment, and there was nothing left to do. I decided to get the shopping out of the way. But Lord, those two blocks from the grocer's just about killed me in this heat. How about taking these and letting me in? Or do I just stand here and melt?"

"Oh, sorry, babe. I wasn't thinking."

She wearily raised an eyebrow and shook her head as I took the bags from her and set them on the counter. She eased her way past me as I opened the fridge and popped a cool one for her. She kicked her shoes off and took a swig.

"I got a call from the Averys this morning." Pausing to take another swig, she closed her eyes for a few seconds to savor the cold brew. "Rina told me they'll be back in Charleston this afternoon."

"How's Tom's father doing?"

"We didn't really get into that too much—she was calling from the airport. But it sounds as though it wasn't as bad as they first feared."

"That's great. Tom was worried sick."

"Yes, he certainly was." She began putting the groceries away. "Anyway, they want us to make a reservation at the Sailfish restaurant at nine tomorrow evening for six people."

"Boy, that's late. I'll be starving."

"I know," she said. "We'll have a snack in the afternoon to tide us over."

"Did Rina say who the other two people will be?"

"Yes. The new chair of the history department at the college and his wife. They're French."

"Ah—that explains why we'll be eating so late. Different dining customs. But darn it, I was hoping to get some one-on-one time with Tom."

"Keep your knickers on. These people sound interesting, and they just might be fun to be with. You'll have plenty of other times to be alone with Tom."

"I guess you're right."

The next evening we were sitting out on the deck of the busy restaurant. We awaited our friends, and I watched the copper sun descend toward the horizon. It cast the last of its soft rays on the tranquil Folly River, the apple-green marsh grass swaying lazily in the light wind. The serene scene contrasted sharply with my thoughts about the recent murders of three civil rights workers in Mississippi and a week-long race riot in Harlem, which I knew would have had my mother in a tizzy. Most of all I was worried about the thousands of new troops being sent to Vietnam. Spike had been right when he'd told me we were fixing to get into a big fight there. The possibility that I could be called back to active duty angered me—especially if Julie were pregnant. Damned if I would go!

My somber thoughts were happily interrupted when the Averys appeared with an older couple in tow.

Tom said, "Mike, Julie, I want you to meet Jean-Luc Baptiste and his wife, Marie Claire." We all shook hands, smiling with the polite reserve of people meeting for the first time.

After we were seated, a waitress arrived, handed around menus, and took our drink orders. Julie and Rina decided on colas and Marie Claire a ginger ale. Jean-Luc, Tom, and I asked for ice water.

After several minutes of small talk, our drinks arrived, and the waitress asked if we were ready to order.

"Not yet," Tom said. "Give us a little more time, please."

When the waitress left, I asked Tom if he had brought the bourbon.

"Of course, Mike. Did you bring the Scotch?"

"Yeah."

Taking our flasks from our jacket pockets, we poured according to everyone's mix preference—except me. I threw out the ice water into a handy planter and poured myself a generous shot of Scotch. I always thought it was sacrilegious for anyone to dilute a good whiskey with ice or water.

Looking somewhat disgruntled, Marie Claire raised her bourbon-spiked drink and looked at it. "*Dieu merci* for small favors. If I had known this state was so dry, I never would have left New Jersey."

"It really isn't that dry," Tom said. "What we're doing right now is called brown-bagging, and it's legal."

"I see no brown bag!" she grumbled.

Attempting some comic relief, I said, "We gentlemen carry flasks," which got laughs from everyone except Marie Claire. Clearly she was becoming increasingly annoyed. Coming to her rescue, Jean-Luc explained to her in French what it meant.

Tom said, "Some businesses just operate illegally, and the local cops turn a blind eye. Others get around the law by becoming private clubs."

"Either way, I think it is stupid and uncivilized," Marie Claire said with finality.

Everyone agreed, and then the women began chatting among themselves.

I asked Tom how his father was doing.

"Better than we hoped. Apparently he had a minor heart attack, and the docs just prescribed a couple weeks' rest. They told him to lose some weight, do light exercise, and stop smoking those dreadful cigars. As if he's going to do that."

"Is he still going to be able to sit on the bench?"

"He fully intends to. I think it'll be important for him to do so. A man like him would wither and die without his work."

Jean-Luc nodded in agreement.

Turning to him, I asked, "So what brought you to Charleston, sir?"

He said, "It's a long story, as you Americans say. But I will try to make it short so as not to bore you."

I detected a faint grin on Tom's face.

Resting his chin on his clasped hands, Jean-Luc began his story. "Many years ago I acquired a degree from the Sorbonne in international law. I had an eye toward serving my country in the diplomatic corps, but this plan was rudely interrupted when the Bosch invaded. I joined the resistance—what the allies called the French Underground."

"What did you do?" I asked.

"My comrades and I ambushed convoys carrying war materials and troops. Also we blew up transportation lines and communication systems. We fed intelligence information to the Allies. This was especially important before and during the Normandy invasion."

Wow, this little guy with wild gray hair and spectacles hanging from the tip of his nose is something else.

"When the war ended, I realized my earlier ambition, and I served several ambassadors around the world as a legal attaché. However, after those years, I became disenchanted by my government's policies. Also I was tired of upsetting my family with the constant moves they had to make, so I tendered my resignation and came to America. I taught international studies at Princeton University. When the position of chair came up here at the College of Charleston, I applied and was accepted. *Et voilà*. Here I am."

"Boy, you have had one heck of a life," I said.

He smiled graciously. "Michael, most of us who lived through the Great Depression and fought the fascists for years had—as you say—one heck of a life. But enough of me. Tell me a little something about yourself."

I laughed. "There's not much to tell."

"Come on, Michael."

"OK," I said reluctantly. "I was born and raised in New York City. At sixteen I was thrown out of high school. I worked odd jobs for two years, helping out my family. Then at eighteen I lucked out and got a job working in a fancy gym called Vic Tanney's. I loved working there. I rubbed elbows with professionals and celebrities. One night I had an interesting conversation with a well-known movie star, a notorious womanizer. I learned a few things, to say the least."

Grinning from ear to ear, Jean-Luc said, "*Vive la différence.*"

"Yeah." Tom had that sly look men give each other when discussing women.

"At twenty," I continued, "I was shanghaied into the marines. Then one day—"

"Whoa, hold on, Mike," Tom interrupted. "What do you mean, shanghaied?"

"I actually wanted to join the air force. I go to the recruiting station in Times Square, but the air force guy isn't in. I'm told by the marine and army recruiters that he'll be back in twenty minutes tops. Half an hour goes by, and I'm getting fidgety. The marine recruiter comes over to me and says, 'Why do you want to join the air force?'

"I reply, 'I like planes. Maybe I can become a pilot.'

"He returns to his desk and comes back with a colored brochure showing a jet taking off and says, 'We marines have our own air force. Why don't I give you a test and see if you qualify?'

"I take the Mickey Mouse test, and he grades it. He then announces it's the highest grade he's ever seen. Yeah! I'm pumped up! And bingo, I'm in the infantry, roasting and freezing my balls off, being eaten by insects, and crawling through mud."

"Damn, I can't believe they sandbagged you like that," said Tom.

"They did, and they're still not through with me."

"How so?"

"I'm in the reserve for two years. If the idiots continue to escalate the war in Southeast Asia, they could activate me."

Jean-Luc gazed at me pensively. "Michael, I share and understand your concern. Your government has engaged in an exercise of pure folly that will inevitably result in the loss of many lives. In the end it will almost certainly result in defeat, as it did for the French."

"Yeah," I said, shaking my head. "I was such a fool joining up that way."

"Don't be so hard on yourself, Michael," Jean-Luc replied. "We're all naïve and foolish when young. Unfortunately most people never stop being so, allowing the powers that be to exploit them. It is one of the great tragedies of history." He paused and cocked his head slightly. "Tom told me you like to read, especially history and philosophy. Why?"

"I'm looking for answers as to why the world is what it is and why I am who I am."

Jean-Luc looked at me over his spectacles, brow furrowed. "What motivates you to do so?"

I took time to collect my thoughts. "I'm tired of all the bullshit that passes for truth out there."

"Can you elaborate?" asked Tom.

"Come on, Tom, you know what I mean." All these questions were starting to irritate me. "I'm trying to free my mind from all the damn lies and prejudices fed to me and most people in this country—by our families, religion, schools, and the politicians—so I can see and know things as they truly are."

Pausing, I grabbed my last weed and crumpled the pack. Tom lit me up. Blowing smoke upward, I watched it swirling around the ceiling fan before being whisked away like a ghost.

I managed to say, "At least I know some of the crap I'm up against."

"And what is that?" Jean-Luc asked.

"The money class. The fat cats have all the power, pull all the strings, and make all the fixes. I have to get my own without using a gun or losing my decency." I fixed my gaze on Tom and Jean-Luc. "Let me put a question to both of you. How the hell does anyone in this country—anyone who is honest—make it big when they have nothing to start with and a deck that's stacked against them, especially those in the minorities? I read an article recently that said most people in America will die in the same class they were born to."

"A government of the rich, by the rich, for the rich shall never perish from this Earth," uttered Tom sonorously.

Jean-Luc looked away and then turned; he was about to say something when the waitress reappeared to take our orders.

While we waited for the food, Rina engaged us in conversation about the weather. We all agreed that it had been too damned hot for too long and wondered uselessly when it would end. That topic exhausted, Marie Claire described her recent experience of swatting and only wounding a flying roach the size of a bat that had sought sanctuary in her generously sized bra.

Jean-Luc, grinning, said, "I was deeply honored when my fair lady asked me to rescue her from her tormentor."

"May I say," she said, "he did so with the utmost delicacy."

"Oh là là!" Rina giggled.

More stories about the winged devils ensued. I recounted the time at Parris Island when, just before lights-out, Sergeant Gaynor was smacked square in the face by one. He was flailing, ducking, and running away from the flying beast. We were all trying mightily to control our laughter while standing at attention as though nothing was happening to our beloved drill instructor. When the attack ended, the embarrassed sergeant said, "I'd rather face a hundred charging Japs than one of those fuckin' things!"

The appetizers arrived, and the conversation quieted. Favorable comments were made on the she-crab soup. I stuck with a shrimp cocktail, as did Julie, which we especially appreciated given the weather. During the main course, I was the only one to partake of a land animal—sirloin—not being particularly enamored with seafood overall.

While we were chowing down, Marie Claire looked up from her plate. "I overheard part of the conversation between you gentlemen about how fucked up this country is."

Julie and Rina looked stunned, as I surely did too. It wasn't considered appropriate for a lady to use the four-letter word in mixed company—or for a man to do it, for that matter. Jean-Luc, not at all fazed by the indelicate term, said, "Yes, *ma chérie*, we were, but I don't believe it would be of any particular interest to you, Julie, or Rina."

Marie Claire's dark eyes narrowed, and a flush rose in her cheeks. She was an exotic beauty. "*Zut alors*, you think we have no interest in the growing war?"

Julie stiffened, not having heard the recent news that Congress had passed the Tonkin Gulf resolution, giving the president broad military powers in Southeast Asia, short of dropping a nuke.

Marie Claire eyed her husband. "You should know better about us women and our interests. Did we not fight side by side with you men in *La Résistance* against the Hun? Were we not tortured, wounded, and killed like any man? And who covered your asses with the sniper rifle while you were running around blowing things up? Hmm?"

Jean-Luc looked at her, his eyes softening. "*Mon amie*, to you." He raised his glass in a toast.

Julie had said these people might be interesting, but this would be a night to remember.

As we left the restaurant, Jean-Luc turned to me. "So are you prepared to do anything about the injustices of which you spoke?"

The question took me off guard. Before I could come up with a response, he said, "Don't try to answer now. Take your time. Think about it." Then they drove off in Jean-Luc's Peugeot.

Julie and I stood in the parking lot.

"Hey, baby, it's a beautiful night," I said. "How about a little stroll along the beach?"

"That sounds nice."

Heading down Folly Road, with Julie cuddled up close to me, we listened to our song, "Blue Moon," on the radio. Nearing the beach we saw Folly Plaza—the bright lights, the Ferris wheel, other amusement rides, and concessions. As we went closer, we saw the crowd whooping it up to beach music on the boardwalk. We turned left, away from the merriment, to seek out a quiet place to park near the beach. How many of the revelers behind us knew anything about the island's varied and sometimes gruesome past? Gershwin writing *Porgy and Bess*, the Union encampment during the occupation of Charleston, and, worst of all, the poor, sick souls who were dropped off by incoming ships and left to die of various plagues along that narrow stretch of sand.

We parked the car well off the road and walked the soft sands barefoot and hand in hand, enjoying the soothing sound of the surf under the clear, starry night lit by a full summer moon. Moments like these were reason enough to be living in Charleston.

Thirteen

Over the next three weeks, I settled in comfortably at the job. My sales increased as the people got to know me better. Julie was happy with her work, although she didn't appreciate the low pay, and was enjoying her occasional lunches with Rina and Maggie.

On Wednesday afternoon, I sat at the thickly lacquered, wooden bar in Moses's Grill. Moses Radcliffe was a short, dark colored man with a hard face and jaundiced eyes. He took time from stocking his bar to pay his premium and gave me a cold beer on the house. After I marked his receipt book, he excused himself and went back to work. Left alone in the quiet, empty club, I sipped my brew and enjoyed the refrigerated environment. I was at peace with myself. The mood was broken when two white men entered the club, one as thin as a rake, the other short, fat, and piggy eyed. Both walked quickly through the bar and into the storage room at the back without pausing or saying a word. A minute or so later, they came out, straining under the weight of two cardboard boxes, and then left. Moses didn't give them the slightest recognition.

"Hey, Moses. Who the heck were those guys?" I asked.

"Cops," he grunted.

"What were they doing?"

"Getting paid off in booze."

"What do you mean?"

He looked at me as if I were an idiot. "It's their payoff, man, for not rousting me and allowing me to operate like I want."

I wondered exactly what that meant. Prostitution? Operating outside hours? Selling booze illegally? All of the above? He cut me off as I opened my mouth again, and in a gritty voice he said, "Enough questions. I gotta get back to work."

Whoa! I'd made him angry—or at least the cops had. My uncle Luca, a cab driver in New York, always talked about cops being on the take; it seemed to be common knowledge in the blue-collar neighborhood where I had lived. Why should it be any different down here in the Bible Belt, where the Southern Baptists ruled in judgment of sin and morality?

I finished my beer, bid a hearty farewell to Moses, and headed for Jacob's Row. Earlier in the week, Catherine Dupree had promised me that if I made a return trip she would pay up all her insurance that was in danger of lapsing.

Large drops of cold rain began to fall, pummeling me like small pebbles. I picked up my pace as I entered the row. Residents, visitors, pimps, prostitutes, gamblers, and thieves headed for cover as lightning flashed, and it began to pour. A communal fire pit smoldered behind one of the tenements. A picnic table with benches was abandoned. However, the usual craps game went on under the protection of a large porch.

I made it to Catherine's place at a run and was just about to knock when I heard the sound of a pistol shot, then another. I turned tail and raced away, believing in the moment that her crazy boyfriend must have killed her, and I could be next if he saw me there. I looked over my shoulder and saw the door opening. Catherine stood there in a thin, pink slip and blue robe, her face bloodied and bruises forming on her cheek. Then she slumped against the jamb with a gun pointed down at her side.

"Catherine! Are you OK?" I asked, as I cautiously approached her.

She didn't reply. I peeked behind her into the room and saw the animal lying on his back on the bed in his underwear, bullet holes in his stomach and chest. A tide of blood pooled into the mattress.

"Put the gun on the ground, Catherine."

She didn't respond.

"Put the gun on the ground!"

She lifted her head, turned in my direction, and dropped the weapon. I kicked it away from her as she slid to the ground, trembling in the pelting rain.

I stepped over to the next apartment and pounded on the door. Thunder rolled around the city. There was no answer. I banged on the door harder. A terror-filled voice screamed, "Go away! Go away!"

"It's me!" I yelled. "The Cardinal State Insurance man."

Slowly the door opened, chain in place. Seeing me, the woman closed the door briefly and undid the chain.

"Ma'am, will you please call the police?"

"What happened?"

"I think Catherine killed her boyfriend."

"Thank God," she said, putting her hand over her heart. "You call, sir. They never seem to listen too closely to us coloreds."

I made the call. They assured me that someone would be arriving soon.

Neighbors looked on from doorways and windows. Some stood in the rain. Minutes later cops arrived. One of them, a sergeant, came over to me. In an irritated voice, he asked if I had been the one to call in.

"Yes."

"Tell me what happened." He took out his notebook.

I gave him what I knew, and he took my name, address, and phone number. I asked if I would have to go down to the station to make a written statement.

"I doubt it," he replied. "This appears to be a clear case of self-defense." He gave me a long look. "Besides, these niggers are always killing each other off, so whadda we care? The more they bury, the better for us. She'll probably be out in a couple of days."

His callous words resonated in my mind as he walked over to Catherine. She was now in handcuffs, and another cop stood over her. Grabbing her roughly by the arm, he shoved her into the squad car and took off. Two other cops stood by, waiting for the meat wagon to pick up the sorry corpse.

Cold and soaking wet, I quit the bleak scene with scores of dark eyes following me out of the alley. Drained, I headed for my apartment through the rapidly flooding streets that would soon resemble the canals of Venice. I was glad to be home and took a long, hot, therapeutic shower, poured a large Scotch, and slumped on the couch, shaken by the surreal experience. The day was over for me—debit or no debit.

Fourteen

I didn't sleep well on the nights after Catherine's ordeal. However, on Saturday morning, Julie and I both managed to sleep late. I awoke first, reveling in the knowledge that we had absolutely nothing important planned. Julie was lying next to me, partly covered by a sheet and nothing else. I gathered her toward me, and she smiled drowsily, running her hands down my back. Then she stilled, and a disconcerted expression flitted over her face. She tumbled out of bed and ran to the bathroom. Through the open door, I heard the unmistakable sounds of retching. When I reached her, she was sitting on the floor by the commode, a sheen of sweat on her pallid face.

"Are you OK? What's happening?"

"No idea. Maybe it's something I ate. Do you feel all right?"

"I'm fine. Can you get up?"

"Yes, I think so. Whatever it was, it seems to have passed. Maybe I'll just lie down for a bit."

I helped her to her feet and into the bedroom. "Can I get you anything?"

"Some water would be nice, thank you."

As I turned for the kitchen, I caught her staring wide eyed into space.

Julie began throwing up each morning. She went to the doctor on Wednesday. When she returned, she walked in the door, looked at me almost shyly, and took a deep breath.

"Well, Michael, it turns out I'm pregnant!" Her cheeks were rosy with excitement.

"I can't believe it—I'm going to be a father!" Running to Julie, I picked her up by the waist and spun around the room, laughing with joy.

"Put me down! I'm getting dizzy. And you're holding me much too tight. You don't know your own strength."

I released her. "I'm sorry, honey. That was stupid of me."

"Stupid?"

"You're pregnant. I could have hurt you or the baby."

"Don't be silly. It's too early to worry about things like that."

"Are you sure?"

Still aglow, she chuckled. "Yes."

I hurried to the phone.

"What are you doing?" she shrieked.

"Calling everyone to let them know the good news."

"No, no, not yet. Hang up."

"Why not?"

"Because I want to make sure that everything's OK."

"What do you mean?"

"All sorts of things can go wrong in the first few weeks of pregnancy. Let's just settle down and enjoy things as they are, and we'll make sure all's well before we make any announcements."

"Go wrong? Jesus! Like what?"

"Well, you know," she said vaguely. "Sometimes it just doesn't... take. But I'm sure we'll be fine, so don't worry about it. Think of the side benefits."

"What benefits?"

"Wild, unprotected sex!" She grinned.

"Is that allowed? You're with child. You're going to be a mother."

"With child? For heaven's sake, Michael, don't turn me into some kind of Madonna figure. It could be a real passion killer. Sex won't hurt the baby or me. I'm still Julie, and you're still Michael. I don't want that to change."

"But we'll be parents, and that'll be a full-time job."

"Yes, but we mustn't let it consume us. We'll need to keep a space for ourselves and not lose who we are. How about I go change and we have dinner out to celebrate?"

Left alone, I went out to have a smoke on the rear landing and think about our future. Clearly we weren't going to be a Donna Reed family. But then, would I want that?

Julie's words made sense. How could one ball the Madonna with great passion, if at all? I wondered if there were some vestiges of religious conditioning in me that had made me say she was with child. Nah, couldn't be. It was just a colloquialism. As a kid I'd hated being hauled to church, listening to some priest in drag mumbling mass in Latin, which no one understood. I'd intensely disliked the nuns who had tried to beat Catholicism into me with slaps to the back of my head and rulers across my little knuckles. What great mothers they would have made. But most of all, I despised the church for not allowing my mother absolution because she was divorced. It worried her to no end. Religion, with all its symbolism, would have no effect on me. It was pure voodoo and an insult to my intellect. Virgin birth? Perfect woman? Baloney!

On Friday morning, the office was in a flap. Agents straightened their desks and checked their appearances in a long mirror attached to the inner office door. Written to the side was a list:

Is your hair combed?
Tie straight?
Jacket buttoned?
Pants pressed?
Shoes shined?

There was no such list of questions for the ladies.

The much anticipated visit from the home office big shots was upon us. The staff managers were dressed in their Sunday best and nervous as old hens. But Jim Dawson sat placidly at his desk, reading the newspaper. I went to the outer office to get a cup of coffee and caught sight of Sal, who, despite having a pasty look about him, was chatting in his usual animated way to a group of agents gathered around the coffeepot. We made eye contact, and he nodded. Before I could make my way through the crowd to greet him, he ducked into the corridor, probably to have a final smoke before the meeting. I sipped my coffee and watched the agents, office staff, and managers scurry about. The scene reminded me of an ant colony disturbed by a misplaced boot. Just when I decided to go back to my desk, the office door swung open. Sal was talking a mile a minute to the honchos from the home office.

"Mr. Romano." I was surprised to see Mr. Tickles—Tylke—approaching with his hand outstretched. He shook my hand vigorously. Turning to the other visitors, he said, "Gentlemen, this is Mr. Romano, one of our new agents. I expect big things from him. Mr. Romano, I want you to meet our vice president for sales, Mr. Madison, and Mr. Polk from Mississippi."

Madison, a balding, overweight man, gazed at me briefly, his eyes flat. He said briskly, "Good. We need bright, aggressive young men to carry the company's banner forward into the future."

"I'll do my best, sir."

"I'm certain you will, son."

It was like talking to a marine general. It made me uneasy and reminded me of all the rah-rah shit that, likely as not, would get you killed.

Our conversation ended when Mr. Randall appeared and greeted the three visitors pleasantly. He invited them into his office and closed the door.

At my desk I pulled out the *New York Times* crossword puzzle I had started earlier. Stuck on a clue, I got up, paper in hand, and walked over to Dawson, who was now leaning back in his chair, staring at the ceiling.

"Pardon me, Jim, but I need the word for the ability to become a werewolf. Got any idea?"

He took the paper from my hand, smiled, and thought for a minute. "Lycanthropy." He wrote it down on a memo slip.

"Gee, thanks, Jim. I never would've gotten it."

"No problem. It's nice to see *someone* exercising his brain around here."

I detected an edge in his voice. Why was it there? I went back to my desk, and he resumed his perusal of the ceiling. I looked at him, becoming more aware of his age and fragile physical condition.

A few minutes later, Mr. Randall and our visitors came into the main office. After the usual sounds of chairs being raked over the floor, coughs, and throat clearings, everyone settled down under the harsh office lighting.

Randall came forward, smiling. "Ladies and gentlemen, I want you to greet our three distinguished guests, seated behind me. Beginning from left to right, Mr. Madison, our vice president, who some of you know already; Mr. Ed Tylke, our director of education; and Mr. Jeremiah Polk, one of our leading staff managers from Jackson, Mississippi."

Everyone applauded politely. The three waved, nodded, and smiled in return. Mr. Randall then calmly announced that he would be stepping down as manager. A chorus of shocked whispers and gasps filled the room, causing a noticeable stir among the three wheels and the staff managers—except for Jim, who sat stoically at his desk. Surprised by the reaction, Randall paused, fingering his mustache, and then signaled for quiet by raising his arms. After a minute or so, order prevailed in the emotionally charged room. "I want to thank you for your support and concern—"

Calls came from around the room.

"Stay in there."

"We're behind you."

"Don't give up!"

He raised his hands again and said, still smiling, "Please. Let me continue."

Silence fell once again except for the barely audible sobs of Kitty Kelley, who was surreptitiously blotting her eyes.

"Over the last four years of my eight-year tenure as your manager, the district's production has stagnated. Heaven knows I tried everything to increase sales, but I had little success. The home office and I agree it would be beneficial to all concerned if I step down and return to a debit."

Hell, I thought, *he's not stepping down but falling to the bottom of the ladder at age forty-four.* I doubted the sincerity of his announcement. For me it was tantamount to believing that a man standing on the gallows would serenely put a noose around his own neck and open the trap door with a smile on his face. Some deal must have been struck. Why didn't they just fire him outright? They surely hadn't kept him on for altruistic reasons. No. They probably needed him to maintain stability during the period of transition to a new manager and afterward. It was the price of still having a job.

Randall sat down, and Mr. Madison strode forward. He said, "I know you're upset. We all like and admire Mr. Randall. But we need to get this district moving. I'm pleased to introduce Mr. Polk, your new manager. I've known Jeremiah since he was first starting out fifteen years ago, when I was regional manager. He has an outstanding record in sales as both an agent and a staff manager. I know he can get the job done." He gestured to Polk, a bandy-legged pipsqueak of a man, to step forward. They shook hands, and the VP returned to his seat.

In the most god-awful hillbilly accent I'd ever heard, Polk said, "I ain't long on makin' speeches. So I'll make it short, lady and gents. I guarantee that y'all are goin' to make a lot of money with me and be happy. So git yoursel's a lotta rest this weekend, 'cos when Monday comes, we're gonna kick the mule in the ass and git goin'. Thank y'all."

God, what were we in for?

After the meeting ended, I went over to Jim. "You knew about this in advance, didn't you?"

"Yes, Mike. The other staff managers and I have known for over a month."

"So that was nothing but a dog-and-pony show."

"I guess you could call it that." He exhaled loudly. "It's a damn shame. The district is turning a profit, but not enough for the money-grubbers in the home office in their Savile Row suits and Italian loafers. They're going to take the company public, and they want the initial price offering to be as high as possible so they can make a ton of money. What happened here today is happening in other districts throughout the company."

"So human beings don't count for much, do they?"

"At one time they did, but the new guard cares only about filling pockets. I know this is all new to you, but that's how America works these days. You're strong; you can make it with the company."

"Maybe so, Jim. I don't think I ever could have made that decision about Mr. Randall the way they did and sleep well at night."

"I have been deeply disturbed myself. The other staff managers are frightened to death about what might happen next, especially Sal. He's at his wit's end."

"I noticed that. So how do you stand with the company?"

"I really don't know, and frankly I don't care. I'm nearly sixty-two years old. I was planning to retire in a couple of years if my health allows me to stay that long. I inherited money recently from the sale of some family land. And I get a small pension from the state of Alabama from my time there as a teacher."

"So you're OK."

"I'll be fine."

"I know it's only noon, but I need a drink. How about it?"

"Sure. But let's make it a couple."

"You're going to need it, Jim."

"Why?"

"Because you're going to have to give me a crash course on how a corporation works. How you take a company public. Who determines the initial price thing."

"Are you buying?"

"I don't expect to get something for nothing."

"You catch on fast. Let's go!"

FIFTEEN

Midweek, the shit hit the fan. Polk fired three agents one afternoon and replaced them temporarily with staff managers who were charged with running their debits and drumming up new business. *Damn him,* I thought as Polk strutted in to speak to us.

"This district got a lot of dead wood that's been lyin' around here, rotting for too long a time." Polk pinched his sweaty nose and fisted his midsection as he spoke. "I will not tolerate that. You thinkin' that y'all can collect the debit, have the occasional sale, and get your base pay, but that ain't gonna cut it no more. I'm gettin' some ol' boys out of Jackson to transfer here and get some real sellin' goin'. Now you know what I'm all about and the way it's s'posed to be. So remember when you're out there today, and every day, my three favorite words are: *sell, sell, sell.*"

He turned abruptly on his leprechaun feet and marched out of the office, leaving some in a state of shock or quiet distress.

Sal leaned over to me. "Ulcer. Betcha ten bucks."

No one else knew quite what to say, or they dared not for fear of repercussions. When would the "you're gonna be happy" speech we heard on Friday kick in? However I wasn't particularly worried. I had a far better motivation to produce than Polk's threats: namely money, especially now that Julie was pregnant. Nevertheless I was going to have to watch myself around the little bastard.

I was readying myself to leave, and Jim wearily rose from his chair. "Hey, Jim," I called out. "How about us going over to Bilbro's for breakfast?"

"Can't. I'm stuck here with Randall and Polk, going over the district books and expenses."

"So you're not among the unlucky three having to dog it out on the debit?"

He laughed quietly. "No. I guess I'm blessed, huh?"

"You certainly are—with brains."

He raised his eyebrows and smiled. "Flattery will get you everything."

"Like you said, I'm catching on." We exchanged amused looks.

As I left I heard a voice calling from behind me. "Wait up, marine!"

I turned to find Burl Woodrow shuffling his bulk at surprising speed toward me. I hoped he could put on the brakes fast enough, or I would be flattened like roadkill.

"Where you going, boy?"

"Over to Bilbro's for breakfast."

"Mind if I tag along?"

"Not at all. I could use the company."

In the restaurant, he lowered his giant frame into a booth with some difficulty, resembling a large teddy bear in a baby chair.

"So whaddya think, Mike, 'bout that toad threatening us?"

"Unfortunately I think his method will work: fear is a great motivator."

"You know what that little squirt had the nerve to get on me about? My dress! He said I looked like I was going out on an African safari. I told him I didn't have my guns with me," he said morosely.

I couldn't help but find it funny, even though he appeared deadly serious. "What did he say?"

"Nothin'. Then I asked him if he'd ever worked a debit on the Sea Islands. He said no. I told him he had no idea what the hell it was like. Rough dirt roads that are impassible without a jeep. And when it rains, which is often, you're up to your ass in mud. When you finally make it to one of those little shacky villages, the kids are running around bare assed with mangy dogs, chickens, and hogs, and there's shit all over the place. You daren't sit down anywhere because of the filth and the fleas that'll eat your hide off. That's why I dress the way I do."

"I've been to Africa, and it sounds worse than what I saw there."

"No kidding! Africa?" He rubbed at the stubble on his cheek.

"Yeah."

At that point, Sal's favorite sweet thing appeared, wearing an outfit that had obviously shrunk in the wash. Having gained a good ten pounds myself since hanging up my uniform, I ordered only oatmeal with raisins and a cup of coffee.

Burl decided on two helpings of the special: six eggs, four sausages, a half dozen flapjacks, orange juice, and coffee. Whoa—I'd have hated to have his food bill. Orders taken, Sweet Thing did her usual brushing of my hand with a foxy grin as she collected menus, and her eyes swept past mine. She was one hell of a tease, and I enjoyed her game.

Burl must have noticed because as she walked away, he said, "I do believe that little gal is in heat for you."

"Maybe...or she's just playing around. Besides, I'm a happily married man."

"What the hell's that got to do with it? A little sugar on the side is just fun and keeps a man from going stale."

I was glad Julie hadn't heard that, but I laughed. "Burl, are you married?"

"Used to be. Three times in the last twenty years or so. I loved them all dearly, but they just couldn't get the hang of me, even when they knew what I was all about. Now I don't buy the cow anymore, especially when I can get all the milk I want for free."

"Sounds more like economics than love."

"I guess at my age, that's the truth. Anyways, about the asshole Polk...I told him to take a day off and come see for himself how things are on Wadmalaw. The wimp heed and hawed. Probably thought I'd butcher him and feed him in little pieces to the gators."

"One can only wish. If you ever have a mind to do so, give me a call. I'll help."

"Y'know, the more I talk to you, the more I'm thinkin' I like you, even though you're a damn Yankee."

"Don't put that Yankee shit on me. When your grandpappy was fighting the Civil War here, mine was drinking wine and chasing chicks down in sunny Naples, Italy, and he was from the South."

Roaring, he hit the table with his meaty hand, scaring the bejeezus out of the customers. "That's a damn good one, son."

In the space of fifteen minutes, I had gone from being a marine to Mike and now his son. Was he planning to adopt me?

"How did it finally end with the imp, Burl?"

"He said he would check out my story with Randall and the other staff managers to see if it's really that bad. But he insisted I dress 'properly' for the Friday meetings. I told him yeah, OK, I'll wear a tie."

"I hope it'll be a real fancy one to go with the safari outfit."

We chuckled, and then he said, "You gotta come out to the island and let me show you around."

"I think I'd enjoy that. I've never been on Wadmalaw. I hear it's strange and mysterious."

"You got that right, son. Just let me know when. I'll make sure the electric's turned on."

Sixteen

The holidays were fast approaching. Julie was doing fine as she began her fifth month of pregnancy, though she was still a bit irritable because she had stopped smoking. Our parents and friends were looking forward to celebrating the blessed event.

My selling continued showing solid gains every week. Polk drank antacid by the gallon and cracked his whip over the heads of agents and staff managers alike, with marked success. President Johnson was solidly in office with his plan for a Great Society, and some rabid segregationist Democrats switched allegiance to the Republican Party, which embraced them, as the divide between northern and southern Democrats widened over civil and states' rights. The Republicans looked as though they might be making a deal with the devil.

On Saturday night, Julie and I were getting ready to go to a dinner party the Averys were hosting. They lived on Tradd Street, in a spacious home that had been beautifully restored, unlike most of the homes in that area, which were in disrepair, their inhabitants living in genteel poverty. Tom and Rina had to have spent some big bucks to resurrect the antique from its doldrums.

I got out of the shower. Julie was in a black cocktail dress, turning from side to side in front of the full-length mirror on the bedroom door.

"You look great, baby," I said.

"Look at this." She pulled the dress tight around her waist. A little bulge appeared below her navel.

"That's great! I hadn't noticed."

"I think I'll wear something looser." She turned to the closet and rummaged around.

"You don't have to do that. You look fine," I reassured her.

"Yes, but I don't want to squash it." Suddenly she froze, a blank look on her face.

"What's happening? Are you OK?"

"Oh, Michael, I think I just felt it move!" Her face flushed.

I put my hand carefully on the bump. "I can't feel anything."

"It was like a little flutter. It's not doing it now."

Fifteen minutes later the bump still hadn't obliged, and we were late for dinner.

"Julie, Michael, how good to see you again." Jean-Luc peered through a haze of pungent smoke as he stubbed out his cheroot in a large, crystal ashtray a hovering Rina handed to him. "It's been a few months since we first met at the Sailfish."

Rina was dressed for the occasion in a gorgeous, pale-blue sarong and fitted blouse, the silk shot through with silver and gold threads that highlighted her dark features and large, expressive eyes.

"Time flies, Jean-Luc," I replied.

"Ah, yes it does, and, for some strange reason, faster the older you get."

"My mother's always saying that, but I, as yet, haven't had that experience."

"Give it time," he said, chuckling.

Marie Claire joined us. "And you, *ma petite*, how are you and the baby doing?" she asked Julie.

"Fine, Marie Claire. I'm so glad to be over the morning sickness."

"*Sacré bleu*, the morning sickness! I thought I would die from it before some Bosch bullet had a chance to kill me."

"Oh my God, you were pregnant when you fought in the Underground?"

"I was, with my darling Françoise. I hid it from Jean-Luc and the others until it became too obvious." She blew out her cheeks, clasped her hands under her slim abdomen as if she were carrying a thirty-pound watermelon, and laughed.

"Why?"

"They needed my marksmanship, as you know, during our raids and ambushes."

"But the baby! How could you take such a risk?"

"I had rather that my baby and I be dead than live with the tyrant's boot on our necks."

Julie and I were flabbergasted, as were Tom and Rina.

Jean-Luc interjected somberly, "Until you lose your freedom and see your people subjugated—living in fear every day and loved ones tortured and murdered—you cannot fathom the anger and hate that swells up in you to fight to the death if necessary to vanquish the oppressor."

The doorbell's ringing broke our spellbound state. Rina went to answer it and returned with a handsome, well-dressed couple in their midthirties. Rina introduced the Baptistes and us to Arthur and Elaine Sutcliffe. She resembled a young Katherine Hepburn—a slender figure encased in red satin; creamy, freckled skin; and bewitching green eyes radiating intelligence and energy. Arthur, in a conservative, dark-blue blazer and light-gray trousers, sporting a yellow cravat that played well against his Nordic looks, could have been a silver screen idol himself.

Small talk took up the next few minutes as we all got to know each other. Then Rina announced, in her soft but strongly accented Burmese tone, that dinner was served. The pale sea-green dining room had white enameled moldings, heart pine floors, and a gorgeous, sparkling chandelier. We took our seats at a large, mahogany table covered in an ivory damask tablecloth, white china, crystal glasses, and silverware.

Tom uncorked two bottles of wine, a Chardonnay and a Cabernet Sauvignon, and poured according to each guest's taste. Julie asked for ice water.

"Anything wrong, honey?" I asked discreetly.

"Just a bit of queasiness. I probably need to eat."

Jean-Luc, sitting to my right, raised his glass to propose a toast to the Averys, their hospitality, and their friendship. We happily followed suit. Jean-Luc, smiling slyly, then said, "Of course in ancient times, the host would drink first to assure his guests that the wine was not poisoned." Amused looks and chuckles ensued.

Each guest was served a light green salad with artichoke hearts and some sort of creamy dressing, with toast points on the side. While I was enjoying the delicious appetizer, Jean-Luc asked if I had considered the question he had put to me when leaving the Sailfish restaurant.

My mind was a blank.

He said, "About your willingness to do something about the injustices in this country."

"Ah, yes. I remember now. No, sir. I have neither the time nor the resources to get involved in other people's struggles, especially with Julie and me just getting started and a baby on the way. But don't think for a minute I don't care about the plight of the minorities and the poor. I see it every day when I sell insurance to the colored here in Charleston. I'm only one rung up on the ladder from most of them—working my ass off day and night, trying to get ahead."

"I'm sorry, Michael, I was unaware of your struggles."

"No need to apologize, Jean-Luc. I intend to change my lot in life."

Elaine said resolutely, "Those of us who *do* have the time and resources have the moral responsibility to get involved."

Jean-Luc nodded energetically.

Julie interjected, "Won't the passage of the Civil Rights bill change things for the better?"

"Not necessarily so," said Tom. "The South has always found novel ways to circumvent federal laws. For instance, we passed the Thirteenth Amendment to abolish slavery, but what resulted from that was a much harder and crueler form of slavery."

"How so?" I asked.

"Several hundred thousand coloreds were arrested over many years throughout the old Confederacy on bogus misdemeanor charges and given long jail sentences. Then their bodies and souls were leased out by the counties and states to private individuals and companies, where they were beaten, whipped, tortured, starved, and worked to death. An estimated twenty thousand of them died."

"Oh my God," said Julie. "I had no idea it was that terrible."

"It was. I won't go into how hideous the torture was. Most southerners knew what was going on and didn't raise a hand to stop it—at least not until much later on."

Where the hell had the federal government been when all this shit was going on? They damn well had to have known.

"Then we passed the Fourteenth and Fifteenth Amendments, which gave them the right to vote and be properly represented. We all know that didn't meet with much success."

"But why, Tom?" asked Rina.

"I want to know too," said Julie quietly.

I was pig ignorant, so I kept my mouth shut.

Tom said, "Well, OK—"

"Pardon me, Tom," said Elaine. "Let this southern girl, whose family, I have to say, prospered mightily off the backs of the coloreds, tell Julie and Rina how it happened."

"I can't imagine it coming from better lips." Tom smiled at her.

"It was really very simple. The states imposed a poll tax, and the majority of those people couldn't pay. There was a literacy test, and most couldn't hope to pass. Then they divided up the voting districts in such a way to guarantee that they would stay in power, and the coloreds would never have their own representation. But that wasn't enough." She grimaced. "The segregationist Supreme Court upheld the 'separate but equal' doctrine, also known as Jim Crow. It was pure BS. Hardly anything about it was equal, especially in the area of education. Many states, especially in the South, relegated the Negroes to a subhuman category, which had—and still has—an enormous negative effect on them. And then, to make sure this evil system would prevail, they had the Klan help reinforce it with all the atrocities known to man. This is still going on as we speak." She paused to sip from her glass.

Out of the corner of my eye, I saw Arthur placidly eating his salad.

Suddenly an enraged Marie Claire rose from her chair, waving her arms and with blood in her eyes. "*Fascistes*—we will never be rid of them!"

Jean-Luc grasped her hand firmly. "*Ma chérie*, please sit and calm yourself."

Everyone stared. How deep the wounds must have been for her, fighting that terrible war, to have caused this outburst. She dropped her arms to her side, took a deep breath, and let it out slowly, just as we had been taught on the rifle range to steady ourselves before firing a shot. Then she sat calmly, looked at her untouched salad, and closed her eyes. I bet Jean-Luc was wishing he had never asked me that question.

But then he surprised me when he spoke. "There are those of us who are historians and believe that the rise of fascism in this country began in the South after Reconstruction ended."

Tom nodded in agreement. "It's a cancer that's most prevalent in the South and needs to be eradicated—or at a minimum confined—so it doesn't spread."

"May I ask," Julie said, "what Reconstruction was?"

"Sorry, Julie. I should have explained," said Tom. "The Thirteenth, Fourteenth, and Fifteenth Amendments are known as the Reconstruction Amendments. Federal troops were sent to the South to enforce them, and for a very short period of time, Negroes had their rights guaranteed under the Constitution. However, when Reconstruction ended in 1877, the government troops pulled out, and the southern states reverted to their old ways and stripped the Negroes of their rights."

"Damn!" I said. "Five hundred thousand men died in the Civil War, and this is what we end up with?"

Solemnly Jean-Luc replied, "Man's history has been a tortuous process. However, that bloody war was a necessary step in moving this country along the path of becoming a truly democratic nation, as we are all witnessing here in our time."

"I hope so, Jean-Luc," I replied reluctantly.

With the subject finally exhausted, tranquility returned to the dining room as everyone resumed eating their salads. Arthur, who had long finished his, now pensively sipped from a tumbler of what looked suspiciously like whiskey. When had that appeared?

After the salad plates had been collected, a beaming Rina came out of the kitchen with a great side of roast beef on a wooden carving board. She placed it ceremonially in front of Tom to do the honors of slicing. The maid followed with roasted potatoes and parsnips basted with butter, parsley, and black pepper. Next came two gravy boats filled with a rich brown sauce to complement the meal.

After a few minutes of silent eating, I asked Tom for a second helping of beef. While he was slicing, Julie laid her fork down, having hardly touched her food. Rina asked her quietly if she was OK.

"I'm just a little under the weather, Rina. Probably some bug I picked up. I'll be fine."

"Are you sure? Would you like to lie down a bit?"

"No, thanks. It's such a beautiful party—I don't want to mess things up."

While we were awaiting dessert, Tom clinked his knife on his glass to get our attention. "I have an announcement to make." Were they pregnant too? Perhaps there was something in the air. "Elaine is planning to run for the state senate in '66." He gestured toward her. "Elaine?"

"Tom, it's still a long way off."

"Please, Elaine."

"If you insist." She glanced briefly at her husband. His expression remained blandly benevolent. "When we were speaking of disenfranchisement, I meant to add that the voting rights bill looks as if it has an excellent chance of passing. If it does, it will eliminate most of the obstructions for the minorities to vote. This will give an opportunity for both liberals and moderates running in southern state primaries and elections to win office with an army of millions of new voters to support them. Hopefully, with time, a more egalitarian Charleston and a new South will emerge."

Jean-Luc rose with great dignity and raised his glass. "*Liberté! Égalité! Fraternité!* I salute you."

We applauded, smiling at each other in a glow of camaraderie. I felt as though I might be witnessing an historic event.

As conversation resumed, Julie quietly excused herself and got up from the table. After a few minutes, Rina slipped from the room. When she returned, she gestured for me to join her in the hallway.

"Michael, don't panic, but Julie isn't doing well. She's bleeding. You need to get her to the hospital."

All thoughts of high-minded politics left me. I felt as though my heart had stopped. Julie emerged from the bathroom, ghostly pale and in obvious pain. I didn't say a word to the others as Rina and I helped Julie to the car. I held her hand tightly as I sped the few blocks to the Medical College Hospital.

As nurses helped her onto a gurney, she smiled weakly at me. "Don't worry, Michael. I'll be fine."

An unknown amount of time later, the doctor found me prowling the waiting room. We had lost the baby.

Seventeen

Early on Sunday morning, I reached for a quarter-filled bottle of Scotch and sloppily poured another drink. I was alone. The apartment felt still and quiet. I hadn't slept. The ashtray was overflowing with fag ends.

As I sipped the amber liquor, conflicting emotions tormented me. Julie would be OK, which relieved me of the dread that I might lose her. However, what nagged at me was that I didn't feel any grief at the loss of our child; I felt only a barely discernible sadness. Why? I had been looking forward so much to being a father. I had been excited and filled with joy when Julie first told me she was pregnant. How could it be that I wasn't now grief stricken—wringing my hands and tearing my hair out—like any normal person?

Maybe I was in some state of shock or denial. No, that wasn't it. Maybe the horrible fear of Julie's dying had overshadowed the loss. Yes, but only at the time when I'd thought she was in danger, certainly not now. Perhaps it was the stress of the ordeal overall that led me to drink and left me devoid of feeling. I did know I was agitated and exhausted, but I had no answers that felt right.

Angry and frustrated, I'd had enough of this shit. I had more pressing problems right then. I would need to look after Julie when she came home. I would have to find someone to cover me on the debit. I would have to put on the right face to the world and especially to Julie. I hated doing that; I was a lousy actor. I needed to find someone to confide in and help me sort myself out.

I dialed the phone apprehensively.

"Mike, what's wrong? It's six thirty in the morning."

"Jim, we lost the baby. I need someone to talk to."

The sounds of his breathing filled a short pause. "Of course. Give me forty-five minutes. I'll meet you at Bilbro's."

"Thanks a lot. Forty-five minutes."

Rising to clean myself up, I stumbled over the coffee table and fell, hitting my head on the wooden floor. Dazed, I realized how screwed-up drunk I was. I staggered into the bathroom, downed a glass of fizzy antacid, clumsily undressed, and took a cold shower in hopes of straightening up a bit.

Feeling somewhat better and one fewer sheet to the wind, I carefully navigated the back staircase to the parking area. I didn't want to be late in meeting Jim. Nevertheless I knew I had to drive cautiously or risk a run-in with Charleston's finest. Pulling out of the parking lot, I was blinded by a ray of sunshine slanting through the ominous clouds gathering over the peninsula. Dammit! Like an idiot, I'd forgotten my sunglasses. Squinting, I drove like a student driver, shoulders back, arms stiff on the wheel, and feeling cops' eyes everywhere. I managed to make it to Bilbro's in one piece.

Jim was sitting in a back booth.

"Good morning," he said as I joined him.

"Hi, Jim. Thanks for coming out."

He nodded. "Judging by your gait and general appearance, I would have to surmise that you are inebriated."

He was a gentleman to put things so politely. Anyone else would have told me that I was fuckin' wasted.

"Sorry, Jim. I tried to sober up a bit before coming over here. That's why I'm a little late."

He reached across the table and patted my hand. "That's OK. You took care of me when I was ill. Talk to me, son."

Tears welled up in my eyes. No one had ever addressed me in such a fatherly way. As I worked desperately to compose myself, a waitress brought water to our table and asked if we would care to order.

"Mike?" Jim asked.

"I'll just have coffee, thanks. Lots of it."

"No, that won't do, Mike. You have to put a little something in your stomach. Trust me, I know from experience. You'll feel better."

It was hard for me to envision Jim ever getting drunk. The man always seemed to be in complete control. Turning to the waitress, he pointed to his menu. "Let me have the breakfast special with bacon, please, and bring an extra order of toast for my friend here." He looked at me intently. "Don't be afraid to tell me everything that happened. I'm here to listen."

Clearing my throat, I related all that had occurred and how confused I was. The only clues to what he might be thinking were in his subtle facial expressions. When I'd finished, he shook his head ever so slightly.

"Michael, there's nothing wrong with you other than being young and inexperienced and being brought up as an Italian Catholic who has to dramatize everything that happens in life like a Puccini opera."

I laughed in spite of my misery.

"Have you ever known anyone who has lost a child in the way you have?" he asked.

"No."

"So why did you conclude that you should be pulling your hair out and wringing your hands? Did you ever see anything like that other than in the movies?"

"I was ten years old. My grandfather died, and my poor grandmother did just that. It was so terrible that my uncles had to drag her off her husband's dead body."

"Latins have a tendency to show great emotion. It's a cultural trait, and the young learn from it. However, it was natural for your grandmother to be grief stricken. She'd lost someone she had shared a long life with. When he died a part of her died too, and all the good memories came back to haunt her. She was bonded to him in every possible way that a human can be. How could your loss compare to hers? You didn't see, feel, hear, smell, or know your child in any way, much less have any memories of it. All you could have felt, at the most, was sadness at what could have been and what Julie was going through. I have known several people who have lost a child like you. Some were my family members. I observed sadness for a while but never true grief."

He looked at me pensively. Everything he had said made sense, especially about my Italian nature. My morbid state was slowly being replaced by a feeling of foolishness.

"I guess I'm stupid and a little crazy."

"There you go again, coming down hard on yourself. Stop the melodrama. Learn from what has happened. And remember this: 'A mind is its own place and in itself, can make a heaven of hell, a hell of heaven.' The poet Milton said that."

The profound words worked their way into my psyche. "I will, Jim. I really will."

Having finished breakfast, I thanked Jim for his help and left for the Battery. I didn't want to return to the gloom of the empty apartment, and I needed to repair myself before I visited Julie. I leaned over the guard rail, looking out toward Fort Sumter and the choppy waters around it. What mattered most now was that Julie recovered.

I arrived at the hospital a few minutes after ten o'clock, breathless from hurrying and clutching a bunch of somewhat bedraggled daisies mixed in with a few anonymous yellow blooms; a *Vogue* magazine; and a microbiology journal that had arrived for Julie on Saturday in the mail. A nurse directed me to Julie's room, where she lay propped up on pillows, staring out of the window. I tapped lightly on the doorframe. She turned, summoning a smile when she saw me, and held out her hand. I sat cautiously on the bed beside her and put my arms around her, careful of the IV tube snaking from her left wrist. My heart turned over; she was still so pale. Neither of us spoke for a few moments.

Then she said, "We're crushing the lovely flowers. You'd better put them on the table until we can find a vase for them."

"In a minute, honey. How are you feeling? Why do you still have an IV going?"

"Michael, don't worry. I'm fine. It's just that I'm still bleeding a bit. They say they'll do something about it if it hasn't stopped by tomorrow." She paused and narrowed her eyes. "What happened to you? You've got a nasty bruise on your head."

"Never mind that. I want to know how you are. I was so scared when it happened and so sad. I know you must be too." I was desperately trying to find the right words.

No more came to me, so I put my gifts on the table and took her in my arms. She rested her head on my chest and began to weep silently as I stroked her hair and crooned endearments.

She raised her eyes to mine and said brokenly, "Oh, Michael, if only I hadn't felt the baby move."

I held her while she cried. A nurse popped her head into the room and then quietly withdrew, pulling the door closed. A radio was playing somewhere nearby, and two women were chattering and laughing in the corridor outside. The rain that had threatened all morning finally arrived, streaming down the window and blurring the view of the rooftops of the old Porter Military Academy below. Eventually Julie stilled and lay back on her pillows.

"So," she said resolutely and then blew her nose loudly. "What did you bring me?"

I couldn't help laughing a little; she sounded like a kid at Christmas. I reached behind me and retrieved my offerings. She raised one eyebrow at the *Vogue*, but she looked decidedly more interested in the science journal.

"Oh, thank you! There's nothing to read in here. This'll be great. Did you see what Marie Claire sent?"

She'd sent an enormous basket of fruit, decorated with a big, red bow. Where on Earth had she gotten such a gift on a Sunday?

"Wow, that's amazing. Can I have one of those bananas?"

"Of course you can. You'd better take the whole thing home with you. I'm on fluids until they decide what to do with me."

I had forgotten about that. "So what are they thinking?"

"If I don't stop bleeding, they'll do a D and C, but even if they do, I'll still be home on Wednesday at the latest. I'll take the rest of the week off though."

"A what? Is it an operation?" My blood pressure was rising again.

"It's a routine procedure, nothing to worry about."

That sounded vaguely ominous to me, but I decided to leave it alone.

She said, "Rina came by this morning before visiting hours started, but they let her in. She knows some of the nurses on this floor. She said she and Tom will come by this evening."

We talked of this and that for a while. She started yawning.

"You'd better rest, honey," I said. "I'll be back this evening."

"You'd better be or else!" That sounded more like my girl. "And by the way, I expect you to tell me what you got up to, getting that bang on your head."

I waved her words away. "I love you so much, Julie. We're going to be fine."

Her smile looked a bit wobbly. "I know we will. I love you too," she murmured.

Eighteen

Almost a month had passed since we had lost the baby. Julie was still recovering from the terrible ordeal—how much I couldn't tell for certain. However, I'd already reconciled myself to the blow fate had dealt us. Julie had written to her mother, Winifred, with the news, and assured her that she was fine, worried she might feel she had to jump on a plane to the States to look after her. Winifred was crestfallen but optimistic, reminding her that she had lost a baby before Julie was born. My mother, deeply saddened, told us it was God's will. She would pray for the baby and light a candle for its soul.

Thanksgiving was only two days away. All of our friends were out of town or visiting their families, but we were content with the prospect of spending the holiday alone together, watching the Macy's parade, eating leftover lasagna, and taking a long walk on the beach.

I needed to double up on my collections because of the long holiday weekend. I knocked on the torn screen door of the Chavis family's home. Pinky Chavis, a frail, coffee-colored girl in her teens, answered, her cat, Marmalade, weaving itself around my ankles on the termite-ridden porch, purring loudly. Pinky was uninsurable because she had sickle cell anemia, a disease Julie had told me was prevalent among people of African descent. She lived with her mother and helped take care of her two nieces, whom her drug-addicted sister had abandoned. Their only source of income that I knew of was her mother, who worked two jobs as a maid and was away from their small apartment most of the day and part of the night.

Smiling, Pinky greeted me. "Hello, Mr. Mike. Hope you're havin' a fine day, sir."

"So far, so good, Pinky."

She handed me the receipt book. While I marked it, she untied a knotted white handkerchief containing two dollars and eighty five cents, all in coins, and handed it to me. I counted it out and put the nickels, dimes, and quarters in my right pants pocket, which hung heavily against my thigh like Friar Tuck's purse.

I returned the book to her. "So Pinky, are you and your mom ready for Thanksgiving?"

She looked away, twisting the handkerchief in her hands. "Ain't goin' be no Thanksgivin' around here, Mr. Mike."

"Why on Earth not?"

"We ain't got no money to buy a bird, and besides, Momma got to work part of the day helpin' Miss Lucy get ready for her turkey party."

Damn! I hoped I hadn't embarrassed her by asking that question. Not knowing quite what to say, and eager to leave, I said, "You have yourself a good rest of the day, Pinky. I'll see you next week if the devil doesn't get me."

She laughed. "You gotta keep a good lookout for him. He always creepin' around some corner, lookin' for another soul to take."

Having finished the day's work later than usual, I returned to our apartment and found Julie in the living room, watching Charlie Hall on the channel five evening news. When she saw me come in, she clicked off the TV and asked what I would like for dinner.

"Pizza," I replied hopefully.

She put her hands on her hips and got an amused look on her face. "And where in this town are we going to find that?"

"Caruso's," I replied. "Let's try it. I'm in desperate need."

"You must be. You get upset every time you try anything that's remotely Italian down here."

"We've gotta keep looking. Besides, Sal told me months back that they make a good pie."

"OK. But I don't want to hear you complaining for hours on end if it's not good."

We were seated at a table for two in the cozy pizzeria. Candles set in Chianti bottles gave off a dim light. We ordered a large pepperoni pizza and two colas. Picking abstractedly at the congealed, multi-colored wax on the bottle, I told Julie about my experience that day with Pinky. She gazed at the candle flame and joined me in scattering waxy flakes on the checkered cloth.

"Michael, I know it would change our plans somewhat for Thanksgiving, but what d'ya say we cook a bird with all the fixings and take it over to Pinky's family?"

"Whoa, that sounds like a heck of a lot of work. Why not just buy a turkey and give it to them? Let them do what they want with it."

"But you said the mother will be working a good part of the day. It would be hard on Pinky. She's only a kid, after all, and not well. She can't do everything on her own. Besides, all you have to do is help me with the shopping. I'll take care of the rest."

"OK. If that's what you want, it's fine with me."

Our pizza arrived within fifteen minutes of our placing the order, which was nice since the place was packed with hordes of Citadel cadets and others, with more people still crowding in. Pulling a slice away from the aluminum tray scored with a thousand cut marks, I folded it and took a large bite. *Mamma mia!* It was delicious. A perfect blend of a tasty, crisp crust; a quality mozzarella; and a rich tomato sauce. I closed my eyes and savored the wonderful flavors. I was in heaven, as was Julie, who was quiet and two bites ahead of me. Finally I had found an Italian oasis in the land of grits.

Late on Wednesday afternoon, Julie and I were rolling a shopping cart around old Mr. Davies's store, picking up groceries for Pinky's Thanksgiving dinner. As we strolled down an aisle, we ran into Mr. Davies himself. We stopped and exchanged greetings.

"My goodness," he said, looking at our cart, "you must be planning to invite the Pilgrims over, given the size of that bird."

"Something like that," I replied, "but we won't be at the feast."

He looked confused. "How's that again?"

Julie told him of our plan.

He scratched his thinning hair and peered again through his horn-rimmed glasses into the cart. "Please wait here. I'll be back in a moment."

Julie said, "What's going on?"

"I haven't the foggiest," I replied.

He returned with a price list in his hand and his son, Tom, who greeted us affably.

Mr. Davies said, "Allow me to contribute to your laudable deed."

Taking out a pencil, he wrote on a slip of paper the items in the cart destined for a Thanksgiving dinner. He handed it to Tom. "Give this to Karen at the checkout. Tell her we are charging Mr. and Mrs. Romano our cost for the bird, and the rest of the items on the list are on us."

"Gee, thanks, Mr. Davies!" I said.

He smiled. Julie kissed him on the cheek, catching him off balance. He blushed and excused himself, saying he was needed up front to help with the bagging.

The next morning, hugging Julie's soft, scented pillow, I was stirred awake by delicious aromas emanating from the kitchen and the sounds of pots and pans rattling. I wanted to sleep longer. I burrowed deeper into the bedclothes, nodding off again. Sometime later I awoke to a gentle nudging of my shoulder and the delectable scent of strong coffee.

Smiling, Julie said, "Wake up, you lazy bugger! It's almost ten o'clock."

"Holy mackerel! We're missing the Macy's Thanksgiving Day parade." I bolted past her into the living room and turned on the TV.

We watched the parade together while the bird roasted, drinking coffee and dunking doughnuts. A wave of nostalgia hit me, remembering my uncle Luca, who owned his own Checker cab back in New York City. I had seen my first Macy's parade with him and my two cousins as we balanced on the roof of his cab, bundled up against the freezing weather to watch the marvelous floats and colorful, huge balloon figures pass by. Luca took pity on me since I had no father, brothers, or sisters around; he took every opportunity during holidays and birthdays to include me in his family's festivities.

He was gone now, having worked himself to death pushing a hack night and day all over the city to provide a life for his wife and children that I could only have wished for. I missed him.

Julie knocked on the Chavis's door around noon. She was holding a large shopping bag in one arm while I stood behind her, gripping a covered roasting pan loaded down with an eighteen-pound turkey and sweet potatoes. Emily and Doreen, the five-year-old twins, opened the door. One of them—I could never tell them apart—yelled into the house, "Pinky, there's some white folk out here on the porch!"

Pinky was confused to see Julie and then surprised when she recognized me. She opened the creaking screen door.

I said, "Pinky, I want you to meet my wife, Julie."

She hesitated for a second or two and then said shyly, "Pleased to be meeting you, ma'am."

Julie extended her hand to Pinky, who took it gingerly. "I'm happy to make your acquaintance, Pinky."

I wanted to get things moving. "Julie and I know how tough things can get at times. We couldn't enjoy Thanksgiving without doing something for your family. So this dinner is as much for us as it is for you."

Pinky pursed her lips and looked at us squarely. "My family is truly thankful and much beholden to you, sir."

"Forget the beholden stuff, Pinky. You owe us nothing. Just tell us where we can put this stuff down. It's getting heavy."

"Oh," she said. "Come with me into the kitchen, and put it on that table there."

We unloaded the dinner in a small, yellow kitchen with aging, white appliances.

I said, "Pinky, we gotta get going. Our family's coming over for dinner."

Julie looked at me askance. I was sure she knew I wanted to leave. As we turned to go, one of the twins, who had been surreptitiously eyeing Julie as though she were an exotic creature from another planet, took Julie's hand and looked up at her, a smile on her round face. The other twin grabbed her other hand. Julie knelt on the worn linoleum floor and put an arm around each one of their tiny waists as they touched and examined her hair.

"You are such darlings," she said. A minute later she rose. Tears welled in her eyes. "I'm sorry, little ones, I have to leave now."

NINETEEN

On Saturday night, the city was spruced up for Christmas, which was less than a week away. The weather was mild if not balmy as Julie and I sauntered into the Francis Marion Hotel. We were a good half hour early for the office Christmas party, so we sat in the spacious, chandeliered lobby, which was tastefully decorated with holiday cheer.

"Michael, may I have a cigarette?" Julie asked.

"Sure, babe."

I could tell she was uneasy. She wouldn't know anyone at the party and was worried about making a good impression. I tried to reassure her that she would be a big hit, but I seemed only to make things worse. But she did look great in her cocktail dress as she sat erect, with her shapely legs gracefully to one side and her skirt arranged to show the lacey trim peaking below the hem.

After about fifteen minutes, Jim Dawson came into the lobby through the Calhoun Street entrance. I rose from my chair and hailed him. He looked dapper in a beautifully tailored dark suit and silver tie.

"Julie, I'd like you to meet Jim."

He took her hand gently. "Julie, I must apologize for my not meeting you sooner. I had planned sometime back to take you and Michael out to dinner. However, changes in the office, which I'm sure you're aware of, and matters of health and family have made it difficult."

"No apologies are necessary, Mr. Dawson." She smiled warmly.

"Please call me Jim. No need for formalities. Michael has told me you're a research technician with the ambition of securing your master's degree."

"Yes. A bachelor's degree won't allow me to perform my own research. Actually I'd like to go further and get my doctorate eventually."

"I applaud your aspirations." Jim looked at me. "I've wondered at times if it might not be advantageous for Michael to go to college himself one day."

"No way in hell, Jim. I haven't got four years to waste trying to get some fancy degree and having to hang around with a bunch of seventeen- and eighteen-year-old kids. Besides, I learn better on my own. All I need is books."

Julie raised her eyebrows.

Jim chuckled and shook his head. "On second thought, I do believe that you will probably get to wherever you want to go without a degree."

He paused to check his watch and then offered his arm to Julie with a gracious bow. "May I escort you to the ballroom, my dear?"

"Why of course, Jim." She had a sparkle in her eye and a delighted smile on her face.

The three of us found a table where Sal Fanelli and P. J. Lucas, a former professional wrestler, and their wives were already seated. After greetings and introductions, we were stilled by our illustrious leader, Mr. Polk, taking the floor in high holiday spirit.

"Ladies and gents, I wanna wish y'all durin' this blessed time of the year, as we celebrate the birth of our Lord and Savior, Jesus Christ, a merry Christmas."

Jesus Christ? This little bastard ruled through fear and intimidation. He had no idea of Christ's message of love, compassion, and forgiveness.

He droned on. Few if any of the agents or their spouses seemed to be paying much attention. He finally ended by saying, "Let's give thanks to the Lord and our wonderful company, who allow us to put bread on the table for our families."

Now the Lord was working through the company? Did he hold any stock options?

Polk received lukewarm applause and some smiles and handshakes from his cronies, and then he returned to his table. Then Mr. Randall rose to say grace. Everyone bowed their heads obediently like little children receiving their First Communion, including me, as he intoned the prayer.

Amens sounded throughout the ballroom. The waitstaff circulated, depositing mixed green salads with blue cheese dressing in front of each guest. P. J. stabbed at his salad and said, "Thank you, Lord, for the sixty-plus hours I work every week as a lowly staff manager, busting my ass for the company and the glory of Polk."

"Now, now, P. J., mind your p's and q's," Jim said, patting him on the back. We all chucked at his silly joke.

Notwithstanding the bizarre introduction, the company had gone to great expense to treat us to a wonderful mignon with béarnaise sauce, roasted potatoes, and steamed vegetables. Dessert was chocolate layer cake with a scoop of vanilla ice cream. However, the Lord hadn't seen fit to turn the iced tea into wine.

As the waitstaff served coffee, Polk walked to the front to join Ida, our secretary, who was holding a cardboard box.

"Ladies and gents, we come to the most important part of the evening," Polk announced. "The recognition of our three leading agents. Miss Kitty Kelley, please come forward."

Kitty, resplendent in a long-skirted dinner suit in midnight-blue brocade, made her way to the front, smiling widely. Ida handed Polk a plaque out of the box.

"Miss Kitty, on behalf of our great company, I'm very pleased to award you this fine plaque that recognizes you as the top agent in our district and a check for three hundred dollars."

Enthusiastic applause and wild whistles erupted as she raised the plaque on high and said, "Thank y'all very much!"

As she turned to leave, Polk said, "Please stay, Miss Kitty." He indicated a spot to his left.

"Our second leading agent is Mr. George Simmonds." Following the same ceremonial procedure, George collected his plaque and a check for two hundred bucks.

Polk then looked over in our direction. "Mr. Romano, please come forward. You are our third leading agent."

I was floored. I'd had no idea.

Polk handed me a plaque. "Considerin' that Mr. Romano had only a half year to compete, I consider this to be quite an accomplishment."

I almost could have kissed the little prick on his lips. Then he handed me a check for a hundred dollars, which I waved in Julie's direction. She proudly waved in return, a huge grin on her flushed face.

"Let's all give a round of applause to our three stars," Polk shouted. I had to admit I liked it.

After we said our farewells to Jim and the Fanellis, P. J. said, "Mike, do you and Julie like to dance?"

"Yeah, why?"

"Bobbie Jo and I are headed out to a honky-tonk called Rahaley's. It has a great country-and-western band and serves liquor."

He came up close to my ear and nudged me. "They also have a blackjack game going out back and some of the hottest-looking snatch in the Lowcountry."

"Sounds like fun, P. J." I figured I might make a few bucks playing cards while we were there.

Bobbie Jo, a five-foot-two, blue-eyed southern doll, regarded us suspiciously. "What are you boys plotting?"

"Nothing, sugar. Honest!" replied P. J.

She crossed her arms and stared him down. Then she looked at Julie. "I bet they're up to no good."

Julie seemed oblivious and just shrugged her shoulders. I figured P. J.'s interest had more to do with the hot snatch than booze, dancing, or gambling. Perhaps Bobbie Jo was aware he had a wandering eye. I had heard rumors around the office that he was a ladies' man. Nevertheless I felt good and wanted to party. I asked P. J. where the joint was.

"Just a short ride from here, out in North Charleston."

"Whaddya say, Julie? Feel like boogying?"

Her face lit up with a smile. "We haven't danced since our wedding."

"OK, let's go!"

After following the lights of P. J.'s car for more than a half hour, we finally pulled into the dirt parking lot of Rahaley's, just short of the Dorchester County line. The white stucco building, with its large, green-and-white neon sign announcing the nightspot, reminded me more of a truck stop than a place of entertainment. We weaved our way in the dark around cars, pickup trucks, and semis parked in every direction. The girls found it difficult to maintain their balance in their high heels on the rutted surface. We finally made it to the entrance.

Once inside we scanned the large, dimly lit, smoky club, looking for a place to park ourselves. As luck would have it, a group was breaking up at a table near the dance floor. We raced over to it. Just as we were settling in, a harried young waitress appeared to take our orders.

"Beers all around!" I announced.

She dropped her order pad into her short, black apron, cleared off the table, and wiped it down with a soiled, white towel. Hearing the cries for more brew from a boisterous lot at another table, she was off like a sprite.

We didn't want to leave our seats until the drinks arrived, so we watched the dancers grind away slowly to the romantic music of "Stand by Your Man" sung by a Patsy Cline lookalike. After several minutes, our drinks still nowhere in sight, two rough-looking characters approached our table. The bigger of the two, standing more than six feet and carrying more fat than muscle, said, "How 'bout you gals doing a whirl with us? Looks like you got two left-footed dudes there that probably can't walk straight, much less dance."

I chuckled in spite of the insult, but Bobbie Jo glared at him. "Get lost, road rat. You're stinking up the place." Much to their chagrin, we all laughed except Julie.

The big guy grabbed Julie's wrist and said, "Let's go, baby." His partner moved toward Bobbie Jo.

Caught off guard, I didn't react until Julie yelled, "Let go of me!"

Getting out of my chair quickly, I hit him with a roundhouse elbow to his nose. Releasing Julie, he staggered back, holding his nose while blood streamed through his fingers. Then, like a snake on shit, I nailed him with a right cross to the temple that drove him up against the wall. P. J. picked up the other asshole and body-slammed him onto a table, sending bottles, chairs, and occupants flying in all directions. I got too close to my punk; he wrapped his arms around me and bit me hard on the shoulder, like a rabid dog. Rage took hold of me as I broke free. I grabbed the back of his head with two hands and shoved his face down as I came up hard with my knee. He went limp and sagged to the floor. I started to kick the hell out of him, yelling, "I'm gonna kill you!"

It ended when three guys pulled me off him, holding me back by both arms until I calmed down. One took me aside and growled, "Listen up. I'm the owner of this place, and I want your asses outa here right now. I saw what happened—you and your pal just whupped up on two of the meanest sons of bitches in the county. They're part of a redneck gang that'll come after you if they know who you are. So git! And don't never come back to my place again."

I rushed over to Julie, grabbed her hand, and shouted to P. J., "Let's haul ass!"

We made it back to our cars and headed for home. Julie sat quietly.

"Are you OK, baby?" I asked.

I got no response. I turned on the radio to a music station, to lighten the mood.

After a while, she said, "I don't want to go to a place like that *ever again*! I'm glad to have a man who can protect me; but it really upset me seeing how violent you became. Please try not to let that happen anymore."

"I'll do my best, Julie, but I didn't make this world we live in."

"It's not the only world, and it's certainly not mine. We can choose *which* world we want to live in."

Twenty

As the year drew to a close, an arctic cold dipped deep into Dixie. It was New Year's Eve, and I wasn't dressed warmly enough for the weather—I hadn't thought to buy an overcoat to go with my new wardrobe. I raced through the debit with my jacket collar turned up against the frigid wind. I wanted to get home early, to rest up before going to a party at the Howard mansion, the Sutcliffes' residence on East Battery. Julie and I had been surprised to receive the engraved invitation. We had only met Elaine and Arthur once, on that terrible night when Julie had miscarried. However, we were excited about being invited. Tom and Rina would be there, and we would be bringing in the New Year with one of Charleston's most prominent families.

As I worked, I thought about what Julie had said about choosing the kind of world in which one wished to live. I enjoyed the world of fancy dinner parties, good clothes, and intelligent people. I aspired to become a part of it, and these people offered me a bridge.

Some of my customers insisted on having holiday drinks and chats with me, and I ended up running an hour behind the time I had told Julie I would be home. I was shivering and half buzzed when I knocked on the door of Dorothy Wright's funeral parlor.

When Dorothy saw me, she said, "Get your white butt in here, boy, and warm up a bit."

Dorothy was a large, straight-talking Negro woman in her fifties who had managed her own business for more than twenty-five years. She took no guff from anyone, colored or white. Even the thugs in the neighborhood respected her, knowing that if they ever crossed her they might get a rolling pin to the side of the head. That she was the proud owner of a .357 Magnum helped too. I liked her, and we got along fine, especially after she had found out about Julie and me making the Thanksgiving dinner for the Chavis family.

Shuffling her heavy body on gauze-wrapped, diabetic legs, she set two water glasses and a bottle of first-class Scotch onto the kitchen table. Then she poured us both a generous amount, went over to the icebox, and got out a bottle of milk. She cut her liquor with it.

She gestured with the bottle and asked if I wanted the same. I hesitated. She said, "It's a good mix. It smooths out the Scotch and cuts down on the bite."

"OK. I'll try anything once."

I was surprised. It was a good drink—far better than eggnog.

"What're you planning for New Year's Eve, Duke?"

Duke? Had I heard her right? Had she confused me with someone else, as old people do sometimes?

She must have read my face. "Don't you know that the folks 'round here call you the Duke?"

"No, why?"

"You look like an aristocrat, always duded up in fancy clothes like you're going to a wedding or a funeral."

I chuckled while she drank her high-octane milk. "Thanks for telling me. Now I feel like a real cool cat."

"You are, and some of the colored girls have an eye out for you."

I blushed as she laughed, seeming to enjoy my uneasiness. I decided to get back to her question. "I'm going to a party at the Sutcliffes' house on East Battery."

Dorothy looked impressed. "Boy, you sure moving in high society! How did a Yankee like you get to know them?"

I told her, and she surprised me by asking if I was happily married.

"Yes, ma'am."

"I do know something about Elaine Sutcliffe. She was a wild one when she was young. She might just have a hankering for a good-looking buck like you." She cackled, adjusting her bulk on the chair.

"No, that's not it. She's going to run for public office. I suspect that she believes I'll be able to get her a few votes with the people I know."

"I could be wrong, but a lot of those cotillion belles and their men-folk like to mess around and cause all kinds of mischief. My advice to you is to keep your tallywacker in your pants until you get home and have legal right to use it."

I laughed. "Thanks for the advice. Now I've gotta get going."

Picking up my glass as I stood, I threw down the remainder of the potent mix and wished her a happy New Year.

"Same to you, Duke. Remember to look out for yourself."

Back out in the biting cold, I headed for my car with a now larger buzz on, making me feel as though it were closer to midnight than five in the afternoon. I entered the apartment quietly, figuring Julie might be resting. I needed to get some sleep for the long night ahead.

Lying down fully clothed, I fell fast asleep next to Julie. At seven, the alarm clock went off. I swung my legs over the side of the bed and lit up a cigarette, trying to get my bearings. I had a slight headache and a parched mouth. Julie was in the shower, singing.

I finished my smoke, got up, and went into the kitchen to get some aspirin. I popped two into my mouth and washed them down with a large glass of water. Still thirsty, I poured myself a cold slug of orange juice. When I returned to the bedroom, I found Julie, with her head wrapped up in a towel, wearing her satin robe.

She said, "I thought you would be home by four. I waited, but got tired and decided to nap."

"I got held up by some of my people offering me drinks and wanting to talk. I didn't want to offend them, so I obliged."

"That was wise. After all, you make your living through them. So when did you get in?"

"A little after five."

"Good—you got some rest then. Why don't you take a shower to freshen up? It's after seven, and I need the bathroom to put on my makeup. I figured you'd be hungry, so I made you a ham and Swiss sandwich."

"Great, honey, I'm famished. I'll eat it after I clean up."

Thanks to Julie's penchant for long, hot showers, not having experienced them in England or South Africa, where bathtubs were the norm, the remaining water was barely warm. I toweled myself off and headed back to the kitchen, patting Julie on the behind as she passed me on her way to the bathroom.

"Don't do that," she yelped. "You know it irritates me."

I shot her a bratty grin.

Sandwich in hand, I wandered over to the living room window and peered out onto the dimly lit Rutledge Avenue. I couldn't believe what I saw. Quarter-sized snowflakes fluttered silently down onto the street. I opened the door and stepped out into the cold air, seeing and feeling the snow as it fell on my upturned face.

I yelled out to Julie to come to the front door. She rushed into the living room with a worried look on her face and a lipstick in her hand.

"What are you doing with the door wide open? Are you crazy? You're letting all the heat out," she said, coming over to me. Then she saw, as I had, that for the first time since we had arrived in Charleston, it was snowing.

We watched the rare and beautiful scene for a while like little children wanting the day off from school, hoping it would snow harder and settle on the ground. But we had to get ready for the party.

"Michael, you have to go get dressed now. I want the bedroom to myself."

"Yes, ma'am."

I knew she wanted to surprise me with the new floor-length evening gown she had bought—the only one she'd ever bought—at some fancy shop on King Street for the gala event.

I dressed posthaste and left the bedroom to her. Still thirsty, although my headache was almost gone, I decided that one beer couldn't hurt. I went back into the kitchen, popped the cap, and then jumped back like a matador as the amber brew exploded with volcanic force from the bottle, just missing my black, pin-striped suit and maroon tie.

The radio was playing softly in the living room. Good grief, didn't they know Christmas was over? There was only so much "Deck the Halls" a man could take. However, they did announce that they would be broadcasting live, at eleven thirty, the Guy Lombardo band, direct from the Waldorf Astoria in New York. What would New Year's Eve be without Guy? I had heard him first as I'd left my mother's womb in 1940, and I was certain he would still be there as I took my last breath in 2040.

Firing up a smoke, I admired my new Italian-made shoes, which had cost me a fortune at twenty dollars. I was fast becoming a crass materialist. Why not? There was nothing wrong with wanting and having beautiful things in life. Then Julie appeared, twirling in front of me, and banished all other thoughts.

Her dress hugged her breasts and waist and then fell in folds of aqua shades to her feet. She had pinned her hair up in wild curls, and her blue eyes shimmered with shadow. Her cheeks flushed with excitement, or rouge, giving her a rare allure. This was a woman who was lovely without any makeup, and tonight she was stunning.

"Do you like it? I got it on sale for twelve dollars." She poked a foot out from beneath the dress. "And the shoes cost only four." They were satin pumps in a shade of blue that picked up the same color in the gown. "They're really uncomfortable. I'm going to be limping before the end of the night."

My twenty-buck shoes began to pinch.

Even though the party had begun at eight, we arrived a little before nine at the Howard mansion. Elaine and Arthur welcomed us warmly. After a few genial words, Arthur told us that drinks and hors d'oeuvres were available in the living room. We thanked him, and Elaine and Arthur turned to greet other guests.

We made our way into the noisy living room. A jazz combo was playing "Sweet Georgia Brown," and dancers were shaking it up. Others talked loudly, holding their drinks none too steadily. Most of the men wore tuxedoes, and the women were in slinky gowns and were dripping in gold, diamonds, and pearls.

Feeling somewhat underdressed and not seeing anyone we knew, we picked up a couple of drinks and roamed through the palatial residence, admiring the gorgeous furniture, oriental carpets, and what looked to be paintings of long-departed ancestors.

In the cherrywood library, we scanned an entire wall of leather-bound books. Seeing some of interest, we cautiously leafed through the crisp pages that had clearly never been turned before.

"Michael, look! A first edition of Jane Austen's *Pride and Prejudice*!"

"How about that. I'm looking at one by Sartre that might be a first; however, it's written in French. Can you translate it?"

"Sure. Let me see."

Reading, and murmuring to herself in French for a few moments, she said, "Yes. It's a first. *Being and Nothingness*, 1943."

"You know, it wouldn't surprise me any if we ran across a Gutenberg Bible in this collection."

She laughed and knuckled my shoulder.

We carefully slid the books into their original positions, turned to leave, and were confronted by a short, heavyset man who I guessed to be in his midfifties. He was dressed in an old-fashioned tux with large silk lapels.

"Good evening," he said, "I'm Elias Pendergast. I do hope I'm not disturbing you. I couldn't help but notice your interest in this wonderful book collection."

"No, we were just about to leave and find our friends," I answered.

"May I ask who they might be?"

"The Averys and the Baptistes. And we're the Romanos, Mike and Julie."

"Ah, the Averys—a fine old Boston family. I know Tom well."

I thought about poor Rina.

"So I take it that one of you may be connected to the college?" He took a cigar from his jacket, studied it, and then began to unwrap it.

"No, we're not," I answered.

Continuing his interrogation, he addressed Julie. "And you, Julie, you must be English?"

"Yes, I'm a Yorkshire girl," she answered pleasantly.

"Great people! I have some relatives who live in Leeds. Who knows? We might be cousins." He smiled. "My family is originally from Wales. And you, Michael, you must be a Yankee."

"Yeah," I said. If I lived to be a hundred, I would always be "that Yankee" in Charleston. Curious, I asked him what *he* did for a living.

"My family is in real estate."

A bell went off in my head. I visualized many real estate signs with the Pendergast name prominently displayed.

"Also, I'm chairman of the Republican Party here in South Carolina. So what brought you to Charleston, Michael?"

"Employment opportunities," I responded dryly. "I was originally stationed here in the marine corps."

I got the usual look of respect. I could tell Julie was growing tired of the conversation.

Smiling, he handed me his business card. "If you're ever in the market for real estate, please feel free to call on me."

Turning to leave, we were happily interrupted by the arrival of the Averys and the Baptistes.

"Julie, Michael," said Tom. "How in character to find you both in the library. And Elias. Are you the self-appointed librarian for the evening?"

"No, Tom. I sought refuge here to escape the hubbub and to smoke a cigar in peace. However, when I saw these two delightful young people so engrossed and excited looking through these books, I felt the need to introduce myself. As you know very well, not too many in our circle of friends have any real interest in literature."

"Unfortunately that's true," Tom replied ruefully.

Julie nervously interjected, "I know we were being naughty, exploring the books, but we just couldn't resist."

Elias said, "Don't fret, my dear. I'm sure Elaine and Arthur wouldn't mind. What's the point of having books if they aren't read?"

Jean-Luc cleared his throat.

"Oh," said Tom, "forgive me, Jean-Luc. I haven't introduced you and Marie Claire to Elias Pendergast. Elias, Dr. Baptiste is the new chair of the history department at the college."

Elias nodded cordially.

Marie Claire, elegantly adorned in silk and pearls, announced, "I'm famished! I've eaten nothing since breakfast, and I'm so hungry I could eat a horse."

An impish grin lit up Jean-Luc's face. "Marie Claire developed a taste for that four-legged beast when we were short of meat during the war."

Looks of distaste were apparent on everyone's faces except mine. I had eaten horse a few times at Aunt Livia's family dinners, the meat prepared in a ragù and served with pasta. As my aunt said, a horse was a lot cleaner than a pig, and a pig was a lot smarter than a horse. And most folks had no problem eating pork. With that in my mind, I followed the others into the dining room, where the crowd picked and ripped at a pig's carcass, its roasted head intact, one eye drooping in a grotesque way and an apple in its mouth. Now *that* I found truly disgusting.

Julie and I steered clear of the ravaged beast. She filled her plate with shrimp, asparagus, stuffed tomatoes, and canapés; I headed for the roast beef.

We and the Baptistes stuck close to the Averys, who introduced us around. After a while, feeling less ill at ease, we all broke off and mingled with the crowd and introduced ourselves when opportunity allowed. We met bankers, lawyers, judges, and politicians. We spotted Elaine, dressed seductively in a close-fitting, emerald-green gown. She was talking to a frizzy-haired, plump woman wearing a long, blue skirt and a plain, white blouse. Although she was wearing little makeup, I noticed she had remarkable light-blue eyes. It was getting close to midnight, and Julie and I wanted to take the opportunity to thank Elaine for inviting us to the party. Rather than interrupting her, we hovered, hoping we could catch her eye.

"Julie, Michael," she called, waving us closer, "are you enjoying the party?"

We responded enthusiastically, which made her smile.

"By the way, this is my close and dear friend, Elizabeth Alcott. We were roommates at Radcliffe. Elizabeth is going to manage my political campaign." Suddenly looking stricken, she said, "Oh, Julie. I'm so sorry, my dear. How are you?"

"It's OK, Elaine. I'm fine now. I've decided it's time to work toward getting my master's degree."

Both women appeared impressed. Elizabeth said, "We need more women in all fields, professional and otherwise. I applaud you."

I asked, "So what are the chances of Elaine eventually becoming governor?"

Elaine and Elizabeth looked at each other, and Julie raised her eyebrows.

Elizabeth regarded me steadily for a moment. "Are you serious, Michael?"

"Certainly. There won't be any significant changes made, especially here in the South, until women take top leadership roles."

Elaine turned to Julie. "You're lucky to have this one."

"I know." Julie smiled. "He's a real rebel."

Elizabeth turned to Elaine. "I believe we have found two kindred spirits tonight. We'll have to get together again soon."

As others approached the group, we broke off.

At one minute to midnight, the excited countdown began. What made a date on a calendar and an hour on a clock so special? Were we rejoicing that we had survived to see another year? Was it hope that the New Year would bring better fortune? Or was it merely an excuse to allow the god Bacchus full rein over us as we engaged in abandoned revelry?

Three! Two! One! Cries of "happy New Year!" erupted in the crowded living room. Streamers flew in every direction, wrapping the guests in a web of bright colors. Noisemakers sounded throughout and beyond the room, paying tribute to the incoming year. Strangers kissed and hugged while Julie and I swayed in a tight embrace to the music of "Auld Lang Syne."

"Michael, it's really warm in here, and I need a breath of fresh air. Can we go outside for a while?"

"Sure, honey." I took her hand, and we walked out onto the wide piazza. Snow now fell heavily on East Battery, covering the walks and rooftops in a soft, white blanket, sparkling in the lamplight. We marveled at the scene and were oblivious to the cold until Julie began to shiver. I took off my jacket and draped it over her shoulders, drawing her close to me.

She turned to me, and I whispered as I held her in my arms, "I love you, baby."

TWENTY ONE

The winter months faded into history with the Four Horsemen of the Apocalypse still circling the globe, wreaking their endless havoc upon humanity. However, they were far from my mind on a glorious April morning as I sprinted past the flurries of red, white, and pink azaleas that ringed Hampton Park, not far from the military academy. I finished my last lap out of breath, and I decided to rest awhile on an inviting patch of green grass.

I stretched out on my back near a moss-draped oak, where two Carolina wrens were busily flitting about, building their nest. I heard the clarion call to mess and the youthful cries of hundreds of Citadel cadets filing out of their barracks into platoons and marching off to breakfast. After I relaxed for several minutes in the hazy, early morning sun, my heart rate slowed to normal, and the tightness in my legs eased up.

I rose and checked my watch. I had an hour to shave, shower, dress, and get to the office by eight o'clock to meet with Polk. For some reason, he had decided to work the week with me on my debit. Usually a staff manager, much less a district manager, worked with an agent only when he was failing to produce or if there were some irregularity with his books. However, I was in a three-way race with Kitty and Harmon Bodine, Polk's henchman, for leading agent for the first quarter, and everything on my debit was hunky-dory. His decision didn't bother me, but I was curious to see what the little devil was up to.

After a short office meeting, Polk decided we should have breakfast at Bilbro's. Taking a booth close to the waitress station, he hailed Sweet Thing to come take our orders. She sashayed over with her pad at the ready and said, "Y'all in a hurry today, boys?"

"Yeah," replied Polk, "we gotta git goin'. Gotta helluver lot to do today."

What the heck was he talking about? Monday was just a normal day—there was no real rush to do anything. But then he was always in a hurry, from the way he talked to the way he walked. He was a hot engine, always overrevving and burning rubber.

As Sweet Thing took our orders, old Burl Woodrow appeared from out of the men's room, drying his hands on the front of his shirt. The establishment had a bad habit of not attending to the facilities often enough.

He looked over at us and walked to our table. "I hear y'all going to be hitched together this week."

Polk picked up the menu and appeared to be studying it in great detail. I laughed and said, "I guess Mr. Polk is going to teach me a few things on how to run a debit. I'm still new to the business and open to any advice."

Polk slapped the menu down. "At least there's some around here willin' to listen and learn." He made angry eye contact with Burl. "Cain't you at least clean that swamp mud offa your boots before coming into the office? It's bad enough I gotta look at you in that damn safari outfit."

"Hell," said Burl, "ain't it good enough for you that I'm wearing this fine polka-dot tie that I bought at Woolworth's for eighty-nine cents? My island niggers think I'm in high fashion!" He snickered.

Polk shook his head in utter frustration, probably wishing that Wadmalaw Island had never existed or would sink into the sea. Burl was the one person he could never get the upper hand with. Luckily the tense exchange ended when Burl tried to pinch Sweet Thing on her butt as she returned with our meals. She dodged his attempt with the speed and agility of a quarterback while still balancing our grub on her tray. I chuckled, and Polk smiled in spite of himself.

Burl shrugged off his failed attempt with an unrepentant smirk, threw a kiss to Sweet Thing, bid us "hasty lumbago," and shuffled his bear-sized ass down to where Kitty and P. J. sat waiting for him. They greeted him with ribald laughter, having witnessed the escapade.

I soon realized eating with Polk was an experience I would not want to repeat too often. Taking his knife and fork in hand, he cut up his over-light eggs, mixed the runny mess with his grits, and then liberally shook salt and pepper over the whole thing. This I didn't find distasteful; it seemed to be a common practice in the South. It was a variation on what we Yankees did when we swamped our eggs and fried potatoes with ketchup. What I did find disgusting about his eating habits was the way he grabbed his spoon in his fist and shoveled heaping amounts of food into his mouth at light speed while hunched over his plate like a Neanderthal, never pausing to blot his lips.

Rising, Polk dropped six bucks on the table, leaving a generous tip for Sweet Thing. At least he wasn't cheap.

We rode downtown, not saying much. Polk asked me to turn on the radio to a country-and-western station. After a couple of Roger Miller and Loretta Lynn numbers, the news reader came on, announcing in a matter-of-fact tone that twenty-five thousand members of the Student Democratic Society were demonstrating in Washington, DC, against the Vietnam War.

"Damn those pinko, snot-nosed college brats coming out against the war and burnin' their draft cards," said Polk. "It must really get you hacked, Mike, seein' as how you were a marine an' all."

"Not really," I replied.

Giving me an irritated look, he said peevishly, "Why the hell not?"

Boy, were we getting off on the wrong foot this morning. But I was determined, boss or no, to let him know what I thought.

I recounted what Spike had told me about his experiences in Vietnam. Polk became quiet for a moment. Then, in a tone that exuded frustration, he said, "But dontcha think we still have to stop them Commies no matter what?"

"Maybe so. But you have to ask yourself why people choose Communism in the first place and why it's spreading. Just take a look at Cuba."

"Well, I don't rightly know," he said. "You tell me, boy. You got more book learnin' than me, and you've been around a lot more. I got no higher than the fifth grade. I had to help my family with the sharecroppin'."

"The imperialist powers throughout the world exploit the natural resources and labor of other countries and leave the majority of the people with little hope for better futures. But you know what? Those bloodsucking governments, with their greedy capitalist systems, did the same to their *own* people during the Industrial Revolution and right into the early part of this century."

He looked taken aback by my aggressive tone.

"Let me give you an example from right here in this country. When the Great Depression came, better than one third of the population was starving."

"Yeah," interrupted Polk, who was tearing at his thumbnail with his teeth. "My family always had a hard go of it, but that time was the worst of all."

"Well, anyway," I continued, "the government refused to open the national granaries to feed them, fearing that a little socialistic help, which the people were entitled to by way of their tax dollars, would somehow threaten to overthrow their avaricious system in which one to two percent of the population controlled all of the wealth in the country at that time. Christ! What about humanity? Did they ever consider that?"

I expected a response from Polk, but I got none. Not knowing what he was thinking made me uneasy. He just continued to gnaw away on his mutilated thumb. I turned up the radio to mute the deafening silence. An old Tennessee Ernie Ford number was playing—"Sixteen Tons." How appropriate.

When we finally reached our destination, Polk broke his silence. Speaking more to himself than to me, he said, "You gotta look out for yourself. Nobody else goddamned will. Make all the money you can. That's why I'm always yellin', 'Sell, sell, sell.' That's what gets you the bucks you need to live right and feel secure."

Well at least we had one thing in common!

Having ended as abruptly as he'd started, he was out of the car before I knew it, looking up and down the street, raring to go.

Several hours into the debit, with the sun beginning to relinquish its benign hold on the day, Polk was antsy. He hadn't made a single sale. He had insisted on taking the lead, and I wasn't about to argue with him. It would be his funeral if the week turned out to be a dud. His sales approach was hokey and disrespectful. He treated everyone as if they were none-too-bright children, sometimes joking with them and other times scaring the hell out of them.

He kept saying, "You gotta back the hearse into the living room when you're sellin' insurance."

On the last call of the day, desperate for a sale, Polk knocked on the door of Annie May Lupton's tiny back house, once the servants' quarters of a grand home and now reduced to a tenement. She answered, receipt book in hand. Polk took the book, marked it, and then checked mine to see if it matched. He had done this consistently throughout the day.

"Annie May," he said, "y'all have only two hundred fifty dollars' worth of insurance. That ain't gonna get you properly planted. Prices have gone up for buryin', y'know. Y'need twice that amount to give yourself a fittin' goin' out. You'll be lucky to get an old pine box, which will rot before you do, with no marker to say you ever been."

"Sir," she replied with dignity, "I don't care 'bout no fancy box or marker liken most folks do. I'll be safe with the Lord in His heaven."

"Mebbe so," Polk said, "but you're bein' right selfish. You owe it to your kinfolk to have a proper send-off. I believe you need a visit from the root man to set you straight."

She flinched and flung up her hands defensively. What the hell was going on? Then she said, "I ain't got 'nough money to hardly eat on. Mr. Mike know that. Root man or no root man, I'll trust in my dear Jesus to see me right."

She closed the door politely but firmly. As we turned to leave, I could hear her singing some old Negro spiritual in a haunting tone that followed us down the path and onto the street.

"Mr. Polk," I asked, "what was all that root man stuff?"

"You don't know 'bout the root man?" He smirked, clearly amused. "Well, I reckon not, you coming from up north an' all. Back in olden slave times, when they first started bringin' Nigras from West Africa, they toted their own beliefs with 'em. Even after they'd been Christianized, quite a few practiced their jungle ways, right into today. A root man is a witch doctor who can cast good or evil spells on a person."

I couldn't believe what I was hearing. "You're talking voodoo?"

"Now you got it, Romano."

"I thought that shit died out sometime back."

Leaning against the car fender, Polk pulled out a pack of unfiltered cigarettes and offered me one. I hated them—they made me cough—but I accepted it, not wanting to rub him the wrong way.

He lit up. "It's very much alive, boy, along the Mississippi Delta and them bayous in Louisiana. Some folks believe in it in these parts too. And it ain't only the niggers, neither."

"How did you know to bring it up with Annie May? Were you just guessing?"

"Oh, no," he said cockily. "When I got to seein' that blue paint around them windows and doors, I knew she were a believer."

"Whaddya mean?"

"That color keeps evil spirits away. I'm suspecting next week when you come back to collect, she'll be takin' out more insurance." He laughed. "Look, find yourself a root man, and pay him a buck or two. I did it back in ol' Mississippi, when I ran a debit. He did half the sellin' for me."

I flicked my half-smoked weed into the gutter and picked flakes of tobacco off my tongue. This man would go to any ends to make a sale.

On Wednesday morning, Polk was on tenterhooks and looked ghostly pale. The only sale we had chalked up so far had been mine, to Mrs. Lottie Bouchon on Tuesday, which managed to infuriate him to no end. Seeing Polk in operation on Monday had convinced me that I had very little to learn from him, and what I had learned I would never use. I was worried he was having a negative effect on my insured, and it might come back to bite me in the ass. So on the previous day, before we'd knocked on the door to Mrs. Bouchon's beautiful Victorian home near Hampton Park, I'd showed Polk a completed application for an education policy on her newest grandchild. A week earlier she had requested, of her own accord, that I should prepare it for her signature. I asked Polk to please allow me to complete the transaction on my own with no interference from him. He agreed, albeit reluctantly.

Mrs. Bouchon was a self-made mulatto woman who owned four Laundromats. She was prominent in her community and active in her church. Within a few months of my becoming her agent, we had discovered through casual conversation that we held a lot in common, especially in the area of politics. We became friends, and she often invited me into her gorgeous home for coffee, tea, or a stiff drink when the occasion called for it. Moreover she provided me with good leads to new clients.

Polk, after promising he would not interfere, suddenly interjected himself into the deal, trying to up the insurance amount. I cut him off, saying, "Mrs. Bouchon is a businesswoman who knows what she needs and wants. We needn't be telling her otherwise."

Polk looked flabbergasted by my audacity. I was surprised too; the words had flown out of my mouth before I knew it.

Coming to my rescue, Mrs. Bouchon said, "I hope, Mr. Polk, that you realize you have a very good agent here. I know most of the people in this area, and they hold him in high regard."

"Yeah," said Polk grimly, clearly smoldering. I had made an enemy, not meaning or wanting to. I worried how he might take it out on me somewhere down the road.

Mrs. Bouchon signed the application and handed over the money. Then she opened the door and briskly ushered us out, appearing to want the undercurrents of tension gone from her home.

In a state of apoplectic rage, Polk headed down the path at almost a run, with me close on his heels. Suddenly he stopped, turned to me, and shouted, with eyes glaring and shoulders rolling. "Damn you! Don't you ever do that agin! I'm your manager, y'hear?"

"Yes, sir. I know you're my manager, but you butted into my deal when you promised not to."

"Shit," he yelled. "You're an uppity son of a bitch."

Jesus Christ! What an asshole.

"OK, Mr. Polk, have it your way. You're the boss."

"You bet your sweet ass I am!"

The rest of Tuesday was pure hell. We didn't speak to each other, and I think neither of us felt like selling.

Compared to the events of the previous afternoon, Wednesday should have been an easy collection day. The weatherman had predicted a late-morning rain. I hoped it would pour so I could be rid of Polk early. Two hours into our work, neither of us talking much, we rounded the corner of King onto Spring Street to collect from Dorothy Wright at her funeral parlor.

Standing on his crutches in his usual spot was Joshua, the gum man—a one-legged, colored Korean War vet who sold sticks of spearmint gum out of a tin cup. On his faded army jacket were pinned the Purple Heart and the Bronze Star with V, which he had earned for bravery during the battle for Pork Chop Hill, just a few bloody days before the armistice. I always made it a point to spend a little time with him and pass him a few bucks.

Polk stared at his jacket. "What's them medals for?"

Joshua told him.

"Damn," said Polk. "Don't the guvment give you enough money, bein' messed up the way y'are?"

"No, sir," said Joshua, shaking his head.

"Shit," said Polk. He pulled out a twenty and tucked it into the cup. We turned to walk away. "How can the guvment not take care of a man like that, so fucked up?"

"I don't know. Ask your congressman."

Polk had become an enigma to me. One minute he was a dictatorial bastard, and the next he was a caring, generous man. I thought of Socrates, who said that no man does evil knowingly. I argued that back and forth with myself many times with no real conclusions reached. However, like all of us, Polk found justification for what he did, good or bad.

A block away from where we left the gum man, I greeted Dorothy Wright at the entrance to her funeral parlor.

"Dorothy, this is Mr. Polk, my district manager."

She just nodded, shifting her weight to her better leg.

"How's business?" asked a grinning Polk.

"Dead," she said, her face expressionless. Polk took her receipt book to mark it, noticing the dozen or so names listed as insured.

"Looks like you got a lot of kinfolk insured here, Dorothy." He winked at her.

She gave him a condescending look and took in a quiet, deep breath.

"Tell you what I'm gonna do, Dorothy. For fifty cents a person, I'll double everyone's accident insurance."

"I got enough insurance," she said.

"Hell, Dorothy, you know better'n that, bein' in the buryin' business an' all. You can never have enough insurance. Look, since you're such a fine customer, for twenty-five cents apiece extra, I'll increase everyone's insurance to five hundred dollars."

I could tell he was getting her dander up as she tightened her lips and narrowed her eyes. Oblivious, Polk forged ahead, taking an application from his briefcase. Implied consent at its finest.

"Stop right there!" Dorothy barked, startling him. "Where you from, Polk?"

"Mississippi," he replied nervously.

"Hmm. That figures. Polk, you ain't talking here to some dumb-ass Mississippi nigger behind a plough who you can browbeat into buyin'. Me and most Charleston City coloreds got more sense. And we don't take kindly to the likes of you. If I'm buyin' any more insurance, it'll be from the Duke here," she said, casting a veiled look in my direction and confusing Polk further. "Not some goddamned peckerwood like you!"

She slammed the door in our faces.

Polk was incensed. Wheezing, with flecks of spittle on his lips, he unleashed a torrent of expletives that would make a marine drill instructor blush.

Catching his breath, he clutched his midsection in obvious pain. Massaging the affected area, he hissed through his teeth, "Romano, I've had it with you and your fuckin' niggers today, especially that coffin-pushin' bitch! Take me back to the office. And I'll be expectin' you to keep yer trap shut on this. You got it?"

"Yes, sir. I got it."

While dreading yet another day with Polk, I was happy to meet up with Jim Dawson in the company parking lot. As we headed toward the office, I asked him how his week was going.

"Fine," he replied, "or at least it was up until yesterday afternoon, when Polk started throwing up blood in his office. It was a real mess in there." He winced.

"Christ, what happened?"

"Sal and I had to rush him over to the emergency room at Roper. Apparently he has a bleeding ulcer. He's in bad shape. They're going to operate on him today."

"Any idea how long he'll be out?"

"A month or more," he replied glumly.

"Who'll be taking over in the interim?"

"I will," said Jim, not looking particularly overjoyed by the prospect.

"Great!" I responded enthusiastically. "I hate to see anyone get that sick, but let's face it, Jim, we can all use a break from him."

"How magnanimous of you to feel that way about the dear man." He raised an amused eyebrow. "I expect that when others find out, like Burl, Miss Kitty, and P. J., there will be candles lit at Satan's altar and prayers offered up for his demise."

Laughing, I said, "How about you, Jim?"

"I respectfully decline to answer on the grounds that it might tend to incriminate me." His lips twitched.

"I thought only we Italians took the Fifth."

Grinning, he replied, "Your brethren are wise to do so, and others have learned well from you."

Jim stopped halfway down the corridor, his demeanor changed. He looked around, making certain no one was within hearing distance.

I sensed that something was wrong. "What's up, Jim?"

He peered at me seriously over his glasses and asked if anything unusual had happened the previous day that might have upset Polk.

"Why do you ask?" I said uneasily.

"When Sal and I got back to the office, the secretaries told us that Polk was really agitated when you dropped him off. He was cussing everyone and everything in sight."

"I know he was upset about having a lousy week, but then so was I. Nothing more than that, at least that I know of."

I couldn't tell Jim the whole truth, and that disturbed me. I suspected he knew I was holding back, but I couldn't risk Polk's wrath if the incident at the funeral parlor got out. More important, I didn't want to lose the ace in the hole I was holding against Polk.

Two agents interrupted our conversation as they passed us by and bid us a good morning on their way to the office. Taking advantage of the break in our discussion, and wanting to end Jim's questioning, I preempted him by asking why in the hell Polk was out there with me in the first place. Jim was clearly taken aback by the question and the sharpness of my tone.

He took off his glasses and stared down at them as if they held the answer. Then he primly replaced them on his face. "Mike, you operate in a way that is entirely different from that which is the company's—and especially Polk's—norm. They believe you should pressure people into buying. You and I know that you convince people to buy based on their needs and their abilities to pay. To use an industry metaphor, Polk and some others believe in throwing a lot of mud on the wall, hoping that some will stick. You throw very little, and most of it sticks. Furthermore you have one of the lowest default rates I have ever seen in this business. Polk believes you were using your own money to keep business on the books and induce people to buy."

"Holy shit! That's stupid. Why would I do that?"

"To advance yourself in the company."

"Well, that bastard and the company have found out otherwise."

"Exactly, Mike. But I couldn't tell you in advance. I was worried it might affect your actions during your week with Polk."

"Well, let me tell you something, Jim. Fuck that little shithead for trying to discredit me. He couldn't sell for beans on my debit. After Monday's experience with him, I held back prospective buyers, knowing he would screw up my deals. But now that he's waiting to get his guts cut, I'm going back today to write them up. You know what the kicker is?"

I opened up my attaché case and pulled out a completed application for a whole-life policy in the amount of $50,000. The application was in the name of Dr. Thomas Avery.

Twenty Two

"Cast off!"

The *Tempest* eased its way out of the Charleston Marina onto the Ashley River and headed for the inland waterway. I stood at Arthur Sutcliffe's side and watched noisy seagulls whirring above the blackwater tidal river that ran for more than twenty miles from the great cypress swamps to the Atlantic. Arthur adjusted the throttle to a speed that would accommodate other craft in the area. The sleek, forty-foot cabin cruiser responded smoothly. Its white bow cleaved the waters, leaving in its wake a wave that slapped the shorelines of the peninsula city and James Island.

I turned to see how Julie was faring. She wasn't too fond of being either on or in any waters other than her bathtub's. She appeared to be fine, engaged in animated conversation with Rina, Elaine, and Elizabeth, Elaine's campaign manager. Wanting to be with her and the other guests, I told Arthur I needed a drink and asked if I could I bring one back to him.

"No, thanks, Mike. Not while I'm skippering. Go and enjoy yourself. As you may have gathered by now, I'm not a great conversationalist. I have only two loves outside of Elaine and the children: the sea and a good martini once on shore."

This was an honest man who had no ambition, no job, and great wealth, and who was content with his life. I envied him.

As I descended the bridge ladder onto the teak deck, Tom called me over. He was talking with a couple we had met briefly before embarking, Ira and Ruth Bloom.

Ruth grinned. "You're obviously not a southerner, Mike. I would guess you're from either Brooklyn or Queens."

"You nailed it: Queens. Just a hop, skip, and jump from Manhattan and Greenpoint, Brooklyn. When I was a kid, I would wake up smelling either the Silver Cup bakery or Cooper's glue factory."

They both nodded in recognition.

Ira was a rotund, balding guy who was sporting a blue blazer with white trousers; he looked like an admiral's aide. He began the usual conversational dance to ascertain where I stood in the social and economic pecking order, ending with an inquiry about which college I had attended.

With a smile, I answered, "The good ol' USMC."

Ira looked confounded, and Tom laughed. Ira said, "Oh, how many years did you serve?"

"Four."

"Are you safe from being called back, with the war escalating in Vietnam?"

"I try not to think about it. What will be will be."

Ruth, a rather dowdy-looking woman in her midthirties, shot him a reproachful look, perhaps detecting my discomfort. "You don't appear to be a military type, especially a marine."

"Mike," Tom said, "consider that a compliment."

"I do." Reflecting in that moment, I hoped that the hold the corps had on me was losing its grip, like a cancer in remission.

"So Ruth," I asked, "what brought you two to Charleston?"

She smiled as I looked down at her. She was maybe five feet tall, if that. "I was born and raised in Charleston; my family has been here for many generations. I've been gone for fifteen years, going to school and practicing law in New York City—mostly civil rights law. Ira was a stockbroker on Wall Street and decided to throw in the towel."

Ira grimaced and downed the last of his mimosa. "If I hadn't, the rat race would have given me another coronary."

"So here we are with Arthur and Elaine and you all, enjoying the good life on a gorgeous, warm Saturday morning, on our way to Beaufort."

New York was a million miles away. I was having a great time.

Conversation ceased when the engines suddenly died back. All hands steadied themselves as the craft began its turn southward onto the inland waterway.

Looking Julie's way, I caught her eye. She beckoned me over, waving her empty champagne glass.

Ira laughed. "I believe you're being summoned!"

"It seems my lady is in need of more refreshment."

I bowed out and hailed George, the Sutcliffes' ancient Negro cabin boy. He approached with a silver tray, and I grabbed two glasses. I thanked him and walked carefully over to Julie, balancing myself with the glasses held out from my sides like a tightrope walker.

Shortly after noon the *Tempest*'s horn sounded twice as we prepared to dock thirty-odd yards from the marsh shoreline. Working the engines fore and aft, Arthur deftly brought the boat to rest against the tire-lined dock. Tom and I jumped off and tied the craft securely to the dock cleats. Several colored servants ran down the boardwalk to greet us and then assisted us with our overnight bags. Clustered together, we and the other guests walked from the dock up to Arthur's ancestral home, a white clapboard plantation house that predated the Revolutionary War. The house was nestled in a grove of huge magnolias and azaleas. Ancient live oaks draped with Spanish moss gracefully rested their boughs on the ground to each side of the compacted, earthen walkway.

We ascended the tall steps to the wide entrance of the house. Other servants greeted us and escorted us to our rooms to freshen up before lunch.

Minnie, a young, slender ebony-skinned girl dressed in a white maid's uniform, placed our bags on the four-poster, mahogany bed. She turned to us with her hands clasped primly in front of her and said, "Is there anything more I may do for you, Mr. and Mrs. Romano?"

"No," said Julie, "but thank you."

Minnie bobbed a curtsy. I reached for my wallet and extended a couple of bucks to her.

"No, sir," she said, "that won't be necessary."

"Come on, Minnie, take it. Buy yourself a little something."

She looked uneasy at my insistence and replied firmly, "No, sir, but thank you very much." She glanced at the door and then back to us. "Are you sure there isn't anything else I can do for you?"

"No, thanks," I said. I felt bad that I'd made her uncomfortable. She smiled and left the room. Looking at Julie, I shrugged. "What was the big deal about refusing the tip?"

"It must be some kind of house rule," Julie said as she opened our bags.

"Can I help you unpack?" I asked.

"No, it'll take me only a few minutes. I just want to hang up my dress before it gets all wrinkly."

"OK, I'm going to grab a breath of air and have a smoke."

Opening the jib doors, I walked out onto the piazza and then lit up. I leaned on the balustrade railing, gazing out at the serene waters and the dense foliage on the far bank. It was reminiscent of Africa, especially Sierra Leone. It was little wonder that many of the slaves taken from there had no idea they had ever left. I loved the Lowcountry, as I had Africa. One had a better sense of self here and fewer intrusions from the modern world.

Back in the bedroom, Julie was bustling about on those shapely, long legs in white shorts. My body responded accordingly. Unable to control the urge, I snuck up behind her, grabbed her around the waist, and began to nibble her neck and shoulders.

"What the heck do you think you're doing?" she said.

"Do you need a blueprint?" I said, still holding her tightly as she tried ineffectually to twist away.

"Michael, we have to be downstairs for lunch in less than ten minutes. Stop it!"

Ignoring her, I ran my hands under her thin cotton tank top and gently cupped and caressed her naked breasts as she arched back against me. Then she turned and kissed me open mouthed. I picked her up and laid her on the bed, where she wiggled out of her shorts and panties. I dropped my pants and shorts to the floor and kicked them away. She grabbed at me and said with barely suppressed laughter, "Little Mickey wants to play, so let's play!"

And so we did, all inhibitions gone until she began to yell, and I had to quiet her with my hand cupped over her mouth while suppressing my own primal need to cry out. We climaxed at the same time. I toppled off her, completely spent and brain fried. She arose quickly, and I soon heard the sounds of the shower. When she came out, I was still lying there dazed.

"Come on, cowboy. Hitch up your pants, and get your boots on. We need to git moving."

Obviously Julie had been watching too many TV Westerns, especially *Rawhide.*

Somewhat bedraggled, we raced down the stairs to the dining room. Everyone was already waiting.

"Sorry we're a little late," I said. "The time got away from us in unpacking and freshening up."

Elaine smiled. "Come sit next to me, Michael. Julie, could you please sit next to Arthur? Now that we're all here, let's start lunch."

She rang the silver dining bell. Two servants quickly appeared from the kitchen, laden with large pitchers of iced tea.

Darn, mimosas at sea and iced tea on land. Maybe blue laws didn't apply off South Carolina shores.

"Michael," Elaine said with a sly grin, "you have a very healthy glow about you. To what do you attribute it?"

Elaine was one perceptive woman, probably recognizing the signs of a recent amorous interlude.

I raised my eyebrows and smiled blandly. "I'll never tell." I gave a wink.

She laughed wryly. "I do like you, Michael. You have a bit of the devil in you." Then she put her hand lightly on mine and pressed it.

Tom Avery, sitting across from us, gave me a questioning look.

As if nothing had happened, Elaine drew everyone's attention by tapping her fork against her water glass. "Arthur and I must apologize for not getting together with all of you sooner. Our trip abroad, along with getting the children off to boarding school, has consumed most of our time recently. But now that we're back, we'll certainly be seeing each other more often, especially those of you who will be helping me organize my campaign. So without further ado, let's enjoy lunch and each other's company."

She nodded to three servants poised in front of a buffet table. They sprang into action, quietly picking up platters and bowls of food, and then moved gracefully about us at the table, serving us a wonderful meal of roast pork, yams, collards, and buttermilk biscuits on the side.

Tom asked Elizabeth if she and Elaine had decided on the main issues on which they would base their campaign.

Resting her knife and fork precisely on her plate and turning toward Tom, Elizabeth said with barely restrained fire in her voice, "There are several. First we have education. We rank very near the bottom in comparison with other states."

Elaine interrupted, sotto voce, "Thank God for Mississippi and Alabama!"

"Exactly," said Elizabeth. "Without raising our educational standards, South Carolina has no chance to compete with other states in attracting new industries and businesses, and our youth will be forced to move elsewhere to seek job opportunities. The second issue is health care. We have one of the highest infant mortality rates—not to mention venereal disease rates—in the nation. These two issues alone make it understandable that most of the country thinks that we in South Carolina are backward hicks. Unfortunately many in the current leadership are contented with the status quo. But third, and perhaps most important, we have to make sure that all our citizens have the right to vote and be represented fairly if there is to be any real change."

Rather pedantically Tom interjected, "South Carolina, like the South overall, draws much of its inspiration from the past and is threatened by anything new that might change its antiquated culture and prejudices."

Leaning forward to look down the long table at Tom, Ruth Bloom said, "Unfortunately you're right, Tom. We are an inbred society made uneasy by outsiders, new ideas, and new philosophies. As a matter of fact, we're downright hostile toward them."

"Hopefully with new leadership, that will change," said Tom. Some around the table nodded in agreement.

Elizabeth picked up her knife and fork and resumed eating, followed by the rest of the company, other than Arthur and me. We had already finished the food on our plates and were gesturing to the servants to bring us more.

"My word, Michael, you have a healthy appetite," said Elaine, looking me over appreciatively as though I were a spicy meatball.

"I work out a lot," I replied. "It makes me hungry."

"That's obvious, given your physique." Then, abruptly changing focus, she said, "Tom tells me you're doing quite well in the insurance business."

Tom looked up but said nothing.

"I'm doing OK, making a few bucks."

"Better than OK from what I've heard—I understand you're the leading agent in your company?"

"Actually no. That's not quite right. I'm leading agent in my *district*, which takes in Charleston, Dorchester, and Berkeley counties. I have no idea how I stand in the whole company. That would cover many states."

"I also hear you have won the trust of many of the coloreds in the city of Charleston."

"I wouldn't say the whole city, but a fair-sized chunk of it."

"That's hard for any white person to do. Why do you think you have succeeded?"

I thought briefly. "I treat them like human beings and not like some subspecies, which most people around here seem to do."

She visibly stiffened, which surprised me. I thought she would understand best of all, given her remarks at the Avery party, that her family had prospered mightily on the backs of Negroes. I thought of the servile demeanor of her staff. Did Elaine truly believe they were equal to whites as human beings?

Relaxing again, Elaine asked if I would be willing to campaign for her among my colored insured.

"Yes," I said, "but only if *you* are willing to come out with me and meet with these people."

She looked surprised by my boldness, and she hesitated before responding. "Michael, do you really believe it's all that important or necessary for me to do so?"

"Without a doubt. You have to see and feel firsthand what life for them is really like. With all respect, you can't do it riding through the slums of Charleston, viewing them from the comfort of a Bentley."

Elizabeth interjected, "Michael's right. Unless you take the time to talk to them individually and hear their grievances, you will never really understand what we're fighting for. You'll never win their trust."

Ira Bloom spoke up. "I also agree with Elizabeth and Mike. There's a simple political adage that describes what they're talking about: if you want to get the votes, you have to be willing to go out and press the flesh and kiss the babies."

Effectively cornered, Elaine said irritably, "OK! Maybe I don't fully understand all the problems that are out there. I'll do it."

TWENTY THREE

As the *Tempest* wended her way back to Charleston under windswept clouds the following day, I thought on and off about Elaine. She was an intriguing woman. At first glance she appeared to be in complete control of herself and all around her; however after the experience at lunch, I saw a woman not quite sure of what she was getting into, caught up in a web of her own making. Something in her character and behavior provoked a need in me to challenge her. Up until the time I told her my terms for helping her in her quest for public office, she had been toying with me and treating me as a source of amusement that could also bring in a few votes. But now things were different; we were on a more equal footing, and I intended to use her for all she was worth in helping me obtain my own goals of achieving wealth and status.

Late in the afternoon, a fierce wind blew down the river as we were nearing the last leg of our voyage. Julie slipped her arm under mine. She had become quieter since our arrival in Beaufort. Most of our conversations had been inconsequential, with the exception of our discussion of her parents' visit several weeks back. Julie was thrilled by the idea that after seeing the historic district of Old Point in Beaufort, her father, Geoff, had talked about possibly moving there or to Charleston when he and Winifred retired.

After disembarking we all thanked Elaine and Arthur once again for a wonderful weekend and bid our fellow travelers farewell.

Elaine came over to me. "Michael, I know it's early yet, but let me know when would be a good time for us to talk about our part of the campaign."

Before I could reply, Julie said, rather pointedly, "Michael, let's go! It's about to rain, and we've got to go to the grocery store if you want to eat tonight. And *some* of us need to get ready for work tomorrow."

I looked over at her. "OK, baby."

Elaine smiled as she glanced between us. "I'll call you."

We headed for our car, and threw the bags in the back.

While we rolled homeward, Julie fidgeted. Finally she blurted, "I don't know what to make of that woman."

"Who?" I asked.

"Elaine, for God's sake! Who the hell do you think I'm talking about? From the minute we boarded the bloody boat until five minutes ago she was coming on to you. And don't tell me you didn't notice. As a matter of fact, I believe you were encouraging it."

"Hell no, baby! I was just playing around. That woman's a habitual flirt. Tom told me that's her style with most men—including him when they first met."

"Well, I don't like it. And I don't like her. What's more, I think it may be more than that with you."

I reached out to put my arm around her. "Hey, honey, she's too skinny for me. She doesn't hold a candle to you in any way."

She batted me away and said scathingly, "Too skinny my ass! Well, you'd better keep your little Mickey under lock and key, or I'll cut it off."

I flinched at the thought, and little Mickey retreated like a turtle for deep cover.

As we glumly climbed the rear staircase to our apartment, we heard the phone ring in the kitchen. Rushing to catch the call, I opened the door and made a dash for the phone. "Romano here."

The voice on the other end was one I had never expected to hear: Kong's.

"Romano," he said in a gruff voice, "where the hell've you been? I've been trying to reach you since Saturday."

"I've been partying in Beaufort. Why? What's up?"

"You mean what's down," said Kong morosely. "Pug's dead."

"Don't fuck with me, Kong!"

"I'm not. Pug was killed in a motorbike race."

Julie whispered, "What's happened?"

Strangling on the words, I told her.

She wailed, "Oh my God!" She brought her hands to her mouth.

I turned back to the phone, with Julie leaning close, listening in. "How did it happen?"

"It was going to be his last race. He told me he was going full out to win. Then he was going to sell his bike. He was riding like the very devil was on his tail."

"So you were there?"

"Yeah. It was horrible. He was out in front every lap, with only a few more to go to win. Then he skidded coming into a high turn. I thought he was going down but he managed to muscle the bike upright, causing it to snake into the path of another bike which clipped him hard, sending him flying over the bars. He broke his neck." He choked. "I got to him first; he was dead."

"Oh, Jesus. How...how's Maggie doing?"

"She's a freaking wreck—what do you expect? She and her family saw it all, and she's blaming herself for allowing him to race."

Julie was weeping, and I was numb with disbelief.

"Romano, you still there?"

"Yeah," I replied.

"Maggie asked me to call you. You'd better get back to her."

We hung up.

I was deeply shaken and dreading having to talk to Maggie. "Julie, I think it would be better if you called, rather than me. I haven't the foggiest idea of what to say to her."

Sadly Julie replied, "I will, but there's nothing anyone can really say or do to help, other than to be there and listen and hope that with time the grief will lessen. However, I'm not really a great believer that time heals all wounds." Then she said with trepidation, "Michael, I don't ever want to lose you. I wouldn't know how to keep on living."

My voice broke as I said, "I'm not going anywhere. We'll be together forever."

We held each other tightly as our tears fell.

Under an azure sky, with warm breezes blowing gently, six marines in dress blues carried Pug's flag-draped casket from the black hearse. As they proceeded to the grave site, fellow marines snapped to attention and saluted. Standing behind a dozen white chairs where the immediate family was seated, I felt out of place not wearing the uniform. Being a civilian somehow diminished my sense of belonging and participating in the somber event, even though most there knew I had been Pug's best friend.

Coming to a halt, the marines placed the casket carefully over the grave site. As they did, Gunny Starr, who had led the procession, came to attention at the foot of the casket and saluted slowly—a deliberate motion to magnify the honor and appreciation for a deceased comrade. Then the pallbearers reached down and gripped the flag firmly in white-gloved hands and spread it over the coffin. As they did, a minister stepped forward to say the last words and prayers over my friend's body.

As he spoke of Pug, a person he had not known other than through what others had told him, sobs and nervous coughs provided background, especially when he brought out the time-worn cliché of a young man being cut down in his prime. The minister was part of the necessary ritual that tried to give some meaning to the life of a man who was only twenty-two years old and to give some solace to those who loved him and called him a friend. Nearing the end of his eulogy, the minister said that Pug was in a "far better place," where he waited to be reunited with loved ones. Maggie, who up until then had managed to keep up a brave front, broke down, weeping inconsolably. If it was such a wonderful place, why not skip the shit down here altogether?

However the thought of Pug picking up a new Harley as he entered the pearly gates and riding it like the devil himself wherever he wanted brought a reluctant smile to my face and more tears to my eyes. Julie glanced at me and clasped my hand, squeezing it tightly.

When the minister had finished, a bugler stepped forward and began to blow taps. As he did, the marine pallbearers began folding the flag into thirteen perfect triangles, ending on a blue field with the white stars. Then the last man handed it to Gunny Starr, who took the flag against his chest and tightened the folds. When the last sweet note faded, Gunny marched slowly over to Maggie, went down on one knee, and said gently, "On behalf of the president of the United States, the commandant of the marine corps, and a grateful nation, I present this flag to you."

Maggie took the flag and buried her face in it. Then Gunny rested his hand on her shoulder and said a few quiet words to her. She raised her head and nodded faintly.

He rose, saluted Maggie, did an about-face, returned to the burial detail, and marched them off, leaving one man behind to see that Pug's body would be properly interred. As the gathering broke up, Kong came over to Julie and me.

"So whaddya think, Romano?"

"It was a great send-off for a great guy."

"I feel the same."

"Anyway, how're you doing, Kong?"

"Fine. I'll be out in two weeks and going back to Montreal."

"What're you going to do?"

"Join the mounties."

I started to laugh.

"What's so funny?" he said with his usual scowl.

"You in a red uniform, wearing a Yogi Bear cap and singing opera to Jeanette MacDonald."

He chuckled in spite of himself, and again, as we had done several months back, we said our farewells. However, this time I knew it would be forever.

When Julie and I returned to our car, Gunny Starr was close by, talking to a bunch of marines and having a smoke. Seeing us, he broke away from the group and came over.

He nodded to Julie. "Ma'am." Then he said, "Staying out of trouble, Romano?"

"The best I can, Gunny."

"You got yourself a fine lady here. Take care of her, and make sure you go to church regular."

I took a deep breath and wisely didn't reply to that.

"You must be getting close to retirement, Gunny."

"Yeah, just a little less than two years to go. But I got my orders to ship out to the First Marines and prepare to go to Vietnam."

Julie and I were silent for a few seconds. "Well," I said, "I don't have to tell you to keep your head down and come back and see us when your tour is finished."

Julie said, "Gunny Starr, would it be improper for me to ask you what you said to Maggie at the grave site? She and I are close friends."

"I told her to be strong, trust in the Lord, and believe that he has a purpose in all he does."

I bit back a silent cry. What fucking purpose could my friend's horrible death serve?

TWENTY FOUR

I was still shaken by Pug's death. Jim Dawson came over to my desk and said, "Mike, what's wrong? You're awfully quiet this morning."

"Yeah, Jim. I lost a close friend in a motorbike race on Saturday. It's sucked the very spirit out of me."

"I read about it; it was a terrible accident."

"I don't know if you can really call it an accident when it involves racing a bike at eighty to a hundred miles an hour on a dirt track—not when the odds are so high that you'll be killed or badly hurt. An accident is slipping on a bar of soap."

"Good point. Look, why don't you come to breakfast with me and the gang? P. J. just announced that he and his wife are going to be having a baby. I thought it would be nice to celebrate this morning. I'm picking up the tab."

Despondently, I said, "There must be more to life than just eating, drinking, and screwing—and then, like a puff of smoke, you're gone."

"There is," he replied. "Art transcends the mortal thread and uplifts the human spirit. But more important, loved ones and good friends who enjoy your just *being*. C'mon, let's go."

Seated at the back of Bilbro's, P. J., Burl, Sal, and Kitty were engaged in animated conversation.

P. J. trumpeted, "The dynamic duo has arrived."

Jim grinned. "Which one of us is Batman?"

Kitty answered, "You, Jim, of course; but I'll take Robin—he's much younger and cuter."

Taking a seat next to P. J., I fanned the cigarette smoke engulfing the table away from me and lit up. I cracked, "What's an old dude like you doing having a baby, P. J.? By the time the kid is five, you'll be on Social Security."

"Hey, watch what you say, Yankee. I'll have your Confederate green card revoked and you deported back to New York."

"Oh no, please, forgive me. Don't do that! It would be a fate worse than death."

As they all chuckled, Burl said, "But y'know, he has a point, P. J. How the hell does an old dog like you get it up? You using a splint?"

"Look who's talking, you cantankerous old fart. Your pecker must be limp as a wrung chicken's neck."

"I beg your pardon," said Burl pompously. "That of which you speak is a goddamned rooster."

Kitty almost spat out her coffee.

"Speaking of peckers," Burl said, "would anyone know when Polk is coming back?"

"Unfortunately," replied Jim, "next week."

"Hell," said Burl, "I was hoping the son of a bitch might die."

"He almost did," said Jim soberly. "He lost a lot of blood."

"Well, I got an idea," said Sal cheerfully. "Let's get him to go out with Mike again."

"Hey, don't put that shit on me, Sal."

"Why not, Mike? He worked a couple, three days with you, and it almost killed him. Just think what you might be able to accomplish if you had a whole week."

The table quieted a bit when Sweet Thing arrived. My God, I thought, her uniform had shrunk yet again. How had she gotten into it? All the guys ogled her as she moved around the table, taking orders, especially

Sal. Kitty had an amused look on her face, probably wondering at the condition of the attendant peckers.

While Sweet Thing poured coffee in Sal's cup, he remarked, "Y'all know that Mike has been hobnobbing it with the Sutcliffes?"

"Damn," Burl bellowed. "I've lived here for near twenty years, and I don't believe I've ever come within ten feet of any of those aristocrat types. Tell me, Mike, does their shit smell?"

"Burl, I've dined with them on a couple of occasions and recently visited Arthur Sutcliffe's ancestral home in Beaufort for a weekend."

They all raised their eyebrows as I continued.

"However, I've never visited a privy with any of them, and no one has farted in my presence. I really can't tell you, pal."

Burl's deep laugh boomed over the table.

Incredulous, P. J. asked, "How does a guy like you, who's been down here for less than three years, with two of those in the marines, get to know folks like that?"

"Lucky connections, good looks, and a charming disposition."

Jim shook his head, and Kitty smiled.

"Since Sal brought up the subject," I said, "and it seems to be of some interest here, I want to take the opportunity to make a request that might prove beneficial to you, your families, and the state. Elaine Sutcliffe is planning to run for public office. Right now she seems set on being a state senator. However, when I met with her campaign manager on New Year's Eve, I suggested Elaine should eventually run for governor. The idea tickled both Elaine and her manager. I think something may come of it."

"Ain't never gonna happen, Mike," said Burl, shaking his head slowly. "You'd probably have a better chance runnin' a barefoot nigger."

P. J. laughed. "I'll second that!"

Kitty said wistfully, "Wow! A woman governor. That would be a first."

"I understand your positions. You may have a point. But I really believe that things are changing to make it possible for a woman to obtain political office. Look, let's cut to the chase. I'm asking you all to help Elaine take her first step into the political arena."

"Why the hell should we?" asked P. J. "What's in it for us?"

"Without me giving you her whole political platform, I'll tell you what I consider the most important point: education. With a better-educated citizenry, industries are more likely to locate here. That will mean more and better-paying jobs for your children and grandchildren and get us off the federal dole down here."

"Whaddya mean?" said an indignant Burl. "Dole?"

"Let's face it, Burl, without the navy base and shipyard, we wouldn't have a middle class here in the Lowcountry."

"I don't consider that being on the dole," huffed Burl.

"What else can you call it when a state or county can't survive without those federal dollars? But y'know what gets me? All those assholes in Columbia always yelling about state's rights but holding their hands out for the federal bucks. Isn't that hypocrisy?"

"Mike's right," said Jim firmly. "When you think of all the military facilities we've got in South Carolina—and the private industries and businesses that depend on them—we'd be up shit creek if we ever lost them."

"What do you want us to do?" asked Kitty.

"Drum up support for Elaine on your debits, in your churches, and with your friends."

"Hold it, Mike!" said Sal. "Most of the folks we have insured are coloreds and poor whites who don't vote."

Jim interjected, "That's because the corrupt political system has disenfranchised the coloreds and poor."

"Right, Jim," I said, "but that's coming to an end with the Civil Rights Act in place, and soon the Voting Rights Act will pass. Once that happens millions of people throughout the South will be able to vote for the first time. And people who've never been able to obtain office will have the chance to do so. I bet you dollars to doughnuts that quite a few of them will be women."

"Hell, Mike, are you telling me I'm supposed to get behind some goddamned woman by supporting niggers? Well, I ain't gonna do it!" said Burl, glowering.

"Burl, you got it backward. The Civil Rights and Voting Rights Bills are for all of us who are behind the social and economic eight ball. Don't you want women to be able to obtain office and have equality in the workplace?"

"I don't know 'bout that," he said with a frown.

Flushed with anger, Kitty pointed a shaking finger at Burl. "Goddamn you, Burl, you ignorant son of a bitch! We birthed you men, suckled you, tended to your every need, and loved you, and you don't think we deserve equal rights? Me and my daughters have been abused by the very system that Mike and Jim have been talking about. Don't you believe that we should have the same opportunities as men in our jobs? And get the same pay for doing the same work? Mike, count me onboard, and if the rest of you agree with this fat, old toad here and are willing to condemn your mothers, sisters, and daughters by supporting the status quo, know that you'll never see me again at this table. And you, Burl: forget about coming around sniffing at my front door anymore."

"Calm down now, Kitty," said Burl, nervously rolling his stogie between his fingers. "I never had it put to me that way. It's the Negro thing that's got me twisted up."

"Well, you should know better. Your daddy was a sharecropper in Kentucky—dead behind the plough by the age of forty. Your mother worked her fingers to the bone. And you got no more than a fifth-grade education because of all that. Had to run moonshine to make ends meet. So if anyone should know about a system that works against you, it should be you. Your folks were the poor whites that Mike's been talking about, and I bet they never got a chance to cast a vote or have a say in their lives."

"Kitty, you know I love you, darlin', and I'd never want to hurt you. You're right. I guess my head's been screwed on backward. Mike, tell that skinny bitch—excuse me, woman—if she's willin' to get her ass bounced around Wadmalaw in my muddy ol' jeep, I'm willing to introduce her to the natives. Goddamn it, I need a drink."

Kitty looked at him. He patted her hand, and her anger seemed to be fading somewhat.

P. J. rose abruptly from the table. "I'll have no play in this shit," he said. "I like things just the way they are. I don't believe we should be messing around with the natural order of things." Angrily he threw a few dollars onto the table and stormed out.

Dumbstruck, we sat silently.

Sal stirred his coffee anxiously. "Darn it. I wish I'd never brought up the damn Sutcliffes."

"It's not your fault, Sal," said Kitty, blotting her eyes. "But why the hell did this have to happen? This was supposed to be a happy occasion."

Jim said, "It was bound to occur sooner or later. You can't have titanic changes like we're going through now without blowups and hard feelings. It's like the Civil War—brother set against brother in a bloody struggle over pretty much the same issues."

Jim's words helped ease my guilt over the incident and ended my conspicuous silence.

"Jim, I'm worried there'll be a lot more blood spilled before this is over...if it's ever going to be over," I said.

Sal stubbed out his cigarette, "What d'ya think P. J. meant when he talked about the natural order of things?"

Jim answered, "I guess he was referring to what some people in this country believe, especially here in the South, that a colored man should still be a slave, a white laborer should be a serf, and women should be chattel."

Burl continued to fidget with his cigar. Kitty let out a deep sigh, shaking her head.

TWENTY FIVE

An action-packed year had sped by since I'd gotten out of the corps and begun work at the Cardinal State Insurance Company. Having some vacation time coming to us, Julie and I decided to celebrate by buying the fastest stock car in production, the GTO, and taking a trip down the coast, visiting Savannah, St. Augustine, and Daytona. The trip would recharge our batteries and put a rough patch in our lives behind us. On Friday, with my books balanced and money turned in, I bid farewell to Jim.

He said, "Take it easy driving down south, and don't forget to visit Blackbeard's Tavern. It has great food and the best bloody Mary in all Savannah."

"I won't forget, Jim. Be looking for a postcard from us."

I left to pick up Julie. A little later, rolling up to the entrance of the Medical College, I was tickled at the sight of Julie hiking up her skirt to show a bit of leg, thumbing a ride from me.

"Where you headed, sweetheart?" I asked.

"Anywhere you are, handsome." She hopped into the car and flung her white lab coat onto the rear seat. "Hell's bells! It's bloody hot out there. Am I glad we're getting a new car with air."

Remembering the previous summer, I certainly wasn't going to argue with that.

"Let's go," she said. "I can't wait to see the selection of GTOs. And don't forget—I get to pick the color this time."

"Yeah, but remember, anything other than pink."

She sucked in her cheeks and gave me her *nitwit* look. Riding along to the Pontiac dealership on Meeting Street, I reminisced about Pug and me racing each other late at night along a narrow stretch of road in the Neck Area of Charleston. Pug always won, beating me and other daredevil racers by a good length or more in his hot Chevy. If he were still around, he'd be tweaking his 409 engine, knowing he would have his work cut out for him trying to outrun my GTO.

"What's so funny?" Julie asked.

"Oh, I was just thinking about Pug and how we used to race each other."

"You still miss him a lot, don't you?"

"Yeah." I sighed.

"I miss him too. But please promise me that you won't race again. I know that with a GTO, you'll be tempted."

"Don't worry, honey, I won't," I said, lying through my teeth. I couldn't wait to rev it up, let out the clutch, and watch other dragsters eat my dust. I wasn't worried about an accident or dying. I was convinced that the gods had something special in store for me other than crashing and burning.

"Wow!" Julie cried as we entered the showroom. We saw a burgundy GTO convertible with its white top down, showing off its black interior and bucket seats.

She bounded over to it. "Michael, I don't believe it—that's my favorite color, *and* it's a convertible. Isn't it just gorgeous?"

"No doubt about that, babe. It's one cool machine."

I hadn't planned on a convertible, but this car was something special, guaranteed to catch the attention of all who saw it. I liked that.

I opened the car door to examine the interior more closely. Damn! It had automatic transmission. That would kill my ability to maximize its speed; I would be laughed off the track. I wondered what to do. Then a young, eager salesman came over faster than a jackrabbit with a coyote snapping at its ass.

"Hello there! My name's Hank. This is a real beaut, isn't it?" He smiled, probably tasting a sale in the making.

"Absolutely," said Julie. "I love it, and I can't wait to drive it."

Damn! There goes all my bargaining power.

Hoping against hope, I asked, "Will it do zero to sixty in five point eight seconds, as advertised?"

"Oh, no, sir. That only applies to hardtops with four on the floor. Even if you got this model with a manual transmission, you wouldn't be able to do it because a convertible is much heavier. The best you could expect is seven seconds."

"Michael, what difference does it make? You're not racing this car. Let's take it for a test drive, and if we like it, let's buy it."

I'm screwed!

It handled beautifully, and forty-five minutes later we were rolling down Meeting Street toward our apartment, Julie driving and me thinking that the gods did indeed work in strange and mysterious ways. And clearly in Julie's favor.

As we reached for our packed bags set by the front door, the phone rang. Julie answered.

"Oh, Elaine."

Damn.

"How nice of you to call," said Julie, a note of sarcasm in her voice. "Unfortunately, we are just about to leave for vacation."

I knew that Elaine's call would annoy Julie, and I would pay the price.

Julie said politely, "I'll be sure to tell Michael. We'll give you a call when we get back."

She hung up, and I waited warily for a tidal wave of invectives from Julie.

Calmly, she said, "That was Elaine."

"Well, I kinda guessed that. What did she want?"

"Other than you? She wanted us to go over tomorrow to meet with some new people, along with the Averys, Baptistes, and Blooms, to discuss her campaign *yet again*. Apparently she has it on good authority that the voting rights bill will be passed by the House within the next couple of weeks."

Mystified by her relaxed demeanor, I asked, "Are you OK, honey?"

"Michael, I'm fine. She's definitely too skinny for you!" She smiled sweetly. I knew she was smoking me.

I blew out a breath and picked up the bags. "Let's get the heck outta here!"

The big 389 engine purred as we cruised, top down, along Highway 17 under a lush canopy of trees casting shadows on us and dappling the sunlit road. About sixty miles out of Charleston, we came to a fork in the road where a small Esso gas station was located. Thirsty, I pulled into the dirt parking area away from other cars and trucks, worried about getting dents in our new car. Julie headed for the john in the back of the building while I went into the station to pick up a couple of sodas and a candy bar. At the counter I noticed a headline on the front page of the daily paper. It announced that President Johnson had ordered an increase in troop strength in Vietnam from about 75,000 to 125,000 men, and he had asked that the draft be increased from 17,000 to 35,000.

Shit! Tell me we aren't in a war that isn't going the right way.

The good news was I had less than a year to go in the reserves. Given the increases in the draft, I was reasonably sure I wouldn't be called up. Besides, who would want a twenty-five-year-old who's almost four years out of a line outfit for combat duty? Gunny Starr had once told me, "Order an eighteen-year-old to attack a hill where the enemy has the advantage, he'll charge. Order the same marine three years later to do likewise, and he'll tell you to go fuck yourself." That would certainly be the case where I was concerned.

Back at *my* beautiful car, Julie shouldered me aside and leaped into the driver's seat. As we drove the last forty scenic miles to Savannah, we luxuriated in the cool breeze from the AC.

A little before five, we checked into a fairly new-looking two-story motel on West Bay Street, overlooking the Savannah River, and not too far from the center of town. After we put our clothes away, I turned on the TV in hopes of getting the results of the Giants' game. After several fruitless minutes, I gave up and switched off the tube. "Julie, I'm going to take a shower."

She cracked, "If everyone in America took as many showers as you do in a day, the reservoirs would run dry!"

"Good! I don't like to drink water anyway. After all, little fishes make love in it."

"Smartass!"

After a long shower, my stomach was growling, and I was ready to eat the wallpaper off the wall. We had bypassed lunch with all the goings on.

"Let's get going, Julie. I'm starving."

Out the door we went, and several minutes later we were circling the crowded parking lot of Blackbeard's Tavern, looking for a spot. Finally one came up, and we pulled in quickly. Inside, after standing in line to get our names on the waiting list, we were told it would be about thirty minutes before we could be seated. By then I was ready to chuck it in and go get a burger, but Julie was all dolled up, and I didn't want to disappoint her, so I dogged it out.

To reduce the tedium of the long wait, and to have a little fun, Julie and I played Holmes and Watson, trying to determine a person's background by his or her clothes, grooming, and who he or she was with. Searching the crowd for a likely subject, I was surprised to see Elias Pendergast, of all people, with a drop-dead gorgeous blonde half his age at his side. Our eyes made contact, and a look of uncertain recognition passed over his face. We had met for only a brief time at the Sutcliffes' on New Year's Eve. Julie and I decided it was only appropriate that we go over to greet him.

"Hello, Elias. Good to see you again. You may not remember us: Mike Romano, and this is my wife, Julie. We met at Arthur and Elaine's house."

"Ah, yes. How could I have forgotten the two bookworms?" We chuckled, and then he said, "Allow me introduce you to Miss Melissa Reddick. She manages my office here in Savannah."

Nice manager. Melissa was a long-legged babe wearing a scanty silk dress with white pearls, and there was enough gold on her to sink a pirate ship. She offered a limp hand in greeting, and with an educated southern accent she said, "So pleased to make your acquaintance." She had some class!

Elias said, "If I recall, Mike, you're in the insurance business."

I nodded.

"So how're things going for you?"

"Well," I said. "My bank is happy."

He and Melissa laughed; Julie smiled pleasantly.

"But what gripes me is I had to pay one heck of a lot of taxes on money I worked so hard for."

He and Melissa glanced at each other, and then Elias said, "You know, there's a way around that."

"Well, tell me. I'm all ears."

I listened closely, and I saw that Julie was on alert.

"Buy rental real estate. You get a lot of depreciation that you can write off the top of your income, and if you can buy enough, you can zero out your income and pay no taxes."

"Damn! It really works that way?"

"Yes; it certainly does. If you're interested, I can have one of my agents contact you, and I'll give you the name of a good tax attorney."

"Elias, I'm more than interested. Please have your agent call me toward the end of next week."

"Do you still have my card, Mike?"

"Yes, right here in my wallet."

"Excellent." He nodded. Turning to include Julie in the conversation, he asked if we had seen the Sutcliffes since the first of the year.

"Yes, we have," she replied.

"You know she's running for political office?"

"Yeah, I'm going to be helping her out somewhat," I said.

He paused for a beat, pulled out an expensive-looking cigar, wet its tip, and then lit up.

"That's interesting, Mike. How so?"

I apprised him of my intended role.

After thinking awhile, he said, "I take it then that you're a Democrat?"

"Yes and no. If you mean a northern Democrat, yes. A southern one, absolutely not."

He laughed. "It's all very confusing at times, isn't it?"

"Certainly is," I said. Both women regarded us curiously.

"Maybe you would consider the party of Lincoln, Mike?"

"With all respect to you, Lincoln would be rolling over in his grave knowing that South Carolina has the most rabid segregationist in all the land wearing his party's banner. How can that be, Elias?"

"Expediency," he replied, "pure and simple. Might I suggest you read the Lincoln-Douglas debates? They might enlighten you."

I sensed Julie getting edgy.

"Look, Elias, I'm not very political. I kinda got roped into this thing with Elaine. The bottom line for Julie and me is equal rights for all. We'll back any candidate, Republican or Democrat, who is willing to fight for that."

"Sounds to me like you're both more nonpartisan than anything else."

"Probably." I shrugged. "And I hope this doesn't put a wedge between us."

"No, no. I understand your positions, especially given that you're both so young."

Condescending prick.

"However, you and I share some important common denominators," he continued smoothly. "We both like the idea of making money, living well, and not paying taxes. And we Republicans hold all that dear."

"Well," I said, dragging the word out to three syllables in the ol' southern way, "you got me on that one."

Grinning, he extended his hand to me. "It will be a real pleasure doing business with you. I'll be interested to watch your progress in the coming years. I do believe you have the makings of a good Republican."

"Don't bet on it."

He smiled again with the assurance of someone who was holding a crystal ball. Then, like a bell ringing to signal the end of a boxing match, his name was called to be seated.

We were finally left alone. Julie said, "Well, that was interesting."

"Sure was, honey."

"I liked the way you talked to him. I do believe you're developing some diplomatic skills here."

"Who, me?" I mugged. "Are you kidding? Anyway, he's certainly clever; no telling what we can learn from him."

"Actually I rather like him in an odd way. I think more is going on behind that Republican façade than we think."

"Yeah. Maybe he's a closet liberal."

TWENTY SIX

We returned a couple of days earlier than planned. Julie got badly sunburned and bore a marked resemblance to a boiled lobster. We hunkered down in our apartment with the phone off the hook so she could rest and recover.

Overall we'd had a wonderful vacation. In Savannah we'd walked the once elegant city that was in a state of disrepair, much like Charleston. Then we'd driven down to St. Augustine. We took in many of the beautiful sights and especially enjoyed touring the historic district and visiting the Ripley's Believe It or Not Museum. On our first night there, we ate in a small, romantic Spanish restaurant that served us a fabulous paella with a bottle of fine white wine. A Spanish guitarist serenaded us. Afterward we returned to the motel and made sweet, lazy love and slept in late the next morning.

Two days later we left the old Spanish town and headed for Daytona Beach, where we laid out on the white sands, frolicked in the water like teenagers, and read our books.

However by the second day, I was getting bored and restless, and I decided to occupy some time by taking long runs on the beach, checking out bikini-clad chicks, and hanging out at the hotel bar overlooking the ocean. From there I could keep an eye on Julie while chatting with fellow drinkers and baseball fans. Unfortunately Julie, who was determined to get a good tan, was out in the blazing sun, reading her mystery novels for hours on end, believing the gallon of suntan lotion she had sloshed on her pale skin would protect her from the powerful rays. Well, it didn't work. So there we were, five days after we had started our vacation, back in our apartment, with Julie in pain, trying to read in bed, and me twiddling my thumbs in the living room.

I walked into the bedroom. "Honey, we're almost out of cigarettes, so I'm going to take a walk and pick up a couple of cartons."

"Please do. You must be going bonkers hanging around here." Her face took on a mournful look. "I'm so sorry for screwing up our vacation. It was really stupid of me to stay out in the sun that long."

"Hey, baby, look on the bright side. We had five great days together. You just rest, and I'll be back in a little while."

"OK, but don't rush. Take your time, and enjoy your walk."

As I strolled along King Street on my way to Wentworth, the stench of rotting buildings permeated the air, reminding me, as I passed the many vacant storefronts, that the city was in increasingly rapid decline and was in danger of becoming one large slum. However, the city fathers seemed unable to do anything to reverse the gangrenous trend.

After walking several blocks, I entered a tiny store on Wentworth, not too far from the corner of King Street, which sold cigars, cigarettes, and newspapers; after the liquor stores closed at sundown, it became your friendly neighborhood bootlegger. On occasion, when I ran short of booze, I would go there to pick up what I needed, as did many other Charlestonians. You could simply place your order, which would be called up to the second-floor liquor warehouse and then sent down via a hand-operated dumbwaiter, bagged and ready to go.

Charleston had many clever ways to deliver illegal services, whether it was prostitution, booze, or gambling. In some ways it operated like a small, underground Las Vegas.

Cigarettes in hand, I turned to leave and bumped into Kitty. She looked exhausted.

"Mike, what're you doing back in town? Jim told me you were vacationing down in Florida."

"I was, but Julie got sunburned in Daytona and is now lying in a bathtub of cold cream."

She chuckled and then said hurriedly, "Forgive me. That's awful but it sounded funny."

After picking up a cold bottle of pop, blotting the sweat from her face with a handkerchief, and smearing her makeup, she said, "You missed one helluver week."

"What happened? Did Polk jump off the Cooper River Bridge?"

"Unfortunately no. But one can always hope."

"Don't keep me in suspense, Kitty. What happened?'

"Polk went bananas at the Tuesday-morning meeting, lambasting all of us for not working hard enough, including the staff managers, who he threatened to replace if production didn't pick up. Mr. Drury—who's been a staff manager for ages, as you know—suddenly broke down crying and shaking like a leaf while Polk was ranting. It was dreadful, Mike, just dreadful. We all sat there, looking on in horror, not knowing what the heck to do, except Sal, who rushed over to the poor man, trying to console him, rubbing his back and saying, 'Don't cry, Joseph. Everything'll be OK. Please try to calm down, friend.'

"Well, he didn't calm down. He just continued to cry and shake uncontrollably. Then Jim went over and helped Sal lift Drury out of his chair, and he and Sal walked him out of the office to Jim's car. Then they took him home.

"A day later Mrs. Drury called the office to inform Polk that her husband had suffered a complete nervous breakdown and wouldn't be able to come back to work for quite a while."

"Damn!" I said. "He's got two kids in college and a wife to support."

"Well, this changes everything for them. They're all going to have to pitch in to survive."

I sighed. "What a bloody rotten shame. Did Polk show any remorse?"

"None that I could see."

"Well, that figures! I guess Polk and the company will chalk it all up as just another corporate casualty."

"Unfortunately," said Kitty, "we're all replaceable where they're concerned."

"Any word on who's going to replace Drury as staff manager?"

"Mr. Randall." She beamed.

"Wow, I can't believe it! But y'know, it makes sense. Randall helped Polk learn the ropes and, with Jim, writes most of his communications with the company."

"Any wonder, Mike? I haven't heard that man utter one grammatical sentence since he arrived here."

"You're telling me. After working three days with him, neither could I. But Randall has helped Polk a lot, especially running interference between him and the agents."

A flash of anger crossed Kitty's face. "But why did the stupid company have to send such an asshole to us in the first place? Look at all the harm he's caused."

"Come on, Kitty. You know why—production! As long as he's making them a profit, they couldn't care less about his grammar or foul personality. And let's face it—the district is up twenty percent since he's taken the reins."

Shaking her head, she put her soda down with a clunk on the glass counter, stubbed out her cigarette, and reached into her substantial leather purse to pull out another weed. I flipped open my Zippo and lit it for her. She blew the smoke out of the side of her mouth, away from me, and then rested her eyes on mine.

"Mike," she said seriously, "I believe that a lot of that so-called *increase* is pure bullshit."

"Whaddya mean?"

"Listen to me, honey. I've been with this company for nearly eighteen years, and I know this business inside out. Many of the agents are my close friends. Some of them, shall we say, confide in me. Quite a few are frightened to death of losing their jobs. So what happens is they try to secure new business by offering to pay the initial application fee themselves. They hope that these newly insured will appreciate what they've done and will keep up the payments. Sometimes it works, but most of the time it fails. On top of that, they start paying for the policies about to lapse on other folks in hopes they too will bring their premiums current. If they don't, it will be subtracted from their commissions and from the company's yearly record. After a time these agents will get to feel that it just isn't worthwhile. Then I'll expect to see a sizable dent in that increase."

"I hope the dent will be big enough to get rid of that little shit."

"We can only hope and pray. But Mike, a guy like you can do a lot better than working for some nickel-and-dime insurance company. No matter how the company tries to break into the monthly business, the much larger companies will freeze them out. What's more, there's only so much business you can squeeze out of these old debits each year. I'm too far on in years to make a change. I have too much invested in the company toward my retirement. But you're young and have very little invested. Take what I am saying into consideration."

I appreciated her advice. "Yeah, thanks. I'll think about it."

Swigging down the last of her soda, she sighed tiredly. "I've got to get going. I have a couple of chronic arrear cases I have to get to before I can go home and rest my bones."

She smiled and said good-bye.

As I walked back home, I mulled over what Kitty had said. Maybe she was right about the company and its limitations, but for now I felt pretty good with the money I was making and didn't want to risk changing anything, at least not until I had something in hand that I knew was better.

I checked my watch. It was only half past two. I figured that Tom Avery might still be at the college. The conversation I'd had with Pendergast was nagging at the back of my mind. So I headed toward the college to seek out Tom and the Lincoln-Douglas debates. As I passed through Porter Lodge on my way to Randolph Hall, I was reminded by a brass plaque on its wall that the college was 180 years old and the oldest municipal college in the country. I climbed the curved, worn stone steps of Randolph Hall and then turned under the portico to view the beautiful campus, with its evergreen oaks; reddish stucco buildings; high walls; and large, iron gates. In a different life, I might have found myself there, studying in its small, quiet library, attending classes, and maybe even teaching.

I climbed to the second floor and knocked on Tom's office door. I waited a few seconds and then knocked again. Disappointed that he wasn't in, I was turning to leave when Jean-Luc Baptiste peeked out of his office down the hall.

"Ah! It is you, Michael. Are you looking for Tom?"

"Hello, Jean-Luc. Actually I am."

"I am so sorry, but you missed him by about fifteen minutes. Is there something I might be able to help you with?"

"Possibly. D'ya know anything about the Lincoln-Douglas debates?"

Smiling and nodding, he waved me into his office.

I followed him into the musty room and marveled at the tall bookshelves lining three walls, loaded with books, photos, and bric-a-brac, and an ancient desk stacked with more books and precariously balanced papers. I took a seat. Peering at me over his spectacles, he said, "Well, as you Americans say: shoot."

I told him about my recent discussion with Elias Pendergast.

"Ah, I see." He lit up one of his god-awful smokes, belatedly offering me one, which I politely refused. "Lincoln became an emancipator in the end, but the man was never for equality of the races. In one of the many debates in Charleston, Illinois, he made his opinion very clear that Negroes were inferior to whites and not entitled to the same rights. He was a segregationist, not too unlike the present-day segregationists to whom you referred when you spoke to Elias."

"So all that stuff I was taught in school was a myth?"

"*Mon cher,* many grade-school teachers, not knowing better, believe in that same myth. But sometimes myths inspire us to make them come true, as we are now witnessing in the civil rights movement. What matters is what *you* think and can support with *your* intellect and moral strength, not what Lincoln thought or, for that matter, the Founding Fathers, who wrote a Constitution that applied only to white male Americans of European descent." He paused to stub out his cigarette. Then he said firmly, "Tom and I believe, as you do, that no good can come from inequality. Battles are raging in cities and towns across America as we speak. What matters is that good people must be ever vigilant and not shrink from the fight against the never-ending injustices."

We stared at each other for a few moments. Jean-Luc rose from behind his desk, and I hastily followed his example.

"Thank you, Jean-Luc, for educating me. I really appreciate it."

"No, Michael, thank you," he replied. "Teaching, after all, is my life."

"Would it be an imposition to ask you to get a book for me out of the college library that covers the debates? I'd really like to read them for myself."

"It will be my great pleasure. I would expect nothing less from you than to study the matter further."

As I walked home, carrying a carton of cigarettes in one hand and a book in the other, I thought about Elias. He had gone easy on me in Savannah. He could have embarrassed me, given my ignorance, but he hadn't. He was a real enigma.

TWENTY SEVEN

The two weeks after our vacation had ended were historic. The voting rights bill was finally passed into law. A few days later, Watts, California, experienced one of the worst race riots in American history. The aftermath saw thirty-four dead, a thousand injured, and tens of millions of dollars in property damage. The scenes Julie and I witnessed on TV for six days were those of a war zone: buildings burning and Negroes battling it out with police and National Guardsmen in the conflagration.

Aware that tensions were running high in Charleston between whites and coloreds following these incidents, and not wanting to get caught up in any arguments with my fellow agents, I decided it would be wise to duck out after morning meetings and take my breakfast alone at Walgreen's on Savannah Highway. Walgreen's not only served up a great breakfast but also sold a couple of national newspapers I had been reading in an attempt to gain perspective on the root causes of the tragedy. From what I could glean, it came down to discrimination that disallowed the citizens of Watts to have access to good education, jobs, and housing. That, along with a planned policy of intimidation by the LAPD to keep the Negroes in their place, had finally culminated in fiery rebellion.

One afternoon I was going into Jacob's Row to make a collection. An angry colored man with a livid scar running from his forehead to his cheek accosted me. He rushed toward me with his fists clenched, screaming, "Get your fuckin' white ass outta here!"

Luckily for me a woman ran up behind him and grabbed his arm, pulling him back. "This man ain't done nothin' against you, Spider. Let him be." Turning to me she yelled, "Go!" Which I did as a small, hostile crowd began to circle around us.

I headed straight for my car. It was time for me to buy a gun. Even the friendliest of my insured were reluctant to talk other than to greet me. How could you blame them after all the beatings, hangings, murders of women and children, and bombing of churches and now the nightmare of Watts? I wondered if the firestorm would come to South Carolina and Charleston.

Given the volatile climate in the city, I told Elaine Sutcliffe about my recent experiences on the debit and advised her to put off her visit there until things calmed down. Nevertheless she insisted we and others get together at the Palmetto Yacht Club to discuss the situation.

A few days later, arriving several minutes late to our meeting at the prestigious club, I recalled Jim Dawson telling me that you had to have either a certain pedigree or a ton of money to become a member.

Inside, Elaine, Elizabeth, Ruth Bloom, and a dynamite-looking chick I'd never seen before were seated in the lounge area, casually chatting and sipping on drinks. Was I going to be the only swinging dick at this party? But what the hell. I enjoyed the company of women far more than that of men.

Elizabeth got up and welcomed me with a firm handshake. The other women remained seated and gave me various greetings and smiles. I took a seat between Elizabeth and Elaine.

Elaine said, "We do appreciate your taking the time from work to be with us."

I just nodded.

"Michael, what can I get you to drink?"

I looked at my watch. "A ginger ale will be fine, thanks."

Elaine waved over a gray-haired, colored server and gave him my order. Then she said, "Michael, you know everyone here except Debbie Mobley from New Orleans. She'll be my political strategist. She will work closely with Elizabeth and Ruth, who'll be our legal counsel."

This was going to be one heck of an estrogen-driven campaign. But then maybe it had to be that way, given the dispositions of men toward women in politics.

I got up from my chair and reached over the glass table as Debbie, still seated, leaned forward and shook my hand, affording me a whiff of her subtle, expensive perfume. She was a truly gorgeous young woman with shiny, black hair cut in a short bob; large, gray eyes; and a decidedly firm chin. While the other women were dressed casually in light summer dresses, she wore a silk blouse tucked into a demure navy skirt, her only ornamentation a simple sapphire pendant around her neck. No rings, wedding or otherwise, adorned her slim fingers.

I asked, "So, Miss Mobley, I assume you had political experience in Louisiana?"

"I did. I assisted in two successful campaigns."

"So this is your first time coming up to bat on your own?"

Her face expressed that she didn't like the question. "Yes."

Realizing that my remark might have offended her, I said, "I guess there's a first time up for all of us, especially me. I know squat about politics and less about running a campaign. At least you have experience."

She smiled. "I'll do my best, but given the short time we have to prepare before the election and the fact that I don't know the lay of the land here yet, I think it's going to be extremely difficult, if not impossible, for us to win."

I noticed a faint but definitely disdainful look cross Elizabeth's face.

"Why?" I asked.

"First of all the voting rights bill took longer than we expected to pass. Without it, it was impossible for us to go up against an entrenched senator like Aloysius Simmons in the June Democratic primary."

"So if we're not running as Democrats, does that mean we're Republicans?"

Everyone chuckled kindly at my confounded expression.

"No," said Elaine. "I'll be running as a write-in candidate."

"Boy, that's a relief. My family in New York would have killed me if they knew I was backing a Republican."

Elaine said, "I know it's rather confusing, but what we want to do for now is get the maximum number of votes in the few months remaining before the general election and make a credible showing. Two years from now, when we're better prepared, with a solid Negro vote behind us and our liberal friends, we'll be able to run again and hopefully kick that fanatical segregationist son of a bitch Simmons out of office."

I was more puzzled than ever. "I thought state senators were elected for four years."

Ruth, tucking one short leg under her butt while the other dangled a foot from the ground, said, "Providentially, due to a change this year, it's for only two, but in '68 it'll revert to a four-year term."

I didn't ask why. I was getting buggy with all the chatter and wanted to end the meeting by getting down to brass tacks. "Then what's the big deal about getting out on the debit now? Especially when it may be unsafe, given the unease out there about what happened in Watts."

Perched primly on the edge of her seat, Debbie replied, "It's as Elaine said. We have to make a good showing in the general election, and that won't happen unless we get as many coloreds and others registered as soon as possible and behind us. Time is important here. Anyway, most of our friends and supporters seem to believe there's no need for alarm, and everything appears as usual in the colored neighborhoods."

I bellowed, "Your friends must have their heads up their asses! Debbie, there's something you may or may not know. About three years ago, we had a large demonstration by coloreds here in Charleston that took the locals by complete surprise. They were frightened to death that King Street might go up in flames. Let me ask you something.

How can you trust these people when it's their segregationist policies and enforcement of them that are at the root of the problem?"

"Michael's right," said Ruth firmly. "My mother called me every day from New York during that time, worried sick that something terrible was going to happen. Ira and I felt the same way during the Harlem riots, concerned that it might well spill over into our neighborhood. And now a militaristic group has arisen within the movement. They believe that the only way to get real change is through violence, not unlike Denmark Vesey in the 1820s."

"Who on Earth was Denmark Vesey?" asked Elaine.

"Didn't you Radcliffe girls read any American history?" countered Ruth wickedly.

Elaine narrowed her eyes, looking annoyed. "I found the Greeks and Romans much more interesting."

"Denmark Vesey," Ruth continued, "was a Negro who put together a large band of coloreds, numbering in the hundreds, with a plan to kill every slave owner in Charleston. If two of his followers hadn't betrayed him, he would most likely have succeeded, and you and I, Elaine, wouldn't have been born or sitting here now. After all your family was one of the largest slave owners in the Lowcountry. Mine was involved in the slave trade."

I'd had no idea the Jews had been involved in slavery.

"And by the way, Elaine, weren't you frightened back in '63?" asked Ruth.

"Well, not really. Actually I was in France at the time." Looking frustrated, Elaine continued, "It's my decision whether we go out there on Michael's debit or not, dammit! I didn't want to do it at first, but now I realize how important it is. I need to see the plight of these people firsthand if I'm going to be a credible candidate."

"Oh, no, Elaine. It's not your decision; it's mine," I said forcefully. "I say whether or not we go. So just sit tight."

No one said a thing.

"However I might have hit on something else," I said. "I've been speaking to Mrs. Bouchon, a Negro woman who is very prominent and influential in her community. She and a Negro minister named

Billy Hazard are willing to meet with you and give their support if you fit their bill. I haven't met him yet, but I know that Hazard is now the pastor of one of the biggest colored congregations in all of Charleston."

Debbie shot out of her chair. "That's just the kind of inroad I'm talking about. When can we meet with them?"

"I'll give them a call and see if I can set something up for next week. And there's more. Mrs. Bouchon told me there are a bunch of Young Turks who have formed a coalition with some Negroes to get progressive candidates elected to office. You're not alone in this."

"Young Turks?" asked Elaine. "What are you talking about?"

"I really don't know, but according to Mrs. Bouchon, it's a group of primarily liberals from all walks of life who want change."

Elizabeth added, "The term originated in Turkey during the Ottoman Empire, when a group of young people tried to modernize the country along European lines. These days it's become synonymous with any group advocating political and social reform."

"Well, that's what we're all about," Elaine mused.

"Do you know who these people are, Michael?" asked Debbie.

"No, not yet, but I'll find out. Look, I hope this information will be useful to you ladies. But please understand I have to make a living, and there are only so many hours in a day. After I hook you up with these people, I'm out of it other than talking it up and the excursion with Elaine through my debit, conditions permitting."

I rose, and everyone reluctantly got up. Debbie and Elizabeth shook my hand and thanked me warmly. Ruth said, "Well, I do hope you'll stick with us, Michael. See you and Julie soon."

As I turned to leave, Elaine put her hand on my arm. "Mike, I need to speak to you alone." She guided me out the large French doors at the back of the club and down to a long pier and dock where several small sailing vessels were being batted about by the river current. We stood at the edge of the dock. Strong gusts whipped her auburn hair and full skirt about her.

Elaine turned to me. "You're a pirate. You know what you want, and you're determined to get it. In many ways we're alike, you and I."

She took my hand and drew me toward her. We stood motionless for a few seconds with our bodies touching, saying nothing. I eased my hand gently from hers and stepped back. "Look, Elaine, I make no bones that I'm attracted to you. Any man would be. But I have everything that I want or need in a woman in Julie."

She smiled unrepentantly. "Too bad for both of us, for now. But I'm not giving up on you."

TWENTY EIGHT

On Wednesday morning I called into the office and made the excuse that I wouldn't be in because I had a doctor's appointment. I had a lot on my plate for the day. I had to collect my debit, sign a real estate contract, and meet with Elaine at Mrs. Bouchon's home at three. Starting early, I moved through the debit quickly.

On Coming Street I knocked on David Scruggs's first-floor apartment, hoping he wouldn't be working that morning. David caught jobs on and off as a mason. He was a quiet, thoughtful young man, totally unlike his fiery mother—the loud, angry woman who made me come back time after time to collect her insurance at her small beauty parlor.

He opened the door in his pajamas and did not seem surprised—as others had been—by my early appearance. "Mr. Romano, are you here about my mom?"

Confused, I answered, "No. Why?"

"Then you haven't heard about my no 'count bum of a father killing my Momma?"

"Good God, David, what happened?"

"All I know is he emptied his gun into her and then sat and waited for the police to come. Momma wasn't an easy woman to get along with, but he had no right to do her that way. She had a tough life running that little business of hers. She worked herself hard, day in and day out, to make enough money to keep us all fed and clothed. It tuckered her out and made her short tempered, but she sure loved her family and tried to do right by us."

He turned his head away from me and let loose a river of tears, which he tried to wipe away with the backs of his hard, calloused hands.

I rested my hand on his shoulder, trying to offer some quiet consolation.

In a broken voice, he asked, "Will you be taking care of Momma's insurance, Mr. Romano?"

"Of course. Do you know where she kept her policies?"

"At the house."

"Good. Please get them for me when you have a chance."

He nodded.

"Also, we're going to need her death certificate and possibly a police report."

A look of panic crossed his face. "Sir, that's all going to take a long time to get. We need the money now to give Momma a proper funeral."

"Easy, David, don't worry. Do you know which funeral parlor you're going to use?"

"Dorothy Wright's."

"Great. I know Dorothy well. When I tell her that your mother's insurance is in full benefit, she'll move forward to take care of everything."

"Oh, thank you, sir. That takes a load offa my mind."

"Stay cool. Everything will work out. I'll be in touch soon. Again, I'm so sorry for your loss."

As I turned to leave, he said, "Mr. Romano, ain't you goin' to collect my insurance?"

"Sorry, David. How could I have forgotten?" I marked his book and left.

Close to noon I had all my collections out of the way and informed the office of Mrs. Scruggs's death. I headed for the Medical College to pick up Julie for lunch and then the signing of our real estate contract. For nearly three weeks, we had been looking for a property to buy in the city. Finally we had narrowed it down to one on Tradd. It was an ideal location for us, only a few short blocks from White Point Gardens, which would afford us the opportunity to take quiet, late-night strolls through the park and along the Battery and enjoy the cool winds gusting down the rivers.

It was a three-story, turn-of-the century apartment building with wide porches. We would live on the third floor and rent out the others. It was in reasonable shape and was a good deal at $23,000, which we managed using my VA benefit. What made the deal even sweeter was that the other two apartments would generate enough rental income to cover our mortgage and still give us a cool hundred bucks a month in income. Each apartment consisted of a spacious living room, a dining room, a kitchen, two bedrooms, and a large, old-fashioned bathroom with a claw-footed tub that could accommodate a whale. We couldn't wait to move in.

With Julie riding beside me and the top down, we decided to have lunch at the Port City Drive-in. After we gave our orders to a teenage waitress with a bad case of acne, Julie said, "Guess what, Michael? I'm finally registered to begin my master's program next semester."

"That's great, baby! We should have gone somewhere we could have had a drink to celebrate. How many hours a week will it take?"

"About four hours of classwork and three hours of lab a week. I should be finished in fewer than two years."

"That's terrific, baby." I was beginning to repeat myself.

"And Dr. Herschaft has been so wonderful, sponsoring me and allowing me flexible hours at work. He'll be my thesis advisor. He's calling me his Madame Curie."

"And rightly so. What's your thesis going to be about?"

"I want to study the *Pseudomonas* bacterium. It's a common problem in burn patients, and it produces some toxins that haven't been studied too much. I'll be looking at how they act."

"I have absolutely no idea what you're talking about, but it sounds like high-powered stuff to me."

She smiled. "I'll take care of the science; you make the money."

When we had finished our lunch, the waitress removed the tray from the car door. Off we sped to Pendergast Realty on Broad Street, where Mrs. Pringle, the neatly dressed receptionist, welcomed us. Smiling, she said, "Please follow me."

Trailing her, we entered a conference room and took our seats at a highly polished table. Mrs. Pringle offered us a choice of tea or coffee, which we declined. She quietly left the room and closed the door.

After a minute or two of waiting, Julie and I roamed the room, looking at some oil paintings by an artist named William Halsey.

Julie commented, "I wouldn't mind having one of these."

"Yeah, one day, when our ship comes in."

The door opened. Our real estate agent, Mr. Waring, a tall, handsome man in his forties, greeted us. Julie had been quite taken with him when we'd first met.

"How are you both doing on this lovely afternoon?" he asked, smiling with the straightest, whitest teeth I'd ever seen. How much had he paid for them?

"Fine, thanks," I replied as we took our places opposite him. I could tell Julie was a bit nervous; so was I.

"Good. This won't take very long, and it's quite painless." He smiled again and pulled out a one-page contract from a folder and passed it across the table to us. "Take your time reading this. Most of it is what we have already gone over, but please ask any questions you might have."

We read through the contract carefully while conferring with each other. Then we told him that we understood it.

"Excellent." He pointed a manicured finger at where we were to sign, which I did with a flourish, followed by Julie. Bingo! It was over with in fewer than ten minutes.

We all rose from the table. Mr. Waring congratulated us, and we thanked him with hearty handshakes.

Elias greeted us after we left the room. I assumed he had been waiting for us to emerge so we could chat.

"Congratulations, Julie and Mike! You are now on the road to becoming property owners in our fair city."

"Thank you, Elias," said Julie. "We really appreciate all your advice. Mr. Waring and your staff have been great."

"I can't tell you how pleased we are that you and Mike are living and investing here in Charleston, especially when so many of the old families have abandoned it for the 'burbs."

"They'll probably rue the day that they sold," I said.

"Why?"

"The time will come when other carpetbaggers like me will realize there's a fortune to be made in buying these old homes."

"Ah, it's interesting that you see it that way."

"I probably wouldn't have if you hadn't advised us on buying real estate for tax purposes. But after three weeks of hunting for investment properties and seeing so many of these old houses up close, especially South of Broad, it seems obvious."

"I think you're right. It may take many years, but you're young, and one day you'll reap big dividends. Also you confirm my belief that you will be making many return visits to my office."

I laughed, but Julie was quiet, probably worried about us overextending ourselves. "Well, Elias," I said, "as long as we keep getting the loans, we'll be back."

"Then we must make every effort to see that you do."

"How's that? Do you have the keys to the vault?"

"No, but I do have the combination." He winked.

TWENTY NINE

"Mrs. Bouchon," I said, "permit me to introduce Mrs. Elaine Sutcliffe, Miss Debbie Mobley, Miss Elizabeth Alcott, and Mrs. Ruth Bloom."

"Welcome to my home. I'm very pleased to make your acquaintance," our hostess replied.

"Thank you, Mrs. Bouchon. We do so appreciate your inviting us to your beautiful home," said Elaine graciously. Each woman took the measure of the other—Elaine in peacock-blue silk and chunky turquoise jewelry, Mrs. Bouchon in fine black linen, small diamonds winking discreetly at her ears.

"Well, Mrs. Sutcliffe—"

"Oh, please call me Elaine."

"Certainly, Elaine. I do hope that our time and effort today will prove to be of consequence in expeditiously restoring the rights of my people that were lost after Reconstruction."

Whoa, there wouldn't be any prevaricating today.

"Now," said Mrs. Bouchon, "if you all would be so kind as to follow me into the living room where the others await us."

Did I hear that correctly? Did she say others? I thought we were meeting only with the Reverend Billy.

Elaine and Debbie paused stiffly in the doorway. We hadn't expected to encounter this group of a dozen or more people standing, sitting, talking, and drinking iced tea. However, Ruth and Elizabeth stepped forward with aplomb. I just tagged along. The group quieted as they became aware of our presence.

Mrs. Bouchon introduced us as a group. Then she said, "Elaine, I want you to meet the leaders of our church. First our pastor, the Reverend Billy Hazard."

I wanted to prompt Elaine to press the flesh. I hoped she would stay cool and not treat these people as if they were her servants.

The others in our little group mingled and began to talk to the assembled church people. I tried to position myself close enough to overhear their conversations, but an ancient-looking colored woman tottered over to me, leaning on a cane. Her face resembled old oak bark.

"You must be that Yankee they call the Duke Miz Bouchon been talking about."

"Yes, ma'am, I'm Mike Romano," I replied.

Shakily she grasped my wrist with her free hand to steady herself. "Well, I just wanted to meet you and thank you fo' trying to help us colored folks out. I know it cain't be easy for no white man to do that down heah."

Without saying another word, she slowly made her way off and collapsed onto a large wing chair that swallowed up her tiny body.

I moved closer to Elaine and the reverend. Now that I was able to get a good look at him, he reminded me of a dock worker, with his strong, squat build and loud, resonant voice. Elaine appeared frustrated, unable to get a word in edgeways, as he embarked on a hell-fire-and-brimstone sermon directed at her and her alone. She could do little more than maintain her pleasant smile, nod, and shake her head.

Mrs. Bouchon came to the rescue and cut him off smartly by saying, "Reverend, time is pressing, and Elaine has to meet with others."

Looking rather affronted, he said to Elaine, "Well then, read the Bible, woman. It will guide you into the ways of the Lord."

After Elaine had completed her round of the church officials, Mrs. Bouchon once again called on everyone for their attention. "Mrs. Sutcliffe, who y'all know is running for the Senate, now wishes to address you. Elaine?"

"Thank you, Mrs. Bouchon, and all of you who have given me this opportunity to speak with you and tell you why I'm running for the Senate. For too long the state of South Carolina has denied you your rights as citizens—those rights guaranteed to you under the Constitution of the United States. However, these are times of historic change. New laws in are place. With the courage of your people, along with fair-minded whites such as our late beloved President Kennedy and the majority of the Congress, the tyrant's yoke is in the process of being lifted from your backs.

"Unfortunately, as we have seen all too often in the past, that tyrant has found clever ways of keeping that yoke in place. I pledge to you that if I am elected to office, I will fight to prevent that as long as I have breath in my body."

Many applauded enthusiastically. Others said amen, and the little old gal came out of her chair waving her cane, crying, "Halleluiah!" Only Mrs. Bouchon and another woman mused in silence.

Overall, I thought Elaine had done a good job: short, sweet, and straight to the heart.

Elaine gestured for silence. "The question is, how do we do this? With your permission, I would now like to ask members of my staff to address you. Ruth?"

She bowed out as Ruth took center stage.

"My name is Ruth Bloom. I am a civil rights lawyer and a Jew. Everyone here knows the plight of my people throughout history, especially during the Holocaust. We Jews recognize that our fate is inextricably linked to that of any group of people persecuted for any reason, whether it be race, religion, or ethnic origin. A government or system that allows or condones such persecution is fascist by definition and threatens us. That is why so many of us are active in the ACLU and have worked closely with the NAACP. I did so for several years when I was in New York.

"I know, as a member of Elaine's campaign, that *I* have an individual stake in *your* freedom. I will make certain that no one will interfere with your rights, either in registering to vote or at the ballot box. If anyone tries it, I assure you they will find themselves in front of the Supreme Court of the United States."

Ruth bobbed her head in response to the polite applause, and then Debbie stepped forward and introduced herself as the political strategist for Elaine's campaign. After delivering a lengthy explanation of why Elaine would be running as a write-in candidate and fielding many questions, she summarized the strategy we had discussed at the yacht club.

"One: build name recognition for Elaine. Two: make a credible showing in the election to demonstrate that she is a viable candidate. Three: build a strong political base over the next two years to include disenfranchised Democrats, Republicans, Independents, and Negroes. Four: run under the Democratic banner in the 1968 primary against Senator Aloysius Simmons."

A young man in the back of the room said, "OK. Let's say you win the '68 primary. What about the Republicans in the general election?"

"Good question!" Debbie responded briskly. "The Republicans haven't been able to do much in fielding a worthwhile challenger since the end of Reconstruction. Usually they don't put anyone up. However, as we have recently seen, our erstwhile revered Democratic senior senator in Washington has jumped ship to join the Republican Party. I expect that many Democrats at all levels of government down here in the South will eventually do likewise over the next few years.

"However, it will take time for them to organize, given all the political confusion that's going on, never mind the infighting among the leadership of both parties."

Suddenly Debbie paused and started laughing and shaking her head. What was she up to?

Then, serious again, she continued, "Something has just occurred to me. Given what I said about Democrats jumping ship, if there is a Republican who might be running against us in '68, it could be Senator Aloysius Simmons himself. And I hope he does. After all, voters usually vote their party lever, and since the Democratic Party holds the overwhelming majority, the rest I leave to your imagination."

Those of us who had grasped what she had said smiled at the irony while others were left somewhat bewildered.

She ended by saying assertively, as her gaze fell deliberately on each of the people seated in front of her, "No matter what happens, if we have the support of the Negro community as well as that of the other groups I mentioned, I believe we will win and usher in a new era of South Carolina politics."

Still leaning casually against the wall, applauding with the others, I was relieved. It had gone well. Now maybe we could wrap this thing up and go home. I was getting hungry.

Rising from her chair, Mrs. Bouchon said, "Now I would like to ask my friend, Mr. Mike Romano, who is responsible for bringing us all together today, to say a few words."

I froze. A few moments into my hesitation, she urged me on with an encouraging wave of her hand. "Don't be shy, Mike."

I took a deep breath. Then my lips moved while my thoughts raced, trying to catch up.

"I grew up in an all-white neighborhood in Queens, New York. One day when I was very young, my mother and aunt took me to Macy's department store to see Santa Claus. I saw a colored family for the first time in my life. I asked my mother, 'Why are those people black?' She said, 'God made them that way the same as he made you white. They are just like us—human beings.' That simple, direct answer sufficed for me, both then and now. However, coming to the South years later as a marine, I saw the disturbing truth of inequality in a segregated society.

"I reflect on stories my grandparents, who came from Italy, told me and how they were discriminated against in many ways, such as you are today. Why? Their skin, hair, and eyes were dark. They wore different clothes and had different customs. They were relegated to the status of inferior beings and were called guineas, dagos, organ grinders, and dirty, filthy wops. They lived in a ghetto on the Lower East Side of New York with Jews and Chinese, who suffered equal discrimination. Gangs attacked them if they made the mistake of wandering onto their turf. My great-uncle, who lived in New Orleans many years ago, told me of how a lynch mob took three Italian shopkeepers and two innocent bystanders in Tallulah, Louisiana, and hanged them for serving colored people. Nothing was done to bring the murderers to justice.

"Let's end this corrupt rule that threatens all of us, whether we're black, brown, yellow, or white, or one day we may each find ourselves dangling from the end of a rope."

Rising heavily from his chair, the Reverend Billy boomed, "I say unto you: the Holy Spirit has spoken through this young man. We must support these people. We have nothing to lose and everything to gain."

Mrs. Bouchon said with calm authority, "I concur. May I have a show of hands from all who are in support of Mrs. Elaine Sutcliffe's candidacy?" Quickly scanning the room, she pronounced that the vote was unanimous.

The reverend said, "I will contact my brethren ministers and our civic groups, informing them of our meeting and our decision and urging them to have Mrs. Sutcliffe come speak to them."

He lifted his hands. I felt a lengthy sermon coming on, but mercifully he merely delivered a short blessing.

Thirty

Excited chatter filled the room, and I took the opportunity to nip out onto the porch. As I was lighting up, I heard the door open behind me. Elizabeth walked over to my side. To my surprise she accepted the cigarette I offered.

"I don't often smoke, but this seems like a good time." She smiled. "Michael, I think you carried the ball over the goal line for us."

"You won the game before you walked in."

"What on Earth do you mean?"

"Mrs. Bouchon had already made up her mind. We had a long conversation earlier this week. Like the reverend said, they have everything to gain and nothing to lose. And Mrs. Bouchon has Billy Boy in her pocket. She is, after all, the biggest contributor to his church. Look, they don't have any real political organization yet, much less a candidate they could hope to run. Even if they did, they represent only thirty percent of the population. And the voting districts are gerrymandered against them. They couldn't elect a dogcatcher to office."

"Even so, I was really moved by what you said about your family and the discrimination against the Italians. I had no idea."

"Well, a lot of it wasn't actually true."

She gave a short huff of surprise. "Which parts?"

"For one thing my mother and most of my family are bigots. They don't like or trust people who they perceive as being different from them, including the Sicilians—they call them *melanzanes*. They were horrified when I started dating a lovely Puerto Rican girl, a 'spic,' and succeeded in running her off with spiteful looks and false courtesies. And the only great-uncle I had lived in a tenement on Mulberry Street on the Lower East Side and hardly ever ventured out of the Italian ghetto. However, the part about what happened in Tallulah was true."

"So how did you know about that?"

"Tom Avery told me. And the discrimination my grandparents described and experienced firsthand was absolutely true as well."

The door opened again, and Elaine sauntered out, followed by Ruth, Debbie, and Mrs. Bouchon.

Elaine lifted her brows in mild surprise to see Elizabeth and me standing together. "What are you two doing out here? Michael, I thought you had abandoned me."

"We were just talking. I wouldn't leave without saying good-bye to you and Mrs. Bouchon."

"So what were you discussing?'

Elizabeth answered smoothly, "Cooking. Michael was telling me how he makes his own sausage and tomato sauce from scratch. I told him how much I adore Italian food."

This was getting really thick.

"And he invited me to dinner tonight."

What the heck? Dinner?

"So there's no need for you to drive me back, Elaine."

Ruth's face was a picture as she looked back and forth between us. An expression of great irritation flowed briefly like a wave across Elaine's face before she assumed a polite mask. "Well, Elizabeth, have a pleasant evening."

Once in my car, Elizabeth turned to me and grinned. "Sorry about that. I hope this'll be OK with Julie. I really want to talk to you some more."

"You're not sorry at all," I scolded. "And Julie will be delighted. I hope you like bangers and mash."

"I love them—whatever they are! By the way, what does *melanzanes* mean?"

"Eggplants. They have a black skin."

"Black as in Negro? That's terrible!"

"Yeah, I know."

On the way back to the apartment, we stopped briefly at the Piggly Wiggly, where Elizabeth insisted, over my protests, on buying a peach pie and a tub of vanilla ice cream. When we got home, Julie was already there in the living room, surrounded by cardboard boxes. She bounced up as we walked in, gave me a quick kiss, then turned to Elizabeth and said, "It's great to see you again! Sorry about the mess. I thought I'd get started early on packing for our move. We signed a contract for our new place today. It's incredible how much *stuff* you can accumulate in such a short time. Can you stay for dinner?"

Somewhat to my surprise, the women were hugging like old friends. Elizabeth had lost her usual reserved air and looked relaxed and happy. "I have a confession to make. I already invited myself, but I come bearing dessert."

"Oh goody—peach pie. You're always welcome, Elizabeth. I'll put the ice cream in the freezer before it melts." They walked off into the kitchen, where I could hear them chatting away. I was thinking about getting a beer but decided to leave them to it for a while. I was poking through boxes, making sure Julie hadn't thrown out anything I wanted to keep and listening to their conversation with half an ear as Julie was describing our new apartment on Tradd. She asked Elizabeth where she lived, and I perked up, realizing I didn't know either.

"I have a little house on Lamboll Street. It's very convenient."

Julie exclaimed, "That's only a few blocks from where we'll be! I hope we'll be able to see more of you."

I gave in to my thirst and walked into the kitchen. Elizabeth had shed her light jacket and was standing at the counter, peeling potatoes. Next to her Julie was snapping green beans.

Julie said, "Michael, if you're going for a beer, I think we could use one too, unless—is that OK with you, Liz? Something stronger or a soda?"

Liz?

"Beer would be great, thanks."

"And while you're at it, Michael, could you get the sausages out of the fridge?"

Elizabeth started laughing helplessly. "I wondered about the bangers but didn't dare to ask."

An hour or more passed as we ate the plain but tasty meal, drank lots of beer, and enjoyed lighthearted conversation. A chance remark by Elizabeth about Ruth Bloom had Julie sitting up straight with a stricken look on her face.

"Oh, Michael, I completely forgot. How did the meeting go this afternoon?"

"Actually, it went well. I think you would have enjoyed it, especially the Reverend Billy's oration."

"What Michael fails to mention, being so modest"—Julie snorted at this in a very unladylike manner—"is that he himself gave a very powerful speech," Elizabeth said.

Trying to divert her, I asked, "So what did you want to talk to me about, Elizabeth?"

"Please call me Liz. That's what my family has always called me, and I like it. Elizabeth sounds so prim."

"So Liz, what's on your mind?"

She looked a little uncomfortable. Julie stood and began to clear the table. "You guys relax and talk while I wash up," she said, smiling at Elizabeth, "and then we'll have pie and ice cream."

"No...no, Julie, you don't have to leave—unless you don't want to hear any more political nonsense."

Julie hesitated and then sat down again.

"Elaine and I have known each other since the day we became roommates at Radcliffe. I was shy and didn't make friends easily. I preferred studying to socializing. Elaine studied very little and was the belle of the ball wherever she went. She befriended me and dragged me around with her to meet people and go to dances, parties, and so on. I must admit my life was much happier—certainly more interesting. We became close friends, telling each other our life stories and spilling our hearts, as girls will. So when Elaine called me last year asking me to help her with her ambition to become a public servant, I gave up my teaching position at a small liberal arts college in Maine."

"I imagine that must have been hard to do," Julie commented.

"Not really. When someone you care about, someone who has done so much for you...well, this was my chance to do something for *her*. We had never lost touch and always managed to visit each other several times a year. We went on vacation together a few times."

How was she supporting herself without a job? I wasn't about to ask.

"What did you teach?" asked Julie.

"Philosophy."

"Oh no." Julie gave a mock groan. "Now I have two philosophers to deal with."

"Did you study philosophy in college, Mike?"

I laughed. Obviously she knew very little about my past.

Elizabeth looked a little confused, and then Julie silently pointed to a bookshelf stuffed with my well-worn philosophy and history books.

"Let's get back to you, Liz," I said.

Liz toyed diffidently with her napkin. "Well, frankly...I'm beginning to wonder if the real motivation behind Elaine's running for public office is not so much that she wants to make a difference but that she's bored and frustrated with her life."

Julie said contemptuously, "Bored? Frustrated? Doesn't she have enough in her life with all the parties, trips abroad, and hobnobbing it with the South of Broad crowd?"

"Unfortunately not, Julie." Her tone sounded defensive. "To give you an example in Elaine's own words: if you want the worst food, worst booze, or worst conversation, go to a South of Broad party."

I laughed. "Hey, lay off the South of Broaders; they make me feel real smart!"

Julie shot me an irritated glance.

Elizabeth shrugged. "She's burned out, I think, on the life of luxury and privilege."

"Oh, poor little rich girl," Julie said sarcastically. "Liz, why don't you tell her to take better care of her kids rather than abandoning them to some boarding school? That would end her boredom and maybe give her bloody life some real meaning." Pausing, Julie gave a short sigh. Her face hardened. "Liz, you undoubtedly have gathered by now that I dislike your best friend with a passion. She humiliated me in Beaufort, making a blatant play for my husband all the time we were there. And don't tell me you didn't see it."

"Unfortunately I did, Julie." A pained look surfaced on Elizabeth's face.

"And by the way, what the hell gives with dear old Arthur? Is he blind or just complacent?"

"I think he just chalks it up to benign flirtation. It happens all the time."

"Well," Julie said, "I think that's terribly sad and pathetic."

"Julie," I said, "please calm down and let Liz get to the point of why she's here."

Still seething, Julie took a deep breath and went silent.

"What I said about Elaine's motivation doesn't mean she doesn't genuinely care about injustice. I believe that her life of privilege, and what it was built on, does cause her guilt. What I'm concerned about is that she can be easily swayed by those closest to her. And now Debbie has been advocating that Elaine make deals with one and all to get into office. But choosing that course will water down our positions and beget very little in real change. We must stick to our plan and build a viable coalition. We need to steer clear of the old party machinery.

"Mike, you have proved to be more influential than any of us could have imagined. When Elaine finds out that your help arranged the outcome of today's meeting before we even walked into Mrs. Bouchon's home, I know she'll be as impressed as I am."

Julie looked up with interest but said nothing.

"I believe that if you stay with us and don't bow out as you planned, you, Ruth, and I can dilute most if not all of Debbie's influence and win the election in '68 with the coalition we started building today."

"Thanks, Liz, but all I did was set up the meeting. The rest just fell into place. But my relationship with my wife is far more important to me than Elaine's ambition or any cause—no matter how noble it may be. So I must decline."

"Hold on, Michael." Julie sighed. "This *is* a noble cause. Having lived in a country that is even more segregated and unjust than this one, I couldn't in good conscience tell you not to help Liz and Ruth. However, Liz, if Michael decides to go with you on this, you tell Elaine that if she makes a play for him again, I'm knocking her bloody head off."

Grinning in spite of everything, Liz said, "So what do you say, Mike?"

"Well, OK, I'll help. But I'm certainly not about to devote my life to this thing."

"All I ask is that you make the meetings and speak your mind."

I nodded.

Turning to Julie, Liz said, "I have to tell you—the time we spent in your kitchen and at this table tonight has been the happiest since I moved to Charleston. I hope you can separate our relationship from mine with Elaine. I do want us to be friends."

"Me too." Julie gave her a warm smile.

THIRTY ONE

Time sped after the political do at Mrs. Bouchon's. The gods decreed that I would not be taking Elaine around to meet my insured—or at least Debbie did. In one way I was disappointed. I wanted Elaine to get to know people who overall hated the color of their skin. But I also felt relieved. What might have happened between us if we'd been left alone for four days? I needed Elaine to continue to open doors for me, both social and economic. But I strongly suspected that if I rejected her advances again, her itch for me would turn to disdain, and those doors would slam shut. Anyway she was meeting far more people through speaking engagements than she could ever see in any given week with me. As Debbie put it, it was now a numbers game—the enlightenment of Elaine would have to take second place. Also her being hooked up with the Young Turks through Ruth's efforts had added to Elaine's support base and hectic schedule. They were making big demands on her time to meet with them, embroiling her in all kinds of political skullduggery not only involving her campaign but also in the targeting of many local, county, and state representatives for removal from office in the near future.

For the moment I put politics aside. Julie and I were making last minute preparations for our housewarming party, putting out napkins, plates, flatware, and glasses. To make things easier, we had Indigo Kitchens do the catering.

Julie was really excited. It was the first time we had ever held a party. For me the occasion was a time to shine and to celebrate my departure from my lower-class roots. However, I had many rungs yet to climb to get the respect and power I wanted.

Around six, as we opened the doors to the wide piazza, we heard our first guests climbing the stairs, chattering, laughing, and complaining.

"Jesus Christ," groused Burl at top volume. "If I'd known I was going mountain climbing, I'da brought my gear! Why didn't Mike take the first floor, dammit? He owns the freakin' building."

"Hush now, Burl," uttered Kitty in a theatrical whisper. "They'll hear you."

"Well, hold up a bit, girl. I gotta catch m'breath and hitch up m'pants."

Finally they made it to the third floor. Kitty called out, "Mike, Julie, we're here!"

"Come on in, Kitty," I said. "We didn't hear you coming." Julie and I exchanged surreptitious smiles.

The women embraced. Julie stood back and held Kitty by the shoulders. "My, you look absolutely splendid! That's a beautiful gown." I had to agree. Kitty twirled in her full-skirted, silky silver dress, pleased as a debutante at her first ball.

"Burl, I don't believe it." I laughed. "You're not wearing your safari outfit. You look great in that green jacket. Are you a member of the Hibernians?"

"Hell no! I'm English through and through. At least a couple generations back."

"And what's that on your tie?"

"You blind, son? It's a picture of a nekkid gal. I picked this up some years back on a trip to Vegas."

A look of consternation crossed Kitty's face. Julie covered her mouth, struggling not to laugh. Oblivious, Burl handed over a bottle of bourbon. "Just in case you run out of gas."

We heard the sounds of more people arriving, and Julie and I excused ourselves from Burl and Kitty. From the apartment door, we looked down to see a small crowd ascending the stairs. Tom, Rina, Jean-Luc, and Marie Claire led the way, bearing gifts. Julie ushered them in while I waited to greet the Fanellis, who were climbing the stairs with some difficulty. They waved cheerfully when they saw me. The Sutcliffes followed next with Elizabeth and Debbie. Trailing them were Melanie with her beau, Eric, complete with guitar. I welcomed them all and directed them down the hall to the dining room, where Julie was offering drinks. At that point I needed a drink myself. As I was pouring a Scotch, another group came through the open door and paused in the hallway. Mrs. Bouchon walked briskly toward me, with Mrs. Wright in tow, carrying a potted fern. As we said our hellos, Jim Dawson and Lloyd came in behind them.

Mrs. Bouchon said, "Greet your guests, Michael. We'll talk later."

A buzz of conversation was coming from the group of guests. I walked back with Jim and Lloyd to the dining room, which was beginning to look like Grand Central Station. Burl chatted with Elaine, showing her his tie. Sal hovered over the food, helping himself to mounds of shrimp and roast beef. Rina presented Julie with a box. She opened it and oohed and aahed over its contents. Elizabeth was engaged in earnest conversation with Mrs. Bouchon while Eric was tuning his guitar in the living room.

As the party spread throughout the apartment, I didn't notice the arrival of Elias Pendergast and the Blooms until they came over to us.

"Mike," Elias said, "may I introduce you to my wife, Patricia?"

I put out my hand. "Very pleased to meet you, ma'am."

"Do call me Trish. *Ma'am* makes me feel ancient."

"OK, Trish."

I reached down to embrace Ruth, who was still a foot shorter than me in her three-inch heels. I then turned to greet her husband.

"Ira! Haven't seen you since Beaufort."

"Been busy, Mike. I'm in the process of setting up a small investment group."

"I thought you retired."

"From Wall Street—but not from the business."

Reaching into the same admiral's jacket he had worn on the cruise, he produced a silver card case and handed a business card to each of us.

"I like the name," said Elias. Then he read the card aloud. "'Bloom Investments: a better strategy for the future.' Has a good ring to it."

Ira had managed to get out the first few words of a sales pitch when Ruth broke in. "Enough of this business stuff. Where's Julie, Mike?"

"Last I saw, in the living room."

She took Ira by the hand and firmly pulled him away, like a row-boat towing the Titanic.

Elias said, "Mike, you've done a great job on this place—and in such a short time too. I hardly recognized the building when I drove up."

"Thanks. I had a couple of colored guys help me out with the painting and carpentry work."

I glanced over at the dining table; the roast beef slices were running low, and I excused myself. As I carved away, I recognized Elaine's perfume before I saw her.

I laid the knife back on the platter and said in my best Bogey voice, "Of all the beef joints in all the towns in all the world, you walk into mine."

She looked up at me from under her lashes and purred, "Only if I can play Bacall. Just whistle!"

"Wrong movie, sweetheart," I responded with as much finality as I could muster.

"I could be whoever you want."

"No, lady, you're too hot for me."

Laughing lightly, she said, "Oh, Michael. Whatever am I to do with you?"

"Remember me in your will."

"You are impossible."

"Yeah, that's what the corps said about me too."

Just then Lloyd sauntered over to us. "Elaine, darling, you look absolutely divine."

Elaine's eyes widened. "Lloyd? I didn't expect to see you here."

"Mike's a good friend of mine. Oh, I'm so thrilled you let me give you that new cut," he said, lightly fingering back the wings of her hair. "It's truly befitting the style of a senator. It's *soooo* difficult to achieve that worldly look with grace and beauty."

What the hell was he talking about? Most senators I knew were either bald or looked like a lawn mower had run over their domes.

"But do come in to see me, dear lady." His tone took on a stage whisper. "Your roots need just a *tiny* little touch-up."

As Elaine stood speechless, I was surprised and ecstatic to see Julie leading Maggie into the room.

I looked at Maggie and realized I was totally at a loss for words. All I could do was put my arms around her, and we embraced gently. I finally found my voice. "We missed you, girl."

"I know," she said quietly.

As I relaxed my grip and let go of her, she continued, "It's taken me such a long time to accept the fact that Pug is really gone, and I have to go on with my life. I'm really sorry I turned down your attempts to see me. I wasn't ready."

"Oh, Maggie, we understand. You don't have to say any more." In an upbeat tone, I said, "Let's get you a drink. I'll introduce you to some of our friends."

Glasses in hand, we went into the living room. Melanie's beau—Eric the Red, Inarticulate Protector of our Coastline—was readying himself to play. I didn't know if he'd be good enough or if I would have to throw his ass out.

Julie introduced Maggie to her boss and a new postdoc in the lab, Mark Newman, whom I had never met. At that point I heard a beautiful, classic guitar melody being played in the living room. People were gathering around, entranced. Melanie looked as proud as a peacock as she sat next to Eric.

Mrs. Bouchon appeared next to me. "You have a wonderful and interesting group of friends, Michael."

Dorothy Wright added, "This sure is unlike any party I've ever been to."

"Well," I said, "you're a part of it all. There'll be many more."

A good three hours into the festivities, only the Fanellis, Mrs. Bouchon, and Dorothy Wright had left, claiming fatigue due to age. Jean-Luc also pled weariness, much to the chagrin of Marie Claire.

"*Sacré bleu,*" she muttered as they said their good-byes and made their way out the door. "This is what you get when you marry an old man."

Then the party was picking up steam. People were becoming noisier and more animated. The gods of the grain were reigning supreme. Going to the bar to pour myself another drink, I passed Elaine, Arthur, and Debbie at the dining room table.

Arthur called out, "Great party, Mike."

I raised my glass and twirled it in response.

I looked around for Julie and found her in the kitchen, having a chat with Elizabeth. I fired up a fat cigar and joined in.

"Blimey! Where did you get that thing?" Julie wrinkled her nose.

"Elias gave it to me as a housewarming gift." I puffed out a giant cloud of smoke. "It's really good."

"I hope this isn't going to become a habit. I don't want you stinking up the house with those horrible things. Please go out onto the porch to smoke it."

"Hey, if I'm to be part of all the backroom politics going on around here, I need to look the role."

Elizabeth laughed. "I hope we women don't have to smoke cigars." Then more seriously she added, "A couple of things are going on that you need to know. Elaine is planning to invest a ton of money in a vicious media blitz targeting Senator Simmons."

"Well, the son of a bitch deserves it," I responded. "He's a bigot who cares only about power and filling his pockets—a perfect tool of the money class. What else is going on?"

Chuckling, she said, "You're not going to believe this. Elaine has some of the Republicans behind her, with Elias Pendergast's help. He figures that anything that weakens the archaic rule of the Democrats down here is good for the Republicans."

"I wouldn't be so certain about Elias's motives. He holds his cards pretty close to his chest. Mark my words, there's going to be a battle between the forces of light and darkness in the GOP. It'll being interesting to see who's left standing. So you're OK with all of this, Liz?"

"I've learned to accept reality, Michael."

"Yeah, nothing's lily white."

Julie fanned the cigar's smoke away from her. "Michael, please get rid of that wretched phallic symbol."

I took the offending stogie out of my mouth, examined it closely, and then held it up to her. "It's too small for that."

Elizabeth chuckled. Julie quipped, "Who are men to judge?"

Grinning, I held my precious smoke under the faucet. "There, are you happy now? Lay one on me, baby."

She turned her face from me. "You'd better go brush your teeth if you want to play around tonight."

I smacked her lightly on the butt. "I'll leave you ladies to yourselves," I said and headed for the bathroom, where I brushed my teeth furiously and rinsed with a gallon of minty mouthwash. Then I heard what sounded like a cat yowling on the piazza. I was violently allergic to them and certainly didn't want one in the house. Going out to shoo it away, I found Arthur with Debbie pinned against the wall, her luscious, black-nylon-encased legs wrapped around him in the throes of passion while he pumped away. Embarrassed and hoping they hadn't seen me, I ducked back inside.

I heard Arthur call out, "Mike?"

I stopped dead in my tracks and turned. Arthur appeared, zipping up and buckling his belt. An awkward moment of silence passed.

"Mike, I hope we can keep this between ourselves."

"Sure. It's none of my business. Besides, I can understand how this sort of thing can happen, especially with a babe like Debbie."

"Thanks. I owe you."

"Hey, you don't owe me a thing, and I don't want you thinking so. OK?"

"OK, Mike."

As I turned to leave, Debbie appeared from the porch, flushed but not flustered. She leaned casually against the doorjamb. "This wasn't planned, Mike."

"Isn't that the way it usually goes, Deb? Especially when you're boozed up? Look, both of you, do me a favor—just forget it, all right?"

I walked back into the party and headed for Julie, who was deep in conversation with Maggie and, to my surprise, the postdoc, Mark. I planted a big kiss on Julie's lips.

"What's that for?" She giggled.

"You forgot already? You ordered me to go brush my teeth, so I did. And drank a bottle of mouthwash on top of that."

"You know, you're crazy. If you were still in the corps, they'd hand you a Section Eight."

Maggie said, "Mike, Julie, it's been a wonderful party, and I can't tell you how good it is to be with you again. It's the best evening I've had for...a long time." She swallowed. "But it's getting late, and I have to go."

"Late?" I said, putting my arm around her shoulders. "It's only eleven, Maggie. The evening's still young, and there's still plenty to eat and drink. Why don't you sack out here if you're worried about driving?"

"Mike, you'll never change. I know you're ready to keep going full blast until the sun comes up. But I promised Mom I'd go to early mass with her. Besides, I'm tired. It's been a hard week at the bank."

I said, "But we're getting together soon, right?"

"Yes, sir." She saluted.

Mark laughed. "I'm leaving too. Maggie has been kind enough to offer to drop me off at my apartment."

Dumbstruck, I said, "I thought you came with Dr. Herschaft."

"I did, but he left an hour ago; his wife's sick."

"I'm sorry I didn't get to talk to him. "

Julie said,"Well, Mark, I hope we'll see *you* again."

After they had left, I turned to Julie. "What the hell's going on there?"

"Michael, are you blind? They've been talking to each other most of the evening."

"I was too busy running around."

"Hush! Keep it down." She looked around to see who was within earshot. "You heard what Maggie said about this being the best night for her since Pug died. We may be watching the beginning of a happy relationship here."

"Christ, Pug's body isn't even cold yet."

"What's wrong with you? Don't you want her to be happy?"

"Yeah, but this strikes me as too early."

"There you go, Italian to the core. What do want her to do, wear black for two years? Not go anywhere or see anyone? Forbid laughter, like your family did after your grandparents died? Remember how your uncle slapped you upside your head because you turned on a radio to listen to music six months after your grandfather passed?"

"I guess you're right, but it still upsets me to think that if I were dead, you'd be going out with another guy less than a year later."

"I love you, but by the same token, if *I* died I wouldn't want you to be alone and suffering. I would wish for someone to come into your life and make you happy." She smiled. "As long as she was really ugly."

I knew she was trying to cheer me up, but I ignored it. "There's a big difference, Julie. I know there could never be another person who could replace you."

She sighed. "It's the same for me." Then she said, "Come on. It's been a great evening. Let's get back to our guests."

A little after midnight, the festivities began to wind down. As the last of our guests made their way out, I told Kitty not to worry about Burl, who had passed out on the living room sofa, a spent bottle of booze cradled in his lap.

"I'm so sorry I didn't watch him more closely. I should've known better after all these years."

"Kitty, he was the life of the party with all his shenanigans. He was making everyone laugh, especially when he pinched our next senator on the butt."

"Oh, that was so embarrassing!"

With a gleam in her eye, Julie said, "I loved it." Jim and Lloyd agreed enthusiastically.

"Look," I said, "Burl will be out for at least eight hours. When he wakes up, I'll feed him a good breakfast and drive his ass back to Wadmalaw."

"Thank you, Mike." Kitty embraced Julie and said good night to Jim and Lloyd, who were the last in line to leave.

"Mike, this had been a truly extraordinary party. I thoroughly enjoyed it."

"You must have, Jim," said Lloyd. "I've never known you to make it past ten."

"Hush, Lloyd, and let me finish. Michael, you and Julie have surrounded yourselves with an interesting group of friends. I must commend you for inviting Mrs. Bouchon and Mrs. Wright. It may be one of the few times that Negroes have been guests at a South of Broad party."

"I didn't even think about that. They're my friends. We invite who we want. To hell with what some people might think."

Gripping my arm, Jim said enthusiastically, "Good for you, Mike. Good for you."

THIRTY TWO

The day before the election, I was throwing darts with a college kid at Toby's Pub just a few blocks away from the campus. I was to meet Tom for lunch.

Tom walked up as I let the darts fly. "Mike, you really have a most unorthodox way of throwing darts. I don't think I've ever seen anyone throw underhand before."

"I sort of picked it up while in the corps; you'd be surprised at the accuracy and power you get throwing a Ka-Bar that way."

"What the heck is a Ka-Bar?"

"It's an all-purpose marine utility knife—it can open cans or cut throats."

The kid's face blanched, and he turned away.

I paused to take my last shot, which missed the bull's-eye by two inches. I thanked the boy for the game and took a seat with Tom next to a table with two guys drinking beer and engrossed in a chess game.

"Lunch is on me, buddy," I said. "Thanks for the client you sent me. He took out a ten-thousand-buck policy. What are you having?"

Tom replied, "The usual, thanks. Ale and the ploughman's lunch."

At the copper-topped bar, a handful of dedicated smokers silently nursed their drinks. I gave the bartender the order for two ploughman's, and he yelled it in to the kitchen. Back at the table, ales in hand, I asked, "How's it going with Elaine?"

"The college is buzzing with her campaign. I don't think this town has ever seen so much money spent on TV and radio ads by any political candidate. There's a rumor going around that Aloysius Simmons doesn't know whether to shit or go blind."

I laughed at hearing that old marine expression coming from Tom's lips. "According to Elizabeth, Debbie believes she may get forty percent of the vote."

"Phew! Now that would be something, considering Elaine was virtually unknown a couple of months ago."

"For me it's a real eye-opener as to what money can do in politics."

"Romano, order's ready!" came the shout from the bar. I picked up the lunches and asked for two more ales. At our table two young coeds had engaged Tom in animated conversation.

"Excuse me," I said, squeezing my way between them.

"Sorry, Dr. Avery," said a giggly brunette wearing a kilt-like skirt anchored with a huge pin up around her ass. "We didn't mean to interrupt your lunch, sir."

"That's OK, ladies," answered Tom in a serious, professorial tone. "The exam will focus primarily on the Investiture Controversy, so make sure you study."

The girls thanked him in chorus and left.

"How do you stand it, Tom, surrounded by pussy like that every day? Must be hard."

Catching on, he turned to make certain they were out of earshot. "You bet it is!"

"You know, a hard cock will always trump the intellect."

"Without a doubt. A few professors I know have screwed up that way. It cost them their jobs and their families. Talking about femmes fatales, how about that Debbie? She doesn't say much unless it's about politics, but even then, the way she postures and looks at you is sheer pornography."

"Without a doubt, she's a real turn-on. But where I'm concerned, there's only one really dangerous woman out there: Elaine."

"Oh, come on, Mike, I told you back in Beaufort: she's a chronic flirt, a real cockteaser. She gets off on unnerving men and seeing how far she can push them. Anyone who's known her for a while doesn't take her seriously."

"You try telling that to Julie!"

"I had the same problem with Rina when we first met Elaine. And here we are, years later, with nothing happening, and we're all good friends."

"Sorry, Tom, but I know when a woman's screwing with me and when she's not."

"All I can tell you is there's been no scandal where she's concerned. Don't you think that if something were going on, Arthur would know and take action?" Tom dabbed at his upper lip with his napkin before taking a long swallow of his ale.

I held my tongue about Arthur's romp on my porch and Elaine's come-on to me at the yacht club.

I said, "Well, you've heard the old saying—the husband is always the last to know. Or is it the other way around? So, what's with this Investiture Controversy that has all the little cuties tracking you down? Does it have anything to do with what's going on in today's world?"

"Talk about switching tracks! One minute femmes fatales, the next minute medieval history?"

"You brought up the femmes, not me. I can't help that you're hot for Debbie."

"I didn't say that, Mike."

"Yes, you did, in so many words. Don't worry. I won't tell Rina."

"You'd better not—it would be the end of all your free history lessons."

It was interesting to see him smoothly donning his academic mask.

He said, "It was the most significant conflict between church and state in medieval times. To put it simply, the church challenged the authority of the monarchs to appoint bishops and abbots."

I warded him off with an upraised hand. "Go no further. Let's get back to sex and dangerous women."

Later Julie and I were spooning chili into bowls at the dinner table. I filled her in on my conversation with Tom, including his current infatuation with Debbie. Julie appeared interested but offered no opinions.

I asked, "So when you women get together, do you talk about men the same way we talk about women?"

She stared at me blankly.

"What?" I said.

"I'm sorry. I was thinking." She took a long drink of icy beer and barely managed to suppress the inevitable burp. She picked up a piece of corn bread and crumbled it onto her plate.

"Well?" I persisted.

"Michael, I'm trying to think. Honestly I don't remember ever having a conversation with a woman about men and sex. We might notice a good-looking guy walking by and comment on his attributes, like you men do about women, but I don't think I've ever heard anyone say anything of a sexual nature. Nearly all the women I know socially are married, and we certainly never discuss our husbands that way. What happens between a man and wife is none of anyone else's bloody business. I would be absolutely mortified if I knew you were talking about me like that."

She shifted uncomfortably in her seat.

"Although," she said slowly, "there was this one girl I knew in South Africa. She seemed nice enough—you know, little white hat and gloves. One day I agreed to meet her for a drink, and she was with this group of really unpleasant women. After a couple of cocktails, they really got going."

"What happened?"

"They began teasing one of the girls about how she'd been working her way through the entire soccer team. Far too many details, real or imagined. I didn't join in, and that was when they turned on me, calling me little Miss Prude, among other choice names, and pushing me to tell them juicy stories about myself. They used words I'd never heard spoken aloud and haven't since."

"What did you do?"

"I made up an excuse about having to get home for dinner with my parents and left."

She looked so embarrassed and dejected, I felt terrible. "I'm sorry, Julie. That must have been awful."

"Do you think I'm a prude, Michael?"

"Hell no, baby. I love you just the way you are."

"What I find so awful about people who talk about a wife or boyfriend, whatever, like that, is..." She was trying to collect her thoughts. "It denigrates the whole point of a true relationship. Some women seem to have no concept of what that might be, even if they don't indulge in such gossip." She looked me square in the eyes. "Like Elaine, for example." Then she looked at me uncertainly. "Do you agree?"

I got up from the table and lifted her up into my arms. "Julie, I can honestly say that since you came into my life, I have never wanted another woman. Looking is one thing; doing is another. I would never risk what you and I have, I promise. I love you, Julie. This is forever."

THIRTY THREE

"Romano, get in here—now!" Polk barked.

We stood face to face in his office. "I don't like your attitude! You think you're the cock of the walk around here and that the rules don't apply to you."

"Excuse me, sir, what are you talking about?"

"Like you missing meetings and not coming into the office regularly."

"When I haven't come in or missed meetings, it's been to attend to important family matters that are really none of your business, or my being sick and having to see a doctor."

"You smartass sumbitch! Who do you think you're conning?" His face was beginning to take on a purple hue. He was flipping out again and not making any sense.

"Sorry, Mr. Polk. I really don't know what the hell you're talking about."

"And your production has dropped off too."

"What? It's fractional compared with what the district is down."

"There you go, wising off again!"

Now he was really beginning to piss me off.

"Ya just listen to me, boy, and keep yer trap shut!"

That did it.

"No! You listen, Polk. I don't know what the hell is bothering you, but you don't talk to me that way. Understand?"

He inched away from me, a look of surprise on his face.

"You may be able to bully others around here, but not me. If you're so mad at me for God knows what, just fire me, and go fuck yourself! I'll get a job with one of the national insurance companies. With my record they'll be happy to have me." I took a step toward him. "Do you remember Dorothy Wright? Would you like that little story to get out? You peckerwood. Get off my back!"

He glared silently at me, a pulse throbbing at his temple.

Before he could say another word, I turned and walked out of his office, through a crowd of agents who probably had heard everything from outside the door. I headed for Bilbro's.

"What're you having today?" asked Sweet Thing—bless her.

"Give me a ham and cheese omelet with buttermilk biscuits, please."

She didn't brush her hand against mine when she was picking up the menus, as she usually did. Her crisp, peach uniform, new and rather loose, showed clearly that she was pregnant. She looked lovely, and her face was devoid of makeup. Gone was the little flirt we had all enjoyed, transformed by imminent motherhood.

Still incensed by the morning's events, I was restlessly stirring my hot coffee when Jim and Sal arrived and sat opposite me.

"Are you OK, Mike?" asked Jim.

"Just need to calm down some. That little prick doesn't know how close I came to snapping his neck."

Neither man spoke, but I noted their subtle shift away from me.

After several tense seconds, Sal opened up. "He's angry, Mike, because you didn't invite him to your party. He's been smoldering for nearly a month now."

"Oh, for God's sake. Screw him! Why should I invite someone I dislike and risk ruining the evening? Could you imagine what might have come out of his mouth when he met Mrs. Wright? Or Mrs. Bouchon? Or Elaine?"

They nodded slowly in agreement.

"By the way, what were you inferring with your comment about Mrs. Wright?" Jim asked.

Not giving a damn any longer, I described how she had confronted him at the funeral parlor.

"That might explain why his ulcer popped that day. So are you going to quit?" asked Sal.

"I don't know yet."

"He won't fire you—you must know that. He'd have a real hard time explaining it to his bosses. The company wants to keep young men like you."

"I'll probably stick around for a while. See what happens. But he'd better stay away from me, or I swear I'll hurt him."

"My God, Michael, I've never seen this side of you," said Jim.

"You don't know everything about me, friend. I'm truly sorry if it upsets you." I wanted to drop the subject. I said, "So, Sal, d'ya still want to get it on with Sweet Thing?"

Jim snorted his coffee out of his nose. The bad spell was broken, and we all relaxed.

As I got up to leave, I reminded Jim and Sal that they were invited to Elaine's election party at Alhambra Hall later that night.

"Count me out," said Sal. "I'll be dog tired after a day's work, and I hate driving that damn bridge at night. But please give Elaine my best."

"What about you, Jim?"

"Unfortunately I have a long-standing dinner engagement. However, Lloyd is really excited about going. He loves the idea that he may be a senator's hairdresser!"

I laughed. "Maybe he'll create a new trendy hairstyle. He could call it the Dixie bob."

"Tricky, Mike—I like it. Be sure to tell Lloyd when you see him, and enjoy your evening."

Loud music reverberated from Alhambra Hall, and the two-story white edifice was lit up like a beacon. Julie and I paused just inside the grand entrance and scanned the crowded hall for anyone we knew.

We made a beeline over to Jean-Luc and Marie Claire, who were chatting with Elaine and others.

"How're you doing tonight, senator?" I asked.

"That has a good ring to it, Mike. I think I could become used to it."

Turning to Julie with a big smile, Elaine enthused, "I just love your new look! That short skirt is something else!"

"It's called a mini," Julie said demurely.

"It looks great with those long boots."

"Thanks, Elaine." Julie sounded surprised. "They call it the Chelsea look. It's taken Europe by storm and is just appearing here in the States."

"Ah, yes, *ma chérie*, the look is fine, but one must have the figure and the youth to wear it, as you do," Marie Claire said. "It wouldn't look so good on older women such as me or Elaine."

"What do you mean?" said Elaine indignantly. "I'm only thirty-seven. However, I couldn't possibly wear such an outfit now that I'm running for public office."

Jean-Luc chuckled. "In my country such a look could—how do you say it?—make you win by a landslide."

I said, "The same applies to the Italians."

Ruth sighed loudly. "Will we women ever see an end to this chauvinism?"

"Well, I absolutely love it," said Debbie. "Where did you get it, Julie?"

"At good old Belk's. Where else?"

"Debbie, I hope you're not thinking of wearing anything like that while we're out stumping," said Elaine, frowning.

Was this the same Elaine I had met several months back, now seemingly so worried about propriety?

Elizabeth burst out, "What the hell? Julie looks great. What does it have to do with the rest of you? We're here because of the election, for God's sake." She checked her watch. "The early results should be coming in any minute now."

As if a bell had rung, everyone headed across the vast room, to where televisions had been set up. Party activists were calling in to the precincts to try to determine what was going on and if there had been any problems or irregularities.

"Michael," Julie said quietly, "I need to go outside for a bit. I'm getting really claustrophobic in here."

We left the hall and walked out back, toward the edge of the marsh. We gazed out onto the harbor, lit by a full platinum moon. The sound of rocking buoys drifted over to us, and the lights of two freighters awaiting the harbor pilots to guide them safely down the river twinkled in the distance.

"It's so beautiful," said Julie, "especially at night."

"Yeah, it's gorgeous."

"So what do you think is going to happen tonight?"

"I have no idea other than she won't win." After a while I said, "Are you feeling better, baby?"

"Yes, I just needed to get out of there for a while."

We headed back to the bar area for our long-awaited drinks.

"Michael, Julie," came a call from somewhere behind us.

Looking back in the general direction of the voice, Julie said, "It's Lloyd."

I was busy grabbing a handful of peanuts. "Where? I don't see him."

She pointed him out as he stood, waving, behind a group of people. "There he is—in the pink tie."

"That's not him. That guy's got short, brown hair."

"He just did that last week. I must say I preferred him blond."

He squeezed his way through the crowd toward us. He gave Julie a big kiss and then surprised me by throwing his arms around me. I stiffened. I wasn't used to guys grabbing me that way, especially one who was light in the loafers. But what the heck—he was a nice man and couldn't help the way he was wired. Finally he released me. I looked him up and down.

"Lloyd, that's a beautiful suit. You look like you work for Goldman Sachs."

"Oh no," he said conspiratorially. "I envision myself in this look as a movie mogul."

"Ha! Would you still be doing hair?"

"Of course. That's the whole point of it. Just think of all the movies made with all the different periods and hairstyles. Everything from Queen Cleo to Marilyn Monroe."

Laughing, I said, "How about from Caesar to Rock Hudson?"

"That goes without saying. And by the way, Michael, I must say with all due respect, whoever is doing your hair belongs in a butcher shop. Come in one day and let me fix you up, free of charge."

"Oh, Michael," said Julie, "that would be such fun. You loved the Mary Quant hairstyle he did for me."

"You won't catch me in a ladies' salon under a hair dryer, listening to gossip about who's doing the vicar."

"Michael, I do understand," Lloyd responded earnestly. "You're the personification of male rugged individualism. It's too bad. I could have made you even more handsome than you already are."

I couldn't come up with a reply to that.

Lloyd, glancing at Elaine weaving through the crowd, excitedly excused himself and took off like a shot.

Julie, of course, succumbed to a fit giggles.

"What's so funny?"

"You and Lloyd—you're so...cute together."

"Yeah, well, I'm glad you think it's amusing. Try being on my end sometime."

In a third attempt to get a drink, I grabbed Julie's hand and bogarted our way to the bar.

"So what's the score?" I asked an elderly fat guy propped up next to me.

"Whaddya mean?" he replied.

"The election returns."

"Last I heard Simmons had fifty-three percent of the vote."

"You got to be kidding me."

"Actually the lady, Elaine, is doing surprisingly well. Some analysts are saying she may have a chance of winning because of poor voter turnout for Simmons. So many thought he was a shoo-in."

"No shit?"

Possibly affronted by my indelicate response, he excused himself and vanished into the melee.

"Julie, let's get to the front," I said, "so we can hear what's going on."

"No, you go. I'm happy to wait here and nurse my drink."

"Are you sure, baby?"

"Yes. I know you're excited to find out what's happening."

"I'll be back in a little while. Don't pick up any strange guys."

She laughed. "Take your time."

I edged my way slowly toward the front and ran into Mrs. Bouchon.

"Michael," she said excitedly, "who would have thought a few months ago that this would have turned into such a close race?"

"I guess more people want change than we anticipated."

"Talking about change, let me introduce you to the leader of Citizens for a Better Charleston, Leo Dukakis, and his wife, Lydia Lesser."

"Hi," I said as we shook hands. "I'm Mike Romano. So you're the leader of the Young Turks?" I liked his firm, dry grip.

Lydia took my hand. "Mike, we've heard quite a lot about you from Ruth Bloom. She thinks highly of you. You played an important role in getting the ball rolling for Elaine."

"All I did was arrange for some people to meet; the rest was pure luck."

"We heard it was rather more than that."

I shrugged.

"And guess what?" said Mrs. Bouchon, barely able to contain herself. "Mr. Daniel Rivers and I will be running for seats in the General Assembly in the next election."

"You're kidding!"

"Lydia and Leo have talked me into it. If either of us wins, it'll be the first time since Reconstruction that a Negro has held public office in South Carolina."

"That's even bigger than what's happening here tonight."

"Exactly," said Lydia quietly.

"Well," I said, "count me in to help you in any way I can."

"Thank you, my dear. I know I can depend on you."

Suddenly a roar erupted from the crowd up front. We all turned, anxious to hear what had happened. The word spread like wildfire that the race was now 51 percent to 49 percent in favor of Simmons. The gap was closing, with more precincts yet to report.

Leo said, "Getting people registered to vote and overseeing the write-ins is paying off even greater dividends than we had hoped."

I began to edge away to get closer to the action.

"Hold on," said Leo. "Let me give you my card."

"Me too," Lydia said.

Taking both, I glanced at them: Lydia Lesser, attorney at law; Leo Dukakis, ship's chandler. Very interesting.

"Sorry," I said, "I don't have any cards. My business doesn't really require it." Maybe it was time I got some.

Lydia took out another card and asked for my phone number and address. "We'll be in touch."

I didn't need either a lawyer or a boat engine.

I finally made it to my destination with bruised elbows. I stood next to Elaine and Elizabeth, whose eyes were fixed, trancelike, on the television screens. They didn't notice my arrival.

I did my Bogey again for Elaine. "Sweetheart, if I'd known this would be such a close race, I'd have placed a five-dollar bet on you."

"Quiet! This is too important to fool with."

"OK, I'll rejoin the unwashed masses." She ignored me as I walked away.

Three hours later Julie asked impatiently, "*When* will this blooming thing be over with? It's getting close to midnight. I've got class tomorrow."

"Soon," Tom responded. "A few irregularities at the polls needed to be worked out."

I laughed. "Yeah, I'll say. Two poll managers duked it out, one breaking the other's jaw and both ending up in the hoosegow."

"You've got to expect that sort of thing, Mike. No one thought this would come down to a dead heat. There's a lot riding on it for both sides."

"Well," said a testy Rina, "I'm bored and tired of all this too. And if nothing happens in the next fifteen minutes, I'll drive Julie home. Mike can give you a ride whenever this circus is finished."

I had to take a leak or go blind, so I excused myself and headed for the john. When I was halfway there, pandemonium broke out. I turned to see Elizabeth being helped onto a table, a mic in her hand.

"Quiet, please! Quiet," she shouted. "It's now official. Elaine has won the Senate seat by two hundred eighty-six votes!"

The crowd roared in delight, and the band struck up "Happy Days Are Here Again."

I had only ever seen something like this in a Hollywood movie. Full bladder and all, I stoically turned back, not wanting to miss any of the action.

Signaling the band to stop, Elizabeth said, "Ladies and gentlemen, I give you Elaine Sutcliffe, our new state senator from Charleston!"

She handed the mic down to Elaine, who stood with Arthur at her side, and more cheers erupted from supporters, who moved in close to get a better look at her.

Flushed and breathless, Elaine said, "Thank you all for your unwavering faith in me. I especially want to thank my wonderful staff—Debbie, Ruth, and my lifelong friend, Elizabeth—who have worked tirelessly to make this happen. I also thank the grand coalition of liberals and minorities whose support made this possible."

Putting her hand over her heart and gazing mistily somewhere beyond the crowd, she said, "I pledge myself to represent all the people of Charleston and this great state of South Carolina."

That was going to be tricky to do given that most of those who had voted against her abhorred the idea of integration, and many considered that the lower classes, the poor, and minorities were a drain on society. Nevertheless her victory surely signaled that changes were taking place, whether the bigots or the hucksters liked it or not.

Having finished her blessedly short speech, Elaine moved through the crowd, shaking hands, hugging, gushing, and thanking her supporters.

Julie said, "Can we please go now?"

I hesitated for a moment, wanting to bask in the glow of the political victory I had played a part in—but then I thought better of it. We said good-bye to the Averys and slipped out back, where I hosed down an old oak that had to have been a sapling at the time of John C. Calhoun's birth.

THIRTY FOUR

A few days before Christmas, my happy holiday mood was shattered. I discovered that Polk had cheated me from being leading agent for the year. Seeking revenge in the best way he knew, he had arranged for his henchman and fellow Mississippian Bodine to load up his books with bogus insurance sales. The more I tried to convince myself that it didn't matter, the more upset I became. I wanted the company plaque that named me number one.

Growing up I'd been made to feel that I would be a failure. One of my uncles had told me repeatedly that I'd wind up like my old man, a loser pushing a cab around New York City. Worse than that I'd found out that some folks in the neighborhood speculated that one day I'd end up in the penitentiary. The plaque would have proven them all wrong, and I could have stuck it in their faces. Depressed, I quietly left the office to begin my day's work.

Around noon I walked into Moses's joint out of the rainy, cold day. He pulled out a beer and plunked it down on the bar. We had become good friends over the two years I had been servicing his insurance. Occasionally, when he wasn't busy, and I had the time, we would play a couple of games of checkers in the midafternoon, talking, drinking, and smoking.

As I sat down, he said, "What the hell's wrong, man? You look like you been at war with the devil himself."

I gave him the picture of all that had been happening.

He leaned his meaty arms on the bar. "A beer ain't good enough for that. Let me get you and me a whiskey."

We raised our glasses to each other and threw the liquor down fast.

Pouring another shot, he lit up a stogie and squinted at me through a cloud of noxious smoke. "Duke, you'll never be a free man working for the company. All you'll be is just some fancy slave in a suit. When the company's tired of you because they cain't suck no more of your blood, they'll turn you out like some old mule to go die in the field. If you're smart enough to do the job for the man, why the hell don't you do it for yourself? Do like me. I learned the bar business when I was working for one of the meanest niggers you could ever imagine. He worked me to the bone day and night. Finally I'd saved up enough money—and stole enough from him—that ten years later I owned my own place. So here I am. Fifteen more years have passed. I got me a brand-new Caddy out front, a contented wife, two kids in college, and a house free and clear."

"You're right, Moses. I am a slave. Never thought of it that way. I just have to figure a way to get free and do my own thing."

He nodded slightly. As he began to pour us both another shot, the door was blasted open by a guy pushing a heavy dolly loaded with boxes of beer.

"Damn that son of a bitch!" Moses shouted. "If I've told him once I've told him a hundred times: go easy on that door! One of these days he's goin' to rip it off the hinges."

Charging out from behind the bar, he read the delivery guy the riot act and then told him where to unload. Swiveling my stool around to watch the action, I spotted a discarded newspaper at one of the tables. The headline screamed, "Off-duty Cops Caught in Early Morning Burglaries of Stores and Warehouses by Fellow Officers!"

How ironic, I thought, chuckling to myself. Further reading revealed that the city administration had promised a full investigation and shake-up of the police department.

Moses returned to the bar, yelling over his shoulder to the delivery guy to be careful on his way out. The man nodded sheepishly as he backed out the door.

"Asshole," Moses grumbled, picking up his cigar.

"Talking about assholes, did you read the paper?" I asked, pointing to the headline.

"Yeah, don't surprise me none. In one way I'm glad they're gone; in another I'm not. I sure don't need some sheriff in a white hat tryin' to clean up Dodge to make all them righteous folk happy. Duke, they's goin' to be doin' some hard time in the joint, and I don't just mean time. The cons up there don't much care for the dirty cops. Wouldn't surprise me any if you might hear someday that one of them died with a crowbar shoved up his ass."

The thought made me flinch.

"Columbia's a bad prison," I said. "Reminds me of a dungeon."

"So how you know that, man?"

"I was up there when I was a marine prison guard, learning some of their techniques on how to manage and control inmates. It's one ugly place. When some of the other marines and I were speaking with one of the guards, he pointed to two chain-link fences with concertina wire coiled across the top. He told us that the previous day, a prisoner had tried to make a break. The man cleared the first fence, but the guard in the tower blew his head off just as he reached the top of the second one. The guards were hacked that they had the unpleasant duty of cutting the corpse free and washing bits of brain and blood off the wire. They don't fuck around."

"Was the prisoner white or black?" asked Moses.

"We never thought to ask."

Dropping the subject abruptly, he said, "Do you have some time for a game of checkers?"

I looked at my watch. I really didn't, but I obliged him.

He beat me in less than ten minutes. As I bowed out and headed for the door, he called out, "Don't forget, Duke. If you're goin' to be wearing chains in this life, make sure you own them."

Halfheartedly going about my work, Moses's words rang in my ears. I decided to take a break and get a cup of coffee at the Fort

Sumter Hotel. Comfortable in a quiet corner of the restaurant that afforded me a view of James Island, I watched some dedicated fishermen baiting their hooks and casting their lines into the river. How might I go about establishing my independence? Thirty minutes passed with no epiphany. I rose in frustration to leave, and out of the corner of my eye I saw a car pass by with a sign on the door advertising Pendergast Realty. Eureka! I would start my own real estate company. After all selling was selling, whether it was insurance, cars, or real estate. Didn't my mother always say I could talk the birds out of the trees?

With that thought in mind, I set off eagerly to see Elias Pendergast.

"Mike, to what do I owe the pleasure of this surprise visit?"

"I've come to pick your brains about how to start a real estate company."

He looked at me blankly for a second or two, and then he laughed. "You've come seeking information from me...in order to become...my competitor?"

Shit. "Sorry, Elias. I really didn't think about it that way."

Smiling broadly, he said, "I know you didn't. Come into my office, and tell me what's got you so fired up about going into real estate."

I took a seat across from him as he sat behind his large, mahogany desk.

He said, "So what's going on?"

I told him about the day's events that had finally led me to him. He listened patiently without interrupting, and when I had finished he said, "Your manager sounds like a complete imbecile. My God, good salesmen are hard to find in any field. But Michael, you can't just snap your fingers and boom! You open a real estate company. It takes two years working under a broker and three exams before you can get your broker's license. *Then* you can open your own office."

"Dammit, I had no idea."

"Obviously not, Mike," he said wryly. "May I ask you what you're making annually in the insurance business?"

"About fourteen thousand dollars."

"That's a lot of money. Not something you want to give up that easily. Most agents who make it in real estate average about ten thousand, and I can tell you that the vast majority who get their first-year salesman license quit because they can't make a decent living."

"It's that hard?"

"It really is. Out of the two dozen or so agents I have, six are responsible for seventy percent of my company's total production. It's not an easy business. But I'll tell you what I can do for you."

He reached into his desk drawer and pulled out a small red book and handed it to me. It was titled *First-Year Salesman Examination*.

"Study this," he said. "Pass this exam, and get the clock ticking toward the two-year requirement to become a broker. Keep your present job, since it pays so well, and work under my banner to sell real estate on the side. Or you can refer clients to me, which will earn you twenty-five percent in commissions from any sale I make off them. This way you'll learn the business, become known as an agent, and put extra money away until the day comes when you know you want to set up your own company."

"That all figures, Elias. Thank you. I really appreciate your advice and help."

"Well," he said, laughing, "I hope I won't regret it and find myself working for *you*."

I rose to shake his hand. I noticed a photo of a young soldier on the bookshelf. I asked who it was.

"My son, Jeff," he replied quietly. "He died after the Korean War. When he came back, he wasn't Jeff anymore. We couldn't reach him no matter how hard we tried. He dove into a bottle for a couple of years and then one night put a gun to his head and ended it all on the beach."

"Oh, Jesus, Elias, I'm so sorry." I wished I hadn't seen the picture.

"It's been fourteen years. Not a day passes that Trish and I don't think about him," he said somberly.

"Do you have any other kids?"

"No, we couldn't have any more." He sighed heavily. "By the way how do you stand with the marine corps? Any chance they might call you up?"

"There's always a chance, but I doubt it. Four more months, and my obligation to them is done."

"Good. War is...such a waste."

We parted with promises to see each other for dinner soon.

"My God, Julie, this veal is excellent."

"Well, it should be. I had to beat it to death for an hour to get it tender enough. It would have been a heck of a lot easier to make a shepherd's pie," she grumbled.

I ignored that comment. "And the sweet sherry was a good substitute for Marsala in the sauce."

"Hey, we have to improvise down here. Not that I've ever tasted Marsala wine."

"Yeah," I replied. "And I'm tired of having to use cottage cheese instead of ricotta when we make lasagna. Maybe one day the stores down here will start carrying the stuff we need."

"Don't hold your breath, Michael. It may take decades."

"So how did your day go, honey?"

"Fine," she replied casually. "Nothing big to report. I went to class and finished my experiment in the lab. How was yours?"

"Bittersweet."

"Uh-oh. What happened?"

I began to recount the day's events.

"That little pissant!" Julie hissed.

"It's OK, baby. Could you pass me the Parmesan, please?"

"How can something that awful be OK?"

"I considered what happened to be providential," I said rather loftily.

Peering at me while sipping her wine, she waited for me to follow up. I described my conversation with Moses.

"Well, I think he's spot on," said Julie. "You're not cut out to work for a company, and I like you for it. You won't let anyone force fit you into their mold. You stand up and fight."

"I love you, baby," I said, relieved that she was behind me.

"Same here," she responded briskly. "So what are you going to do?"

I told her about my visit to see Elias. The plan of action to set me free intrigued her. Then she looked a little worried and chewed slowly. "But can you put up with bloody Polk for two more years?"

"I will if I have to. As the cons say, I can do the time standing on my head."

As I heard my own words, it hit me: Polk was the personification of the slave in the suit. Controlled by bone-crushing fear to produce, he ruled others the same way, making their lives equally miserable. It had robbed him of most of his humanity and his health. He was the perfect company man.

Thirty Five

Julie, Kitty, Burl, and I were in high spirits as our plane touched down at the Miami airport on a fine March morning. We picked up our luggage and hailed a cab to take us to the fabled Fontainebleau Hotel. Even though Burl hadn't qualified for the all-expenses-paid, three-day holiday for top agents in the company, he claimed he had come along as Kitty's chaperone and bodyguard. We checked in after a twenty-minute ride and agreed to meet at one that afternoon for lunch. Kitty and Burl walked off, squabbling over whether they should go first to the bar or their room.

A hovering bellhop picked up our bags and escorted us to our suite. As he opened the door, I swept Julie into my arms and carried her across the threshold like a new bride, spinning her about in the room.

Embarrassed and pulling down her skirt, she yelled, "Put me down!"

"OK." I dropped her on the bed like a rock.

Amused, the Latino bellhop asked if there was anything more he could do for us.

"No, thanks, pal." I slapped a dollar into his palm. "But if I need anything later, you're my man."

He tipped his cap and left.

Sitting on the edge of the bed, looking a bit ruffled, Julie said, “You know you’re barmy, don’t you?”

“I must be. You keep telling me so.”

She shook her head and unwittingly echoed Elaine’s words. “You are impossible!”

Still wanting to tease her, I pointed to the bags. “Well?”

“Well what?” she said, a glint in her eyes.

“Aren’t you going to unpack like a good little squaw while I take a smoke out on that nice balcony?”

“Squaw, my arse.” She hurled pillows at me.

Ducking, I rushed her and wrestled her to the mattress while she tried to wriggle away.

When I finally released her, she sat up and said breathlessly, “When the big chief goes beddie bye tonight, he may wake up in the morning and find one of his big feathers cut off.”

She took my proffered hand, and we walked out onto the balcony.

“Isn’t it just gorgeous, Michael? The ocean here is such an incredible color—a mixture of sapphire and emerald.”

“Sure is. I haven’t seen waters like this since I was cruising the Caribbean.”

“It’s so different from Charleston, with all these modern hotels and art deco buildings. I like it. It has an eye to the future.”

I was feeling weary. I hadn’t slept well the night before. I pulled up a deck chair and propped my feet on the balcony railing.

Julie wrinkled her nose. “Oh well. I guess I’ll have to do the unpacking.”

I smiled at her, closed my eyes, and soon nodded off while listening to the rhythm of the surf.

“Michael,” I heard a voice calling me from outside my pleasant reverie. I felt a hand gently stroking my shoulder.

“Michael, wake up. It’s time to go for lunch.” The strokes turned to rather firm pats. Still bleary-eyed, I asked Julie how long I’d been out.

“About forty-five minutes. You were dead to the world. But we’ve got to get going. Throw some water on your face.”

Back in the lobby, we headed for the restaurant. Seated at a round corner booth were Burl and Kitty, decked out in beach attire. Julie was in her white shorts and a loose tank top—I was the odd man out.

"Hey there, boy," said Burl. "Don't you have any fancy Miami duds like we do?"

He was dazzling in a multicolored Hawaiian shirt, shorts drooping down over hairy legs, and disreputable leather sandals with black socks.

"He fell asleep and didn't have time to change," Julie said rather defensively.

"I thought you marines were tough. A little plane ride got you all tuckered out?"

"I guess they don't make 'em like you any more, Burl," I said.

Kitty, wearing a pretty green sarong over her black bathing suit, said, "You got that right! But I guarantee he'll be in bed by nine o'clock."

Ignoring her remark Burl took a long suck on a horrible-looking blue beverage decorated with little flowers and a paper umbrella, all arranged in a Dali-esque glass. He nearly poked his eye out on the umbrella and pulled it out in disgust.

"What the heck is that you're drinking, Burl?" I asked.

"I don't rightly know. It's got some fancy island name. It's kinda sweet, but I tell you, after three or four of these you won't care what they call them."

"Well, hell, I'll try one," I said.

Opening her oversized, straw bag, Kitty handed Julie a schedule of events that agents and spouses were required to attend.

Julie scanned the list. "This is great. The agents have only a one-hour meeting tomorrow at nine. Then we all get together on Sunday at seven for a gala dinner where the president gives a keynote speech to agents and spouses. Other than that there's nothing we have to go to."

"Hey, since today's free, why don't we rent a car and tour Miami together?" I said.

"Mike," said Kitty, "you and Julie are young. Go out and have a good time. Burl and I are happy just to lie around the pool and enjoy this great hotel. Besides, knowing him, he'll be ready for a nap after lunch."

"What're you talking about, woman? I ain't got my ass in second gear yet."

"That's because you don't have a second gear anymore, you old coot."

Burl tried unsuccessfully to keep a stern frown on his face as we laughed.

Then he said, wiggling his unruly eyebrows at Kitty, "That's a maybe, but me and my first gear wouldn't mind a bit of a lie down on that big bed this afternoon."

Kitty flushed prettily and sat up straight. "I think we all need to eat. Let's order!"

An hour after finishing lunch, Julie and I were cruising Biscayne Boulevard in our rented Chevy. We passed by a good-looking dame in a stunning, hot-pink bikini and high heels walking a white poodle clad in a tiny mink drape. Even though the temperature was already in the high seventies, the chick looked cool to me.

"You'd never see that in Charleston," I said. I watched her shapely behind in my rearview mirror.

"I don't think you'd see it anywhere else but here." Julie laughed.

"How about Vegas?"

"Yeah, maybe. Perhaps we should go there and check it out."

"You've got to admit, she looked great."

"A little too garish, don't you think, dear?"

"Well, maybe she's working for the chamber of commerce."

"Hmm. Like a neon sign for a family vacation."

After touring the swanky Miami Beach area, we decided to go into the city. I had read that it had been heavily Latinized since the Cuban revolution, and in an odd way I felt connected to its people, having been in and out of Gitmo for more than two years and participating in the blockade of the island during the missile crisis. Besides, I thought, it would be fun to visit Little Havana and have dinner there, then go dancing at one of the hot nightspots I'd heard about.

As we walked hand in hand along Calle Ocho, Little Havana's bustling main street packed with shops and restaurants, Julie glimpsed a beautiful sapphire and diamond ring in the window of a jewelry store.

"Oh, Michael, isn't that elegant?" she said wistfully. "I bet it costs a fortune."

"You never know, honey. Let's go in and take a look at it."

We pointed out the ring to the mustachioed older man behind the counter, who took it out of the display. A little tag attached to it indicated a staggering price of $800. He took Julie's hand, bowed slightly with an air of old-world courtesy, and slid the ring onto her finger. It fit perfectly; no sizing would be necessary.

"How much?" I asked, hoping I had misread the price.

"Only eight hundred, sir."

Julie pulled the ring from her finger. "I'm sorry; that's more than we can afford. Thank you anyway."

"You look like a nice young couple, and I'd like to make you happy. I'll discount it by seventy-five."

"Thanks," I said. "We'll have to think it over."

Back out on the street, I said, "Honey, if you really like that ring, we can buy it."

"No, it's absurd to pay so much for a piece of jewelry. You could buy a good secondhand car for that. Anyway, I'd be scared of losing it."

"So would you rather have a car?" I acted confused.

"No! I don't need that either."

I knew her; she wanted the ring. She was just being her usual practical self.

As we strolled down el Calle, we passed old men with leathery, sun-browned skin playing dominoes on the sidewalk. Needing some cigarettes we went into a small tobacco shop. Cigar rollers were engrossed in their work. We picked up four packs of smokes and handed the cashier two bucks. I asked him where would be a good place to eat.

He said enthusiastically, "Casa Adolfina." He wrote down the address for us.

I thanked him, and we headed back to the hotel to take a shower and change into evening attire.

At seven thirty Adolfina's was packed. The predominant language being spoken was Spanish. We were told we would have to wait at least half an hour, but if we wished we could have a drink at the bar until a table came free. We made our way through the smoky haze and were lucky to snag two newly abandoned bar stools.

The two bartenders frantically working the noisy bar took no notice of us. After several minutes, I'd had enough of waiting and yelled out for service. Finally the younger of the two came over with many apologies, and we ordered. As we settled in, we looked the place over. It wasn't too impressive. White masonry walls enclosed mismatched tables and chairs. Brown wrapping paper covered the tabletops. There were few decorative touches—some forlorn candles sputtering in jelly jars and a tattered travel poster showing a sultry dancing girl in a low-cut, frilly dress holding a couple of maracas. But the food going out looked good and smelled even better.

Then I spotted a large, black-and-white photograph of a young man hanging on the back wall. A black drape hung across the top of the frame. When the bartender returned with our drinks, I asked him about it. He said it was the son of the restaurant owner, Señora Adolfina. He had died at the Bay of Pigs, in the failed effort to liberate Cuba from the tyrant Fidel Castro.

I wanted to ask him more, but he was hailed by a group of loud, burly men at the other end of the bar.

"It must be terrible to lose a son in that way," Julie said.

"And for what, Julie? So they could overthrow a socialist government that just got rid of a capitalist one that exploited its people and kowtowed to US business interests? To end right back in the same boat? I'm glad Kennedy didn't back them up. It could have gotten me killed and hundreds of others like me, and for nothing more than to protect the fat-cat Cubans and Americans. The way I look at it, you've got either the tyranny of the right or the tyranny of the left. Take your choice. Either way the people get screwed in the end."

"Which one would you choose, then?" Julie asked.

"Both. The two aren't necessarily incompatible. But with honest government, they could be the left and right hands of a good system."

"You're talking about a symbiotic relationship between organisms. But left to their own individual devices, they would each become parasitic in the end, destroying both themselves and their hosts."

"I've never heard it put that way, Julie, but I think you've hit the nail on the head. Maybe you should give up microbiology and become a politician."

"Not on your sweet life. I'll leave that to the Elaine Sutcliffes of this world."

Just as we finished our first round of drinks and were considering another, we were informed that our table was ready. We were led through the crowd to a rickety corner table next to a raucous group of Cubans that included a woman laughing like a hyena. With that and the racket of an ancient wall air conditioner close by, hearing each other was nearly impossible. Nevertheless the food was very good and brought to us promptly. Julie had half a roasted chicken covered with a spicy brown sauce, served with black beans, white rice, and fried plantains. I, less adventurous, had a flank steak covered with onions, served with the ubiquitous white rice and black beans and a salad, which we shared.

We were stuffed by the time we finished and decided to bypass dessert and coffee. We wanted to leave the noisy, hot environment. We paid the bill and left the elderly waiter a generous tip for his excellent service.

As we wandered up the street, looking for a place to boogie, we heard music drifting toward us through the soft night air. We followed the pulse of bongo drums and came upon an open patio with a bar filled with chattering people. Inside, couples were dancing to hot Cuban music played by a quintet of guys in loose, white, embroidered shirts and tight, black trousers.

We watched the action for a while, and then I said to Julie, "We can do that! Just keep your caboose loose."

"Michael, this caboose was designed to be loose. It's yours you have to worry about."

We shimmied onto the floor. How easily she moved her hips seductively to the beat, flowing with the music, her arms held out wide and her white skirt swirling around her hips! I was getting hot watching her, and I noticed other guys ogling her movements. As she continued to dance, losing herself in the hypnotic beat, she was the epitome of pure sensuality. I had never before seen her dance like that.

When the music ended, we headed for the bar, breathless.

A voice behind us called, "Hey, amigo."

I turned and saw a tough-looking guy waving us over to a large table where several couples were already seated.

"You dance pretty good for gringos," he said. "Pull up a chair. Let us buy you a drink."

Julie and I collapsed into empty seats, and a Hispanic beauty asked her when she had learned the Cuban dance.

"Just five minutes ago." Julie laughed.

"You're a natural," she said, surprised, "But with all respect to your boyfriend, he needs to take lessons."

We introduced ourselves. Our host, Armando, asked what we would like to drink.

"Two beers will be fine," I responded.

Armando, looking over at another guy, said, "Ernesto, go pick up the beer." He handed him a fistful of paper. Then he said, "You are obviously not from around here. Are you vacationing?"

I told him we were from Charleston on a business trip.

"Hey, man, I don't mean where you living now, but where you from? Your lady seems to be Inglesa."

"Yes," said Julie, a bit peeved that she was being excluded from the conversation.

"And you, Miguel?"

"New York."

"Ah, a true Yankee! So what brought you to the South?"

"The marine corps."

In the ensuing silence, Armando pushed up the short sleeve of my summer shirt and examined the tattoo on my arm.

"How many years did you carry a gun for your country?"

I replied, "It's your country now too, isn't it?"

They all nodded yes.

"So how many years?" he asked.

"Four."

"Where were you stationed?" the inquisition continued.

"With the Second Marine Division at Camp Lejeune."

"Ah, so you must have been doing business in the Caribbean?"

"Yeah, for more than two and a half years. Almost all the major Islands: Puerto Rico, Dominican Republic, Jamaica, and Cuba."

"So you were around for the Bay of Pigs?"

"I was on Vieques, playing war games."

"You were playing while our amigos were being cut down on the beach in the Bay of Pigs?"

The increasingly hostile questions were making me edgy. "Hey, I didn't even know that shit was going down. I only found out when I got back to the States."

"Well, if you marines had backed us up, I'd be drinking in Havana tonight—not here." He made a sweeping gesture encompassing the bar, the street, and the city.

"Marines follow orders, like any other good soldiers. If you want to know why we weren't there, ask Kennedy."

"Kennedy's dead," came the hot reply.

"Right. So we'll never know, will we? But I'll tell you what, *amigo*, if they had turned us loose, a week after our landing, Fidel, Raul, and Che would have been hanging dead by their feet in the Plaza Viejo in Havana, their bodies torched."

I had seemingly won him over with those fiery words. He locked his arm behind my neck and pulled my head to his. Tears welled in his eyes. "If only it could have been so, man. If only it could have been."

Then he yelled out, "Another round of drinks for all of us!"

By midnight I was shit-faced with my new compadres, trying to sing some Spanish song along with them. Julie snagged the car keys from my pocket, grabbed my arm, and said firmly, "Time to go. You've got a meeting in the morning."

Everyone rose and hugged like family.

Armando's final words, as he swayed in the gateway, were, "May the Holy Mother watch over you on your travels through life."

Not suffering too much from the previous night's excesses, I parked myself next to Kitty in the large meeting room. I asked if she had seen Polk.

"Yes, when I first came in. I think he's sitting somewhere up front. Did you have fun last night?" Kitty asked.

"You wouldn't believe the fun we had. It was an incredible night."

"Maybe Burl and I should have gone out with you. Tell me what happened."

Just as I had begun to fill her in, Mr. Tylke went to the podium and tapped the mic to get everyone's attention.

"Tell you later, Kitty."

"Ladies and gentlemen, welcome to Miami Beach. I hope you're all having a good time."

Enthusiastic applause and hoots rang through the room.

"You're here because you are all winners. Not content with mediocrity, you persevere until you succeed. You're the cream of the crop in our great company. This holiday is our way to honor and thank you. And now, with no more ado, I give you...our executive vice president, Mr. James Morse."

I'd never met Morse and was struck first by his good looks. He was tall and lean and had a full crop of wiry, gray hair. In his tailored, dark-blue suit and pale-blue tie, he projected an air of confidence and power.

Pausing briefly as he looked us over, he said in a commanding voice, "All of you stand up and give yourselves a round of applause."

"Oh, Jesus," moaned Kitty, as we stood reluctantly, feeling like schoolkids as we obliged him.

Then he signaled to us to be seated and began a lengthy oration about how wonderful the company was and how great we were. The audience was eating it up.

Not paying much attention and clapping like a robot when others did, I heard Kitty grumble, "I hope this is over soon. I really need to go to the ladies' room."

I crossed my eyes at her, making a goofy face. "Me too," which set her laughing and earned reproachful looks from those around us.

Finally Morse uttered his last words, which I didn't hear, and handed the microphone back to Tylke, who said, "You are all winners."

This was getting really repetitive. He needed a new speech writer.

Tylke paused, searching the audience. His eyes fell on me. He said, "But even among the best, some stand out. I want to take this opportunity to call one young man up here. He is unaware that he is about to address you today. He is the leading agent among all our new agents in the company. Mike Romano! Come up here and say a few words to the folks."

Stunned, I looked at Kitty, who grinned broadly and nudged me to stand up. What the heck was I going to say? Tylke shook my hand and then gave up the podium to me.

As I paused, trying to find the right words, the comic in me came to the rescue.

I took a deep breath. "Ladies and gentlemen, I want you all to know that if you send me back to Congress, I promise on the head of my blessed mother that I will steal less money from you than I did in my last term."

Everyone cracked up, including Polk, who I could see shaking his head and no doubt thinking, *That sumbitch!*

I gestured like a true politician for the audience to quiet down. Then, serious, I said, "As you heard from Mr. Tylke, this is a big surprise to me, so what I have to say won't take long."

Starting slowly, I said, "Care about the people who you sell to and serve. They are more than just a commission that you put in your pocket. Take a genuine interest in their lives. Show compassion in their times of trouble. Help them in any way you can when they are in need, no matter the color of their skin, economic status, political beliefs, or religion. And never, *never* sell them more than they can afford. Stay after them to keep their insurance current, reminding them how important it is. If you do all this with true sincerity, you won't have to sell: they will come to you to buy."

Ending on that simple message, I stepped away from the podium to a round of polite applause.

Mr. Tylke and Mr. Morse rose to congratulate me and shake my hand. Tylke presented me with the much sought-after plaque that I had wanted.

Then Morse stepped forward and said, "The company has something for you, Mr. Romano." He slipped his hand into his inside jacket pocket and pulled out a cashier's check for $1,000.

Delighted, I thanked him and then made my way back to my seat. Some agents stood to congratulate me, patting my back and shaking my hand.

"You deserve it, Mike," said Kitty. "But don't forget what I told you that day about moving on to something better."

Soon after, Tylke closed the meeting by saying, "Work hard, and qualify again. Next year New Orleans!"

Saying good-bye to Kitty, I dashed off to find a hotel phone, hoping that Julie hadn't yet left for the pool, where I was supposed to meet her. Luckily she was still in the room.

"Hey, baby, I'm going to be hung up for a while. Some of the big wheels have insisted that a few of the new agents join them for a drink at the bar. So you might want to consider putting off going out until I get back."

"I ran across some really nice women after breakfast, and we agreed to meet at the pool. So take your time, and for heaven's sake, don't drink too much, It's only just after ten."

"Don't worry. I'll stick with ginger ale."

"Uh-huh," she replied, her bullshit meter seemingly working just fine.

"OK, honey, I'll see you when I see you. Have a good time."

Hanging up, I headed for the desk manager to see about getting my check cashed. After a pleasant exchange of greetings, I told him what I needed and handed him the check. He eyed it a bit dubiously and then enquired if I was a guest at the hotel.

"Yes, room twelve fifteen."

He asked for identification, and I gave him my driver's license. Flicking the corner of the check with his finger, he said, "I'll be right back, sir." A few minutes later, he returned and counted out ten big ones for me. I thanked him and took off like a shot, burning rubber back to Little Havana.

"*Buenos dias, señor,*" said the ebullient, mustachioed Pete. "Are you here to buy that lovely ring your charming wife adored?"

"Yes," I replied, slapping six C-notes on the glass counter top.

"But *señor,* I told you seven twenty-five only yesterday."

"I know, but I'm saying six, in cash, right now."

He hesitated, looking at the greenbacks, but then came back with his seven twenty-five.

"I understand, sir," I said, scooping up the cash. "You have overhead and a family to feed. But so do I. No hard feelings, my friend?"

As I headed to the door, he said, "Six seventy-five. I cannot go lower without losing money."

I knew that was a con, but I turned back to him. "OK. We have a deal."

I peeled off the cash and handed it to him.

"But *señor,* the price was for the ring only. It did not include the sales tax."

Damnation! I was a real dummy for forgetting that. Nevertheless, I coughed up, knowing I would have given him the full price if he had insisted. I wasn't about to let that ring get away from me.

Back at the Fontainebleau, I roamed the large pool area, looking for Julie. I finally found her chatting with two other women, lying on her front on a lounge chair.

"Hey, baby, I'm back."

She rolled over, propped herself up on her elbows, and then gazed at me over her sunglasses.

"You faker, you! What've you been up to? I heard about what happened in the meeting."

Grasping at straws, I said, "I ran into the lady with the poodle. We had a long conversation about dog grooming."

She laughed out loud. "Come on, you can do better than that."

Her new friends were looking back and forth as if they were at a tennis match.

"Come on, Michael, come clean with me."

I knew the game was up. I was caught in my own web. I pulled the little box from my pocket. As I did, she breathed, "I suspected as much, you wonderful fool!"

Unwrapping it under the close watch of the two gals, she brought her hand to her heart and took a deep breath. "It's even more beautiful than I remembered!"

"You lucky girl," one of the women said enviously.

I took the ring from her and placed it on her left ring finger, next to her wedding band. She lifted her hand to the sunlight, admiring the color and brilliance of the stones. Then she got up and gave me a long, loving kiss as she pressed her cold, wet bathing suit against me.

THIRTY SIX

After more than an hour in line outside the South Carolina Highway Patrol building behind Pinehaven shopping center, I was still waiting to get my '66 license plates and only halfway to making it inside the squat, one-story building. Upset, as were others, by the long line, I engaged in conversation with those in my immediate vicinity. Exhausted with venting our frustration, we agreed to hold each other's place in line to give a break to take a leak or buy a cup of coffee. Taking my turn to go get a soda at Patrick's Deli, I saw Sergeant Lopez leaving the building. I hadn't seen him since the day I'd gotten out of the corps.

"Sergeant Lopez!" I called out.

He turned and looked at me blankly, not recognizing me. I guessed it was the long hair and the suit.

"It's me," I shouted. "Corporal Romano."

"*Dios*!" he said as he walked briskly over to me with his hand extended, and then pumped my arm in a hearty handshake.

"So, what's happening, Romano? You look good!"

"Hey, do me a favor. The name's Mike."

"OK. So you call me Roberto—or Bob—yes? Y'know, I'll soon be a civilian like you," he said cheerfully.

"How long d'you have to go?"

"Seven months, twenty-four days," he checked his watch, "thirteen hours," he dropped his arm quickly like he was starting a race, "and...five seconds!"

I cracked up. I'd never seen this side of him before; usually he was very serious. I offered him a smoke, which he accepted, and, cupping my Zippo against the steady April wind, lit us both up.

Taking a long drag and then exhaling, he bowed his head and said quietly, "Mike, I want to apologize for not making it to Pug's funeral. The guy who backed me up in the galley was on leave, and you know how tough it is to get out three squares for more than seventy men."

Made uneasy by his unnecessary confession, and not wanting to offend him by telling him I hadn't noticed his absence, I said, "I understand, Sergeant, er, Bob. You were a good friend to Pug, as you are to me."

Wanting to drop the sad topic, I asked him for news of the command.

"Well, your nemesis, Sergeant Pratt, retired and got himself a job somewhere in the South as a security guard."

"Holy shit! God help those people wherever he is, with him wearing a badge and carrying a piece!"

"Yeah. He's a real prick."

"Anything else?"

"Unfortunately, yes. We lost Corporal Bell."

"What happened?"

"He got killed just before Christmas at Da Nang, during a mortar attack."

"*Damn!* He had a wife and a kid."

"Yeah, but there's more bad news. Gunny Starr's back. He lost both his legs."

"Oh shit, no! *No!* How, for Christ's sake?"

"I don't really know the details, but he and his men got ambushed when their Huey set down in a hot landing zone."

Still stunned, I asked, "What's he doing back here? I thought he and his family had moved out to the West Coast when he got his orders to go to 'Nam."

"No, with being so close to getting out, they thought he'd never be transferred again. They'd bought a house here. They wanted to make Charleston their home. Starr even had a job lined up to work as a guard at the county prison farm. You might want to look in on him—I know you were friends. I do occasionally. But be prepared—he's in a bad state. Angry and depressed most of the time. Hitting the bottle pretty hard. He's bent on destroying himself and refuses to go see a shrink."

"But what's a shrink going to do for him? Grow him a new pair of legs?"

"Yeah, yeah, I know. But he won't do any physical therapy either. He's withering away...He's not the man we once knew."

"What about his wife?" I asked.

"She holds down a job at the Kress department store, trying to make ends meet. So when she's off at work and the kids are at school, he's left alone, brooding. He curses God and the country for his troubles."

"Hell, can you blame him? He's been fucked by both."

We stood silently. Then I said, "Look, I've got to get back in line. We'll finish this some other time. Where's he living?"

"West Oak Forest, on Lord Byron Drive. I don't remember the number, but you can look it up."

"Thanks. Let's make sure we stay in touch, Bob. I'll call you."

An hour later I had my plates and registration and headed back to the debit. I had a lot of work to catch up on. Even so, my thoughts kept going back to Gunny. I owed him.

At dinner I told Julie about my chance meeting with Lopez and asked if she knew anyone at the hospital who might be able to give me any information on wounded veterans.

"I don't. Look, I know you want to help him, but if he's refusing to see a physical therapist or psychiatrist, what can *you* do?"

"I don't know, but I'm trying to figure something out."

"I realize that, but I don't want you to depress yourself by trying." Picking up the dinner plates, her hands shook. She blurted out, "It could have been you. I don't know how his poor wife and kids can cope. Damn this war, Michael, and all the others! It's such a horrible waste of lives on all sides. When will we ever learn?"

The next day, around noon, I picked up a six-pack and headed for West Oak Forest. Apprehensive, I rang the doorbell a couple of times. There was no answer. But I knew he had to be in. I walked around to the back of the house and heard a dog barking urgently and Gunny's gravel voice yelling, "Calm down, Basilone!"

Startled by my sudden appearance, he just stared at me, as did the German shepherd, who sat beside his wheelchair.

Casually holding up the beers, I said, "Where's the refrigerator? These are getting warm."

He pointed to an open sliding glass door that had a ramp connected to it. I found my way to the kitchen, put four in the box, and took the other two back outside. Sitting across from him on a wooden bench, I made a point of not looking at the stumps revealed by his shorts. He said nothing, just swigged his beer.

I broke the silence. "You got a nice place here, Gunny."

He still didn't respond, just looked at me expressionless.

I pulled out a pack of smokes and held them out. He just shook his head. Man, he wasn't making it easy for me. Somehow he was punishing me for seeing him this way. So I took another course—a hard one.

"So what the fuck are you going to do with the rest of your life?"

Angrily he wheeled his chair close to me, the big dog rising and coming even closer. I readied myself to roll with whatever blows were coming.

When we were nose to nose, he said, "You were a pain in the ass in the corps, and now you're breaking my balls as a civilian!" The dog growled softly in agreement, his yellow eyes never leaving my face.

"Can't help it, Gunny. Wherever I go, I got a knack for that."

"Jesus fucking Christ," he said, wheeling the chair in reverse.

I relaxed somewhat; I wouldn't be needing a surgeon.

"Why are you here?" he asked.

I told him about my meeting with Lopez.

"Damn that little runt! He won't leave me alone."

"He cares about you, Gunny. He's a lifer like you. If things were reversed, you'd be doing the same."

"So this is a damn social visit?"

"No, it's more than that, and you know why."

He threw down the rest of his beer. I got up and fetched him another.

"Well, what the heck do you think you can do for me, Corporal?"

"I don't know. But I can tell you what I hope for—that you'll get up out of that chair and walk again."

"What makes you think I want to do that, huh?"

"Because you'll never stop being a marine. You were born to it. There are many young kids out there who've been wrecked by this war. They need a gunny to look after them, like you did me."

He closed his eyes and let out a desperate sigh. "Romano, I got no fight left in me."

"Give it time, Gunny. It's there. I know it's there. Now I've got to get back to work. But for God's sake, please allow me to drop in on you now and then."

"OK. But next time bring a case of beer, you stingy bastard. And get your hair cut. You look like a fuckin' hippie!"

Thirty Seven

It was a typical August. Uncomfortably sticky from the immoderate morning temperature, I decided to go home for lunch and take a shower to freshen up. Stopping to collect the mail, I found a slip notifying me that I had a certified letter. I set off immediately to get it. I was a little worried. I'd never received such a communication before.

It was a letter from a law firm named Bowman and Schultz, located in Jacksonville, Florida, informing me that my father was deceased. I was an heir to his estate, and they were acting as executors and all other matters pertaining thereto, and so forth. They requested that I contact them as soon as possible.

Back home in a flash, I dialed the law office number with only mercenary thoughts in my mind. Why not? My father owed me for the scars he had inflicted on me and my mother.

After a few rings, a pleasant female voice answered. I told her who I was and about the letter I'd gotten from Mr. Bowman. Put on hold, I lit up a cigarette and inhaled deeply in anticipation. A long minute or two passed. Then the attorney came on the line and greeted me.

"We had to do a little detective work to locate you, Mr. Romano." Getting right to the point, he said," I require you to come to my office as soon as possible to go over some important aspects of the estate and certain documents you will need to sign.

"However, more important in the immediate," he continued, "is that you notify the Equitable Insurance Company of your father's death. We are holding two policies in the sum of forty thousand dollars each, of which you are the sole beneficiary. But since your father died in a car accident, that amount will be increased to eighty thousand dollars, due to his having added an accidental death rider."

I hadn't thought to ask how he had died.

He gave me the policy numbers and said he would send copies of the death certificate to me and the company. Then he asked me to give him a date when I could go to his office. I told him I would have to check with my employer and my wife and would get back to him the next day.

Hanging up, I was euphoric. I couldn't believe it. What a piece of luck! I wanted to call Julie, but she'd still be in class. Then, on impulse, I left the house, forgetting lunch and the shower, and made tracks for the office.

"Ida, have you seen Jim?"

"Yes, you just missed him. He's over at Bilbro's."

I dashed across the highway and plopped down across from Jim in his booth.

Startled by my unexpected appearance, he said, "What's going on Mike? You look harried."

"I just got news that my father died."

"Good God, Mike. I'm so very sorry to hear that."

"Well, I'm not. He left me some insurance money and a part of his estate."

I could see he was taken aback by my flippant attitude. I gave him some background on my relationship with my old man. When I had finished, he said, "Well, I understand, but he was still your father, Mike." He gazed at me quizzically.

"Yeah, you're right. I'll make sure he gets a nice headstone. Look, I need a favor from you. Can you cover for me on Thursday and Friday?"

"I believe so, but what for?"

I filled him in on my conversation with the attorney.

"I see," he replied. "Well, I don't think it'll be a problem."

"Great! Thanks a million for helping me out, Jim."

Before we could say more, Sweet Thing's replacement, Bertha, interrupted us. She weighed at least two hundred pounds and had the disposition of a pit bull. Business in the diner had dropped off, and Sal had been conspicuously absent from the breakfast table.

Back downtown working, I couldn't stop thinking about the eighty grand. I would finally have the necessary stake in life to catapult me on the way to realizing my dream. What other surprises might be ahead for me in Jacksonville? I decided not to call Julie; I would surprise her in person.

"Hey, forget about cooking tonight, honey," I said. "I've got a strong yen for pizza. We didn't go last week."

"OK with me. I'm bushed."

"Well, maybe one day when we're rich, you won't have to work."

"What makes you think that if we were rich, I'd want to stop working? I enjoy my research."

"Oh, I just meant you'd have the freedom to choose. Maybe go to Rome on a vacation, things like that."

"Dream on! That will be a long way off."

"Well, you never know. Stranger things have happened."

She gave me a suspicious look but said nothing.

"Let's get going before Caruso's gets too crowded," I said.

After we ordered we began our usual ritual of picking the wax off the Chianti bottle candle holder. Then I began to hum loudly, "Arrivederci Roma."

"Michael, you're embarrassing us. What's with this Rome thing anyway?"

"We hit the jackpot, Julie. Eighty thousand worth!"

"Stop your fooling. It's irritating."

"No, I really mean it, baby. And it'll probably be more than eighty. I got news from an attorney earlier this afternoon that my father died, and I'm part heir to his estate."

"Oh, Michael, I'm so sorry!"

I didn't respond to that but brought her up to date on the day's events and asked if she could get the time off to go with me to Florida.

"Certainly, even if I have to lie. I'll tell them I'm going to your father's funeral."

"In one way we are. I want to see his grave site."

"I understand. You need closure, and I want to be there with you."

"It's not closure I need, Julie. I want to make sure the son of a bitch is dead."

We left for Jacksonville on Wednesday after work, so we'd be rested and alert when we saw the lawyer at ten the next morning.

We ascended rapidly in a walnut-paneled elevator to the twelfth floor and exited into a plush corridor. My deadbeat father had been doing business in a place like this? That was ironic. The whole building smelled of money and power, as did the offices of Bowman and Schultz.

"May I help you?" inquired an attractive, red-haired receptionist seated at a modern, glass-topped desk.

I recognized her voice; it was the same pleasant one I had heard when I'd first called.

"Yes, we're the Romanos. I know we're a little early, but we have an appointment with Mr. Bowman."

She smiled. "We've been expecting you. May I get you anything?"

"No, thanks, we're fine."

"Then please take a seat, and make yourselves comfortable."

She went back to her work, whatever it was, while we restlessly scanned magazines. Twenty minutes later a door opened in the hallway. Two impeccably dressed men appeared. One looked as though he had seen the ghost of Christmas past. The other was saying soothingly, "Don't worry now, Frank. I've got everything under control."

After Frank left, the receptionist rose and introduced us. "Mr. Bowman, Mr. and Mrs. Romano are here for their ten o'clock appointment."

"Ah, yes," he said, shaking our hands. He led us into his office, which was lined on three sides with leather-bound law books and various framed degrees here and there, attesting to his competency. One shelf behind him prominently displayed a photograph of a younger version of himself in a tackle position, surrounded by a bunch of football trophies. A bag of fancy golf clubs leaned against one corner.

He pulled out a legal folder from his desk and quickly got down to business.

"The estate of Mr. Romano senior is equally divided between you as his son and his sister, Anna O'Reilly. It breaks down as follows: a home located here in Jacksonville, which is free and clear of all mortgages and encumbrances, appraised at twenty-eight thousand dollars; cash in the bank in the amount of fourteen thousand nine hundred eighty-two dollars; and a small fleet of cabs valued at one hundred and twenty thousand dollars, for which we already have a buyer."

Astounded, Julie and I looked at each other. How the hell had my father amassed all this wealth? He was a drunk, a woman chaser, and a guy who was always short on paying the bills when we had been a family.

Pulling myself together, I asked the lawyer if my father had had any other children.

"No, he didn't, although he was married four times. Allow me to add some pertinent details as to how he acquired this estate, since you had not been in contact with him for a long while. His last wife, now deceased, owned the cab business and the home through *her* deceased previous husband. She bequeathed them to your father upon her death two years ago."

"I see." Things were becoming clearer.

He slid a document across the table to me. It stated that I agreed to the liquidation of the cab company and the house. Then he handed me the two whole-life insurance policies. Now this was something I knew and understood. I scanned through the pages and ran across the names of the designated beneficiaries—only to discover I was the contingent beneficiary. The primary had been his deceased wife.

I may have been second best, but I ended up in first place.

Mr. Bowman said, "I assume you know what to do with these, Mr. Romano, after our earlier conversation." He smiled affably.

"Yes, thank you. I've already informed the insurance company by certified mail that I'm the beneficiary."

"Excellent. And as soon as I complete probate, which shouldn't take too long, we will disperse the assets to you and your aunt."

I asked if he could give me her address and telephone number, and he replied that he saw no reason not to. After he had written the information down on the back of one of his business cards, we all rose and shook hands again, and Julie and I left the office on winged feet.

"Michael, we're rich! It's like a dream," said an ebullient Julie as she sipped her wine in an outdoor café.

"We're not rich, honey; we're well off. Rich is having a million in the bank. We're a long way away from that."

"I must say I'm surprised," she said. "I never knew you wanted to be a millionaire."

"Doesn't everybody? I like the idea of being one and the real power it would give."

Bemused, she said, "Will one million be enough for you, then?"

"Who knows how a person will feel from one day to the next? Right now my ambition is to make that million."

"I guess you need a goal in your life...something to pit yourself against."

"Yes, Julie. It won't be easy, but I figure that if I persevere, with time I'll make it."

After we had finished our drinks, I said, "Let's go back to the hotel, have some lunch, and fool around." Julie cast me a wicked glance.

"And then I'll call my aunt. Hopefully we can see her. I need to know more about my father."

Back in our room, I called the number Bowman had given me.

"Hello?" a man answered the phone.

"May I please speak to Anna O'Reilly?"

"Who's this?" he responded cautiously.

"Mike Romano."

"Blessed Mother!" he said loudly.

In the distance I heard a woman's voice calling, "Who is it, Tim?"

"Oh my God. Anna, *Anna*! Come in here. It's young Mike. Mike Romano!"

I heard footsteps click across a floor.

"Give me that phone, Tim." Then, "Michael, little Mickey, this is your aunt Anna."

"Hello, Aunt Anna. I know this is a surprise, and I apologize."

"Oh no, no. I was so hoping you would call. The attorney told me he had found you in Charleston. What do you do there?"

"I'm in real estate and insurance."

"Are you doing OK?" she asked. I heard the genuine concern in her voice.

"Yes, ma'am. I'm getting by. Aunt Anna, would it be too much of an imposition if I came by with my wife to see you before I leave?"

"You're here in Jacksonville?"

"Yes, I just finished up with the attorney. He asked me to come down to go over the details of the estate."

"Oh, please do come by."

"Will tomorrow be OK?"

"Absolutely! Oh, I'm so excited. I really want to see you. I'll make you and your wife a nice Italian meal."

"What time should we be there?"

"Come at five o'clock. That'll give us plenty of time to talk."

Julie had caught some of the conversation. She said, "Anna sounds like a nice woman."

"Yeah. Too bad my father didn't inherit some of the same genes."

The next day, when I rang their doorbell, I felt both wary anticipation and a degree of excitement. I didn't remember either my aunt or my uncle. Tim answered the door and welcomed us enthusiastically. Not five seconds had passed when my aunt appeared. Without hesitation she threw her arms around my waist, holding me close to her, saying nothing. Then she turned to Julie to give her a big hug.

"Come in, come in," she said. "What are we doing standing here in the hall?"

Julie, Anna, and I took seats in the living room.

Tim asked, "What can I get you all to drink?" He was a burly, bald, freckle-faced man with gentle blue eyes. I liked him immediately.

"A beer, please," I said.

"And you, Julie?"

"A little white wine for me, please, if you have it."

"Do I have it? That's all Anna drinks!"

He disappeared into the kitchen. An awkward moment passed before Anna broke the silence. "So tell me what's happened to you since you were a young boy. I can't believe it's been so long."

"Well, when I was sixteen, my mother got remarried to a nice Italian guy who treated me well. But we never really got close. I was pretty much on my own, working and hanging out in the city at night. When I was twenty I joined the marines."

"I knew you were a marine. Your father had a picture of you in your blue uniform on top of the chest in his bedroom."

"How did he get that?' I asked, surprised.

"I don't know," Anna replied, "but there it was."

Tim came back with our drinks on a tray. My aunt raised her glass. "Here's to my long-lost nephew and his beautiful wife! *Salut!*"

We all raised our glasses, smiling. I had just settled back into my chair when Anna rose. "Now let's all go into the kitchen. The pasta is cooking, and I have to stir the ragù."

I watched my aunt move around the kitchen, testing the pasta, tasting the sauce, and putting the final touches on the salad. She reminded me a lot of my mother. She was petite, standing fewer than five feet tall. She had curly black hair and deep-set brown eyes. She was a Neapolitan through and through.

Finally, when everything was ready, she and Tim placed a large bowl of meatballs and braciole on the oak kitchen table with the salad; the pasta; warm, crusty bread; and a pot of butter. When we were seated, she asked us all to join hands and said grace, and then she crossed herself. We responded with hearty amens. Then she said, "*Mangia*!"

We dug in. The braciole were sweet and tender; the meatballs were spicy and delicious. The sauce—what could I say? It was perfect. I was eating nonstop, engrossed in the feast and asking for more helpings of both food and wine.

"Bravo, Michele!" said Anna.

Tim added, "I'll say! He eats like a horse."

Julie chuckled. She wasn't doing too badly herself.

I finally stopped eating, and I sat back contentedly. "Aunt Anna, that's the best Italian food I've ever had."

"Mickey, stop kidding your old aunt." She was grinning as she fussed around us.

"No," said Julie. "Let me tell you—he's serious. He doesn't give out compliments easily where food is concerned.

Tim said, "So are you two planning to do anything else while you're down here?"

"I'm glad you asked. I need to know which cemetery my father is buried in. I want to visit the grave site. There's a big hole in my life where he's concerned."

"Oh, Mickey," said Anna. "I'm so sorry. I know that my brother was hard on you and your dear mother. He had demons that he fought his whole life. Maybe you should've reached out to him before he passed."

"With all respect, Aunt Anna, your brother was a bastard, a wife beater, and a drunk who one night, in a fit of rage, held a kitchen knife to both my mother's throat and mine and swore he would kill us."

"Mother of God! I swear I didn't know," she blurted out, looking at Tim, who was slowly shaking his head.

I said, "If I had run across him, there's no telling what the frightened child and the angry man in me might have done. There could have been blood."

Anna pressed her fingertips against her temples, her shock at my violent words clearly etched on her face. She sighed sadly. "I know he cared about you, Michael. How else do you explain the photograph of you? And that he remembered you in his will? He told me so many times how proud he was of you becoming a marine."

"I don't know. I'm more confused now than I've ever been."

My aunt rose from the table and rested her arm around my shoulders. She said softly, "Michele, forgive him. You'll never have peace otherwise."

The next morning the clear, blue sky was glorious. Chirping birds darted about in the trees, and the warm sun shone down on Julie and me. We stood beside my father's grave. After a few moments, Julie started weeping. I didn't expect her next words.

"Michael, I can't stand to see your name on a headstone. It's really upsetting me. Please, can we leave?"

"Sure, honey," I held her hand tightly, as though I'd never let go.

I stared at the marker. He and I would have to settle this another time.

THIRTY EIGHT

The devil had taken hold of me.

One morning I ran into Polk outside his office, and I thought I'd screw with his mind, purely for the fun of upsetting him.

"Mr. Polk," I said, "I know we've had our differences, but for the life of me I can't understand how I can be up four percent for the last quarter while the district overall is down eleven percent? You must be under one heck of a lot of pressure from the home office."

"Well, dammit, I am. We've had a shitload of policies lapsing lately. Those wrecked many of the gains we made from when I first arrived. I cain't seem to get this sales force straightened out no matter what I try to do."

"You know, Mr. Polk, sometimes when you're on the ropes, you just gotta tough it out and hope for the best."

Sighing loudly, he began to massage his stomach as one eyelid twitched nervously.

"Mike," I heard Jim say, "are we still on for breakfast?"

I turned to address him. I hadn't realized he was standing behind us, retrieving his mail.

"Sure, Jim," I said.

Polk walked back into his office and collapsed heavily into his chair.

A few minutes later, Jim and I were seated in our usual booth in Bilbro's, drinking coffee and chatting about nothing in particular as we waited for the food to arrive.

When it did, I bellowed, "Hell's teeth! What's wrong with you, Bertha? Are you on the rag or something? I asked for home fries, not damn grits!"

Her face crumpled. "I'm sorry, sir. I'll have them out as fast as I can." She turned and stumbled heavily back to the kitchen.

"Too bad we lost Sweet Thing, Jim. She was good to look at, efficient, and smart. Now we've got to deal with that dimwit block of a woman."

Glaring at me with anger smoldering in his eyes, Jim said vehemently, "What the hell is wrong with you, Mike? What has gotten into you that you think you can talk to her that way? These days you're barking at anyone who ruffles your feathers."

"I'm just sick of having to put up with so many assholes."

"There you go again! Everyone's an asshole! You're angry all the time. Just stop it! Ever since you got that insurance money and the promise of more to come, you've been behaving like you're better than anyone else. Don't you realize how destructive money and power can be? What you're doing now is pure evil."

"Evil? What the hell am I doing that's evil?"

"I overheard your conversation with Polk, you know. You were tormenting him."

"I was just giving him what he gives to everyone else."

"There's a big difference. He runs on fear. You do it out of sheer malevolence. Listen, a month back you would have been sickened to hear someone talk to Bertha like you just did. Yes, she's fat. Yes, she has an unpleasant disposition. Yes, she's inefficient. But she's a human being. She doesn't deserve your contempt. Let me put it another way in case you're not getting the message. You're going around thinking your shit doesn't stink."

I was dumbfounded. His sledgehammer blows fell hard on me.

"Jesus, Jim, you really think I've changed? I'd hate to think of myself that way. You're the closest friend I have."

"I'm still your friend. If I weren't, I wouldn't even bother to talk to you." He paused to let his words sink in. "You need to be aware of what's happening to you before it becomes habit. Snap out of it. Money doesn't make you better than other people. Get back on track."

I hesitated, eyeing my cooling breakfast as it congealed on the plate, my gut roiling. With an effort I stood up to leave. "I honestly didn't realize, Jim. I'm going to have to think about this."

"You'd better," he said, staring at me coldly.

Over the next few days, I steered clear of Jim, Bilbro's, and—when I could—my coworkers in the office. I needed to be alone for a while. I needed to do some soul searching.

I wondered how something I hadn't worked for, the inheritance, had wrought such a change in me. My success as an agent, the recognition I had received, and the good money I'd made hadn't flipped that switch. Then one day it hit me like a brick: in my mind I had been counting, for the umpteenth time, all the money I would be receiving from my father's estate. The sheer magnitude of the windfall would empower me to do pretty much what I wanted without ever having to kowtow to anybody again. I *liked* that feeling. However, like a drug addict, I needed constant reinforcement of my new self-perceived status. I'd done so by manipulating and abusing others.

It was toward the end of the week. I knew business would be slow at Bilbro's. I walked into the diner with the biggest box of candy I could find and looked for Bertha.

"Oh, Mr. Romano," said Bertha, "you didn't have to do this. I screwed up."

"Yes, I do, Bertha. It's been on my conscience that I spoke to you in such a terrible way. I've never done that to a woman before."

"Don't let it bother you. I'm used to it. My husband does it all the time. Quite a few of the guys who come in here do too."

"Well, not me, Bertha. So please, once again, accept my sincere apologies."

She nodded and then suddenly broke into tears. She said, "This is my last day here. I've been fired."

"God! I'm sorry, Bertha."

She sighed and blotted her face with her apron.

"It happens to me real often," she gulped. "I try real hard, but I just can't seem to get things right. I wish I was back on Daddy's farm, doing the milking, helping with the ploughing, and tending to the house and the cooking. But the small farms are disappearing, just like Daddy's. The big corporations are buying them out. I hardly got no education. It's not easy for me to write things down and keep them straight."

"Are you going to be OK?" I asked.

"I guess so. Me, my old man, and the kids manage to put enough together in a week to meet the rent and buy some food. But this is going to make things real hard."

Pulling out my wallet, I gave her the fifty-eight bucks I had in it. "I hope this helps a little."

"Thank you...Oh, thank you, sir."

She grabbed me unexpectedly in a bear hug and lifted me clear off the ground. The few customers in the place just stared.

"Put me down, Bertha, please. I've got to go to work. Good luck to you and yours."

Everybody's got their ton of shit.

Back in the ghetto, I navigated the ramshackle porch of Pinky Chavis's home for the hundredth time. I yelled through the screen door, expecting the twins or Pinky to appear. I was surprised when Pinky's mother answered. She wearily pushed open the door but didn't invite me in.

"Are you off today, Mrs. Chavis?" I asked.

"No, sir. I'm home to take Pinky over to County to get her the new blood. She in awful pain, sir, and it seem she need the blood more and more often. That sickle cell jus' keep on eatin' away at my poor baby. I jus' don't know why the Lord see fit to do that to her. Pinky's one of the sweetest girls ever to walk this Earth." She sighed. "But it must be part of God's plan for her."

"I know, Mrs. Chavis. This must be a terrible burden for you."

"Sir, don't mean to be rushin' you, but I got to get goin' and make Pinky ready. Then later today, we got to go over to Dorothy Wright's."

"Someone in the family die?" I asked. I figured it might be someone I had insured.

"Lord, yes," she said. "My cousin Dorothy. She passed of a stroke just the other night."

I couldn't believe it. "You mean Dorothy Wright herself? My God, I saw her only two days ago. She looked fine to me."

"Well, sir, she dead and laid out in her own place."

"Where's the funeral going to be held?" I asked her.

"At the AME church in Wraggborough, tomorrow. Are you plannin' on being there?"

"Yes, if I can," I replied. She gently closed the door.

It was getting close to ten. I still hadn't been able to find a parking spot close to the church. I was also having second thoughts about the safety of my car. I decided to park in the Sears parking lot on Calhoun Street. Afoot, I quick marched the several blocks to the church through the cold, misty morning with Julie's girly, plastic umbrella tucked under my arm.

Making it into the church with five minutes to spare, I looked around for a place to sit. I walked down an aisle, and many of the congregants glared at me, probably wondering what a white man was doing there. I spotted Mrs. Bouchon standing near the front, talking with a small group of people. Relieved, I walked up to her and greeted her.

When she took my hand, those around us seemed to relax. The few who knew me smiled in welcome.

"Michael, I'm so glad you could come," Mrs. Bouchon spoke clearly for all to hear.

"Wild horses wouldn't have kept me away—you know that. Dorothy and I became good friends during the past two years. She was a fine woman."

"Yes, and she certainly had a way with people. She could talk to anyone and get them to open up. That allowed her to share some of the troubles and heartaches she had borne during her life. Come—sit beside me."

As we made our way into the pew, a hush descended, alerting us to take our seats as the Reverend Billy, in black robes, walked solemnly to the pulpit. The choir, all dressed in white, took up a position behind him. He looked down at Dorothy's open casket, which was surrounded by mountains of flowers, and said solemnly, "Brothers and sisters, we are here today to pay tribute to Dorothy Wright, a mighty force in our community. She was a loving mother, a loyal friend, and a champion for our people against the many injustices that have been heaped upon us."

Hallelujahs resounded throughout the church. Family members began to weep and wail.

When all had quieted, he launched into a fire and brimstone sermon, telling us in a roaring voice how we must all resist the temptations of the devil and do right toward each other and love one another, as Dorothy had, if we were to achieve salvation and be reunited with loved ones in the hereafter.

Then he said, looking heavenward, "Dorothy is still with us. Her spirit is hovering right now over those she cared for, guiding and protecting them."

Pandemonium ensued. Women let out high, piercing cries and fanned themselves. Two of them passed out. Young girls in white dresses rushed to their side, reviving and comforting them.

When things had quieted down somewhat, the Reverend Billy moved away from the pulpit, and the organist began to play the opening bars of "Amazing Grace." A stout, very black lady in the front row of the choir took a step forward, adding her powerful voice to the haunting melody. The glorious sound must have reached out far beyond the walls of the church. Her performance moved me. Never before had I experienced anything like it in a church. When the song ended, she took her place again with the choir as they sang Negro spirituals from times past, with the entire congregation swaying and clapping joyfully. Some were so caught up in the moment that they too burst out into song, adding to the spirited scene.

If Dorothy were looking down from somewhere in the firmament, she would be smiling and laughing to see this white boy so enthralled by the whole thing, rocking along.

Thirty Nine

The Friday morning meeting ended. I was just about to leave the office when Jim pulled a chair up to my desk.

"Mike, can I have a few minutes?"

"Sure, Jim. Is everything OK?"

"Well, no, not really. Polk asked me to speak to you about why your production has dropped off lately. Is anything wrong?"

"No, quite the contrary. Everything's fine. Actually Jim, I've been waiting for the right moment to tell you. I'll be giving my notice to leave as of the middle of January. That should give you and the company enough time to find my replacement."

"May I ask why?"

"I think you know why, Jim. I'm sick of the debit, Polk, and the way this company does business."

He looked at me a bit disconcerted. "Are you looking to work for another insurance company?"

"No. I'm burned out on insurance as a whole—and the idea of working for *any* company. But to be honest, if it weren't for the inheritance, I'd still be dogging it out with the rest of you guys."

"How does Julie feel about this?"

"She's behind me one hundred percent. She knows I need to be my own man."

"So what are you going to do?"

"Sell real estate with an eye to opening my own company eventually. I'll be free to set my own hours and work as hard as I want to. I've already got my first-year license with Pendergast Realty, and I've managed to make a few sales in the short time that I've been there."

"Huh?" said Jim. "Don't you realize that holding another job on the side is grounds for being fired?"

"What the hell difference does it make now?" I laughed. "I'm outta here in few weeks."

He frowned, deep in thought for a while. "Look, Mike. I need you to do me a favor."

"Sure, Jim, anything."

"Can you hold off giving your notice until the end of January? That's only a few weeks' difference."

"Why?" I asked, surprised by his request.

"Because I'll be retired by then and won't have to bust my ass training a new agent to replace you."

"How about that." I laughed. "Both of us will be out of here, free as birds! So what are you going to do when you retire?"

He hesitated, and then he said, "You probably don't know this, but I write. Actually I've had a couple of short stories published. I want to write a novel. Maybe it will be about you."

We grinned at each other, delighted with our conspiracy.

Later in the day, with nothing else to do except pick up a few pizzas around six to take over to Gunny's for a surprise party, I decided to have lunch at Toby's Pub and get in a game of darts. I pulled open the heavy door and faced a wall of serious drinkers. Careful not to upset anyone's glass, I maneuvered my way to the bar and ordered only a beer, having had second thoughts about trying to eat there. Then I heard the familiar laughter of Elaine Sutcliffe. I looked over the crowd. She was sitting with Elizabeth and Leo Dukakis.

Going over to their table, I said, "So how are the Young Turks doing today?"

Leo rose up out of his chair and shook my hand enthusiastically. Elizabeth greeted me with a smile and said, "Great to see you, Mike."

"Where've you been, stranger?" Elaine asked.

"Just seven blocks from where you live, Senator. Where've *you* been?"

"Sorry, Mike. I've been meaning to call you, and Julie of course, about us all getting together, but I've been so bogged down in the Senate I just haven't had a chance. Do bring me up to date with what's been happening with you."

"Not much. I've been busy peddling insurance and selling real estate."

She arched an elegant eyebrow at me. "You're in real estate now?"

"Yeah, I hooked up with Elias a few months back. By February I'll be doing it full time."

"Why are you quitting insurance? You were doing so well at it."

"I figure the big bucks will be in real estate."

Leo said, "Absolutely! I've seen a lot of people prosper in that business."

"That's my goal, Leo."

Turning my attention to Elizabeth, I asked how things were going with her.

"Quite well, Michael. Tom and Jean-Luc managed to get me a few hours teaching. However, a rumor is going around that the school may be taken over by the state. When I asked Tom about it, he was very tight lipped."

"Wow!" I said. "If that happens the downtown area could undergo a real economic boom." I saw large dollar signs.

Tired of standing, and getting hungrier by the minute, I swigged down the rest of my beer and said, "I've got to get going now. Nice to see you all."

"Hold up!" said Leo. He reached into his wallet for a business card and scribbled on the back of it. He handed it to me. "This is my beach house address on the Isle of Palms. I'm holding a party there tomorrow, starting around four. I'd like you and you wife to come if you can. You'll know quite a few of the people there."

Pleased, I said, "Sounds great. I'll just have to check it out with Julie."

"Oh, Michael," said Elizabeth, "please persuade Julie to come. I haven't seen her for ages, and we need to catch up with one another."

Elaine glanced over at Elizabeth, probably wondering how she and Julie had become such good friends.

"I will, Liz. I'm pretty certain we'll be there." I waved good-bye to them and elbowed my way out of the door.

Julie was apprehensive as we turned onto Lord Byron Drive, as I was. We were taking a big chance by going over to see Gunny Starr unannounced, and so was Laura, his wife, in agreeing to it. This could blow up in her face. Nevertheless she was determined to follow through with it, hoping it would break down the barriers Gunny had erected around himself. She had told me once, when I was leaving their house, that he wasn't getting any better, and that life with him had become pure hell; if it weren't for the children and her job she would go mad.

Lopez was waiting with his wife, Consuela, and a marine sergeant in uniform when we pulled up in front of the house. Lopez and I had figured that Sergeant McCants would be our ace in the hole to keep Gunny from exploding and throwing us out. McCants had been one of Gunny's men in 'Nam, and Starr was unaware that he was now stationed at the naval base.

I loaded up with four boxes of pizza, and Lopez and McCants toted beers and sodas. Consuela knocked on the front door while Julie hovered in the background.

Laura opened the door with a finger to her lips. We walked into the kitchen and set everything down quietly. Then she led us into the den, where Gunny was watching TV. Basilone stood at attention and eyed us fiercely, alerting his master that someone was in the room.

Gunny spun his chair to face us and got an astonished look on his face. "What the *hell*?"

"Hell? What?" said McCants as he strode over to him. "Is that any way to greet one of your men?"

He put out his hand. Gunny clasped it firmly with both of his as tears welled up in his eyes. Looking McCants over, he said, "Thank God you made it out in one piece."

Laura quietly beckoned, "Ladies, let's go get the food ready." They filed out. No fool, Basilone followed them hopefully.

Gunny asked, "So what's been going on over there since they cashiered me?"

Shaking his head, McCants said, "Things are going to hell. We're turning on our own. There've been many incidents of fragging...and guys are doing heavy drugs. If we keep this up much longer, it'll wreck the corps."

"Fuck it all, McCants. But at least you got another stripe out of it. And what about that Purple Heart? Where'd you get hit?"

McCants did a precision about-face, dropped his pants, pulled down his skivvies, and pointed to a gash in his butt where the docs had pulled out the shrap. Just at that moment, the women returned with the pizza and beer. Startled by the extraordinary scene and the roars of laughter from Gunny and us, they let loose with shrieks of merriment and fake horror.

McCants pulled up his drawers and said, deadpan, "I guess I won't have to show y'all my baby pictures."

Still giggling, the women laid out the food in front of us and beat a hasty retreat to their hen party.

"So what the hell's this all about?" Gunny said gruffly. "Why you here tonight?"

"Well, Gunny, my TV's broken," I replied innocently. "So I call Lopez, since I want to watch the light heavyweight title bout tonight at Madison Square Garden. He tells me his set's broken too, so I say to him, 'Let's go over to Gunny's, seeing as how he's got this big new television.'"

He leaned forward in his chair and gave me that chilling stare. "If you'd been a better bullshit artist in the corps, Romano, you might have avoided the brig and kept another stripe."

We knocked off most of the beer and gorged ourselves on pizza. Finally it was almost time to watch the match.

"So who's fighting, Romano?" asked Gunny.

"Dick Tiger and José Torres."

"Should be one hell of a bout," said McCants. "Both men are Olympic champions, and Torres will be defending his title tonight."

Taking the opportunity to look in on Julie before the fight began, I invited the ladies to join us. Julie looked up and winked at me. The others waved me off as if I were offering them glasses of arsenic. They resumed their conversation, ignoring me. I went back to the den after my noble efforts to integrate the sexes. The fight had just begun. The boxers were feeling each other out with light jabs and punches with no major consequences.

By the fifth round, it had turned into a real donnybrook. The fighters exchanged hard left hooks, uppercuts, and right crosses that had them rocking each other back on their heels. It was then I noticed Gunny's shoulders and hips moving, with his fists clenched, shadowboxing. He was back in the ring again, as he had been twenty years earlier, when he had won the heavyweight championship of the First Marine Division. When the round finished, he told us in some detail what he thought each fighter needed to do to gain the upper hand.

From the sixth round forward, until the bell rang, ending it all, in the fifteenth, he was lost in the fight, slugging it out from his wheelchair.

"Whooee!" shouted Lopez. "I'm amazed no one went down for the count. They must have heads as hard as rocks."

"No," said Gunny. "They know how to roll with the punches and cover up when they get in trouble. But damn, that was one helluver great fight!"

But it wasn't over, at least where the fans were concerned. A bloody riot broke out in the aisles. Guys were beating each other half to death and throwing bottles into the ring, angry about the judges' decision that Tiger had won. It took New York's finest to break up the riot and disperse the crowd.

Gunny looked over at me and growled, "Crazy New Yorkers!"

I just shrugged, opened another beer, and handed it to him.

After we had drunk ourselves dry, the girls appeared with Basilone, who was licking his chops, having consumed half a pepperoni pizza and two bowls of beer. I would have hated to be around him for the next twenty-four hours! Consuela announced it was time to go.

As we were leaving, Gunny shouted, “I’m glad you all came. Thanks a lot!”

Forty

Caught up in the high winds above the waters spanned by the new Cooper River Bridge, Julie tightened the scarf around her head as we sped toward Mount Pleasant and the islands. It was gorgeous convertible weather, temperatures hovering in the high sixties. Turning the radio down, she asked over the roar of the bridge traffic who would be at the Dukakises' party other than Elaine and her inevitable entourage.

"I can think of two: Mrs. Bouchon and that colored lawyer whose name I can never remember, who's running for the assembly."

"Don't you think it a bit odd that Leo decided to invite us on the spur of the moment? I'm sure he and his wife sent out invitations to others."

"Stop fretting, honey. Relax and enjoy the ride; it's a beautiful day. Besides, you'll have Elizabeth to talk to."

"Yes, but unfortunately Elizabeth comes with Elaine."

"I thought you were over that!"

"Not really. It still riles me just looking at her."

"Well, she hasn't made a move on me for quite a while. Besides, she has to be more discreet now she's in the public eye. And you know, she's the only hen in the Senate with a lot of roosters to pick from!"

Chuckling, Julie said, "Personally I'd rather be locked up in a cage of monkeys."

"I'd rather be wrestling gators."

We were still laughing and kidding around twenty minutes later when we pulled onto a narrow strip of sand-swept beach road that was packed with dozens of cars parked on both sides. Leaving our car a good distance away, we headed for the Dukakises' two-story, white stucco beach house, which stood out like a jewel against the many older homes with their rusting tin roofs built decades earlier. Seeing that the front door was wide open, we walked in. We looked around the modern interior, which was filled with people of all ages wearing everything from casual chic to raggedy blue denim.

We recognized several people. More folks were flocking in behind us, so we headed for the bar.

We were only midway to the bar when Elizabeth, unusually casual in capris, came up behind us and snagged Julie by the arm.

"Hi, Liz," I said. "Can I get you another drink?"

Raising her can of pop, she said, "I'm fine with this, thanks, Mike."

Julie added, "Nothing for me right now. I'll get one in a minute."

After pouring myself a small Scotch at the makeshift bar, I turned and almost toppled Debbie, who was standing behind me. I grabbed her by the waist to steady her. When I released her, she smiled. "Would you like to do that again, Mike?"

"No, thanks, Deb. I got back problems."

She looked at me invitingly and wiggled her butt when she realized I was checking her out in her high-cut shorts and tight-fitting sweater.

"I've never seen so few inches of material stretched so thin!" I said.

"Glad you're enjoying the view."

"What can I say, Deb? So what's brought you back to Charleston? I thought you were in New Orleans."

"I was up until a week ago. Now I'm here to prepare Elaine for her next election."

"That's a year from now. What's the rush?"

"The congressional primary is fewer than six months away."

I couldn't believe what I was hearing. "Congress, as in Washington?"

"Yes, indeed. Elaine is running for the First Congressional District."

"Holy shit! Is she already bored with being a state senator?"

"Actually she is. And she can do far more good for us up there than she can in the state house. Besides, Washington is a much more exciting place. If she wins I'll be living up there permanently, directing and managing her staff."

"Sounds like high-powered shit. Are you readying yourself to become a lobbyist eventually?"

"Why not? That's where the real money's made. Like you, nobody ever gave me anything."

Until recently!

"I grew up poor as dirt on the bayou," she continued, a hint of defiance in her tone.

"If you win you'll be able to make some bucks earlier than you think."

"What do you mean, Mike?" She was suddenly serious.

"You're going to be privy to any deal Congress makes before anyone else knows. When that happens stock prices usually rise on the company involved."

"That would be like insider trading without being dinged by the SEC."

I said, "If and when this happens, let me know when something's going down. I'll place a bet for the both of us."

"You've got the wherewithal to do that?"

"Yeah. I inherited a goldmine in Alaska."

She looked at me uncertainly but was obviously curious.

"Where're you staying now that you're back?" I asked.

"Over in the big house on East Battery, with Elaine and Arthur. She thought it was silly for me to spend money on an apartment when they have so much room."

That would make Arthur very happy.

As we were about to part, I said, "Deb, just stay off the piazzas. There's a lot of traffic on East Battery."

She gave me a cocky look and strutted away.

Julie and Elizabeth were still gabbing away when I interrupted them. "Liz, how come you didn't tell us Elaine was planning to run for Congress?"

Julie's jaw dropped, and she stared at Elizabeth in disbelief.

"Sorry guys," Elizabeth said. "I was sworn to secrecy. How d'ya find out, Mike?"

"Debbie just told me."

A look of consternation passed across her face, and then she said, "Well, that figures. But it doesn't really matter now. In another hour it'll be announced, when the press shows up."

"So *that's* what this party is all about," said Julie, sounding exasperated.

"Yes and no. They'll also be announcing that Mrs. Bouchon and Daniel Rivers will be running for the state assembly. They'll be looking for volunteer workers and financial support."

Julie asked pointedly, "Why weren't we formally invited like everyone else?"

"I don't really know, Julie." Elizabeth had the grace to look contrite. "It surprised me the other day in the pub when Leo invited Mike. He and his wife, Lydia, were in charge of everything. I wouldn't let it bother you; it's probably just a lapse of memory, nothing more. The point is that he did invite you, and you're both here."

Mulling things over, I said, "I just don't get it, Liz. What on Earth makes Elaine believe she can beat an entrenched congressman like Jim Pickens? He's done a lot of good by bringing military jobs to the Lowcountry for the last twenty years, and he is chair or cochair of several really important committees."

"He's ill, Mike, and he won't be able to run for another term."

"I haven't seen anything in the papers about that."

"Trust me, Mike, we know. It'll be coming out soon."

Boy, I was really out of the loop!

I blew out a breath and said, "I can't believe how things just fall into Elaine's lap."

"Nothing's fallen there yet. We expect a tough Democratic primary. A huge prize is up for grabs. And I expect that the Republicans will certainly put up a candidate when the election rolls around. In the last two years, they've made more converts out of Democrats than ticks on a hound."

Julie laughed. "That's a funny southern phrase coming from you, Liz."

Less than an hour had passed. I was working on my third drink and talking to Tom Avery. To the surprise of everyone, the press showed up. Or at least those who weren't in the know were surprised.

Leo took up a position in front of a large, stone fireplace that rose to the ceiling fifteen feet above. "Lydia and I welcome you all to our home on this momentous occasion."

The cameras began rolling, and the reporters primped themselves in readiness. The crowd stirred and looked around, wondering what the hell was going on.

"It is my privilege and honor to announce that Senator Elaine Sutcliffe will be running for the Congress of the United States."

Dumbfounded, as I had been, the crowd didn't react with much enthusiasm, only a few sporadic handclaps. Then, as the message sunk in, the response picked up to a respectably polite level.

Leo, clearly realizing he might have bombed, followed up quickly. "We also have with us today two esteemed candidates known to most of you, who will be running for the General Assembly: Mrs. Lottie Bouchon and Mr. Daniel Rivers."

This was greeted with wild applause, probably to the chagrin of Elaine, who never liked to be upstaged by anyone.

He gestured for Elaine to come forward. She gave rehashed one of her old speeches from her campaign for the Senate. She finished to polite but lackluster applause. When the room returned to normal, the reporters moved in, asking the candidates the usual mundane questions and receiving the usual mundane answers that politicians always came up with.

"Did you know about this, Tom?" I asked.

"Elaine told me last week at lunch. Didn't you know?"

"I heard about it only an hour ago from Debbie."

"It all happened so fast. They didn't have much of a chance to plan anything. They found out about Pickens being ill only two weeks ago." He sounded a bit defensive.

"Hey, Tom—I'm not upset that I wasn't told. I haven't been involved in anything political since Elaine was elected, and the two times I was invited to one of their political meetings, I couldn't go because I was too busy."

That was why we hadn't received a formal invitation. We'd been off the radar screen until Leo had seen me the other day.

Wanting to have a smoke and to go find Julie, I broke away from Tom and tracked her down on the front porch, talking to a group of young people who I guessed were college students. Not wanting to barge into her conversation, I leaned on the railing facing her. A couple of minutes later, she came over. "Are you having a good time?"

I just shrugged and said nothing.

"I thought so. Me neither. Let's go take a walk on the beach before the sun sets."

Making our way along a trampled path through the sand dunes, we ran across Debbie and a few people who were chatting and smoking. Debbie waved us over. Once in their midst, it became clear they were passing a joint around. Julie had never smoked marijuana before and was curious. When the joint came around to us, I took a drag first and immediately felt the pleasant effects. Then I handed it to Julie, who started sneezing and coughing uncontrollably. Pulling a face, she immediately passed it on.

One of the young girls, adorned in full hippie regalia replete with a peace symbol hanging around her neck, started to talk about the war in Vietnam. The others joined in, vociferously agreeing that the war was wrong and that we should get out of it. Then a fat turd mouthed off, saying our troops were nothing more than "baby killers," and he praised the enemy that was slaughtering them.

I had to step in. "Hold on, man. That's too far out, and it's not true. Those kids who are dying out there believe they're fighting for democracy and keeping you safe."

"Bullshit!" he replied. "They're fuckin' murderers, especially the marines!"

Corporal Bell's death and the vision of Gunny in his wheelchair flashed across my mind. Then in a second, without any thought, my hand struck the guy's throat like a cobra, grabbing it in a death grip. Having paralyzed him with the move, I brought him down hard on his back against a sand dune. I crouched over him as he gasped for breath. "I'm one of those marines you're talking about, you little shit!"

Everyone stood frozen. No one moved to help him. Still holding him in the helpless position, I felt a tentative hand on my shoulder and heard Debbie say, "Let the milk-fed son of a bitch go. He ain't worth the killing, Mike."

I let him loose and slowly got to my feet. I looked at Debbie's hard, determined face. She was one helluver tough Louisiana woman.

I turned to Julie and said roughly, "I need to move. Let's go."

Walking the now dark beach with a chilly wind blowing, I waited angrily for the expected onslaught from Julie that I should learn to control my temper. No longer able to stand the silence between us, I stopped and turned to her.

"Why are you so quiet? Are you mad at me?"

"No, Michael," she said quietly, "although I was worried for a moment there that you might have killed that awful man. But whether you want to believe it or not, you're still a marine. You always will be, no matter how hard you try to deny it. And even if you weren't, you couldn't let him get away with what he said. It was wrong! He deserved what he got."

FORTY ONE

The atmosphere was tense as Ed Tylke sat across from me in the manager's office, with his hands clasped firmly on the desk in front of him.

"Mr. Romano, the company is deeply disturbed by your decision to leave us just at the time we have offered you Jim Dawson's position as staff manager. I was ordered by our vice president, Mr. Madison, to make a special trip down here to ascertain the reasons for your resignation. May I ask you a question?"

"Sure. Go ahead."

"Has our company not paid and treated you well?"

"Yes, sir, it has, but didn't I deserve it, given my record? Did the company not benefit more than I did through my efforts? Sir, the company doesn't act out of benevolence when it pays me. I earned every cent. And at some future time, if my production should drop off due to age, illness, or being unable to compete against younger agents or managers coming in, would the company not hesitate to dismiss me?" Before he could respond, I followed up by saying, "I would rather put my future and livelihood in my own hands than risk them with any company. All that the corporations are interested in is a quarterly bottom line to keep their stockholders happy. That ice is too thin to risk my family's future on."

Removing his bifocals and squinting as he polished them with his handkerchief, he said, "So I take it your answer is final?"

"Yes, sir, it is."

With that I rose, reached across the desk, and offered my hand. After a second he shrugged and took it in a last handshake.

On the way to my desk to pick up my gear to leave for the day, Sal stopped me. "What went on in there, Mike?"

"Let's adjourn to our other office, where we can have more privacy and get a good cup of coffee," I replied.

Huddled in a booth, I gave Sal a rundown on what had happened, but my mind was only half on our conversation. I was revisited by nostalgic memories of the times I had spent with my fellow agents and friends there at Bilbro's.

"Mike, what're you grinning about?" Sal asked.

"You and Sweet Thing, Sal."

He laughed. "I sure miss that hot little tamale! And I'm sure going to miss you being around here."

A quick stab of sorrow hit me as I remembered the same words coming from Pug on the day I left the corps.

"Hey, Sal, you don't get rid of me that easily. I'll still be around."

"Yeah, Mike, but it just won't be the same."

"That's only in your mind," I said, knowing it to be untrue. Much of what bonded us together was the company and the everyday trials and tribulations we had in common—especially Polk, who had resigned his position as manager, much to the astonishment and delight of all in the office, and gone back to Jackson.

I finished my coffee and rose. "I've got to get going, Sal. I've an old buddy I have to check up on."

"Dammit, Basilone, calm down! Romano, you gotta stop bringing him those spare ribs. He's getting fatter than a hog."

"Run him around the block a few times, and get him to do a couple hundred push-ups—that'll get the weight off his ass."

Gunny laughed as I began to punch lightly the Everlast heavy bag I had bought for him a couple of months back, which now hung from a porch rafter. As I began to lay into the bag heavily, bobbing and weaving, he yelled at me, "How many times do I have to tell you to keep that left hook close to your body? A good left hook has knocked out more boxers than any right cross ever has."

Ignoring him, I continued to throw punches.

Frustrated, he said, "You just gotta look fancy, don't you, whether you're in the ring or just hitting the bag, trying to look like that draft-dodging son of a bitch Clay—Ali—whatever the fuck he calls himself now."

Exhausted, I stopped and sank heavily into a chair across from him. He reached into the cooler at his side and tossed me a cold one, shaking his head. "Pound for pound, you hit harder than anyone I've ever seen, but you could hit even harder if you'd just listen to me."

"Hey, Gunny, I'm not looking to become a professional. I'm just trying to stay in shape and keep out of trouble. You were the one who told me that when I got stressed out by anything or anybody, I should go down to the gym and pound the bag. Well, I still do. I have a bag just like this one hanging from my rear porch."

After a while we changed the subject from boxing to baseball, speculating on who would win the next World Series. Finally I checked my watch. "Gunny, I gotta get going. We have a dinner engagement at the Fork restaurant."

"Say hi to Julie for me, will you? By the way I'm surprised she still lets you get away with that sissy hair."

"I tell you what: I'll get a crew cut the day I see you get out of that chair and walk."

He scowled at me as I left.

Later on I was coming out of the shower to dry off. Julie primped in front of her mirror. I asked her if she'd heard anything back from Rina about Tom's father's suffering another heart attack.

"No, not yet. It's too bad they can't come along tonight with the Baptistes. We always have so much fun together. You never know what might pop out of Marie Claire's mouth."

"Yeah, she's a real killer."

"Oh, Michael, she's a lovely woman."

"I agree. But as I said, she's a killer."

"What on Earth do you mean?" she said, clearly upset.

"Honey, don't forget that she was a sniper during the war and probably killed a lot of Nazis. I knew a few snipers in the corps, when we were in Santa Domingo. I remember hearing one talking to another, asking how many he had stitched that day. He answered, 'Fifteen cents' worth.'"

"For heaven's sake, what are you talking about now?"

"Baby, fifteen cents represents two kills: the cost of two thirty-caliber rounds."

She covered her face. "That's just horrible!"

"Yeah, but that's what war does, and those guys liked killing. They had a slogan among themselves: one shot, one kill, no regrets."

"Please, can we stop talking about this? I like Marie Claire a lot, and I don't want my feelings about her changed."

"Your feelings don't have to change. Know that she would probably put her life on the line for *you*, just as she did during the war for her comrades. Those two marine snipers killed for the sport of it; she killed to regain her freedom and dignity. Big difference."

The restaurant was pleasantly quiet that evening. After we had ordered our drinks, Jean-Luc said, "By the way I have sad news. I got a call from Tom just as we were about to leave to come here. His father died late this afternoon. He and Rina will be gone for at least a week, making all the preparations for the funeral and taking care of his affairs for Tom's mother. Tom says she's a complete wreck."

"Did he say how Rina's doing?" asked Julie. "After all she's about ready to go into labor."

"Don't worry," said Marie Claire. "Rina is a strong woman, and if the baby comes she'll be in good hands in Boston. They have fine hospitals up there."

"Ah!" exclaimed Jean-Luc, "I almost forgot to tell you, Julie. Rina will call you tomorrow. She has her hands full with Tom's mother today."

"So what should we do?" I asked.

Marie Claire said, "I will see a florist tomorrow and pick out a beautiful wreath and a card from all of us."

"That seems appropriate," said Julie. "Let us know how much it comes to so we can reimburse you."

"No, no," said Jean-Luc with a wave of his hand. "We'll take care of it."

"OK," I said, "but only if I pick up the tab tonight."

Having settled that, I asked Jean-Luc if anything interesting was happening at the college.

"No, not really, Michael. Without an increase in budget, I cannot grow my department, and the college has no chance of expanding the curriculum. As you say here, we are stuck in the mud. I was lucky to find a little money to have Elizabeth teach a few courses. She is a wonderful teacher and completely dedicated to her students. But I have to say I am somewhat worried about her. She seems to suffer from *la mélancolie*. Always upset about the injustices in the world. She says she cannot escape the fear that one day humankind will destroy itself."

"We all live with that possibility, don't we?" Julie commented.

"Ah, yes, *ma petite*," said Jean-Luc, "but most of us are able to put it to the backs of our minds and go on with our daily lives, like the crazy people who live on the San Andreas Fault. Elizabeth always has it at the forefront of her mind. She is always battling to make changes. Unfortunately for her she is a Jeanne d'Arc without armor—an easy target for the bowman's arrows, either real or imagined."

"I don't buy that, Jean-Luc," I said. "I've seen her very happy on quite a few occasions over the last year or so. I believe a lot of this depression you're talking about was caused by her being marginalized when Debbie took over Elaine's campaign. She was fine when we first met her two years ago, before Debbie came on the scene. And a year back, she was really OK when Debbie left. You may not know this, but she came down here specifically out of gratitude and probably love for Elaine, who played a great part in her life when they were young girls together at Radcliffe."

Jean-Luc replied, "I did not know this."

Marie Claire said, "Ah! *Jalousie*! What Elizabeth needs is some real cows."

We all looked at her blankly. Then Jean-Luc chuckled. "*Ma chérie*! Maybe you mean 'cause'?"

Irritated, she said, "Cows! That's what I said, didn't I? Cows!"

"So tell me, Marie Claire," I said weakly, "what kind of cows are you talking about?"

By that time we were laughing uncontrollably. Julie was gasping for breath.

With a very dignified look around the table, Marie Claire said, "Now."

"What now?" I asked. "Or now what?"

Exasperated, she shouted, "NOW! The National Organization for Women. I have joined the fight for the equality of women. Two weeks from now, we'll have the big meeting at my house."

Then, glaring at Julie, and pointing at her like in the old Uncle Sam posters, she said, "Julie, we want you. You will attend and bring others with you." She added belatedly, "I hope. We must grow our numbers so that we can become a...a..." She looked over at Jean-Luc and waved her hands.

"*Une force à ne pas négliger.* A force to be reckoned with," he supplied helpfully.

Without hesitation Julie jumped in. "I certainly will. It's time that we stand up and fight for equal pay, equal promotion opportunities, and equal say in the workplace. I'm so tired of being relegated to an inferior position just because some male, however stupid, believes that a flipping appendage gives him superiority over me."

"*Eh bien*, Julie! You have the fire in the belly that we all need to make changes." She waved her glass recklessly in the air.

"Marie Claire, you are becoming loud and drawing attention to our table," Jean-Luc said gently.

"What do I care? I hope everyone hears me. It's time for us all to cry out for equality!"

Julie nodded in agreement as Marie Claire continued her rant. I hadn't realized until then how deeply Julie was wounded by the cultural maxim that doomed women to inferior positions. Luckily the tirade ended when the waiter approached rather hesitantly, probably fearful Marie Claire would bite off his head.

After we had ordered and things had calmed down a bit, Jean-Luc said, "Marie Claire, your overzealousness may prove harmful to your cause and to the relationships between men and women. Many women, hearing your battle cry and lacking objectivity, may blame men for all the ills that have befallen them."

"Hey, I have to agree with Jean-Luc," I said bravely. "Just hearing you guys is making me uneasy and feeling defensive, and I'm one hundred percent onboard with you."

Jean-Luc said, "So Marie Claire, Julie, please tread carefully and wisely where your cause is concerned. If you do not, it may backfire on you."

Forty Two

As I was rifling through the files in search of a sales contract, Elias Pendergast came over to me and rested his arm on top of the file cabinet. "I heard you bought another rental property yesterday, Mike."

"Yeah, a sweet one-story brick on James Island." I closed the file drawer. "It was going into foreclosure, and I picked it up for a song, with me assuming the loan."

"How many units do you own now?"

"Six, including this one. How many do you have, Elias?"

"Fifty-two, the last time I checked with my manager."

"Wow! I've got a way to go before I catch up with you."

Smiling broadly, he said, "At the rate you're going, it won't take long. Not bad considering you've been in the business only since you started part time last November." He asked if I was able to cover the mortgage payments, taxes, and insurance on the rentals. He was looking out for me, and I appreciated his concern; he was proving to be a great mentor.

"Yes, I am, with plenty to spare. I figure after expenses and downtime on rentals, I'll be able to clear four thousand a year."

"Not bad," he said. "May I ask how you're going about picking up these units?"

"I run an ad every day in the *News and Courier* that simply says, 'I buy houses; give me a call.' When someone calls with the kind of property I want, and it has an assumable note, I buy it. Quite a few of the callers are behind on their payments and want to get out from under the mortgage and keep their credit. Others need to sell but don't have enough equity to sell through an agency and are content to break even and move on. I'm surprised more people don't do what I do."

"Well, Mike, most don't have the cash or the financial statement you have. And those who do hate the idea of being a landlord and having to deal with tenants. The rest just have no idea of how the system works."

"That's fine with me. Less competition. And I hope that in the next year or so, I'll be able to add another dozen to my inventory. By that time I hope to be making more money off rentals, along with the tax shelter they provide, than I did when I was in insurance. And that plus the sales commissions I'm making gives me a pretty darn good income. Elias, thanks to you, Julie and I are really happy about the way things have turned out."

"You've done it all on your own, Mike. Do you have time for lunch today?"

"Sure. Give me ten minutes to draw up this contract. Where do you want to go?"

"I thought we'd try that new place, Max's Deli, over there near the Gaza Strip."

"Gaza Strip? Where the heck is that?"

"Oh, I keep forgetting that you're still fairly new to these parts, Mike. It's in the South Windermere area, where many of the most prosperous and influential Jews live."

"Yeah, I know that area, but I've never heard it called the Gaza Strip. Deli, huh? Elias, the last time I had a hot pastrami on rye was back in New York, just before I joined the corps. I was dating a Jewish chick, Anne Lyman. She got me hooked on that stuff."

"Were there a lot of Jews where you lived?"

"Can't say. I never really thought about it. But two of my best friends were Jewish. We played stickball and went out on group dates together."

A little past noon, we were seated at one of the only two tables available at Max's. We had already ordered our lunches—pastrami on rye with potato salad for me and a Reuben with chips for Elias. The delicious aromas of food cooking on the grill or being heated in pots or steamed wafted out from the open kitchen. Three workers moved skillfully around each other in a culinary dance, assembling sandwiches and salads, dishing out bowls of hot matzo ball soup and setting them all on a high counter for pickup by the fast-moving servers.

"Y'know, Mike," said Elias, "these people know what they're doing. This sandwich is great, and I'm really impressed by the speed of their service."

"Have you ever been to a New York deli, Elias?"

"No, why?"

"Get this picture: you're in Manhattan with hundreds of thousands of other worker bees. The lunch bell rings, and everyone swarms out of the office buildings and stores. There's only thirty or forty-five minutes for lunch, so you go to a deli because they're fast and feed you a good meal at a reasonable price. It wouldn't surprise me if the owner of this operation is out of New York."

As we were finishing our lunch, I said, "Elias, I need a cup of coffee. How about you?"

"Absolutely. I've got a long afternoon ahead of me."

When the coffee arrived, I asked the waitress to tell the owner that I was a New Yorker who was happy he had opened up such a great place. Soon thereafter a distinguished-looking man in his early fifties, wearing a white apron and a short-sleeved shirt, came over to our table.

"Welcome to my establishment, gentlemen," he said, putting out his hand. "I'm Max."

As he did I noticed on his inner forearm a faded tattoo with the letter A followed by a string of numbers. He was one of the few survivors of the hideous Nazi death camps. He was a gregarious, jovial guy. I wondered how anyone could have lived through such an ordeal without going crazy. But there he was, running a successful restaurant and having a ball doing it.

"So which one of you is from New York?" he asked.

"I am," I responded.

"What part?"

"Queens."

"I used to live in the Bronx and worked in a deli for fifteen years, on Third Avenue in Manhattan."

Elias asked, "What brought you to Charleston?"

"My wife heard about it from a friend in New York. She told us that many Jews had settled down here more than two hundred years ago, and one of the oldest synagogues in America, Beth Elohim, is still in use here. We visited a couple of years ago and fell in love with Charleston. Also we were sick of the crowds and the hectic pace of life in New York. So here we are."

"I know what you mean, Max. It's one of the reasons I moved down here," I said.

A large group of people came in, and Max excused himself to greet them.

As we drank our coffee and shared a slice of cheesecake, I said, "Elias, I had no idea about the Jews coming to Charleston so long ago."

"Actually at one time Charleston had the largest Jewish population in all of America. Among the first to come here were the Sephardic Jews, who were mainly from Portugal. Later on the Hasidic Jews arrived."

"Hey, you know your history!"

"I should, considering my family came here from Wales at just about the time of the first Jewish migration. My great-great-grandfather married a Jewish woman called De Costa. So I have a little Jewish blood running through my veins."

"Hell, Elias, that's probably true of many of us. But blood is blood. If I get a transfusion from a Jewish person, does that make me a Jew? It's that kind of thinking that begets trouble. If Max had been raised Christian, none of the terrible things that happened to him would have occurred."

"You're preaching to the choir here. There are those in Charleston who know my heritage and refer to me as 'that Jew.'"

"Damn, I can't believe it."

"Well, unfortunately it's true," said Elias with a rueful smile.

The day had turned out extremely well for me. I had completed another real estate sale and discovered Max's Deli. Arriving home later than usual, I called out to Julie to let her know I was in. As I headed for the kitchen, where I expected to find her preparing dinner, I heard her say faintly, "I'm in the living room, Michael."

"Hey, honey," I said, "What're you doing sitting here in the dark? Are you still feeling poorly?"

"Yes," she responded.

I turned on the table lamp and sat next to her on the edge of the couch like a physician on a hospital bed. "So what do you think it is? A virus or something?" I had learned from long experience through my mother, who had gotten her degree to practice medicine by way of reading the health tips in every *Reader's Digest* published since 1935, that you would be right more than half the time if you guessed a virus for anyone feeling yucky.

"No. I'm pregnant."

Thunderstruck, I bolted upright. "What? How do you know?"

"I missed my period, I've been nauseated on and off for three days, and I recognize the signs."

"But I thought you were supposed to be babyproof with the IUD."

"Sometimes they fail, Michael."

She looked down, running her fingers through her hair. "I'm scared, Michael. I'm so worried about losing another baby."

I put my arm around her as she rested her head against my shoulder.

After a while she looked up at me. "How about you? How do *you* feel about having a baby now?"

"I'm thrilled by the very thought of it, but you are the most important person right now. I'm going to wrap you in cotton wool and wait on you hand and foot if that's what it takes."

"I'll hold you to that," she said, a smile in her voice.

Julie was still fast asleep when I awoke early the next morning. Grabbing my Levis and T-shirt, I dressed quietly in the bathroom and then headed out the door to go grocery shopping at Mr. Davies's store. Even though the Piggly Wiggly was closer, I preferred to support his family run business rather than give my money to a large corporation. After all he was our friend and had treated us well.

When I arrived Mr. Davies and his son, Tom, were busily stocking the shelves.

"My goodness, Mr. Romano! You're up before the rooster crowed," said Mr. Davies.

"I figured that was the best way to get my eggs and milk fresh."

"Where's Mrs. Romano?" asked Tom.

"She's still sleeping. I thought I'd give her a break today and get the shopping done."

"Lucky lady!" chuckled Mr. Davies.

"Yeah, I know," I said with a large grin. "Well, I gotta get moving. I want to get back before she wakes up and surprise her."

I bid them farewell and moved throughout the store quickly, picking up everything I thought we'd need for the week. Checking out was a breeze; I was the only customer.

Returning home with two large paper sacks in hand, I climbed the three flights of stairs to the apartment, puffing a bit by the end. If Julie was indeed pregnant, we'd need to find a new place to live that was at ground level. A big backyard for Junior to knock around in would also be a plus.

Keys and bags in hand, I unlocked the door and slowly pushed it open with my shoulder. Kicking my penny loafers off, I made it barefoot to the kitchen without disturbing Julie. I unpacked the perishables and stored them away in the fridge. Then I put on a big pot of coffee and sat down at the kitchen table, where I began to go through a list of recent real estate comparables of properties in South of Broad, in preparation for my meeting with Elaine and Arthur Sutcliffe at three that afternoon. They had decided to put the old mansion up for sale, claiming the cost of its upkeep had become prohibitive. They had been surprisingly frank about their teetering fortune, the result of Arthur's bad stock investments and having been forced to close one of their textile mills because of foreign competition. It was hard for me to imagine them living in any other place. The lifestyle suited them to a T, like characters in an F. Scott Fitzgerald novel.

"I smell coffee!" Julie said behind me. "What are you doing up so early?"

"Sit down, honey. Let me pour you a cup. You're walking around like a zombie."

She gave me an irritated look as she sat.

"What've you been doing?" she asked.

"I got all the shopping out of the way, and I'm going over a list of comps for the Sutcliffes."

After a moment what I said registered. "You did the shopping?"

"Yep. There's not a thing for you to do. By the way I got you some of those crackers you ate when you had morning sickness before. And last night, after you went to sleep, I dusted and cleaned up in here too. I'll go to the Laundromat tomorrow." I was quite proud of myself.

"Thank you, Michael. I'm still feeling a bit rough."

"Well, you just put your feet up and rest today."

At three I rang the doorbell at the Sutcliffes' home. Their elderly colored butler, Jonathan, greeted me.

"Good afternoon, Mr. Mike," he said. "The senator and Mr. Arthur are awaiting you in the library."

He ushered me in at a snail's pace and announced my arrival to the couple, who were sitting apart from each other on the couch, drinks in their hands and smoking. Arthur rose to greet me while Elaine remained seated, twirling the olive in her martini.

"May I fix you a drink, Mike?"

"Sure," I said.

"The usual?"

"Yes, please."

While he poured me a Scotch, I walked over to Elaine and offered my hand, which she accepted demurely.

"How's the campaign going, Elaine?"

Actually I knew that things were not going well. Elizabeth was keeping me apprised on an almost weekly basis.

"Terrible." She sighed, setting her glass aside. "We've bitten off more than we can chew. We never thought that dying old fart would have so much influence backing that hack of a fisherman, Pruitt."

"Elaine, you're up against the old party machine. Tom Avery and I were discussing that very fact a week ago. A lot of people make their money from the military contracts that Congressman Big Jim Pickens has brought into the district. They want to make sure they have his successor in their pockets. You're an unknown entity, and some of the liberal positions you have been touting have gotten them worried. So what are you going to do?"

"Fight on as best I can. I'll be damned if I'll throw in the towel—even though that fish peddler has a significant lead over me."

"Well, you can never tell. He may just drop dead the day before the election."

They laughed as I took my drink and sat across from them. I opened my briefcase, wanting to get on with business and go home to Julie.

I said, “I’ve filled out this listing agreement for you both to look over. And this is a list of comparable sales.” I handed them the papers. “However, when it comes down to a property such as yours, I don’t believe that any of these comps really apply, so I’ve added another fifty thousand above the best that have sold in the last year.”

As they read I sat back and once again admired the bookshelves, furniture, and priceless antiques that had so impressed me the first time I’d visited their home. What would happen to all those wonderful, lonely books yearning for human hands to turn their pages, allowing them to speak?

“Mike,” said Arthur, “I like your estimate of one hundred fifty thousand, but don’t you think we’ll have a problem with the banks appraising the house for that much?”

“I agree, Arthur. But a rare property like this one will most likely be bought by someone with good taste and the necessary cash to give the banks the cushion they need to make a loan. Anyway I think that with a little luck, we might make a deal for all cash. A house such as this in New York would probably bring close to half a million or more. It would look like a real steal to anyone from up there.”

“Mike’s right,” Elaine said. “Some Yankee carpetbagger would probably jump at it.”

“OK,” said a reluctant Arthur. He signed the listing contract and then passed it over to Elaine. She signed with a sigh and handed it back to me. I filled in the sales price, witnessed their signatures, then ripped out the copy and put it on the coffee table.

“I want to thank you both for choosing me as your agent. I’m certain you know plenty others you could have chosen from.”

“We owe you, Mike,” said Elaine. “You helped immeasurably in getting my senatorial campaign on the right track, even though you aggravated me to the extreme with your bluntness and stubbornness.

Also you kept quiet about Arthur's little dalliance with Debbie the night of your party. If it had gotten out, it could have ruined everything. It was stupid of him to be so careless, but then who could blame poor Arthur?" She looked at him with a smile. "Debbie is such a delicious young woman. Don't you agree?"

I sat rigidly still for a tense and embarrassed second or two.

"To each his own, Elaine," I managed to respond. Arthur smiled weakly.

"Exactly, Mike. To each his own. Who is to judge a person's relationship with another? Arthur and I have our arrangement, as you do with Julie. I really do admire yours—it's so rare."

As I left I remembered Dorothy Wright's words that New Year's Eve at her funeral parlor: *Beware of those cotillion belles and their menfolk! They like to mess around.*

FORTY THREE

I picked up the Sunday newspaper from the doormat and took it into the kitchen, where Julie was busy whipping up a bunch of eggs. As I laid the paper aside to refill my coffee cup, the phone rang.

"Romano here."

Elizabeth, sounding excited, asked me if I'd had a chance to read the paper.

"No, but I have it right here. Give me a sec...Holy smokes!" I blurted as I read the headline: "Congressional Candidate Alan Pruitt Suspected in Drug-Smuggling Ring!"

"Michael, what's happened?" Julie sported a worried look as I walked over, phone in hand, to show her the headline. "Whoa," she said.

I could hear Elizabeth breathing deeply on the other end. Shoulder to shoulder, Julie and I read further.

Alan Pruitt, the owner of several fishing trawlers, had been implicated in a major marijuana-smuggling operation. When questioned the previous night, he had denied any involvement and refused to comment further, upon the advice of his attorney. However, a reliable anonymous source had informed the paper that Pruitt's captain and crew, now under arrest, had said he had full knowledge of the illegal activities.

"He's finished, Liz," I finally said.

"Yes, and don't we know it! Elaine got a call from Congressman Pickens to cut a deal for dropping his support of Pruitt and throwing his weight and influence behind her."

"Well, I guess that does it. Elaine is now the poster girl for the state Democratic Party."

"That's OK with me, Mike," said Liz. "As long as she continues to support our original platform, I'm fine with it."

"Yeah, but don't forget ending the war."

As I hung up, Julie grumbled, "That witch! She has the most incredible luck. I can't believe it."

"Well, she's our witch, and she and Arthur have shown their loyalty to me by giving me the listing on their house."

"Be that as it may, the witch is still a bitch."

Julie didn't know how right she was. Not wanting to upset her and ruin my chances of continuing to do business one way or another with the Sutcliffes, I had never told her about Arthur and Debbie's cavorting on our back porch or that Arthur and Elaine had an open marriage.

Julie slid my breakfast plate across the table toward me and then sat down to eat. "I can't for the life of me understand the depth of Elizabeth's devotion to Elaine," she said.

"Don't you remember her telling us how much she owed Elaine for looking after her during their Radcliffe years?"

"Yes, but to give up a full-time, tenured teaching position? Leave her home state to become Elaine's lackey? It strikes me as being a bit excessive."

"Julie, she's not doing this just for Elaine any longer. She likes living in Charleston. As you know she's hoping eventually to get a permanent teaching position at the college. She told me one day in Toby's that she had no real friends up north and how happy she is to have us, the Averys, and the Baptistes as her friends here. We've become her extended family."

"Maybe you're right," said Julie. "But Elaine is such a phony."

"Julie, let's face it. Your opinion of her was poisoned by her going after me. You liked her when you first met her, didn't you?"

"I guess," she responded begrudgingly.

The phone rang again less than an hour after Elizabeth had called.

Julie picked up. "Yes, yes! We read the article," I heard her say from the kitchen. "Let me check with Michael. He's around here somewhere."

Coming over to me as I was leafing through the newspaper, she whispered, "It's Elaine. She wants us to come over for a little soiree at seven. She said the whole gang will be there."

"Do you want to go, honey?" I asked.

"No, but I know how important it is that we do."

"Thanks—I appreciate it."

Back in the kitchen, she said, "It's fine with Mike, Elaine. And I'm especially looking forward to it! See you around seven."

With a sly look on her face, my Machiavellian wife reappeared in the living room and said, "So how did I do, *darling*?"

"Don't you think you laid it on a bit thick?"

"Not with that one. She's easy to play when something appeals to her ego."

"You're probably right."

"Well, I guess that blows watching *The Ed Sullivan Show*, darn it! I was really looking forward to seeing the Rolling Stones. But I guess I can put up with the phony for a couple of hours."

"She's no more of a phony than the rest of us, Julie."

"What do you mean?" she responded indignantly.

"We're all dissemblers to one degree or another, depending on the circumstances. We put on masks when we sense a threat or change our colors like chameleons to protect ourselves or to get what we want. You just did it a minute ago with Elaine."

As we were heading out the door to go to the Sutcliffes', the phone rang again.

"Let it go, Michael," said Julie, exasperated.

"Better not; it might be important."

I hardly recognized the hoarse, despairing voice on the other end.

"Mike, can you come over? I need you to be with me."

"Sure, Jim. What's wrong?"

"Lloyd killed himself."

"Oh my God! What happened?"

"I'll tell you when you get here."

Julie was fluttering around me. "Michael, what's going on?"

"Lloyd committed suicide. I don't know why. I have to go over there."

"What can I do to help?" she asked in a shaky voice.

"Nothing right now, honey. I'll drop you off at the Sutcliffes'. I'll give you a call there. If it gets too late, ask Tom to bring you home."

Shoulders hunched in grief, Jim's hand shook as he picked up the brandy decanter to pour me a drink.

"Let me do that, Jim," I said.

He nodded as he rested the heavy crystal on the coffee table. He sat back on the couch, drained. As I poured, he said nothing, just looked past me in a daze.

After a somber minute or so had passed, he said in a voice weighted with gloom, "They murdered him, Mike."

Had I misunderstood what he'd said on the phone, that Lloyd had killed himself?

"It wasn't enough that they beat him half to death, urinated on him. Oh, no! The bastards had to carve up his face, horribly disfiguring him."

Sickened and angered by what I had just heard, I was about to ask him more when he broke down, sobbing uncontrollably. I didn't know what to do or say. All I could do was sit by helplessly and wait for him to cry himself out. When he had calmed, I picked up his brandy glass and handed it to him.

"God, Jim. I'm so terribly, terribly sorry."

"I know, Mike." He blotted his eyes on his shirt sleeve and then sipped his drink down slowly.

Gently I asked him who had done it.

"No one knows. It was late at night when he was attacked on Market Street, after leaving a bar he liked to go to. He told the police later that he was grabbed by three men he didn't know and dragged into a dark alley, where they assaulted him."

"What happened then, Jim?"

"Lloyd barely managed to make it back to the bar. The owner called for an ambulance and the police. They rushed him off to the Medical College Hospital, stitched him up, and sedated him. By the time I got there, he was asleep. I never got to talk to him." Jim was weeping again, shaking his head. "Then late this afternoon, he slipped out of his room unnoticed and found his way to the roof. Oh God. He threw himself off. *He threw himself off the roof.* I couldn't bear to go over there today to make all the necessary arrangements. He's got no family, so I'm going to take him back to Alabama and bury him there in my family crypt. Mike, can you help me tomorrow?"

"Of course, Jim. Whatever I can do, I'll be there at your side all the way until this is over with."

"It'll never be over with," he said bitterly. "To do that to Lloyd because he had a different sexual orientation, which he couldn't help, was purely monstrous. He was such a gentle man; he never hurt anyone. If anything he made people laugh and feel good. But the bigots and the religious zealots have reduced people like us to the level of subhuman."

We sat together into the night, drinking, with Jim reminiscing about Lloyd and his own life. I didn't say much, just listened. He needed to work his way through the pain. Weary with grief, Jim said,

"There was an unwritten understanding that we would look after each other no matter what. Now that I've lost him, there's no one to look after me here."

"Jim, you know that I will. I want to."

"No, Mike, you have your own family to care for. I've decided that when this is over I'll move back to Alabama, where at least I have some kin, to live out the rest of my life."

Rising, he stumbled, and I took his arm.

"Mike, I'm bone tired. I need to rest."

"Sure, Jim." I helped him upstairs to his bed, where he lay down flat on his back. I took off his shoes and socks and covered him with the quilt. I turned the light off and could hear him breathing deeply as I quietly left the room and showed myself out.

Forty Four

Two seasons had passed since Lloyd's death. Jim was now living comfortably with his older, widowed sister in a twelve-room house in Mountain Brook, Alabama, just a few miles away from Birmingham.

In the meantime Julie and I had purchased a lovely Victorian home on Colonial Lake. The location was ideal for us not only for the view but also for the fact that I could jog around the lake every morning. Once Julie had the baby, she would be able to do the same. The rooms were spacious, and the backyard was enclosed. Although the kitchen and bathroom fixtures were prehistoric, we planned to modernize them down the road. We had already added four more window air conditioners to make the coming summer months bearable. Julie was happy, healthy, and huge, and she was spending a lot of time with Rina and her adorable infant, Mala, talking mother stuff and doing an inordinate amount of shopping. Who knew that a tiny human would require so many clothes, toys, and pieces of furniture?

Returning home late one afternoon, I found Julie sprawled out on the couch like a beached whale, reading a magazine that on second look proved to be a scientific journal.

"Hey, honey," I said, "is there anything you need? Something to eat or drink before I go out tonight?"

"No, thanks. And please stop fussing over me like a mother hen. Everything is fine, except I can't see my feet anymore when I stand up. And these giant boobs are getting in the way. I can't wait for this baby to arrive. I'm so uncomfortable."

"Hang in there, babe—only six more weeks to go."

Groaning, she gave me a grumpy look. "Oh, by the way, Michael, I've been thinking about Jim and wondering how he's getting on. We haven't heard from him in quite a while. What do you say we give him a call and invite him and his sister down here for the christening when Caroline arrives?"

"Or Michael junior," I responded. It was a recurring discussion. "Anyway that's a great idea. But don't be surprised if he turns us down; Charleston has become a painful memory for him."

Sadly, Julie said, "Yes, I know."

"On another note," I said, "have you fed the puppy yet?"

On cue a little head peeked round the kitchen door, brown eyes shining, one ear up and one flopped down.

We had acquired a dog. Or, more accurately, she had acquired us. Julie had come home one day to find a small, brown furry thing cowering before a large, gray, spitting cat at our front door. At first glance the cat's prey looked like a rat, but then Julie realized it was a puppy. She scooped it up and carried the shivering, quaking, dirty mess into the house. She told me later that when she set it down gently in the kitchen, it spoke.

"Woof," it said plaintively.

When I arrived home that day and opened the door, I was greeted by a tiny fuzz ball of energy that spun in a circle and then squatted and peed on my shoe. Julie informed me that she was called Woofy.

"How do you know? Who does she belong to?" I asked, somewhat taken aback.

"She belongs to us, and she told me her name." Julie gave me *the look*, and then she said, "She's obviously been abandoned. She's only about four weeks old. She's staying."

OK. She was kind of cute. So now we had a new house, a baby on the way, and a puppy. Fortunately I had a good job and money in the bank!

Just as I was about go upstairs to change my clothes, Woofy started whining and skittering up and down the room. "What's wrong with her?" I asked Julie.

As I spoke the house began to shake. The ceiling lamp swung, and pictures tilted on the walls. Dogs began howling and barking outside.

Julie shot up with surprising speed from the couch, stared at me, and said, "What was that? A sonic boom?"

"I believe it was an earthquake."

Almost immediately we felt another unnerving shock. We rushed out of the house, seeking the safety of the street, Julie with a frightened Woofy in her arms. I wondered if this was going to be the big one, like the quake that had wrecked Charleston back in the late nineteenth century. Runners and walkers had frozen dead in their tracks around the lake, some talking excitedly to each other.

After about ten minutes, with no more seismic activity, everything seemed to have returned to normal. I knew all was well when I saw Woofy wagging her tail happily.

When we got back indoors, Julie said, "That was scary, Michael."

"Yes, I know, but what can you do? The planet has been hit with innumerable natural disasters over the centuries. You just have to be fatalistic and hope nothing catastrophic happens in your time. Besides, I feel fairly safe in this house where a quake is concerned; it's constructed of wood, with more modern building technology than those decades-older Charleston singles, especially the brick ones."

Julie looked a bit skeptical, but she nodded and said, "I hope you're right."

Then the phone rang. Julie picked up.

"Hi, Rina...Yes, we felt it. I agree, it was a little scary...Yes, I'm fine. How about you and Mala? Well, if you want to, come on over... See you soon." She hung up.

Laughing, Julie said, "Rina's coming over to look after me, but I think she was more frightened than I was. Anyway we both would have been alone tonight with you and Tom going off to hear Dr. King speak. So wait until they get here, and then you guys can go together."

After donning my black pinstriped suit, I went to the closet and retrieved a locked box from an upper shelf. I opened it and unwrapped the .38 snub-nosed revolver from a white cloth, flipped the cylinder open to make sure it was fully loaded, and then snapped it shut and slipped the pistol into my pocket. Standing in front of the full-length mirror, I buttoned my suit jacket to make sure the gun was hidden from view. I wasn't looking for trouble, but rumors were rife in Charleston that King's appearance could trigger violence, and I thought it prudent to protect myself.

Tom and I had made a point to arrive early at the old County Hall to make sure we got seats. Looking around we spotted Elizabeth, the Reverend Billy, and Mrs. Bouchon huddled in conversation in a row close to the front, flanked by the Blooms and the Baptistes. They all rose and moved to make us a space, and I took a seat between Marie Claire and Elizabeth. I asked her where Elaine was.

Angrily Liz replied that Elaine and Debbie had gotten cold feet at the last minute and decided not to come.

Before she could say another word, Mrs. Bouchon interrupted her. "Don't judge her too harshly, Elizabeth dear. Many of my people aren't here tonight either, fearing retribution."

"Yeah, Liz," I said. "Elaine's probably worried that if she shows up, she'll lose a lot of white votes at the polls."

Elizabeth frowned moodily but said nothing. Clearly something more was bugging her.

Then the Reverend Billy erupted. "Damn all those Negroes in this town who haven't come out tonight! Who are cowed by the white man, hiding behind their doors and shuttered windows. But then look at all those poor, half-starved island brethren, many without a pair of shoes to their name, who did come here tonight and are standing tall outside this hall, surrounded by a hostile police force, and giving their support to Dr. King and our righteous cause."

"Yes, Reverend," I said. "I sympathize with those folks, but they have nothing to lose and something to gain. But as Mrs. Bouchon said, many colored in this city fear retribution and *do* have something to lose!"

"Oh, yes, indeed they do, Duke," he replied darkly. "Their souls, for betraying their people."

"Exactly!" Elizabeth chimed in.

Mrs. Bouchon and I looked at each other in frustration and gave up.

After some time, when the hall was filled to maximum capacity, Dr. King walked to the stage, where various dignitaries and leaders of the movement were already seated in a couple of rows behind the podium. Although he wasn't a big man, King's stature depicted great strength. His voice was powerful and filled with deep conviction. He spoke with pure eloquence and reason combined. No "sound and fury signifying nothing" came from his lips, unlike the rhetoric of most politicians.

Speaking off the cuff, he admonished those Negroes who had made it in America and had forgotten their brothers and sisters, not extending open hands to uplift them from their poverty and misery. Then he chastised those who were advocating violence with their slogan of "burn, baby, burn."

He said, "I'm going to say, 'Build, baby, build.' 'Organize, baby, organize!' I've decided to stick with love. Somebody got to have some sense in this world..."

Striking a strong chord in me, he then hit on the Vietnam War. It was wrong for our country to be involved in a war that was causing the deaths of so many innocent people. He advocated that the money should have been used to fight poverty and hunger at home and to create jobs. This caused a stir in the mixed audience; most Americans, colored and white, felt it was unpatriotic to speak against the war.

As King continued to speak, with his audience listening intently and applauding often, a single loud gunshot sounded from somewhere behind me. As the crowd reacted in shock and fear, I instinctively reached for my revolver. Marie Claire, seeing me pull the gun from my pocket, grabbed my wrist in an iron grip, stopping me with a fierce look and yelling, "No!" I slipped the weapon back into my trouser pocket and stood up to see what was happening.

Someone called out, "It's nothing! It was just a lightbulb. A light bulb!" Others pointed up to the balcony, where some idiot had tossed the bulb down onto the main floor. People around him were now restraining him. Thank God Marie Claire had had the presence of mind to stop me. Who knows what might have happened, with me being white, waving a weapon around at that point?

Nevertheless Dr. King continued to speak, not missing a beat, ignoring the incident entirely. Here, I thought, was a man who had reconciled himself to the possibility of his early death in pursuit of an ideal.

When the meeting broke up, Tom said, "I haven't eaten, Mike. How about you?"

"Me neither," I replied. "What do you say we go grab a pizza at Caruso's?"

After we had ordered, Tom said, "I heard Marie Claire shout at you—what was going on?"

I looked at him, stone faced, and then pulled the .38 partway out of my pocket.

He paled. "Jesus Christ, Mike! What were you thinking?"

"I was thinking like a marine, and it would have been a big mistake."

FORTY FIVE

The baby was due to arrive any day. My mother had come in from New York to lend us a hand and to look after Julie. We needed and appreciated her help, and we knew we would be especially grateful in the weeks after the baby was born. However, from the minute she arrived, she took control of everything, from cooking, shopping, and laundry to rearranging the kitchen and the furniture and demanding I go to Catholic Mass with her every Sunday. It was like living under Mussolini.

Worse, she took every opportunity to complain about family members who had screwed her over in one way or another over the past forty years. Each time she started up, we glazed over. The rant always ended on a familiar note—that she kept getting it in the neck by trying to help others. I never quite knew what that meant, but I assumed it must have been something painful. But I didn't dare to ask her, knowing that if I did, it would start her up all over again. Julie took it all with surprising equanimity but did confide in me more than once that she was really looking forward to her parents' coming for the christening later on.

Julie spent much of her time lying on the couch with her swollen ankles raised, Woofy sitting patiently beside her and watching her every move. The little dog trailed her like a shadow as she puttered around the house or the garden, and she growled softly if anyone came near Julie, even me! She obviously didn't realize she weighed only twelve pounds. As we lay in bed, she would jump up and lie with her head resting against the large bump of Julie's abdomen, almost as if she were listening to the baby's heart beating.

As the time grew closer for Julie to deliver, I fell helplessly into a general state of anxiety coupled with unrelenting macabre thoughts of losing Julie and the baby. Worst of all an irrational fear haunted me that the thoughts themselves might in some weird way bring about a tragic outcome. I was angry at myself, knowing that the fear had no basis in reality, yet it persisted.

Several times I picked up the phone to call Jim Dawson, to hear him tell me to snap out of my morbid routine, but I didn't. He had his own real miseries, dealing with Lloyd's passing.

Staying occupied was the best way for me to cope. Luckily on Wednesday I was busy with engineers, roofers, electricians and plumbers who were inspecting the Sutcliffes' house. They had signed a sales contract with a couple from New York City for just short of ten thousand dollars below the asking price. I hovered over the inspectors nervously, hoping that nothing of major consequence might prevent the deal from going through. It would be a huge commission for me. Reassured that the old place was in great shape, I was about to leave to return to my office when I heard Elaine calling to me.

"Mike? Are you still here?" Her voice sounded small and uncertain.

"Yeah, I'm on my way back to the office. Don't worry; everything checked out fine."

"Please, could I have a few minutes? I'm in the kitchen."

Rather warily I stood in the doorway. Elaine was sitting at the nook table, dabbing at her eyes with a bunch of tissues. She was crying softly. I studied her face; her eyes weren't even pink, and her makeup was intact. No wonder other women disliked her.

"What's up?"

"Oh, Mike, I can't believe I have to leave here. Howard house has been in my family for more than a hundred and fifty years. And bloody Arthur lost it with his idiotic investments," she added with a flash of temper, her tears evaporated. I stayed quiet.

She suddenly flew out of her chair and put her arms around my neck, pressing herself feverishly against me. "Please hold me," she whispered. "I'm so unhappy. Arthur can't give me what I need. All he does is show up to functions and look pretty, and then he drinks too much. I need someone strong and driven, like you."

I disengaged as gently as I could. "Arthur's a nice guy. And you're still married to him."

"My God, we haven't had sex in years! And even when we did, he couldn't satisfy me. I never loved him."

I nearly commented that he was clearly capable of satisfying Debbie but wisely thought better of it. Elaine was still my client.

"I'm sorry, Elaine. I really have to leave. I want to get back to Julie. She's close to the delivery date, you know."

"Why do you always have to bring her up? This would be just between you and me. I promise you will never regret it."

I knew she was blowing smoke up my ass. All she wanted to do was fuck. I was also angry for Julie's sake and for all the other women Elaine's appetites must have injured.

"You and I have a mutually beneficial arrangement, Elaine, no more than that. And I'm warning you right now, if you *ever* come on to me again in Julie's presence or that of our friends, it's over with between us. Good-bye.

I left the mansion.

Our receptionist stopped me excitedly at the door to tell me that my mother had called to say Julie was going into labor. I spun around and bolted out again. A few minutes later, I was home, car keys in hand, asking if we needed to head for the hospital.

Simultaneously Julie said, "No," and my mother screeched, "Yes!"

I looked from one to the other, uncertain.

"Look, Michael," Julie said, "the hospital is what, three minutes down the road? And the pains are at least six minutes apart and really no worse than period pains. We'd only have to come back home again."

My mother stared at me. "We should go now. You never know what might happen." The voice of doom.

Julie sighed, but then she winced as another contraction hit.

"OK, that's it! We're going." I picked up the packed suitcase from beside the door and ushered a reluctant Julie out of the house with Gilda in tow and Woofy barking frantically behind us.

When we arrived at the Medical College Hospital, they called Julie's obstetrician, Dr. Marcus, down to the emergency room. He stayed with her behind the curtains for a few minutes, and when he emerged Julie was behind him.

"She's not ready yet," he informed us. "We'll be here when she is—maybe a few hours from now. There's no point in staying here and getting anxious."

Easy for him to say.

We all climbed back into the car. Once home again, Julie immersed herself in the novel she'd been reading.

She said, "Michael, don't let me forget to take this book with me when we go back."

Restless and fretting, I didn't know what to do, so I talked my mother into a game of Scrabble. I could tell when the pains were coming by the look on Julie's face, and I was timing them surreptitiously. After a while Julie got up from the couch and went into the kitchen.

"What are you doing, honey? Tell me if you need anything."

"Oh, for heaven's sake, I'm just getting a glass of milk," she called back. Then: "Oops! Glad that happened in here."

I rushed into the kitchen. Julie was standing in a large pool of water, a look of astonishment on her face. She turned and politely asked me to fetch her some dry panties and shorts; at that point I realized what had just happened.

"OK, Michael," she said. "Now we go to the hospital."

In the delivery room, Dr. Marcus asked me if I wanted to be present at the birth.

"Absolutely!" I replied. I couldn't have left even if I'd wanted to. By then Julie had my hand in a death grip as she breathed hard against the contractions. I wiped her sweating brow and whispered silly things in her ear. When the time came for her to push, I supported her shoulders and back and felt every pain with her. I saw the doctor reach for a large pair of scissors and wondered abstractedly what he was doing. Suddenly he was holding a tiny, wet, pink being in his hands. The nurse sucked out the baby's nostrils with a tube, and it cried lustily. I smoothed Julie's damp hair as she lay back, exhausted.

The doctor said, "Well, Michael, you missed having a boy by *this much*!" He held up his thumb and finger an inch apart.

"It's a girl?" I said, and everyone smiled. The nurse wrapped the baby in a blanket and laid her on Julie's chest. We both stared in awe at the little, red-faced, squalling infant. The nurse pulled aside Julie's hospital gown and put the baby to her breast.

"Hi, Caroline," I murmured as I fell in love.

We spent about a half hour with Julie and the baby in her room. I watched Julie as she held Caroline, tracing her downy cheeks with her finger and caressing her perfect, tiny fingers and toes. My mother and I took turns cradling the little tot in our arms, Gilda tenderly telling her in Italian how much she loved her. Finally the nurse came in and said, "It's time for Mrs. Romano to get some rest now."

Reaching down and taking Caroline from my reluctant mother's arms, she brought her over to Julie for her first good-night kiss and then to my mother and me for the same.

When the nurse had left with the baby, Gilda patted Julie gently on the cheek. "You're a brave girl." Then, pointing at me, she continued, "When I had that big lug over there, I screamed so loud they heard me clear over in Jersey!"

Julie chuckled. I shook my head, saying, "Always with the wise-cracks, Mom."

She gave me the Italian wave-off and said, "*Andiamo a mangiare!* I'm hungry."

Julie and I held each other tightly, saying nothing, until she gently pushed me away and sighed. "Go on, darling. Please don't forget to call my mum. She said they'd answer the phone anytime, day or night."

"I will, honey. You rest up now, and I'll be back in the morning." I leaned closer and kissed her. "I love you with all my heart."

Back home, while Gilda was in the kitchen heating up an egg-plant dish she had prepared earlier in the day, I began calling around to give Julie's parents and all of our friends the happy news. Then I checked my watch to make sure it wasn't too late to call Jim, given the difference in time zone. I rang him up and announced I was the father of a seven-pound, two-ounce baby girl. He was thrilled.

"That's wonderful, Mike! I'm so happy for you and Julie. Now you have a real mission in life."

"I guess I do," I replied happily. "Look, Jim, your last letter asked us to come visit you when we had the baby, but it's going to be a while before she's old enough to travel. Do you think you and your sister might be able to come to Charleston in April for the christening?"

He hesitated for less than two seconds before saying, "Sure, Mike. We'll be delighted to come."

"Great, Jim! Please forgive me for cutting this short. I've still got a bunch of people to call."

He laughed. "Then get to it, Mike!"

Forty Six

"Mom, the baby needs changing!"

"So change her yourself," came from the kitchen.

"But I don't know how to do it, Mom. Anyway she's pooped all over herself."

"Eh, *Madonna mia!*" she snapped, charging into the living room.

I held little Caroline at arm's length; Mom took her from me with a sniff and laid her on a blanket on the couch. She whipped off the stinky cloth diaper and handed it to me. I held it gingerly between two fingers and took it out to the diaper-service laundry bin on the porch. When I returned, the baby was clean and powdered and smelled a heck of a lot better.

"Look," my mother said, "I've been here for more than two weeks since Caroline arrived, and I'll be going home next Monday. You've got to learn how to deal with this shit yourself. You can't expect Julie to do it every time. Now watch closely, Michele." She folded a new diaper into a triangle and slid it under the baby's butt.

"You got that part?" she said.

"Yeah, yeah, I got it, Ma."

"Now all you gotta do is grab the left side of the diaper like this, pull the middle part up, fold over the right side and pin it all together, like this."

Then she held up Caroline as if she were a trophy. The baby was smiling and gurgling; she looked really pleased with herself, although I couldn't imagine why.

Gilda said, "You don't have to be an engineer to figure this out."

"All right, I got it."

It wasn't the engineering aspect that bothered me. It was the constant production of vast quantities of unbelievably smelly poop that made me gag. Women were supposed to deal with that.

"Mom, did Julie say when she'd be back?"

"No. She left with Rina a little while before you came in. They were going to do some shopping."

Looking in on my little sweetie, who was now fast asleep and parked in her bassinet, I said, "Mom, tell Julie I'll try to be home around five."

"You'd better be," she said, waving a wooden spoon dripping with tomato sauce. "I'm making one of your favorites for tonight. Baked ziti with sausage!"

"Don't worry; I won't miss that."

Enjoying the sanctuary of my little cubicle, with absolutely nothing to do, I decided to call Elaine's campaign headquarters and find out what was happening in the wild world of politics. The election was in three days. I had $500 riding on Elaine. I was worried, given how close the race was, that it might be money flushed down the crapper. The campaign was one of mud-slinging on both sides; someone in the Democratic Party had discovered that the Republican candidate had recently broken off an affair. The woman was incensed, having believed she was going to be the future wife of a congressman, and was all too willing to speak to the press about the affair.

However Elaine also had her problems. Arthur, drunk as a skunk one night, rang doorbells up and down the street in the old village of Mount Pleasant, where they now lived, lost and attempting to find his house. He was arrested for being drunk and disorderly. The citizens of Charleston were having a lot of fun with all that.

"Hello, may I speak to Liz, please?"

"May I ask who is calling?"

"Mike Romano."

"Certainly, sir. I'll put you through to her."

"Hi, Mike!" said Liz. "What's happening?"

"That's what I wanted to ask you, considering all the shit that's flying around in the media."

"I know. Isn't it terrible?"

"Yeah," I responded. "That's why you'll never see me running for office. So how do you think we stand?"

She paused and said, "Hold on. I'm going to close the door."

She came back on the line. "I believe the adultery issue will certainly help Elaine, especially where the women voters are concerned. On our side Arthur's drunken escapades are just a source of relatively mild embarrassment to the campaign and won't count for much. But let me tell you, Mike, it was pure hell the day Arthur was released from jail."

"What happened?"

"Elaine and Arthur got into a terrible fight, both of them hurling profanities and accusations at each other. Arthur blamed Elaine for his drinking, saying she was nothing but a power-seeking bitch. Elaine began beating him about the head with that heavy handbag she carries around. I really think she would have killed him if Debbie and a few of the aides hadn't pulled her off him. But worse than that, we've lost control of running the campaign. The big boys at the state and national levels have taken over. They have the money to make the difference as to whether Elaine is able to win or not. They call all the shots now; we're just puppets. What really irritates me is that Elaine and Debbie are only too happy to oblige."

"Why wouldn't they be? They're getting what they want—the prestige of holding high office and all the perks that go along with it. Why should that surprise you, Liz? You suspected nearly two years ago that their motives weren't altogether altruistic. Remember?"

"Yes." She sighed. "But I hoped I might have been wrong." Then, her voice breaking, she said, "I had wished for so much more, Mike."

"Look, Liz, you've done all you can for Elaine. Call it quits whether she wins or loses. You don't owe her anything any longer."

"You may be right; there's really no more I can do except be her friend. I had no right to expect that *my* idealism could be exercised through her. I guess I've been selfish, expecting too much from her."

"For heaven's sake, Liz! Stop beating yourself up. We all expected more from her. Let it go, and get on with your own life. Do yourself a favor, and get the hell out of there for a while. Go see Julie and the baby."

"I would love to, but not until this is over with. Just a few more days left."

"OK, Liz," I said, frustrated. "Take care." Then we hung up.

As I stretched out in my chair, I thought about Elizabeth, Ruth, Debbie, and Mrs. Bouchon and their efforts to further Elaine's political ambition. I was reminded of Robert Penn Warren's book *All the King's Men*. If I were ever to write such a book, I would call it *All the Queen's Women*. The mystery would be: who would kill Elaine off in the end?

FORTY SEVEN

I washed the dishes, and Julie walked the floor with a screaming Caroline, trying to soothe her. I actually missed my mother's help. Although Gilda was overbearing at times, she had brought order and calm to our household. Now that she was gone, with me working and participating in the cooking, cleaning, and diaper changing, I appreciated her help even more. On top of that, Julie and I were suffering from sleep deprivation, taking turns at night to care for the baby, who was growing like a weed and always hungry.

Caroline woke me the next morning at five thirty, squawking and sopping wet. I got up, changed her, and staggered down to the kitchen to prepare her bottle. I returned to our bedroom, plopped down into a chair, and began feeding her. She greedily latched on to the nipple of the bottle, working at it so hard that she finished the contents faster than a parched marine downing a beer. We must have dozed off, because the next thing I knew Julie was nudging me awake, Caroline still in my arms.

"It's time for both you lazybones to get up. It's eight o'clock."

Half an hour later, I was showered, shaved, dressed, and sitting at the table, half awake, reading the newspaper while Julie prepared breakfast.

"Fuck!" I yelled, startling Julie, who was pouring me a cup of coffee.

"What?" she asked me apprehensively.

"It says here that Elaine is supporting a troop surge in Vietnam. My God. I can't believe it. She's been in Congress for almost three months, doing nothing; and this is the shit she comes up with?"

Julie shook her head but said nothing.

"She's got to be nuts. We've just suffered thousands dead and wounded during Tet and God knows how many innocent civilian casualties." I read for a moment longer. "And now she's lambasting Cronkite as being a defeatist in the face of Communist aggression."

"You supported her. We'll have to suffer another two years with whatever that twit bitch might do next."

I didn't respond. Anger and frustration consumed me.

After breakfast, still quietly smoldering but managing a smile, I headed for the door. "Don't forget, babe—we have a date tonight."

"You bet! Rina will be over here to babysit at seven."

More than six months had passed since Julie and I had been out on a real date together, and we were looking forward to the grand opening of a new nightclub, Rhythms.

I was on my way to King Street with the heater going full blast in the car. I was meeting with Elias, Lopez, and Gunny Starr. I was struck by the way fate and circumstances controlled our lives. Elias, certain that the state would take over the college, had invited me to partner with him in the purchase of a large, three-story brick building on King, only a few blocks away from the school. Our plan was to modernize the old building, which had a commercial space on the bottom floor and large apartments on the second and third floors that we would rent to students. As luck would have it, Gunny had confided in me that his dream was to own a saloon. I called Bob Lopez, who had been gone from Charleston for more than a year. I remembered he had told me he wanted to open a restaurant in El Paso. Again the fates had stepped in: unfortunately Consuela's mother had gotten cancer, and Consuela had tended to her while Lopez was slinging hash in some truck stop. However, the old lady had recently died, and Bob's younger son hated El Paso. So Bob and Consuela were amenable to the idea of returning to Charleston to open a restaurant and bar with Gunny.

What made the deal work, other than the realization of a dream for both, was that the two men liked each other—and Elias and I had agreed to pay for all the necessary construction and give them a low rent.

Hit by a gale-force wind that almost ripped the car door off its hinges, with debris flying everywhere from upturned garbage cans, I dashed across the street into what was soon to become the King Street Tap.

"It's colder than a polar bear's ass out there," I complained.

Gunny glanced at Lopez and then looked at me. He snapped, "Romano, you pantywaist dago, you don't know what the hell cold is. You shoulda been with Lopez and me at the Chosin Reservoir. Half of the casualties we suffered were due to the freakin' cold. You could've filled a truck with the fingers, toes, and ears amputated due to frostbite."

Elias flinched and turned away, undoubtedly remembering his son.

Ignoring Gunny's remark, and eager to steer the conversation along a different path, I asked, "So when do you guys think you'll be ready to open?"

"Around the middle of February," answered Lopez confidently.

"Hey, that's just around the corner. So you're OK with the beer and wine licenses?"

"Yeah, we worked that out," Lopez replied.

"I can't wait to get going," said Gunny. "Just look at the beautiful mahogany bar I designed."

Lopez and I exchanged a smile. Whirling his wheelchair around like a top, Gunny rolled smoothly behind the low bar counter, ran his big hands over the lustrous wood, and ordered Elias and me to sit.

"See? Just the right height for me to serve and the customers to be comfortable."

He showed us how easy it was for him to move around, work the taps, and get bottles of beer, wine, and soda out of the low coolers.

"Looks great, Gunny," I said. "I'll probably drink up enough beer to pay off the cost of the bar within a year."

Chuckling, he said, "That's fine with me. As long as you don't go whipping up on any swabbies and wrecking the joint."

"Hey, that's all in the past," I said. "I'm a respectable businessman now. I keep my hands in my pockets."

A sad look rose in his eyes. "Too bad those days are over for both of us," he said quietly.

Impatiently Elias rose from his stool and checked his watch. "The contractor and fire inspector are late. They should have been here fifteen minutes ago."

"They're probably caught up in traffic," I said. "I heard on the radio coming over here that there've been several accidents due to icing on the bridges and overpasses."

I had just uttered those words when Mr. Bishop, the fire inspector, walked in, apologized for being late, and complained about the weather. A few minutes later the contractor arrived.

"Shall we get started?" said Bishop.

Elias said, "Yes, I've got to be out of here by eleven for a meeting with the mayor."

Half an hour later, with all of us trailing him, Bishop had examined the exit lights, the fire alarm system, and especially the fire extinguishing system under the exhaust hood in the kitchen.

"Looks good, gentlemen," he said. "I'll see to it that your certificate of occupancy is issued by no later than tomorrow."

Bishop and the contractor left. Elias said, "Mike, I've really got to go, but I'll get an ad in the paper for the apartment rentals this afternoon." He too took off.

I was getting ready to head out the door myself, but then I thought to ask about the sign for the outside of the building.

"Any day now," replied Gunny. "You know how it is with these fancy artists—they move real slow." He reached into his ratty briefcase. "Here's the rendering of the sign. Whaddya think?"

It was worked in scarlet and gold, the traditional colors of the marine corps. It read, "The King Street Tap." I laughed when I saw what was written underneath in smaller letters: "All servicemen welcome (even naval personnel). Proprietors: Gunnery Sergeant Starr and Staff Sergeant Lopez, USMC (Ret.)."

That evening, when Rina arrived at the house with her little girl, Mala, Julie was still fussing in the bedroom, getting ready. She finally emerged, looking lovely in a black dress made of some crinkly material that hid the remaining baby weight and a loose turquoise jacket. She was clearly taking this date seriously. She gave Rina the phone number of Rhythms, showed her where the baby's bottle and formula were, checked on Caroline in her crib—again—and generally drove us crazy until Rina, laughing, pushed us out the door.

When we entered the club, we saw Elaine, Arthur, and Debbie being ushered to a table marked "reserved."

Julie spat, "The one bloody night we get to go out, we have to run into Her Highness!" We were quickly seated at another table across the dance floor from Elaine

I rested the brown paper bags containing Scotch and gin on the table and sat down next to Julie. I took in the club's ambience. The owners had obviously poured big bucks into the place; everything spoke of money and class, from the comfortable chairs and discreet lighting fixtures to the raised bandstand, which was constructed in good part of cherrywood, with a dark-red velvet curtain behind it.

"Michael, Melanie and Eric are here," Julie said.

"Where?" I looked around.

"Behind that crowd just coming in."

We both stood, Julie waving to get their attention. They came over, and Julie and Melanie embraced while Eric and I shook hands.

"I haven't seen you in a while, pal," I said.

"Been busy chasing down drug traffickers," he said seriously. "Seems like no matter how many we catch, they just keep coming."

"I guess that's because the money is worth their risk," I commented. "And a lot of people see no harm in smoking grass."

"It's not only grass, Mike, it's heroin, and that's bad stuff."

"Well, I certainly agree with that. So—what are you drinking tonight?"

"Rum," he said, putting the bottle next to the others on the table.

"I used to like rum rickeys," I said, "until I got wasted on them one night in San Juan and wound up with a Puerto Rican hooker holding my head while I heaved my guts up. I've never been able to stomach the stuff since."

He looked appalled. "Mike, seriously, you shouldn't drink like that. It isn't good for you."

Oh boy, the defender of our coastline, health, and morals was back. But who was I to mock him? He was doing a far more dangerous job than I had done in the corps. Besides, he played a beautiful guitar while I could barely whistle.

Just then Maggie and Mark showed up at the table, completing our group. They had been dating since they'd first met at the party in our old apartment. I still felt uncomfortable seeing Maggie with another guy, but she and Mark seemed happy together.

The waiter appeared to collect the seven bucks per person for our setup charge. Setup included a bucket of ice, sodas, and various mixes. It was a small price to pay for having fun.

The girls were already chatting when Julie suddenly let out a most unladylike squeal.

"Maggie! What is *that*?" she said, pointing at her hand.

Everyone turned to look at the simple gold band set with a large, square-cut diamond that dwarfed Maggie's finger. Julie embraced Maggie and then a red-faced Mark. Soon we were all milling around the table, congratulating them on their engagement.

Julie said, "So when were you going to tell me?"

Melanie poked Eric in the ribs and pointedly remarked how beautiful the ring was.

When it was my turn to shake Mark's hand, he said quietly, "Mike, I know how you must feel about this, since you were Pug's close friend. But I promise you, Maggie is the love of my life and will be forever."

I looked him square in the eyes; he meant it. I grasped his hand firmly and wished him and Maggie every happiness.

Everyone's attention was drawn to the bandstand as a beautiful woman in a silver gown tapped the mic to test the audio. She called out, "Are y'all ready to party tonight?"

"Yeah!" roared the crowd.

"Are you ready to dance?"

The crowd roared again, "Yeah!"

"OK! So let's rock with E-Z and the River Boys from Memphis, Tennessee!"

Six colored guys trotted up onto the stage along with a fair-skinned Negro woman in a slinky red dress. Picking up their instruments without saying a word, they struck up playing and singing "Dance to the Music," which had many in the crowd rising to their feet and hitting the dance floor hard.

Wow, this was going to be one hot night. I tugged at Julie's arm, wanting to dance.

"Not yet, Michael. Let me finish speaking to Maggie and Melanie."

We guys just looked at each other, saying nothing, and were left to ourselves as the girls continued to yack away. Scanning the room, I noticed people were still paying homage to Elaine, who was faking smiles and bestowing blessings on her herd of followers. What was it that made people want to kiss the ass of some politician who did nothing for them? I was still sore at myself for the support I had given her over the last few years. I wanted to tell her so, especially now that she had become a hawk in support of the damn war. On impulse, when the music ended, I got up and walked over to her table.

"I was wondering how long it would take for you to come over and greet me," said Elaine.

"Hey, it's a two-way dance floor. Anyway I was busy with my friends."

The band started up again with a slow tune. I ignored Elaine and said, "Let's dance, Debbie."

Rising, Debbie smiled like a cat, glancing at Elaine. "I've been waiting for something like this for longer than you know."

"Well," I said, "now's your chance, *sweetheart*. Let's do it."

As we took to the floor, everyone at our table looked surprised, especially Julie. I gave her a broad wink. She nodded discreetly and raised both her glass and her eyebrows, knowing I was up to something.

As we danced, Debbie tried to draw me close to her. I stiffened and held her at arm's length.

"What's wrong Mike?"

"Everything. I've had it with Elaine."

"What on Earth do you mean?"

"She crossed the line as far as I'm concerned, coming out for the war like she did. Who the hell does she think she is? God? Men are bleeding, dying, and being maimed by the scores every day while she's sitting pretty up there in DC, enjoying the sweet life on the taxpayers' dime."

Defensively Debbie said, "Mike, a recent poll showed that fifty-five percent of Americans are for winning the war. And let me tell you, the numbers are far greater than that in the South."

"To hell with those ignoramuses. The South can't get over losing its own war. Jesus Christ, I expected more from Elaine and from you, for that matter. Basing life-altering decisions solely on a damn poll."

"Naturally we did. If we hadn't we could lose the support of the party and the electorate in the next election."

"So it's all about staying in office?"

"What possible good could we do if we were voted out?"

"Damn all you politicians. I'm tired of hearing that self-serving bullshit that passes for a reason for not doing the right thing."

Angrily Debbie tried to pull away, but I gripped her hard. "Not so fast, honey. Tell Elaine that before she goes to bed tonight, she should envision an eighteen-year-old marine or army kid in some putrid jungle, holding his guts in his hands, bleeding to death and calling out for his mother. And that mother who loved him and raised him will grieve for him until the day *she* dies."

I released Debbie, leaving her standing still and alone while the music played on, and returned to our table, where my guests sat, frozen, silent.

I said to no one in particular, "Well, that's done." Then I held my hand out to my wife as the band began to play "Blue Moon."

"Will you dance with me, Julie?"

She rose in one fluid movement.

"Always," she said clearly, for all to hear.

Forty Eight

I hadn't seen Sal, Kitty, and Burl for a while, so I planned for us to meet for breakfast at Bilbro's on Thursday. They had become family to Julie and me over the last four years, and I didn't want us to drift apart.

"Kitty, where's that man of yours?" I asked.

"Poor Burl. He's sitting at home, recovering from the flu. He says hi, and he wants you to go fishing with him as soon as the weather gets warmer."

"Tell him to set the date, and I'll be there," I lied. I hated fishing; it bored me to death. The few times I'd tried it, I didn't catch anything. However, Burl had proved to be a good friend and was a barrel of laughs. Maybe I would go at that.

"So how's everything with you, Sal?" I asked.

Morosely he said, "Not well, Mike. My son got his draft notice a few days back."

"Ah, shit."

"Yeah, my wife and I are sick about it."

"When does he have to report?"

"A week from now—but he isn't going to."

"Huh?"

Sal said, "I'll be damned if we're going to sacrifice our only son in a useless war. Donald is a gentle boy. Even if he were willing to go, he would be useless to the military. He wouldn't be able to kill anyone."

"What's he going to do?"

"We're driving him up to Montreal this weekend."

"But Sal, if you do that he could be facing some serious jail time."

"Better that than dead! Don't you agree, Mike?"

"Well, yeah, I guess I do."

"Besides," Sal said, "he can stay up there for the rest of his life if he wants. Most Canadians are dead set against the war. The Canadian government, by all accounts, is allowing men who object to the war to immigrate there. Various groups help them find work and assimilate into Canadian society."

"Too bad he isn't going to college," I said. "He could've ducked the draft like so many other kids are doing."

"He was never one for the books, Mike. He's an artist. You've seen some of his paintings—they're really good, aren't they?"

"Yes, they truly are." I meant it. "Tell Donald I wish him the best of luck and that I agree with the decisions you all have made."

When breakfast arrived I asked Kitty how things were going on the debit.

"It's tense," she replied. "The killing of those three Negro college students in Orangeburg and the wounding of a whole lot more has folks angry. I'm worried that something terrible might happen here in Charleston."

Sal said, "Hell! It was murder the way those cops opened up on them with their shotguns, claiming self-defense. No one has reported that those kids had weapons, and besides, enough cops and National Guardsmen were there to keep control."

"You're right, Sal. And the media keep changing the story. Looks to me like a cover-up."

"Please!" said Kitty. "Enough of the doom and gloom, boys. Let's drop it. Mike, how are you, Julie, and little Caroline doing?"

"We're all fine, thanks. The baby's getting bigger every day. And surprisingly Julie is enjoying staying home, being a housewife and mother."

Kitty smiled. "Give it a little more time, Mike. I'm sure she'll want to get back to work at a certain point. I certainly did! It drove me nuts being home all day."

"You're probably right—she takes time out whenever she can to keep up with all her scientific journals, and I know that one day she intends to get a PhD."

"Are you selling a lot of real estate, Mike?" Sal asked.

"Yes, a fair amount. I'm also making some good bucks buying rentals. But I'm really excited about a deal I recently made with Elias Pendergast on a three-story building on King Street. We'll be renting part of it out as a restaurant and bar to two good marine buddies of mine, now retired. The place will be opening soon under the name King Street Tap. So how about drumming up some business for them with the guys in the office and anyone else you know? I guarantee they won't be disappointed, and maybe soon we'll all get together there for lunch. Oh, and that reminds me! Don't forget Saturday, April sixth. It's Caroline's christening at the Unitarian Church, at eleven, and then lunch at our house to celebrate."

"I've already got it down on my calendar," said Kitty.

Sal said, "Kitty, will you please remind me?"

"Good Lord." Kitty laughed. "Not only do I have to look after Burl but you too?"

Sal looked at his watch and sighed. "Time flies. I've got to get back out on the debit with a new agent I'm breaking in."

We separated, and I headed downtown.

"I'm back, honey!"

"Hush! Not so loud." Julie touched her finger to my lips. "Caroline's sleeping in the living room."

"Oops, sorry." I peeked into the room to see the baby and Woofy lying flat on their backs on the play mat, snoozing peacefully.

"Did you have a nice breakfast with the guys?"

"Yeah, but Burl was home sick."

"Not too serious, I hope?"

"Kitty said he has the flu, but he's recovering."

"How are Kitty and Sal?"

"Well, good and not so good."

I told her about Sal's son ducking the draft by going to Canada.

Julie said, "I'm so glad we have a girl and won't have to be confronted by such a terrible situation."

"Honey, even if we had a boy, I'd do exactly what Sal is planning: drive the kid to the border myself. This gung ho bullshit attracts so many young boys into the service and then wastes their lives on some ill-conceived plan to defeat communism or to protect business interests, all in the name of national security."

Julie nodded soberly. "So anything new with Kitty?"

"She's frightened that what happened in Orangeburg could happen here in Charleston."

"Well, rightly so," Julie said. "She collects in the ghetto, like you did. Remember how concerned we were when Watts happened? And that horrible experience with that colored man wanting to beat you up in Jacob's Row?" She hesitated. "Michael, I have to tell you, I'm really worried, being at home alone with the baby all day, especially with all the recent break-ins around here and being surrounded by colored people who must be mad as hell. I know we've been here only a short while and that you love this house and being in the city, but don't you think we should consider moving to West Ashley or Mount Pleasant?"

I was caught completely by surprise, not having realized how nervous Julie was.

"Let's give it some time for things to calm down, babe, before we make such a big decision. I tell you what: I'll be with you every day for the next week. We'll turn this into a vacation in our own backyard."

Julie looked relieved but said, "What about your work?"

"I don't have anything big going on right now, and there's plenty I can do at home. I think it'll be fun. We can take Caroline to the beach if we bundle her up. Woofy would love it too!"

But what was in the back of my mind as I spoke was whether I needed to add some firepower to my small arsenal by getting a twelve-gauge shotgun.

FORTY NINE

It was a case of hurry up and wait as I paced the downstairs hall. I yelled out in frustration, "Come on, everyone! It's time to get going, or we'll be late for church."

"Calm down," Julie cried from the bathroom. "I have to change Caroline. She's pooped again."

"Eh, *marone*!" I muttered.

"Give her to me!" came my mother's voice as she appeared from the kitchen. "You go put on some makeup, Julie. I'll take care of everything."

Julie ignored the rather critical tone in which that was uttered; smiled sweetly, bless her; and scampered upstairs to our bedroom.

Resigning myself to the possibility that we might be late for the christening, I retreated to the front porch and lit up. Geoff, Julie's dad, was already out there, puffing away vigorously. We stood quietly together, enjoying a peaceful moment of masculine unanimity. Thank heavens for nicotine at a time like that! But the stress I was feeling wasn't due only to the risk of keeping all our friends waiting at the church. It was also because my mother was royally pissed that we wouldn't be raising Caroline as a Catholic and that her husband, Arturo, couldn't be with us, being down with gout.

On top of all that, Julie's mother, Winifred, who had been known to display anti-American sentiments on occasion, was sitting glued to the TV, as she had been for the last couple of days, giving out hourly reports on the recent assassination of Dr. Martin Luther King and the ongoing riots busting out all across America. Major cities were burning, including Washington, DC, where marines were manning M60 machine guns on the Capitol steps.

Other than that everything was fine.

Finally everyone was ready, and we piled into the car, the grandparents in the back, with Winifred holding the baby. Making it to the Unitarian church just under the wire, we waved to our many friends sitting in the pews and took our places next to another family who was also having a kid baptized.

The church was beautifully lit by the April sunshine streaming in through the old, stained-glass windows. Caroline was a picture, nestled in her mother's arms, dressed in the lace christening gown Julie had worn, brought over by Winifred from South Africa. Everyone was ready to do his or her part; we had asked Rina and Tom to be godparents, and they had promised fervently to raise Caroline as their own in the event anything should happen to us and to oversee her spiritual life. It belatedly occurred to me that Rina probably wasn't a Christian—I had never thought to ask—but it certainly didn't matter to me.

We all moved toward the font, and I felt a twinge of nervousness. The minister doused the other kid first, and he let out a furious wail, thrashing about and clearly not impressed. When it was Caroline's turn, she opened her eyes, gazed up at the minister, and then began to giggle irrepressibly as the water dripped onto her brow. It was contagious. Everyone began laughing, even my mother.

Soon it was all over, and everyone filed out to their cars and followed us back to the house. While they maneuvered for parking spots around the lake, I waited at the front door to welcome them. Julie, Winifred, and Gilda were bustling around in the kitchen, plating vast amounts of food they had prepared earlier and bringing it into the dining room. Geoff was busy in the living room, breaking up chunks of ice at a small bar we had set up in the corner. He said he liked the idea of tending bar and wouldn't have to wait for refills that way. He was also keeping an eye on Caroline, who was in her bassinet behind the bar. She, in turn, was watching her grandfather with great interest. Woofy, for once, wasn't at her side; the little dog was lurking around the kitchen, hoping for scraps to fall from heaven.

Last of all the guests, but not least, Burl and Kitty arrived. Kitty asked where Julie was.

"In the kitchen."

Without further ado, she took off, leaving me with Burl.

Marveling at his country squire outfit, complete with brown leather elbow patches, I said, "Good buddy, I need to tap your brain about buying a speedboat."

"Where on Earth will you dock it, Mike?"

"Somewhere west of the Ashley, in my backyard."

"What? What's going on? You've just gotten settled in here!"

"Yeah. But we decided to move to the 'burbs. King's assassination and all the other shit that's happened have set off a powder keg in this country. Things just keep going from bad to worse. I won't have my family living under the constant threat of violence in a city where we're surrounded by so many upset and angry coloreds. If what's going on in Washington and across America were to happen here in Charleston, well, I'll leave it up to your imagination what could happen to us."

Burl nodded. "I understand. Even my Island niggers are stirred up, and usually nothing ever bothers them that much. Look, when you've found a new place and are ready to buy a boat, we'll review the sales nationally to find one that suits you." Grimacing, he tugged at the crotch of his new pants and said, just as Elizabeth appeared, "Kitty made me buy these duds special for today."

Looking somewhat embarrassed, Liz said, "Uh...I do hope I'm not interrupting anything important, gentlemen. But should I put these gifts for Caroline on that buffet table over there?"

I looked over and was surprised to see a pile of festively wrapped boxes on the table.

"You didn't have to do that, Liz."

"It's a tradition. Besides, one is from Elaine."

"Really?"

"She apologizes for not being able to be here. She's hunkered down in Washington, probably scared out of her wits."

We hadn't invited Elaine. What was she up to?

Given Elizabeth's expression as she handed me the gifts, I figured she knew what I was thinking. I accepted both pretty packages graciously and placed them on the table with the others.

"When are we supposed to open them?" I asked.

"Later. Then Julie writes nice thank-you notes." Liz smiled at me.

I excused myself to move on to other guests. What kind of gift had Elaine come up with?

As I headed to the bar to grab a drink, Marie Claire called me over to her side. "Jean-Luc and I want to congratulate you on this happy day."

"So do we," added Maggie, who was standing with Melanie.

"Thank you. I still have to pinch myself when I remember I'm a father."

Jean-Luc laughed. "It changes one's perspective on life like nothing else."

"Yeah. Julie calls me Poppa Bear."

Eric, who had been standing quietly at Melanie's side, said, "Mike, I've been looking closely at your baby. I can tell already that when she grows up, she's going to be a real beauty." Melanie caught his hand and looked up at him wistfully as he continued. "You're going to need a shotgun to keep the wolves away."

"I know, Eric. I already have a twelve-gauge pump in the closet."

"Speaking of little girls who'll soon become big girls," Marie Claire said, "I've been trying to get Melanie and Maggie to join NOW. What do you think?"

She already knew my answer and was hoping I would carry the ball over the line for her.

"Well, for me the answer is easy. Without an organization like NOW, women will continue to be relegated to the position of being second-class citizens. And I certainly don't want that for Julie or for Caroline when she grows up."

Jean-Luc added, "Both the culture and the mind-set that disallow women full equality have to be changed—"

Melanie interrupted him. "But Jean-Luc, I don't like the way these feminists are talking. They seem to want to blame men for everything that's wrong with their lives, including their periods."

Maggie said firmly, "That might be true to a certain degree, Melanie, but as Pug used to say, you can't blame the whole organization for the actions of a few bad apples. Of course he was talking about the corps, but it's the same thing. Count me in, Marie Claire."

"And you, Melanie?" asked Marie Claire.

"The whole thing makes me uneasy; I'll have to think about it."

Eric looked at her quizzically, but I never found out what he was thinking because at that moment Caroline woke up and made her presence known—loudly. I left the group to go check on her and was happy to discover she had only peed. I changed her faster than I could assemble an M1 rifle.

In the kitchen Julie was warming up the last batch of meatballs to be put out. I asked her how things were going on her end.

She grinned. "Fine, honey. Everyone seems to be having a great time, especially my mum and the Pendergasts, Fanellis, and Jim Dawson. And Jim's sister's a real hoot! She's been telling embarrassing stories about Jim from when they were growing up in Alabama, which had him blushing! It's obvious that she loves him dearly."

"Yeah," I said, "Jim seems to be his normal self again. But I know that deep down he must still be hurting."

"You never get over something like that. If you're lucky, you just learn to live with it." Julie poured herself a glass of wine from a half-empty bottle sitting on the kitchen counter.

"Anyway what I found most interesting was that a lot of the conversation revolved around the time when they were all young, during World War II. Did you know that Elias joined the merchant navy before America got into the war? He felt it was imperative to get supplies to England, especially at the time when they were only weeks away from starvation."

"No, I didn't. But like we keep saying, there's more to that man than meets the eye. So what did your mother have to tell?"

"You're not going to believe this, Michael, but when my mum was working as a nurse in London during the war and was pregnant with me, she narrowly escaped being killed." Julie shuddered.

"What?"

"One of the nurses who worked the night shift got sick, and my mother had to substitute for her. When Mum came back to the house she was living in with a bunch of other women, she found it had been hit during the night by a German bomb, killing everyone inside."

"Jesus! How come you never told me this before?"

"I didn't know myself until ten minutes ago."

"Any other revelations?" I asked.

"She and Dad were bikers before the war, riding all over England, and Dad would get into pub fights over her when he caught some guy eyeing her."

"Well, there you go. You Yorkshire lasses bring out the devil in a man. But it's hard to believe, looking at them now, that they were ever that way."

She laughed. "Hey, they're still young—lots of miles on them yet! Oh, Michael, it's so wonderful having them here. I do miss them, you know."

"I know, baby. Well, maybe one day they'll find their way here."

Julie said as we walked from the kitchen, carrying two plates of meatballs, "So anything interesting on your end?"

I leaned in and whispered in her ear, "Elaine sent a gift."

"What?" she squeaked. "We didn't even invite her."

"Liz brought it with hers. It's that one over there in the white box with the pink ribbons." I pointed at the buffet table, now laden with presents. "Should we open it now?"

She smacked my arm. "We wait until everyone has gone."

So she knew the *rules* too.

Later in the afternoon, with the party over and our parents, Caroline, and Woofy taking much-needed naps, we quietly went downstairs to open the gift from Elaine. The curiosity was killing us. Julie carefully untied the beautiful satin bow and set it aside. Then, in the way that always irritated me, she tried to remove the wrapping paper without tearing it so she could reuse it later.

"Julie, for God's sake, just rip the wretched thing open! I'll buy you yards of that paper if you really like it."

"Hush! Be patient," she said as she meticulously removed the last of the tape, revealing the pale-blue gift box inside. She opened it and went through the same performance with the tissue paper around the contents.

"Oh my," she breathed. "It's a sterling silver jewelry box with golden inlay. Look! It's beautiful."

She opened the box, which was lined with royal-blue velvet, and said, "Oh! There's an inscription here inside the lid."

"Let me see that," I said.

It read, *For a new daughter of the South, from US Congresswoman Elaine Sutcliffe.*

"It's a bloody peace offering!" said Julie. "She wants you back at her side now that you have money and influence. Throw it in the garbage."

"Are you crazy? It's too beautiful to destroy. Besides, look at this," I said, showing her the Tiffany mark on the underside of the box. "I'll have a jeweler polish out the inscription, OK?"

"No! Just get rid of it. Give it away. I don't want the damn thing in my house."

After thinking for a few seconds about who might appreciate such a treasure, I said, "Pinky!"

"Perfect," Julie said. "She'll love it."

Fifty

I dangled my bare feet over the edge of our dock, watching the tiny marsh crabs scurry about as the water slowly rose with the incoming tide. I was happy in our little piece of America on this hot August day.

"Michael!" Julie called from the first-floor porch of our plantation-style home in the Charleston Country Club. "D'ya mind if Marie Claire comes over later this afternoon? She wants to talk to me about the NOW budget."

"That's OK with me. It won't interfere with my meeting with Elias. Hey, why don't you tell her to bring Jean-Luc along? When we're all finished, we can have drinks together. I'll call Elias and invite him to bring Trish."

We were glad that we had made the decision to move to James Island, away from the constant worry about living in the city. Julie was especially thrilled with the modern kitchen, bathrooms, and central heat and air. The lot was more than a half acre and had plenty of room for Woofy and Caroline to run around in when she found her legs. We had already been enjoying the club pool, where the baby splashed around like a little fish in her inflatable rubber ring. And I was learning how to play golf, trying to hit a goddamned little white ball straight.

When the Pendergasts arrived, the ladies split off from us, heading into the living room while Elias and I went into the den. I gestured to him with a bottle of his favorite bourbon.

"Not now, Mike, thanks. Maybe later."

Then, looking around the room, probably choosing where to sit, he decided on one of two identical club chairs separated by a round table. Anxious to know what he had to say, I bypassed pouring a drink for myself and sat in the other chair.

Leaning forward and turning his head, holding a thick manila folder in his lap, he said, "Mike, sorry to be bothering you on a Sunday, but I wanted to keep this private."

"No problem, Elias."

He cleared his throat. "I'll cut to the chase. I'm here to offer you a partnership in the company. I know that now you have your broker's license, you're probably thinking about starting up on you own."

Not quite believing my ears, I was slow to answer.

"Well...not really. So much has been going on, with having to rent out the old house, buying this one, and managing my rental properties, I haven't given it any thought. Besides, I'm comfortable with the way things are right now. So is Julie."

"I'm delighted to hear that." I detected a note of relief in his voice. "Anyway I have a folder here containing financials and tax returns for the company for the last five years. Don't try to read it now." He passed it to me. "Take your time, and consult with whomever you feel necessary. My offer is straightforward: an equal interest in the company for thirty-five thousand. I believe once you review the information, you'll find it's a very fair deal."

I was surprised, to say the least. "Why are you doing this, Elias?"

"Well, I'm getting up there in years. It's tough putting in sixty hours a week and traveling back and forth to the Savannah office. Also I need to be around more to take better care of Trish. Mike, I'm telling you this in strictest confidence. She's been under psychiatric care since we lost our son, and sometimes she gets so depressed that I fear for her life."

"Good God, Elias. I'm so very sorry."

"Yes." He sighed. "Mental illness has to be one of the worst things to deal with."

Disturbed and saddened, I wanted to end our conversation and get back to the women.

"Elias, I've been in the business long enough to know that your offer is a generous one. Give me a few days to go over things and talk to Julie. I promise I'll have an answer for you by the end of the week."

Back in the living room, Trish was holding Caroline on her lap, laughing in delight as the baby explored her glasses and then, chortling, latched on to the heavy gold locket that hung from Trish's slender neck. When Caroline grasped it in her chubby hands and brought it to her mouth, no doubt to test her new teeth on it, I jumped in.

"Caroline, let go of that! It's not a toy."

Trish said quickly, "No, no, let her be. This locket has been chewed on before. These dents in it were made by our son when he was little."

I looked worriedly over at Elias, but Trish was completely entranced by the baby and looked content. Julie smiled at me and gave a tiny shake of her head that told me to leave them be.

At that moment the doorbell rang. Woofy abandoned her baby-watching post to welcome Marie Claire and Jean-Luc. After the usual greetings, Marie Claire said, "To work! Then we can enjoy ourselves."

"Oh dear," said Trish reluctantly. "I should leave you to it then. Would you like me to take Caroline outside for a while, Julie?"

"For heaven's sake, no! There's no reason for you to go. Why don't you stay with us? This isn't going to take long."

Marie Claire had a predatory look in her eye. "*Mais oui.* Maybe you will find our cows interesting. I would be very glad to hear your opinion of our activities in NOW. Perhaps you might like to join us?"

As Trish looked momentarily perplexed, and Julie hid a smile, we men took the opportunity to troop off back to the den, where I offered Jean-Luc a glass of his favorite merlot and Elias his bourbon.

"So Elias," Jean-Luc said, "are you happy with your party's choice of Nixon to be president?"

In a searing voice, Elias responded, "By no means! *No*! I was backing Rockefeller, who, as you probably know, was for ending the war and wanted to steer the party in a more liberal direction. But in Nixon we have a warmonger who, along with Goldwater and others, has developed what they call the Southern strategy for the party to follow."

"I have not read of this strategy," Jean-Luc said.

"It's a strategy for gaining power in the South by supporting state rights, which begets racism against Negroes."

"Dammit!" I blurted out. "After all the blood that's been spent? This is what we get? More of the same shit?"

Jean-Luc shook his head, and Elias continued. "Now that the Democratic Party and its leadership have moved away from its once racist policy to become the party that supports civil rights, the radical wing of the Republican party is moving in to capitalize on that change and is all too willing to support and embrace the majority of white, southern segregationists by welcoming them into *their* party. I suspect that one day we will see a South that is solidly in the hands of extremist Republicans." He sighed. "So, gentlemen, I have resigned my position as chair of the state Republican Party."

"*Sacré bleu*! It is now even more terrible that we lost Bobby Kennedy to an assassin's bullet," lamented Jean-Luc. Elias nodded sadly.

"So what does that make you now?" I asked Elias.

"An Independent, like you, Mike."

There was a light tap on the door; Julie peeked into the room and said, "Hey, guys, when you're done here, why don't we have a spaghetti dinner? Michael made a huge pot of Bolognese sauce this morning, and it won't take but a few minutes to cook up some pasta and make a salad."

We enthusiastically agreed and joined the women. Marie Claire was working on tearing lettuce while Julie heated up a big pot of water for the pasta. I poured drinks for everyone.

Trish called to Julie, "Where are the clean diapers? This little one needs a change."

I was going to jump in when Julie said, "In the closet in the bathroom down the hall. Thanks, Trish!"

Trish took care of the necessaries without a blink. I guess you never forget some things. Elias watched the proceedings with a look of deep contentment on his face. Jean-Luc moved into the kitchen and started teasing Marie Claire, who turned and slapped him away, laughing. Julie slipped her arms around my waist.

"This is so nice, Michael," she said.

"Yeah, it's good to have friends...no, family."

While I twirled the pasta onto my fork, Trish complimented me on how good the sauce was. All at the table agreed, and Elias said it was the best he'd ever tasted, which was gratifying. Modesty had never been my strong suit.

"Thank you," I said. "I owe it all to my grandmother, Maria, who taught me how to cook from the time when I barely reached her waist. I watched her add ingredients to her sauce, and then she'd let me taste it from an old, wooden spoon. She would tell me, 'Learn how to cook, *piccolo* Michele, especially if you don't marry an Italian girl!'"

All chuckled and looked at Julie, who said defensively, "I make a pretty good ragù myself."

"You certainly do, honey," I responded. "I taught you everything you know," which earned me a hefty smack from her. As everyone laughed, little Caroline bounced up and down in her chair with joy, smearing mushy peas and carrots all over her face and into her hair. Woofy stood on her hind legs and tried to rescue some off her fingers.

The mood at the table was lighthearted until Trish asked if we'd been watching the Democratic convention in Chicago. We all replied yes.

"It sickens me," she uttered, "how those poor people were beaten by the police outside the convention hall. Especially the war veterans in their ragged uniforms, some in wheelchairs and others on crutches, with missing limbs."

Incensed, Julie said, "This country has hit a new low in its history."

"Not really, Julie," Jean-Luc said. "It was far worse during the Great Depression. One incident that has always stood out in my mind was when many World War I veterans, known as the Bond Marchers, who were out of work and impoverished, came to Washington, quite a few with their families, to lobby the government for an early payment of bonuses for their service in the Great War. After heartbreaking months of petitioning their government to no avail, they were routed by a force of tanks and cavalry and were driven out of the Capitol at bayonet point."

"Oh my Lord," said Trish, who was clenching her napkin tightly. "Were there many hurt?"

"Unfortunately yes," replied Jean-Luc. "And the militia burned their tents and all their worldly belongings to the ground. When it was all over, two veterans lay dead, killed by the police. Many others were injured, and two infants died when the vets and their families were gassed. It was a travesty—a black day in American history."

We were all dumbstruck by the images Jean-Luc had so vividly depicted.

Marie Claire shook her head and said, "Fascists!"

"Yes, *ma chérie*, fascists," said Jean-Luc, then he asked me, "Michael, did you ever hear of a marine general called Smedley Butler?"

"Who hasn't? He's a legend—winner of two Congressional Medals of Honor. He hated the fat cats on Wall Street who used his marines to protect their business interests all over the world."

"Exactly," said Jean-Luc. "Do you also know that some of those business interests, those fat cats, approached him to overthrow the government of the United States because they were worried that FDR was leading the country down a socialist path that would take their wealth and power away from them?"

"What?" said Elias. "What are you talking about?"

"A coup d'état. They came to Butler after he had retired from the military to ask him to lead an army of five hundred thousand men, mostly veterans, which they would raise mainly through the American Legion. They intended to use this army to bring down the constitutionally elected government and install a fascist one modeled on that of Mussolini's Italy."

"How do you know this?" Elias asked. "I've never heard of anything remotely like this happening."

"As a historian I have investigated the information available regarding this matter, and I believe there's enough evidence out there to support the validity of the story. Butler himself gave a dramatic public speech detailing the planned coup. The media played it down, and a committee charged to investigate it appears to have whitewashed the whole affair. Eventually the whole matter was dropped. Remember, this was back in the thirties. We may never know the whole truth about what really happened. That being said, we must *never* take our democracy for granted, believing it will endure forever. We must remain eternally vigilant and remember that turmoil always paves the way for the oppressor's boot."

We sat in silence, digesting what we had heard along with our dinner. Caroline, now camouflaged in orange and green and tired of being ignored, decided to fling her bottle halfway across the table, startling everyone and breaking the spell. Julie lifted the sticky baby into her arms and said, "If you'll excuse me for a few minutes, I really should clean this one up and put her to bed."

Trish rose with alacrity, saying, "Oh, let me help you, please." The three of them went upstairs, and soon we could hear the sounds of water running and Caroline giggling.

Elias smiled at me. "You know, I haven't seen Trish this happy for a long time. This has been a wonderful evening and a fascinating conversation."

"Let's round it out with some coffee and brandy on the porch," I said.

We savored the moonlit night and the scent of the ocean. Marie Claire gazed out at the water with a decided gleam in her eye. "I want to hear about this boat you're planning on getting. I hope it will be a speedy boat?"

"*Ma chérie*, I think you mean a speed boat," said Jean-Luc.

"But of course. A speed boat will be speedy, *non*?" said the incorrigible lady.

FIFTY ONE

"Good mornin', Mr. Mike," said George, our office janitor. He was polishing the shiny brass plate to the right of the front door that read "Pendergast and Romano Realty." "A mite cold today, sir, don't you think?" he said.

"Well, you got to expect that, George. It's only two days until Christmas."

"Yes, sir. I 'preciate you and Mr. Elias giving me the week off to go visit my kin. You going travelin' anywhere, sir?"

"No," I replied. "We're staying here in Charleston for the holidays, just enjoying our family and friends."

"That sound real nice, sir."

"Well, George, have a good holiday. I'll see you when you get back."

Checking my mail and my schedule for the day, I saw that I had only a few things to do, mainly signing commission checks for a few agents. Most of our people had already left for the long holiday, including Elias and Trish, who were visiting relatives in Brevard, North Carolina.

Our one remaining secretary for the day sang out, "Mr. Romano, pick up on line one, please. Mrs. Baptiste for you."

Good Lord! Marie Claire calling my office? And at that hour? Must have been something serious.

"Marie Claire! Good morning."

"Bonjour, mon ami! Ça va?"

I had learned enough by then to answer, "Fine, thank you. What can I do for you?"

"I've been trying to reach our congresswoman, Elaine, for more than a month. Every time I call, they tell me she's not here, she's in Washington, she's doing this or that. Do you know where I can find her?"

"Not really," I replied. "I haven't had much to do with her lately, and I don't think her home phone number is listed. May I ask what you want to talk to her about?"

"NOW! NOW! What else? I want her to join us or support us. She's a woman, no?"

"Last time I looked," I said, laughing. "I'll tell you what I'll do. I'll call Elizabeth. She'll probably know how to reach her."

Marie Claire was probably getting the royal runaround. The National Organization for Women was a political hot potato. I was certain Elaine would stay clear of it, not wanting to risk controversy or votes. The little I was hearing from Elizabeth, who Elaine had also marginalized, much to her distress, suggested Elaine was enjoying her life in DC while Arthur had secluded himself in Beaufort and was diving deeper into the bottle. What was more, their oldest son had been kicked out of boarding school for drinking and drugs. Elaine's family was disintegrating as she remained in thrall to Potomac fever, oblivious to all except those who served her purpose.

Around eleven thirty, bored and hungry, I headed out to the Tap, to have lunch and some holiday cheer with Gunny Starr and Lopez. The minute I walked in the place, Gunny started to heckle me.

"Bring out the silver and the good china. The landlord's here!"

Laughing, I took a seat at the bar. Gunny wheeled his way to the cooler to grab me a beer. "To what do we owe the honor of this visit?"

I reached into a shopping bag and pulled out a bottle of single malt Scotch decorated with a pink bow and a long box containing a chef's knife wrapped in a blue bow for Lopez. I set them on the bar.

"What's with the pink bow?" said Gunny, eyeing the bottle.

"I heard from Lopez here that it's your favorite color."

"You wiseass wop! I'm gonna crown you with this!" he said, grabbing my bottle. Then, grinning, he spun around again and snagged a brew for himself and a cola for Lopez. He held his drink out, and we responded likewise, toasting the holidays.

Damn, it felt great being with them.

"What's the special today?" I asked.

"Open-face roast beef sandwich with brown gravy, mashed potatoes, and peas," said Lopez.

"Sounds good. I'll go with that."

While Lopez was busy getting my lunch, I asked Gunny how he was feeling.

"Not too bad," he said, rubbing his stumps, "but I keep getting what the docs call phantom pains, like my legs are still there."

I wished I hadn't asked. What the hell had I expected him to say? That he was feeling great, running six miles every day like we'd done together only a few years back in the corps? However the question hadn't seemed to bother him that much.

Without warning he launched into a tirade. "You've seen those coffins on TV? Coming back from 'Nam by the planeload, draped in American flags?"

"Yeah, Gunny, it pains me to watch it."

"If we keep this up much longer, we're going to lose more guys than we did taking the islands back from the Nips. They've got our kids caught up in a world of shit out there, with no end in sight."

"I know, but what can little guys like us do?"

A silence fell between us: two warriors, swordless, caught up in a system about which we could do nothing. As he stared through me, deep in thought, a dozen people came in, a few heading for the bar.

Lopez set my lunch down in front of me. "Extra beef for you!"

As I finished my meal at the crowded bar, Gunny racing back and forth, slapping beers and sodas on the counter with a friendly word here and there to patrons. When I got up to leave, he yelled out, "It's on the house, Romano. Merry Christmas and happy New Year!"

Filled with holiday spirit, I drove through my old debit on my way to see Pinky. It looked sadder to me, even though I knew it couldn't have changed that much. I chalked it up to having lived outside the city for a while, in comparative luxury.

Continuing on my way, I felt a twinge of nostalgia, especially when I passed by Dorothy Wright's funeral parlor, remembering that first New Year's Eve on the debit, when she'd invited me into her kitchen and gotten me snockered on Scotch and milk. She had been right on the money about Elaine; she had become a curse to anyone who got too close to her.

At Pinky's I pulled out the silver box, which Julie had wrapped in bright Christmas paper, and knocked on the door.

"Hello, Mr. Mike. Are you back to collecting again?" asked the twin who opened the door.

"No, I'm here to see Pinky. Where's your sister?"

"She visiting down the block, playin' with one of her friends, and I'm here a-caring for Pinky."

"Why, what's wrong?" I asked.

"She dyin' in a big way," the child replied softly.

Entering the tiny room where Pinky lay, half asleep, I said, "Hello, Pinky."

She didn't respond.

Then I said, "Pinky, it's Mr. Mike. I have something for you."

She slowly turned her head to see me in the dim, kerosene-lit room. "Momma din't leave no insurance money for you."

Tears rushed to my eyes. She was very ill. She was so weak, she couldn't raise her head from the pillow. I unwrapped the package for her and held out the gleaming jewelry box for her to see.

"What that, sir?" she said.

"A jewelry box for you, Pinky, for Christmas."

"My goodness," she said faintly. "It's beautiful. Thank you kindly. I's so appreciating that."

Unable to suppress the ache in my heart, I placed the box on the table beside her so she could see it. "Get well, honey. I gotta go collecting."

Crossing the Ashley River Bridge into another world on my way home to Julie and Caroline, I thought about my father, who had afforded us the wonderful life we were now enjoying. Yes, he had marked me hard. But that had only steeled me to go up against a hostile world. God only knew what combination of nature or events made him the way he was. Whatever the reason, in the end he sought redemption and probably hoped for forgiveness.

Merry Christmas, Mike! Rest in peace.

Fifty Two

Thursday morning's office meeting dealt primarily with the Fair Housing Act and the implications of any agents violating it. The law had been passed a year back to protect buyers and renters from sellers' and landlords' discriminating practices. However, some agents weren't getting the message.

Shortly after the meeting ended, I heard one of the agents say, "I'll be damned if I'm gonna tote any coloreds around in my Caddy, smelling of cheap cologne and wanting to buy into a white neighborhood! This is a case of pure communism. It's sure gonna hurt the value of real estate in our white communities."

Elias catapulted past me out of his office, beet red in the face. "John, if that's the way you feel, put your license on my desk right now and find another company that might have you."

Cowed, John slumped his shoulders. "But Elias! I know you gotta be feeling the same way."

"Maybe so, maybe not. But it's the law. I'll be damned if this company is going to be sued because of the likes of you."

Elias returned to his office and slammed the door. I headed out to take a brisk walk down to the waterfront. I was suffering from an acute case of cabin fever and calluses on my executive ass, from sitting in an office most of the day, dealing with the problems of others.

John's remarks about hurting the value of real estate presented me with a moral dilemma. On one hand I wanted the minorities to enjoy the same rights as everyone else. On the other I didn't want them or anyone else affecting the value of my substantial holdings. If the situation were reversed, wouldn't the Negroes feel the same way? In the end it came down to protecting your pocketbook, whoever you were. Wasn't that the moral thing to do?

As I passed the First Federal Bank on Broad Street, I heard a voice calling out from behind me.

"Mike! Hold up!"

Ruth Bloom was loaded down with a stack of folders under one arm and a heavy briefcase almost half her size. Moving quickly on her little feet, she caught up with me.

"Mike, how are you? I haven't seen you in quite a while."

"I've been busy running a real estate company and changing diapers."

"Boy, don't I know about that. Working and having a young baby sure cramps your social life."

"You're not kidding," I said. "If it weren't for the TV and books, we'd go stir crazy. So what's happening with you?"

"The usual. Working on civil rights issues, making sure the state stays on track with federal laws. By the way there's a big fight brewing over at the Medical College Hospital involving Negro employees who are demanding higher wages and better working conditions. Do you know there isn't one single Negro doctor over there? And the only Negro registered nurse who *does* work there has been relegated to being an assistant. Their attempts to negotiate with the administration have been met with downright hostility."

"Ruth, did you really expect the segregationist mentality to evaporate overnight? It's not just the coloreds who are being treated that way. They don't pay *any* of the women an equitable wage. Just ask Julie."

"Well, keep an eye out at the end of this month or the beginning of April. The shit's going to hit the fan." She picked up her briefcase. "I have to run, Mike. Give Julie my love, and kiss little Caroline for me. Bye!"

I wanted to speak to her further. What she had said sounded ominous.

When I got back to the office, Molly Pringle, our receptionist, buzzed through with a call on line three.

"Hello, Romano here."

"Mike, it's Tom."

I was happy to hear his voice, at least until he said, "I need you to find me a rental to live in."

"What for?" I was confused.

"Rina wants me out of the house. She found out I've been having an affair with Elaine."

"Shit, Tom, are you out of your mind? After all the conversations we've had about her?"

"I know, Mike. I'm a hypocrite. But I need your help. Please."

"Sure." I felt depressed for my friend and Rina.

"I love Rina, Mike. You must know that. But Elaine is such a temptress, I couldn't resist her. The sex was incredible. I haven't had many women in my life—just one before I met Rina."

I really didn't want to know any details of sex between Tom and Elaine, so I asked him how Rina had found out. It was an old story. Rina had overheard Tom talking on the phone to Elaine one afternoon when she came home unexpectedly.

"Well, to be honest with you, Tom, I think you're an idiot. The fact that you never sowed much in the way of wild oats is no excuse, but it does make it more understandable." After a pause, I continued, "Look, wait before getting a rental. See what unfolds. You could move into a motel for a while. By the way when did this all happen?"

"Late yesterday afternoon. Look, Mike, I don't want our marriage to end. I love Rina and Mala. Please try to explain this to Julie. She knows you had your problems with Elaine too. Maybe she could talk to Rina, if she hasn't already today, to help me make it right."

I didn't point out that I had rejected Elaine. "I will, Tom. I think it would be terrible to end this marriage because of one transgression, assuming it's over between you and Elaine."

"It is, Mike! I swear it is."

I figured I'd better get home before Rina called, so I could explain to Julie what had happened. I faked a call coming in on the other line, and hung up.

Julie was surprised to see me back before noon.

"What's up? Are you sick?"

"Sit down, babe. I have a lot to tell you."

I recounted my conversation with Ruth about what was going on at the medical hospital.

"It doesn't surprise me in the least. They don't seem to care about us white women, so why would they care about Negro workers? Sometimes I think the only way to get their attention would be to set the bloody place on fire!"

She was still sizzling when I continued with some trepidation, "Julie, Rina has kicked Tom out of the house because she found out he's been fooling around with Elaine."

There was a moment's silence as Julie absorbed this news, and then her face flushed scarlet with fury. When the floodgates opened, Elaine was the target, not Tom.

"That...that...horrible...*vixen*," she finally spat.

"Vixen?" I asked.

"I couldn't come up with a rude enough word," she sputtered. "Get me a drink, please."

"How about *black widow spider*?" I said as I headed for the liquor cabinet.

"Not bad." A smile twitched on her lips.

"Julie, Rina's going to call. I believe Tom is sincere; his voice was breaking when he told me. I think we should help them any way we can. It would be terrible if they threw away their eight years together."

She sighed. "But it's going to take time for Rina to adjust to all this."

"Sure! But you're the one person who can work through it with her. She doesn't have family here, and she has Mala to raise. Think of the economic consequences for both of them. And besides, remember what Bertrand Russell said—that infidelity is the poorest of grounds for divorce."

"Bullshit! Don't you ever try it, buster. I'd kick your arse out in a skinny minute."

As I began to undo my tie and unbutton my shirt, Julie asked, "Aren't you going back to work?"

"No, I'm going to put on my sweater and Dockers and take the boat out. I need to unwind."

"Are you sure? Caroline is sleeping. All's quiet. Why don't we take advantage of the moment?" She was already stripping off her T-shirt and eying me speculatively.

"That's a much better form of relaxation," I said.

FIFTY THREE

Some time had elapsed since I had last spoken to Ruth Bloom. During those weeks about a dozen hospital workers had been fired from the Medical College just for seeking decent wages and better working conditions. Many others had been arrested when they picketed in front of the hospital, demanding union representation. However, all their efforts to deal fairly and openly with the administration had been met with contempt and insults. Clearly a storm was about to descend on the peninsula city.

On a Sunday afternoon, Melanie invited us over to her apartment on Rutledge Avenue for a late lunch. While Julie helped Melanie in the kitchen, Eric entertained little Caroline and me in the living room, playing his guitar and singing.

As he set his instrument aside, I asked him what he would be doing when he got out of the Coast Guard in a few months.

"Going back up north to find a job," he said.

"What about Melanie? Is she going with you?"

"I really don't know. We seem to have reached a crossroads. Melanie is determined to stay here in Charleston, and I need to live in a more cosmopolitan environment and a cooler climate. Besides, there aren't any well-paying jobs for an engineer down here."

"Jeez, this has to be rough on both of you."

"Yes. We do love each other, but not enough to want to give up our lifestyles. I think we're both holding out to see who blinks first when the time comes for me to leave."

The girls set the food on the table, and Melanie called out, "Y'all come eat!"

As we were close to finishing a delicious lunch of roasted chicken, mashed potatoes, and corn on the cob, cooked very southern style, I asked Melanie how her nursing responsibilities were being affected by the strike.

"Not well, Mike. We're all having to work our asses off, covering for those monkey grunts out there on the picket line."

"Monkey grunts?" Julie sounded horrified. She obviously couldn't believe her ears. "Is that what you call those people?"

"Yes, Julie. All they're good for is assisting us and cleaning up. They can't help that they're so damn stupid, but now they have the nerve to make it harder for us, having to cover for them because they want more money and some northern union to represent them. They don't realize that the union will only take their money and give them nothing in return."

"Excuse me, Melanie," I said, "you obviously don't know anything about unions! Ask any members of the AFL-CIO, Teamsters, or United Auto Workers if their lot isn't way better now. Before those unions were formed, the workers lived in poverty and were literally worked to death. Today many of those same people enjoy good wages, pensions, and health benefits. Millions of them have joined the middle class."

"There you go, Mike, speaking like a true socialist, northeastern-establishment Yankee."

"If that's what I am, good! So be it."

Eric interjected, "Melanie, calm down. Mike's right, honey. You only know what you've grown up with down here. And I have to say, I think it's horrible the way the leaders here in the South have convinced you and so many others of the inferiority of the Negro race and demonized them in the process."

Caroline started to whimper in the next room. Melanie jumped up and threw her napkin down on the table. "For Christ's sake! Let's just drop it, OK? We're not getting anywhere, and it's ruining our lunch. Julie, could you please help me with the coffee and dessert?" Julie gave her a withering look as she left the room to get Caroline.

Just then the sound of singing floated up to us from the street. At first it sounded like a car radio, but then the singing swelled. Eric went out to the balcony to see what was going on.

Excitedly he shouted back to us, "There are hundreds, maybe thousands of coloreds, marching and singing, coming down Rutledge!"

We all rushed out to look. As the marchers came closer, I recognized Dr. Ralph Abernathy and Coretta King locked arm in arm at the head of the crowd, leading them in singing "We Shall Overcome."

As the ranks of marchers passed by, I saw Mrs. Bouchon and the Reverend Billy striding along purposefully, with looks of great resolve on their faces.

"Mike," Eric said, "this is our moment of truth. If we believe in what we say, we must act."

As Eric turned to head down the stairs, Melanie yelled out, "If you join them, it's all over between us!"

"Melanie," said Eric, turning to look back at her, "it's been over. We just didn't know it until now."

As he bolted down the stairs to join the march, I looked at Julie, who was holding Caroline in one arm and her bag in the other.

"Go, Michael," she said. "Join them."

"My God, Julie," said Melanie, "I thought you of all people would have understood, coming from South Africa."

"I do understand. I hated apartheid there, and I hate it here. I'm taking the baby home now. Thank you for lunch. Good-bye, Melanie," she said with an icy finality.

"Thanks, baby," I told her. "I love you."

Catching up with Eric, I linked arms with him and Mrs. Bouchon. Reverend Billy was on her other side. Mrs. Bouchon smiled at me. I just nodded; we didn't have to say anything.

As the marchers turned onto Calhoun Street and then Ashley Avenue, we passed the Medical College Hospital, heading back to the old County Hall, where they had first assembled. Eric and I broke off a good part of the way back, said our good-byes, and then went back to Melanie's apartment building. He'd parked his car in the rear lot.

Shit! I couldn't believe my eyes: there was Eric's beautiful guitar, smashed to smithereens and lying across the hood of his car, which was badly dented. He was amazingly calm as he stared at his ruined instrument, which dangled in two pieces held together only by its taut strings. I couldn't find any words to say, but I wanted to wring the neck of that magnolia bitch.

He laid the broken Martin gently in the trunk of the car, looking at it as if it were a departed friend. I examined the damage to the hood.

I said, "I know a good body repair shop that could fix this like you would never believe anything had happened."

"OK, but my twelve-string is beyond repair."

I wanted to tell him not to worry, I'd buy him another one, but that would have been insulting. I felt partly responsible for what had happened. If only I had kept my trap shut and not asked Melanie how things were going at the hospital.

"Look, Eric, I don't know about you, but I could certainly use a drink before you drive me back home. I know a place not too far from here, in the Neck area, where we can go. Whaddya say?"

"OK, Mike. Let's go."

Seated in the windowless, dark-purple block building hidden from view by a lumberyard, we ordered.

"It's been one hell of an afternoon for you, Eric," I said.

He sighed. "Yeah. But it's better that Melanie and I flushed out our differences now rather than later. I didn't realize the depth of her prejudices. Thinking back, there were signs, but when you're in love you're blinded to how things truly are."

"Eric," I said, "I've been in the South a lot longer than you—almost ten years now. I've been constantly surprised by people like Melanie, who hate the way they do. Not too long ago, Julie and I were invited by a friend to spend the day at a fellowship gathering put on by his church out in the countryside. We were worried at first that we would be caught up in some prayer meeting, but that wasn't the case. When we got there, we found a large, open field with cars and trucks parked in a circle and tents pitched in the middle. It reminded me of those old Westerns, when the settlers circled the wagons for protection against marauding Indians. Anyway folks were visiting each other's campsites, exchanging food, telling stories, and just having fun. It was one of the most congenial groups of people I have ever met. That was until my friend asked me to meet with a few of his pals who were skulking behind a big semi, passing around a jar of hooch, talking and making jokes."

Eric raised his brows, perhaps wondering where this was leading.

"At a certain point—I can't remember how exactly it happened—one of them said, 'If those niggers start acting up down here the way they have in the rest of the country, we're gonna have to teach 'em a lesson.'

"'Yeah,' said my friend, 'but don't forget those Jews and college liberals who are behind them.'

"'Hell, maybe they learned their lesson back in Mississippi, where a few of those nigger lovers got themselves killed,' said another. They all nodded knowingly at each other and laughed."

Eric looked appalled. "So what did you do, Mike?"

"Nothing. I was worried what would happen to Julie and me being surrounded by these people. I was a coward, I guess. I just walked away when I had an opportunity, fetched Julie, and left."

We spent an hour or more drinking hard liquor and chatting in desultory fashion, with the usually reticent Eric doing most of the talking and telling me about his life. As we got up to leave, he staggered.

"Whoa, Mike. I think I'm drunk. I don't usually drink that much. How 'bout you?"

"I've got a built-in immunity from drinking a lot while I was in the corps. Give me the car keys. I'll drive us back to my place. You need to sleep it off."

We made quite a racket coming through the door. I was propping Eric up.

Julie, startled by our noisy entrance, came rushing out. “What on Earth is going on? Is he drunk? Are you?”

“He certainly is,” I said. “We’ve been to a prayer meeting.”

Fifty Four

The pending storm had finally broken. South Carolinians held their collective breath as they watched the strikers and marchers going at it against the Medical College Hospital and the state government. Those living in the peninsula city and owning businesses there were worried to death. When I drove into work each morning, I never knew what to expect. Militants were setting fires. Vandals roamed the streets at night. A Negro militia was established to protect its people against harm from whites and the authorities. A curfew was set from dawn to dusk, with armored personnel vehicles and troops posted at all the bridges and entrances to the Holy City. For all intents and purposes, we were under martial law, with more than a thousand national guardsmen and state troopers, armed to the teeth, occupying the beleaguered city. Thank God Julie, Caroline, and I had made our move to James Island, avoiding much of the stress and the constant threat of violence that lasted for nearly four months.

Mother's Day saw the largest demonstration by marchers; an estimated ten thousand people participated, many of them coming in from Atlanta and elsewhere, along with the most prominent and influential leaders of the colored movement. Numerous rallies were held and speeches made. I was present at one in particular, at a church in Wraggborough, where a handful of white reporters and I stood among hundreds of coloreds and listened from outside as Hosea Williams's voice boomed out over loudspeakers. He spoke forcefully about the rights of the strikers, and at one point he uttered his contempt for the police that had surrounded the church in great numbers. He said something like, "What kind of man wants to strap on a gun every day to go out and make a living?" Some of the cops were visibly angry as they listened but maintained their cool. They had to: if they didn't, harm would have come to them as well as the demonstrators. The city might have burned.

A group called the Concerned Clergy, comprised of both Negroes and whites of different faiths, came together to preach peace to their parishioners, wanting to avoid the possible loss of life and destruction of property. Despite their efforts, more than a thousand people were arrested, most of them colored.

Finally, with a strategy to boycott all the businesses in Charleston that survived on Negro patronage, coupled with a threat from the dockworkers to shut down the port, and with President Nixon getting involved, a compromise was worked out. The twelve original strikers who had been fired were rehired, and four hundred workers were given better pay and working conditions. However, the strikers failed to reach their original goal of establishing a union.

We were all relieved to see the militia and the state troopers leave. An uneasy peace was restored to the old city.

On my way to work one day, out of cigarettes, I stopped off at Mr. Davies's grocery store to pick up a carton. The old grocer was busily stacking pumpkins outside the store.

"My goodness, Mr. Romano! I haven't seen you in a month of Sundays. How've you been?"

"Fine, sir. Sorry I haven't been around more often, but with us moving to James Island and all, it's been hard for us to shop here."

He said with a note of fatigue, "I understand. And I can't say I blame you for moving. Things just keep going from bad to worse here in the city."

"Were you affected much by the strike?" I asked.

"Not really. People still have to eat. But business has been dropping off rather steadily over the last several years, with both whites and coloreds leaving the city. I don't know how long I can hold on if things continue to go the way they are."

Grasping at the only possible ray of sunshine that might help reinvigorate my friend's business, I said, "Maybe the state taking over the college will help. I understand they're planning on growing student enrollment to near five thousand over the next few years. That's ten times more than they have right now."

"Might help a bit, but students don't usually buy a week's worth of groceries or do much cooking. Besides, that could take a long time, and time is not what I have now."

Time, time! I was counting on that where my own fortune was concerned, hoping that one day Charleston would rise like the phoenix, more beautiful than it had ever been.

The old gentleman became more upbeat when he asked how Julie and little Caroline were doing.

"Great! Julie loves living in the 'burbs, and Caroline has grown so much since you last saw her, I doubt you would recognize her. Can you believe she'll be two years old next month?"

"It seems like only yesterday that my kids were that age, and now they're in their thirties and have their own families. Enjoy it now while you can; time passes by quickly."

Picking up a pumpkin, he excused himself to get back to work. His words were still ringing in my head as I went inside, thinking how much I loved my little girl and how she was filled with wonder and joy as I held her in my arms, showing her the world around her. I wanted to hold on to this precious time forever.

As I was leaving, Mr. Davies called me over and handed me a giant pumpkin. "Wish your lovely wife and baby a happy Halloween from the old man!"

At nine o'clock precisely, Elias and I began our weekly office meeting. I believed the purpose of such meetings was to be informative, solve problems, and, most important, create a sense of camaraderie between everyone working for the company. After all my business fate, as well as that of Elias, was inextricably linked to those sales associates who worked under our banner. A philosopher once spoke of the master-slave relationship; to put it simply, he said that each one has the other by the throat. They need to cooperate to survive.

After the meeting with our agents had ended, Elias and I stayed behind with our office manager to discuss ways of cutting expenses and improving productivity. The local economy was in a slump, and we needed to make adjustments accordingly. After we had determined a plan of action, I left the office on foot to go over to the Tap, to meet with Elizabeth and Tom for lunch. Then we planned to go over to Marion Square, to participate in a nationwide protest against the war in Vietnam.

Pausing in front of one of the finest antiques store on King Street, I admired the beautiful furniture and gorgeous crystal chandeliers on display. Moving closer to get a better look, I caught a glimpse of my reflection in the store window.

My God! A forty-year-old man who was only twenty-nine looked back at me. That guy had a paunch hanging over his belt and a jacket straining at his shoulders. In that moment I vowed to do something about it. Too many business lunches, long hours, and little or no exercise had taken their toll.

Many blocks later I greeted Lopez and acknowledged Tom, who was sitting at a window table.

"Where's Gunny?" I asked Lopez, who was busy flipping burgers. The place was filling up fast.

"He'll be in later today. He's off taking care of some personal business."

"Who's tending bar, then?"

"His wife. She's in the back at the moment, taking a delivery. Those guys always come when we're the busiest."

"Tell Gunny I asked after him, will ya?"

Settling into the chair opposite Tom, I asked, "Where's Elizabeth? I thought she was coming with you."

"Good question. She didn't show up for class today. I tried calling her, but there was no answer."

"I can't imagine Elizabeth missing her class and a lunch date without letting someone know what's going on. How's she doing? I haven't seen her in a while."

"Fine, from everything I can tell. Only a week back, she was delighted when Jean-Luc offered her a full-time faculty position."

It was strange that she hadn't called Julie or me to let us know.

Consuela appeared at our table to take our orders. I asked her what the special was.

"Corned beef and cabbage," she responded, "with carrots and boiled potatoes."

"I'll take that, minus the potatoes," I said regretfully.

"And you, sir?" she asked Tom with a smile.

"I'll have the same, *with* lots of potatoes, if you please."

When Consuela moved on to another table, I asked Tom how Rina and Mala were doing.

"Fine," he said in a clipped tone. "Mala loves her preschool, and Rina's thinking about going back to work."

"So how are things working out between you guys?"

"As well as can be expected. But I'll take whatever Rina wants to give and hope that one day she'll be able to forgive me, though I know she'll never forget. That time I was away from Rina and Mala was pure hell. I was so depressed, I began thinking about ending it all."

"Jesus, Tom! Why didn't you call me?"

"I could barely make it through a day at work, much less talk to anyone, even friends. Only Jean-Luc knew what I was going through. He helped me as best he could."

I was saddened that he hadn't been able to reach out to me. An awkward moment of quiet came between us.

"Have you spoken to Elaine since all this happened?" I asked.

"No. All she cared about when I told her was how it would affect her political career if it got out."

"Does that surprise you, Tom?"

"It did then. I really thought she cared for me," he said sadly.

"Tom, she has a way of making people believe that. All she's interested in is herself. You must know that by now, don't you?"

"Unfortunately, yes," he answered, averting his eyes.

After finishing lunch in silence, we gave our thanks to Lopez, bade him farewell, and headed for Marion Square. We followed a crowd down King Street to join in on the moratorium. A gaggle of college kids passed us, some of whom greeted Tom. Many carried small flags.

"What are those flags, Tom?" I asked.

"They're peace flags. See the white dove on the black field? The students have been passing them out on campus since early this morning. A few others who support the war have been giving out American flags."

"Damn, Tom! That's wrong. I wouldn't want somebody shoving an American flag in my face and having to reject it in the name of peace."

"I agree, but what can we do? They have a right to express themselves."

"Well, let the warmongers find their own fucking flag."

Upon entering the square, I scanned the area for anyone I might know while a crowd of two hundred or more listened to a young man on the bandstand who was making an impassioned case against the war. The sight of a marine in full dress blues making his way toward the stage on crutches caught my eye. As we walked closer, I was taken aback to realize it was Gunny Starr.

"Gunny!" I called out as I picked up my pace to go greet him. Tom was hard on my heels. "What the hell's going on?"

Turning and looking *down* at me for the first time in a long while, with his gimlet eyes fixed on mine, he said, "You owe me a crew cut, Romano!"

Laughing to cover how moved I was, I said, "By no later than the end of this week, I promise!"

Then I introduced him to Tom, who was taking inventory of Gunny's many medals for valor. As he shook Gunny's hand, he said, true to form, "Mike's told me a lot about you, sir. It's my pleasure and honor to finally make your acquaintance."

Gunny replied with a nod and a grunt, probably wondering who the egghead was.

"So why're you here, Gunny?" I asked.

"Are you dimwitted, Romano? I'm here to make my own argument against the fuckin' war! If that pimple-faced windbag kid on the stage ever stops flapping his jaw, I'm getting up there."

He was on fire, ready to fight again, but this time with words and wearing a uniform that represented the utmost loyalty to the flag, the Constitution, and the American people.

When the young man finally ended his speech to sporadic applause and cries of "right on, man," Gunny climbed the few steps to the stage, balancing himself precariously on his crutches and wincing in pain. Most of the crowd stilled, likely surprised to see the old marine standing erect as best he could in front of them.

He began by saying, "I am Gunnery Sergeant James Starr. I have served my country faithfully for nineteen years in the US Marine Corps. I have fought in two wars. I am retired now because I lost both my legs while fighting in Vietnam."

He paused, tapping his left artificial limb with a crutch, which caused a visible and audible stir among the demonstrators.

"I don't want anyone feeling sorry for me. Those who join the corps know they risk early death or terrible wounds. We look on it as an occupational hazard. However, no serviceman should be put in harm's way fighting an ill-advised, stupid war with a nation that does not threaten our national security. Not too long ago, cooler and wiser heads warned of not getting involved in a war in Asia. The policy of winning this so-called police action through attrition is failing miserably. As one commanding officer put it to me one day, coming back from a search and destroy mission, 'They can birth them faster than we can kill them, Gunny.' Our technological advantage isn't worth much when we're fighting in a jungle, where the enemy uses hit-and-run tactics that demoralize our men in much the same way we did when fighting the Brits in the Revolutionary War. Furthermore this is a civil war, and the side we're backing is politically weak, with an incompetent military, while the enemy we're fighting is strong and willing to go to battle for the next hundred years. But what galls me most is that I suspect that many of our political leaders know the war is in vain but are scared to speak out, caring only about saving their political skins. That's why this moratorium is so important. We, the people, must let them know we want this war ended, and if they don't end it, we will end their careers!"

The crowd erupted in wild applause, whistles, and tears. A group of kids began singing the marine corps hymn, with others joining in. Gunny hobbled down the steps. I offered him my hand, but he waved me off with an emphatic "no!"

Tom stuck out his hand. "Gunny, that was one of the most insightful speeches I've ever heard depicting the war as it is and why we should end it."

Gunny shook his hand and gave a brief nod, his face drawn and gray.

With my back to the crowd, I heard a voice behind me yelling, "Traitor! Traitor!"

I turned to see a mean-looking son of a bitch wearing a blue denim jacket cut off at the shoulders and sporting a Confederate flag patch, backed up by a couple of other assholes. When he got closer to us, he reared back to throw a punch at Gunny. I moved quickly to block it, taking the blow to my cheek. Then I pivoted and threw a hard left hook that he didn't see coming, which cracked his jaw and sent him flying into the arms of his fellow thugs, out cold.

Gunny exclaimed, "Damn, Romano, you finally got the hang of that left hook."

A small, beak-nosed guy in civilian clothes ran toward us, waving a badge. "Hold it right there! I saw what happened."

I noticed an Eighty Second Airborne tattoo on his forearm. I laughed and said,"Airborne to the rescue of the marines! Mike Romano, USMC."

"Well, well, well," he said, a smile spreading across his thin face. "Do you want to press charges against this asshole?

"No," I replied. "It's not worth my time. Fuck that reb. He's probably all boozed up anyway."

"Then I guess I'll have to take him in on drunk and disorderly," he said with a wink.

Smiling, I shook his hand and thanked him. One of his cops cuffed the shit and ordered the other losers to leave the park immediately.

Gunny said, "Let's get the hell outta here and head back to my place to do some serious drinking!"

When I finally got home, exhausted from the events of the day, I heaved the huge pumpkin from the trunk. When I carried it into the house, Caroline came tottering over to me, Woofy faithfully following her like a little shadow.

"Hi, Daddy! Daddy, Daddy, what that?" she shouted, flinging her pudgy little arms around my right leg.

I swept her up into my arms and gave her a big smoochie kiss. She wriggled, trying to get free, and said, "Down, Daddy! What that?"

Julie appeared from the kitchen, drying her hands on a dish towel and laughing, and held us both close.

"It's a pumpkin for Halloween from Mr. Davies," I said.

"Oh, good heavens! Well, you can carve it later. I'm making supper," Julie said.

When I set Caroline on her feet, she started to remove her clothes in the middle of the living room.

Somewhat bemused, I asked Julie what the heck was going on.

"It's just something she's decided to do when she needs to go potty. I'm not going to discourage it unless she does it in front of a houseful of guests."

As the disrobing continued, rather haphazardly, Julie brought me a Scotch. Then when the completely naked Caroline took herself off to the downstairs bathroom, Julie announced, out of the blue, "Michael, I've been offered a part-time job in the lab, working with Maggie's fiancé."

"Whoa! Are you ready for that? I thought you loved being home with Caroline."

"I do. But I've been thinking a lot about this. My brain is atrophying, Michael. I need to do something with it, or it may die altogether."

"What about Caroline?"

"Well, you know that woman Helen, who lives down the street from us? She has two kids, and the younger one just started grade school. Their nanny is putting in only a couple of hours a day now in the afternoons, and Helen wondered if we would like to hire her for mornings when I would be working. Her name is Mary; I've talked to her, and she seems like a really nice woman. Helen says she's completely trustworthy. She's been with them for years."

I was taken aback. Julie seemed to have everything organized for a return to work. Then I realized she had in fact been talking about it for a while. I obviously hadn't been listening closely enough to her.

"I want to meet this woman too. Is she like...a mammy?"

Julie looked at me. "You mean is she colored? Yes, she is. She has some education and speaks well. I would prefer to call her a nanny and pay her a decent wage."

Caroline returned, looking triumphant. "Poopy, Mommy!" she crowed.

We congratulated her, and I took a deep swallow of my Scotch as Julie scooped her up to clean off her behind. Time was indeed passing by at a furious rate.

FIFTY FIVE

October 1969

"My dear Michael, by the time you read this letter, I will be dead..."

Elizabeth had killed herself on the day Tom and I were to meet her for lunch before going to the moratorium. The maid discovered her body the next morning, when she arrived to do the weekly cleaning and laundry. Elizabeth was sprawled out on her bed, an empty pill bottle set on top of an envelope on which she had written "Please notify my attorney, Mr. John Roberts" and a New Hampshire phone number.

The news deeply shook and saddened Julie and me. In Elizabeth's self-deprecating way, she had instructed that she should be cremated and her ashes cast upon the ocean—no fanfare, funeral, or ceremony.

Since her death I had agonized over her letter to me, which, bundled with several old and much handled other missives, had been delivered in a large package by mail to my office the day after her suicide. Elizabeth's last written words were so personal in nature—so disturbing—that I didn't even tell Julie. I kept it all to myself, pondering what I should do.

After two weeks I called Elaine to make an appointment with her at her house in Mount Pleasant, with the stipulation that we were to be alone. She asked me what it was about, and I told her it was something that couldn't be discussed over the phone. She reluctantly agreed to see me.

Monday morning was as cold and dreary as my mood. We were seated in Elaine's den, which overlooked the Cooper River. She asked if she could fix me a drink.

"No."

She looked surprised by my curt response. "Do you mind if I do?"

"It's your turf. Do what you want."

After pouring herself a sherry from a crystal decanter, she sat, allowing her skirt to rise high as she crossed her bare legs. "So...to what do I owe this unexpected pleasure?"

"Elizabeth," I replied.

She stiffened. "What the hell are you talking about?"

I was enjoying her uneasiness. I reached into the inside pocket of my jacket, brought out a white envelope, and slowly unfolded its contents. I began to read aloud.

My dear Michael,

By the time you read this letter, I will be dead.

For the last twenty years, I have loved Elaine with all my heart. I thought she loved me the same way. However, she has cast me aside for Debbie and has dismissed me from her life—and her campaign. She recently told me I had been a constant thorn in her flesh and at times had bored her to tears, making her wish she had never met me in those early years at Radcliffe. I now realize that what I took for love was only carnal in nature where she was concerned. She was the center of my universe—that which held my life together. Without her I would have spun off into space. Now she has broken my heart and left me without a real mission in life, and I find I can't go on.

Know that I love you, Julie, and little Caroline as family. I apologize for causing you any pain by my actions.

Elizabeth

Elaine's eyes narrowed, her face contorted in anger. "What do you intend to do with that nonsense? There's no truth to it, other than I dismissed her from my staff for being incompetent and combative."

"Elaine, you know better than that. I have more than a dozen letters written by your hand, with dates, places, and some pretty graphic details of what you were doing with Elizabeth. It took me a good while to figure out why she sent me all these letters. At first I thought she wanted me to use them to destroy you politically and socially—something I still want to do, frankly. However, knowing Elizabeth, I believe she wanted me to use them for good. What good would it do to end your miserable career and have some other asshole replace you?"

Now her jaw was clenched, and she was shaking, but she said nothing.

"If you wish to stay in Washington, you will take up your original so-called philosophy. You will retract your position on the war and come out firmly against it on the basis that you have reevaluated the situation. You will say that as a mother of two boys, you could not bring yourself to send other children to die or be maimed in a wrong war. You will focus on education and health care for the underserved. I don't really care if you believe in it or not. I will be watching every step of the way. And know this: I will bring the hammer down anytime I see you straying from that path. So the drop-dead date for your position on the war is Wednesday, two days from now. I want to see your retraction in the newspaper."

I rose, leaving her bowed over on the couch with her face in her hands. "Remember—Wednesday. No later than that."

On Wednesday morning our family was sitting at the breakfast table. Julie looked up from the newspaper. "Michael, you're not going to believe this. Elaine reversed her position on the war."

"Good Lord! No, really? I wonder what brought that on," I said, smiling. "Is there any more coffee?"

Author Bio

Michael D. Mercurio is a retired insurance and real estate professional, and restaurateur. Born in New York City to a family of Italian Americans, he served in the US Marine Corps for four years and earned a degree in philosophy from the College of Charleston, where he was a member of the honors History and English program, and was deeply involved with a political group that made for social change in Charleston, South Carolina. In later years, he was invited by both the History and Philosophy departments at the College to speak on the importance of studying the humanities. He also served for four years as director of the Liberal Religious Youth group at the Unitarian Church in Charleston. He acted as adviser and fundraiser for State Senator Arthur Ravenel, Jr., in his successful bid for the US Congress.

Mike Mercurio currently lives in Las Vegas, Nevada, with his wife of thirty years.

Made in the USA
San Bernardino, CA
18 March 2015